FLAMES OF REBELLION

THE KNIGHTS OF ENGLAND SERIES, BOOK 6

MARY ELLEN JOHNSON

ePublishingWorks!
love what you read.

Book and cover design by eBook Prep
www.ebookprep.com

May 2021

ISBN: 978-1-64457-196-5

ePublishing Works!
644 Shrewsbury Commons Ave
Ste 249
Shrewsbury PA 17361
United States of America

www.epublishingworks.com
Phone: 866-846-5123

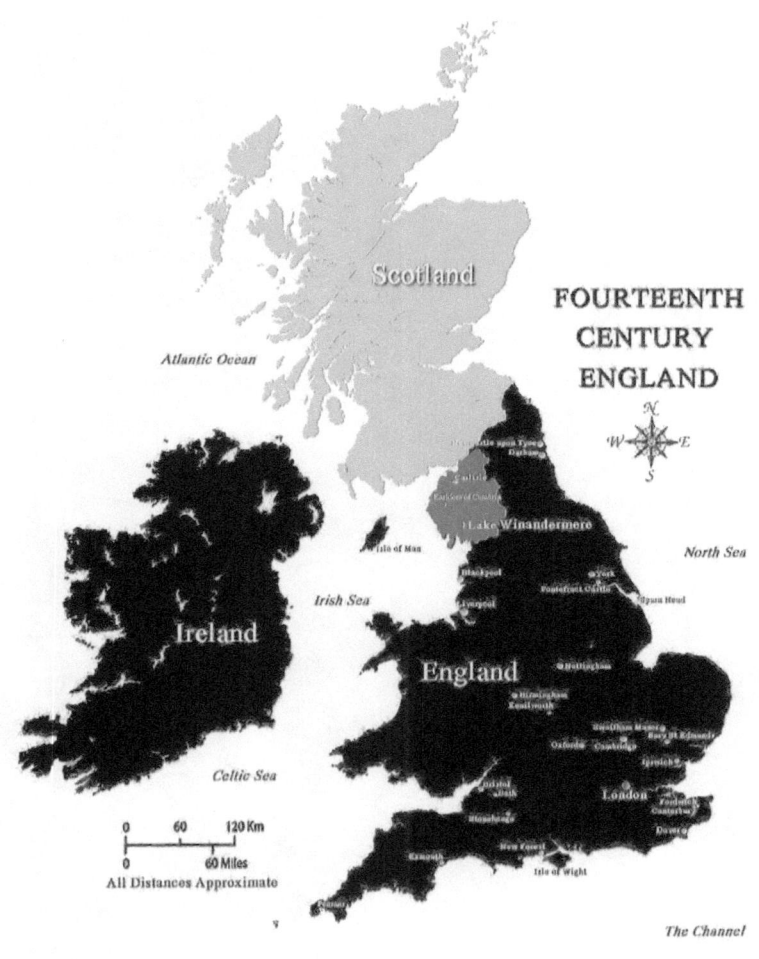

Scotland

FOURTEENTH
CENTURY
ENGLAND

Atlantic Ocean

N
W *E*
S

Newcastle upon Tyne
Durham

North Sea

Carlton
Carlisle of Cumbria

Lake Winandermere

Isle of Man

Blackpool

York

Pontefract Castle

Spun Head

Irish Sea

Liverpool

Ireland

England

Nottingham

Birmingham
Kenilworth

Swaffham Manor
Bury St Edmunds

Oxford

Cambridge

Ipswich

Celtic Sea

Bristol
Bath

London

Fordwich
Canterbury

Glastonbury

Dover

0   60   120 Km
0   60 Miles
All Distances Approximate

New Forest

Isle of Wight

Exmouth

The Channel

PLANTAGENET FAMILY TREE

HENRY III (1207 - 72) = ELEANOR of Provence (1223 - 91)

(1) Eleanor of Castile (1241-90) = EDWARD I 'Longshanks' (1239-1307) = (2) Margaret of France (c.1279-1318) | Margaret (1240-75) | Beatrice (1242-75) | Edmund Crouchback Earl of Lancaster (1245-96) = Blanche of Artois (d.1302)

Thomas of Brotherton Earl of Norfolk (1300-38) | Edmund Earl of Kent (1307-30) = Margaret Wake (d.1349) | Henry Earl of Lancaster (1281-1345) = Maud Chadworth

Eleanor (1269-98) | Joan of Acre (1272-1307) | Margaret (1275-1318) | EDWARD II (1284-1327) = Isabella of France (1296-1358) | Thomas Earl of Lancaster (1276-1322)

Philippa of Hainault (1311-69) = EDWARD III (1312-77) | John Earl of Cornwall (1316-36) | Eleanor (1318-55) | Joanna (1321-62) | Isabel de Beaumont = Henry Duke of Lancaster (d.1361)

Joan of Kent (1328-85) = Edward The Black Prince (1330-76) | Isabella | Joan (d.1340) | Lionel Duke of Clarence (1338-68) | (1) Isabel of Castile (d.1392) = Edmund of Langley Duke of York (1341-1402) = (2) Joan Holland (d.1434)

(1) Anne of Bohemia (1366-94) = RICHARD II (1367-1400) = (2) Isabelle of France (1389-1409) | (1) Blanche of Lancaster (1341-69) = John of Gaunt Duke of Lancaster (1340-99) = (2) Constanza of Castile (d.1394) = (3) Catherine Swynford (1350-1403)

Mary de Bohun (d.1394) = HENRY IV Earl of Bolingbroke (1366-1413) | Philippa (1360-1415) | Elizabeth (1364-1426)

[TUDOR]—[LANCASTER]   [YORK]

MAIN HISTORICAL CHARACTERS

Richard of Bordeaux, (Richard II): (1367-1400) Son of Edward of Woodstock, later known to history as the Black Prince, and Joan of Kent. Ascends England's throne at age ten.

Isabella of Valois: (1389-1409) Second spouse of King Richard II. The French princess marries him at age six; widowed three years later.

John of Gaunt, Duke of Lancaster: (1340-1399) Edward of Windsor's (Edward III) third son. Ambitious for a crown, though not England's. Faithful to Richard of Bordeaux.

Henry Bolingbroke, (Henry IV): (1366-1413) John of Gaunt's oldest son. Born within three months of Richard II. After King Richard banishes him from England for self-serving reasons, Bolingbroke returns and overthrows Richard to be crowned Henry IV.

Henry Percy the Younger, Harry Hotspur: (1364-1403) Skilled soldier who kept the rebellious Scots and Welsh at bay during Henry IV's early reign. Married to Elizabeth Mortimer, who is related to young Edmund Mortimer, heir presumptive to Richard II. That claim, plus King Henry's lack of financial compensation following Hotspur's martial campaigns, causes the Henry Percys to revolt.

Henry Percy the Elder, 1st Earl of Northumberland: (1341-1408) Powerful northern lord. Initially loyal to Richard II, his decision to support the 1399 invasion of Henry Bolingbroke is crucial in deposing Richard. Within three years, schemes to overthrow Bolingbroke.

Thomas of Woodstock, Duke of Gloucester: (1355-1397) Youngest of King Edward and Philippa of Hainault's thirteen children. Ambitious and haughty but also sophisticated, well-read, religious and a courageous military commander. A Lord Appellant. His murder helps lead to Richard II's downfall.

Edmund Langley, Duke of York: (1341-1402) Another of Edward III's brood, positioned between John of Gaunt and Thomas Woodstock. Loyal, able soldier with very little of his older brother's ambition or younger brother's haughtiness.

Richard FitzAlan, Earl of Arundel: (1346-1397) One of the Lords Appellant who curbs Richard's power in the Merciless Parliament.

Thomas Mowbray, 1st Duke of Norfolk: (1366-1399) A Lord Appellant. Instrumental in the death of royal uncle, Thomas, Duke of Gloucester, which eventually leads to Mowbray's quarrel with Henry Bolingbroke... which leads to both of their banishments from England... which leads to the deposition and death of Richard II.

John Halle: Minor play in the murder of Thomas, Duke of Gloucester. Scapegoated and quickly executed, since the truth of the assassination would lead directly to Richard II.

FROM PREVIOUS BOOKS

Edward of Caernarvon, Edward II: (1284-1327) First English king since the Conqueror to be deposed; later murdered. His legacy casts a shadow across the entire fourteenth century, haunting his son, Edward III, and beloved by his great-grandson, Richard of Bordeaux.

Edward of Windsor, Edward III: (1312-1377) Oldest son of Edward II. Reign often compared to that of the mythical King Arthur; ranked among England's greatest monarchs. Begins what is later known as the Hundred Years' War.

Edward of Woodstock, Prince of Wales and Aquitaine, (the Black Prince): (1330-1376) King Edward's oldest son, revered military commander and heir to England's throne. Richard II's father.

John Ball: radical priest who believed that God had created all men alike. After decades of preaching for equality between lords and the rest, Ball's beliefs ignite the Great Rising/Peasants' Revolt. Executed by Richard II.

FICTIONAL CHARACTERS

Characters in A Knight There Was, Within a Forest Dark, A Child Upon the Throne, Lords Among the Ruins, and The Flames of Rebellion:

Margery Watson: Daughter of nobleman Thomas Rendell and a peasant woman. Margery's "mixed" blood accounts for her lifetime of divided loyalties. Matthew Hart's lover for many years; marries him in the aftermath of Great Rising/Peasants' Revolt of 1381.

Matthew Hart: Earl of Cumbria; Margery's long-time lover. Matthew has fought in most of the major battles of Edward III's reign, transforming him from eager warrior to weary survivor. Instrumental in the downfall of Richard II.

Serill Hart: Margery and Matthew's illegitimate son. Heir to the Earldom of Cumbria, Serill is handsome, charming and shallow. Marries Jane le Babbe.

Jane le Babbe: A serious young woman whose romantic nature finds an outlet in fables accompanied by indecipherable drawings. Ever in love with Serill Hart, who seldom takes anything seriously—including his marriage vows.

Lancelot of Glastonbury: Sixth of Elizabeth Ravenne's eight sons, Lancelot makes his fortune via the jousting circuit. Serill Hart's cousin and best friend. Long besotted with Jane le Babbe, who initially dismisses him as uncouth and ignorant.

Elizabeth Ravenne: Matthew Hart's sister. Mother of eight sons, all with names from the Arthurian romances. Lady Ravenne writes verses, is protective of her ward, Jane le Babbe, and enjoys "helping" those she loves, particularly Lancelot.

Viviane Halle: daughter of John Halle, scapegoated for the murder of Thomas, Duke of Gloucester. Of middling lineage with few marriage prospects, Viviane is bossy, opinionated and desperately in love with Lancelot of Glastonbury—who remains enamored of Jane le Babbe.

Gerald Halle: John Halle's son. In Harry Hotspur's service, Gerald vows vengeance against Henry IV for ordering his father's execution.

Reginald Luci: Cousin of the powerful Percy family, the faithless Luci is Viviane Halle's first love. After impregnating Viviane, Luci refuses to marry her.

Fulco the Smithy: An itinerant blacksmith and Margery Watson's one-time lover. Following their summer tryst, Fulco pledged his undying devotion. After the Great Rising, Fulco vows revenge against Richard II.

FROM PREVIOUS BOOKS

Thurold Watson: Margery's radical stepbrother. Follower of the equally radical priest John Ball, who preaches that God created all men equal. Killed by Matthew Hart during the Great Rising.

Lawrence Ravenne: Husband of Elizabeth Ravenne, Matthew Hart's older sister. During the Black Death, Lawrence Ravenne murders Margery's mother, earning him the lasting enmity of both Margery and her stepbrother. During the Great Rising, Thurold kills Ravenne, and is in turn killed by Matthew Hart, who must protect his class, regardless of his private sympathies.

Harry Hart: Matthew's younger brother—charming, vulnerable and rather a wastrel. Marries Matthew's former lover, Desiderata Cecy. Dies during John of Gaunt's Great Chevauchée of 1373.

Desiderata Cecy: Former lover of Matthew Hart; wife of Harry Hart. Last mistress of Edward III. Returns to her native France where she becomes an anchorite. Dedicated to the memory of her dead husband, Harry.

Ralph Hart, Count of Vanves: Son of Desiderata Cecy and Harry Hart. Lives in France, the location of Desiderata's vast holdings.

Maria Rendell: Margery Watson's grandmother. Torn between two men, Phillip Rendell, and Richard of Sussex, illegitimate half-brother of the doomed Edward II, her story lays the foundation for all that is to come in *The Knights of England*.

PREFACE

The Flames of Rebellion is the last installment of my six book series, *Knights of England. Knights* pretty much bookends the fourteenth century, beginning with the reign of the second King Edward, Edward Caernarvon, who is deposed and murdered, and ending in 1403, when Edward's great-grandson, Henry IV, after deposing and murdering another king, successfully fights to retain England's crown at the Battle of Shrewsbury.

Before untangling the skeins of a century's worth of historical as well as fictional events, a few clarifications. While I largely tried to be true to historical dates and events, my fictional characters often elbow aside real figures so the reader can be more personally involved in the story. While I do portray the thoughts of various actual characters, such as Richard II, I've always considered that presumptuous—even blasphemous. I tried to keep such musings to a minimum and in keeping with the individual's character.

Now to specifics:

- Sorting through historical characters of the same name is a challenge. I'm thinking specifically of you, the many Edwards. (And, in *The Flames of Rebellion*, the several Henrys. And Thomases!) The regnal numbers (I, II, III) were not used during this period so I largely confine them to the times when I use the omniscient viewpoint.

- So... Edward Longshanks/Edward I; Edward Caernarvon/Edward II; Edward Windsor/ Edward III (also referred to as England's Arthur). Edward of Woodstock, Prince Edward, was not actually known as the Black Prince until Tudor times. I also sometimes refer to Edward II as the Sodomite King in order to further differentiate him, though that's a bit historically shaky. The belief that Edward's two male favorites were also his lovers, is not universally held. Nor were our ancestors defined so much by their sexuality as they are today. In addition, Edward sired four legitimate children and one illegitimate son, which further confuses the picture. Recent questions have been raised about whether Edward II was actually murdered, but may have lived several more years.
- I will never, ever master the proper manner of addressing the nobility, no matter how many hours I labored over various explanations for titles, etc. I did my best.
- I deliberately made one historical mistake—having women present at Henry IV's coronation feast. Such feasts seemed to have been exclusively male affairs, but I could think of no other way of relaying a bit of royal pageantry while simultaneously advancing my story.
- John Halle *was* unfairly scapegoated and executed for the assassination of Richard's royal uncle, Thomas Woodstock, Duke of Gloucester. Since I could find very little about Halle, I invented most of his biography, including his two children, Viviane and Gerald Halle.

SYNOPSIS OF KNIGHTS OF ENGLAND SERIES:

THE LION AND THE LEOPARD: (1313-1328)

Maria Rendell is the noblewoman who begins it all. After Phillip, her wayward husband, leaves Maria, she turns for solace to Richard of Sussex, Edward II's illegitimate half-brother. Their love affair is played out against the disintegration of Edward II's reign. In 1327, Edward is deposed and murdered. His half-brother and Maria's lover, Richard of Sussex, is killed during a Scottish raid. Maria is reunited with her husband, who was horribly disfigured in that particular raid. The Cherry Fair, which is a constant in the series, makes it first appearance at Fordwich, the family demesne.

A KNIGHT THERE WAS: (1348-1361)

In 1349, the Black Death decimates England, including the village of Ravennesfield, where nine-year-old Margery Watson resides. Margery is the illegitimate child of Maria Rendell's son, Thomas. Margery's peasant mother, Alice, is murdered by Lawrence Ravenne, Margery's overlord and brother-in-law of twelve-year-old Matthew Hart. Margery's stepbrother Thurold vows revenge.

After Thurold and the radical priest John Ball whisk a grown Margery to London, she finds employ at the house of a prosperous goldsmith. Eventually, she and Matthew, who is heir to the Earldom of Cumbria, become lovers. Matthew, the quintessential knight, is often away on glorious campaigns. He counts himself blessed to be living during the reign of England's greatest warrior king, Edward III, and in service to King Edward's eldest son, Edward the Black Prince.

Because the course of true love seldom runs smooth in true life or novels, during one of Matthew's absences Margery is tricked into marriage by her employer, the odious Simon Crull. After Matthew returns, both accuse the other of betrayal. Matthew departs England for Bordeaux and the court of the Black Prince, where he becomes the lover of a scheming Frenchwoman, Desiderata/Desire Cecy.

WITHIN A FOREST DARK: (1367-1377)

Six years pass. Determined to forget the faithless Margery Watson, Matthew's time is largely spent on campaigns, though these campaigns are becoming decidedly less glorious. An increasingly disillusioned Matthew finally returns to England, where he and Margery reunite. After Margery poisons her abusive and increasingly unstable husband, she and Matthew openly live together. Matthew's former lover, Desiderata Cecy, finds herself pregnant and tries to force Matthew into marriage. Instead, Harry, the babe's real father, steps in and marries Desire, making the feckless Harry a very wealthy younger brother. Despite the circumstances surrounding their marriage, Desire and Harry are happy together

In the summer of 1370, the Black Prince, plagued by chronic illness and largely confined to a litter, launches another *chevauchée*. When the French city of Limoges refuses to open its doors to his army, the prince orders the city razed and all its townspeople killed. He orders his most obedient vassal, Matthew Hart, to lead the slaughter.

A tormented Matthew reunites with Margery and their one-year-old son, Serill. With the aging of Edward III and the sickness of the Black Prince, England's golden age has turned to dross. Not only are the campaigns increasingly unsuccessful, but King Edward loses interest in governing. The hedge-priest John Ball, with Thurold Watson at his side, increases his lamentations against the injustices of England's lords.

In 1373, Matthew and his younger brother are once again in France for what will be known as the Great Chevauchée. John of Gaunt leads his army across Auvergne's mountains in winter. Starvation, blizzards. Hundreds of men and horses die. Despite Matthew's many sacrifices upon his brother's behalf, Harry Hart also dies. Worse follows. Matthew receives word that his beloved father is mortally ill. King Edward has slipped into senility. And in 1376, the worst blow of all. The Black Prince, the flower of chivalry of all the world, dies.

Matthew is devastated. On the heels of the prince's demise, the once-great Edward of Windsor, also passes.

The boy king Richard of Bordeaux ascends England's throne.

A CHILD UPON THE THRONE: (1377-1381)

Woe to a kingdom ruled by a child. All the deaths Matthew has suffered, plus his guilt over the slaughter at Limoges, have so distanced him and Margery that they eventually part. Matthew retreats to the wilds of Cumbria, where he lives as a hermit. He knows he must either make peace with his past, the losses he's suffered and the sins he's committed, or he'll be no use to anyone. For how can a man reconcile the whole of his life when everything he once assumed to be true is suspect?

Determined to craft a satisfactory future without her former lover, Margery retires to Canterbury so that she can be closer to her noble father. Here in the summer of 1380, she indulges in a passionate affair with a young blacksmith, Fulco the Smithy. When Fulco asks Margery to leave Canterbury with him, she refuses. She is no longer willing to risk all for love.

Finally, after Matthew exorcises his psychological demons, they reunite. Matthew proposes marriage, reminding Margery that in this new age, merchants are marrying lords and class lines are blurring. Why cannot they wed and retire to a quiet life in Cumbria?

Unfortunately, after decades of preaching about the plight of the poor, John Ball's words have borne fruit and a mob of angry commoners march on London. Fourteen-year-old Richard II repeatedly meets with the rebels, who remain personally loyal to him. However, while Richard makes many pretty promises, he doesn't intend to keep them. The Rising ends in violence, including the death of Margery's stepbrother Thurold. Thousands of other rebels are hunted down and executed, including John Ball, all, Margery laments, for seeking a better life. In this reign of the duplicitous Richard II, can Margery and Matthew even think to share a future?

PROLOGUE

COMBINING EVENTS FROM LORDS AMONG THE RUINS (1382-1396) AND THE BEGINNING OF THE FLAMES OF REBELLION (1397-1403)

*R*ichard of Bordeaux was a man coming into his own. Or more properly, a king coming into his own. For, in the fullness of his thirty years, Richard knew that he'd put himself, his queen, the knights, the bishops and the pawns all into place, moved them so carefully and methodically that there was no way he would not win this match. Against his barons. Against all his enemies. Richard's memory was long, and while he'd had to endure the opposition of so many of his lords even unto the threat of deposition, Richard's position was now much stronger. His royal uncle, John of Gaunt, was simply a dog whose day was past, and the other lords, well, Richard knew the time would soon be at hand when he would extract full measure of revenge.

It was true that Richard's first queen had died without providing England with an heir, but Richard had recently wed the lovely Isabella of Valois. Not only had his marriage to the French princess enriched England's coffers, but it had cemented an alliance between two ancient enemies. Not for Richard of Bordeaux the wars of his warrior grandfather, the third King Edward, or his warrior father, Edward the Black Prince. He was a monarch of the future, with a beautiful royal court, pleasures, clothes and finery, but also fine buildings and entertainments that rivalled the most sophisticated of European courts. And while his new queen was seven years of age, Richard was in robust health —in his prime, really. There would be much time yet for heirs.

For others in his reign, the future was more problematic. John of Gaunt, the great Duke of Lancaster, had grown weary and infirm, putting aside his dreams of wearing a crown—even if it was a foreign one—and hoping to ensure the future of his brood, particularly his first-born son, Henry Bolingbroke, Earl of Derby. Both Richard's nemeses. Though appearances were maintained, the Duke of Lancaster feared for his eldest's future should Richard of Bordeaux ever be able to act unchecked. And Henry Bolingbroke? A crusader, accomplished jouster and a scholar possessing a priest's piety, Henry felt cast adrift. Increasingly, he wandered from his Lancastrian estates in the Midlands to Leicester and Tutbury and back to Leicester, where lay the tomb of his dead wife.

A widower with a brood of six, Bolingbroke often felt as if he were hostage to events larger than himself. He tried to be loyal to Richard even while knowing that Richard of Bordeaux was largely at the mercy of whatever emotion gripped him at the time, spinning like a weather vane, baring his teeth at one moment, showering Bolingbroke and his like with praise and gifts and positions the next. Following the marriage of Richard of Bordeaux in 1396, Henry Bolingbroke had considered going on a second crusade, but instead retreated to his holdings and tried to live the life of son, nobleman and father. The same age as Richard, Henry sometimes felt like a salmon swimming upstream and contemplated that the result would be the same. After spawning his brood, he would simply die.

For Matthew Hart, Earl of Cumbria, he had retreated to his holdings following the wedding of Richard of Bordeaux and Isabella of Valois. Now approaching sixty, Matthew Hart hoped for peace in the kingdom. The wars in which he'd participated during their great king Edward Windsor's reigns might have been legendary, but what had they accomplished? France was retaking territories via this questionable marriage and the increasing disintegration of England's martial prowess. So Matthew, neither a politician nor a diplomat but simply a warrior—or so he liked to say—would delight in the mountains of Cumbria, ride with his beloved wife, the former Margery Watson, to Lake Windandermere, and stay as far away from the doings at Westminster as duty allowed.

As he would stay away from his only son and heir, Serill Hart, who had disgraced the Hart name with his drinking and whoring and refusal to grow up. A grown man of six and twenty, as well as father of three, Serill had carelessly trod upon the heart of Jane le Babbe, the spouse who'd loved him. Now, husband and wife, not having the good sense to keep their quarrels private, were bringing shame upon the Hart name.

Ah, but there were changes in the relationship between Serill Hart and Jane le Babbe. After his father's public shaming and his mother's worried flutterings, Serill Hart had vowed to abandon his wastrel ways. And, while he had despaired of ever reaching a rapprochement with his stubborn Janey, he had returned from the wedding of King Richard and his child queen determined to be worthy of his position as heir to the earldom of Cumbria. Let his wife ignore him; let her perform her hit and run maneuvers. As when Serill had come across her during their youngest child Billy's naptime, when Janey had been cuddling their third babe against her shoulder and crooning a lullaby.

"A maiden mother, meek and mild,
In cradle kept an angel child
That softly slept,
She sat and sang:"
Improvising, Janey finished,
"Papa, Papa, we hate him so
We pray that off to hell he'll go."

Compared to his father and grandfather, Serill had lived a small life. There had been no grand *chevauchees*, no legendary battles named Sluys, Crecy, Poitiers, Najera. But Serill Hart had participated in a crusade. His weapons had drawn blood; he had vanquished enemies in combat. He had bowed his knee before Christ's tomb in the Church of the Holy Sepulchre, something not even his father had done. Serill knew that he'd deserved Matthew Hart's contemptuous slaps across either cheek as if he were a girl, knew he deserved Matthew's challenge to "act like a man."

Serill Hart was determined to do precisely that. He would not further betray his family's illustrious name. Nor would he ever again betray his marriage vows.

Betrayal.

Not knowing that his Janey was determined to betray *him*. With his best friend and her secret courtly lover.

Not knowing, as none of them knew, that the beast called betrayal had been loosed upon England and was on the prowl for them all.

CHAPTER 1

JULY 1397, SWAFFHAM MANOR

*J*ane le Babbe sat on a bench outside Swaffham Manor's Enchanted Cottage. On either side were Guinevere and Alice, while twenty-month-old Billy nestled in her arms. Hadn't she imagined this when she'd been young and foolish—a long bench crowded with her bairns, all sitting so obediently while she enthralled them with her stories? Well, God had blessed her with three children, if not quite the rest.

St. Swithin's Day had just passed, and Swaffham's fields swarmed with villeins cutting hay, weeding other crops and shearing sheep in the pens.

I will cherish this moment, Janey thought. Tomorrow she would be off on "pilgrimage" with her mentor, Lady Elizabeth Ravenne. Which was not a pilgrimage at all.

Nay, I am traveling to my destiny! The knowledge caused Janey's breath to quicken. She could scarce comprehend the magnitude of her daring. Her desperation. The risk to her immortal soul.

She addressed her twin daughters. "Would you like me to tell you a story?"

"Tell us about bees," demanded six-year-old Guinevere.

"Look how they circle the roses." Her twin sister Alice pointed to several flitting around the trellis positioned beside a nearby window. "Don't let them sting me."

"Bees are birds. Very small ones," "Genny" said, for this was not the first time the matter had been discussed. "They come from calves who die. Like the one we saw when we last rode, remember?"

Alice nodded. "It smelled so bad I had to hold my nose."

"They crawl out from all that rotten meat, first as worms—

"Enough!" interrupted Janey. "Let us talk about them after they grow up and become actual bees."

"I hate worms." Alice frowned in the direction of the trellis.

Billy sucked diligently on a corner of *Mon Coeur*, which Janey had earlier given him. *Mon Coeur*, the book she'd so lovingly written and illustrated as a wedding present for her husband. A fabulistic tale involving her and Serill and an enchanted cherry tree. After she'd so shyly, lovingly presented the book to Serill, he had kissed her and promised to carry it everywhere as his talisman. A promise Serill Hart had immediately forgotten, as he'd forgotten all his other promises.

Janey noticed that two of the cover's ornate silver rivets had fallen off, giving her a savage kind of pleasure.

Destroy it all, she silently commanded her son.

Genny tugged her kirtle. "Maman, are you listening?" When Janey nodded, she said, "Tell us about when Papa was a bee who wore a shining suit of armor and arrived at the hive court astride a dragonfly—"

"Just in time to save Queen Isabella," Alice added.

"Not Isabella," Genny corrected. "Isabee, remember?'

Janey shifted Billy in her arms. She didn't want to make Serill Hart, bee or human, hero of anything. Not after all the women he had lain with, including her own sister-in-law. Oh, it was beyond endurance!

"I shall meet the real queen someday soon," Genny said, swinging her legs for emphasis. "I will ask her to show me her doll houses."

"As will I," Alice added. "I hope she likes to share, or we will have to tell the king to scold her."

Janey began, "Bees live in a bee version of London."

"I didn't like London when we visited," Alice interrupted. "It stank. Worse than that dead calf."

"I liked Smithfield and all the horses," said Genny. "And I liked watching Papa at the joust, knocking that knight off his horse with such a crash!"

"Too noisy," countered Alice. "I had to cover my ears." Which she again did for emphasis.

"It sounded just like thunder." Guinevere made an explosive noise. "I want to attend another tournament. Might we attend one soon, Maman?"

Janey sighed. She would not see her babes for perhaps two months, and she would so miss them, but the twins had such a way of meandering through every conversation. "Shall I tell you a story or not?"

Both girls nodded. Fearless, her Bear Dog who lay nearby, groaned in his sleep. Billy chirped, "Dog," before continuing gnawing on *Mon Coeur*.

"Listen well, my pets." Janey told them a variation of other such conversations. Bees were very hard workers, she explained, who created their own houses and cleaned them most diligently. While at their hive court, they performed the same duties as their human counterparts. And when the weather grew cold, the king would send bee scouts on forays to discover warmer climes. Similar to the way the real king and his court traveled about the kingdom. Janey described the bee scouts huddled around tiny campfires at night, warming their bee legs and buzzing about how they missed their flower-petal mattresses.

"Do bees call their king His Majesty the way you and Papa do?" asked Alice.

Janey considered. "Let us just call him King Bee." Even an oblique reference to England's sovereign cast a pall on this July day. Disquieting tales were emerging from London. Three members of the Lords Appellant, the group that during the Merciless Parliament of 1388 had imposed order to the king's erratic rule by banishing or executing his favorites, had themselves been arrested and imprisoned. All three shunted off to the Tower of London on charges of treason. Thomas of Woodstock, Duke of Gloucester and the youngest of Richard's royal uncles, had been pulled from his very bed, or so it was rumored. There was talk of trials, of a monarch who had consolidated his power and was bent on retribution from all he fancied had thwarted him since the beginning of his reign.

"Papa said that when King Bee has some very naughty bee knights who break his laws, they punish themselves—"

"By stinging themselves to death," finished Alice.

Janey frowned. "Did Papa say that?" What did Serill mean? And why was he co-opting her stories?

"Bees have their very own Tower." Alice leaned forward to pet Happiness, the younger Bear Dog gifted them by their *grandpere*, who had roused himself from his place in the sun in order to check on his mistress. "Not like London's Tower, which is very big and seems rather mean, doesn't it?"

"Very mean," Genny echoed, looking pleased.

Janey had a sudden image of bees being led to a chopping block where they would have their tiny bee heads whacked off. She shivered. Real heads, not fantastical, very well might roll... had rolled.

At that moment, Guinevere cried, "Papa!" Leaping from the bench, she raced toward Serill, brown curls bouncing with each step. Janey had been too distracted to notice the returning hawking expedition.

Once Serill and the other riders drew rein, he dismounted and lashed his hawk to the pommel of his saddle. Genny wrapped her arms around him while Alice burrowed against Janey, though she smiled and waved. Billy squealed, dropped *Mon Coeur*, kicked his chubby legs to be let down and tottered toward his father, followed by both dogs.

"Billy-boy." With one arm still on Genny, Serill scooped Billy up by the other and held him round his stomach as if he were a sack of grain.

Billy squealed in delight. After Serill set him back on his feet, he chucked Guinevere under the chin. "And you, *bébé mouton*, you and your sister grow prettier every day."

When Serill straightened, he caught Janey's gaze. "Here, pet," he said to Genny, removing his hawking glove, eyes still on his wife. "Would you hold this for your papa?"

Janey knew why Serill was here, why he'd been hovering about since she'd announced her and Lady Ravenne's forthcoming pilgrimage. An extended pilgrimage to St Michael's Mount, which was near to the ends of earth. Or at least to the ends of England. And, apparently, not far from the manor of Mathilde Cheney and her new husband. Mathilde Cheney, widow of Derric le Babbe, Janey's own father. And who had borne two children that Mathilde-Tillie swore had been sired by Serill Hart.

What a fool you are, Janey thought, gazing calmly into the treacherous face of her husband. Those guileless blue eyes, that charming smile, that thick chestnut hair she'd once so loved to rumple between her fingers. *If you think I'd discomfit myself in order to confirm that you had sired another by-blow?* Serill Hart had no idea of her actual plans.

Serill followed young Guinevere to the bench. He was so used to that stubborn set of his wife's jaw, that distant, sometimes contemptuous look, they scarce registered. Months back, he'd decided, *So be it*, and accepted the reality that they, like so many couples, were in a marriage of business rather than love. While they were both polite to each other in front of their children, Serill doubted they were fooling the twins—or anyone else.

He eased down beside Genny. "We will all escort you to Edmundsbury Castle on the morrow." As if he and Janey were a typical married couple engaged in ordinary conversation. He tousled Genny's hair. "We will make a treat of it."

Edmundsbury Castle was a short ride from Swaffham Manor. There Janey would meet Lady Elizabeth Ravenne, and they would begin their journey to her destiny.

Janey nodded. "If it pleases you."

"And you will be escorted by both Hart and Ravenne retainers throughout."

Janey made a pained face. Serill was used to that face which, maddened, saddened or irritated him, depending on his mood. But times were too insecure to risk her and Elizabeth Ravenne's lives. There was no doubt King Richard was consolidating his power. Royal castles were being strengthened, and it was rumored that the strongholds of the arrested Lords Appellant were already being promised to Richard's sycophants. The king had ordered sheriffs to arrest all the Lords Appellant's followers, who were scattered throughout the kingdom. Which meant England's roads would be crowded with armed men, in addition to the usual noble households, pilgrims and merchants.

"The king has called up two thousand of his Cheshire archers and they are a lawless bunch—

Janey stood, as if to leave. "I'm going nowhere near London—"

"There have been demonstrations across the kingdom against the arrests, particularly that of Thomas Woodstock."

Aye, Thomas Woodstock, Duke of Gloucester. One of Richard's royal uncles. Who had once threatened to depose the king. More fool Gloucester that he and his fellow Lords Appellant had not thought to follow through on their long-ago threat!

"You will be crossing Gloucester's lands—or more properly his former lands. You can roll your eyes all you like, but these are dangerous times—"

Alice left the bench to hug her mother's hips, as if oblivious to the tension between her parents. "Are you really going so far away?" She gazed up at

Janey with solemn blue eyes. Janey tightened her arm around her daughter's shoulders.

Genny scooted closer to her father while cradling his jeweled hawking glove in her lap. "Papa says you and *Tante* Elizabeth will see many old bones and dried blood everywhere."

Billy waddled back to *Mon Coeur*, picked it up by its vellum pages and shook it. "Pretty," he said.

"Papa said *Tante* Elizabeth is going to fetch her son a bride," Alice said.

Janey frowned. "Sir Lancelot is not getting married," she said sharply. Lancelot of Glastonbury was the reason Janey was traveling near to the ends of the earth. Her secret suitor, who acted nothing like a suitor and who fled at the very sight of her. But Sir Lancelot had confessed his feelings and Janey, at the advanced age of twenty-six, had sworn she would no longer live without love.

Billy dropped *Mon Coeur* again.

"If Lance is not getting married, then his mother will be making a very long journey for naught," commented Serill. "Which strengthens my point, does it not, that now is not the time for travel?"

Watching her husband bend to retrieve *Mon Coeur*, Janey imagined herself as one of the archers who practiced weekly on village greens across England. Imagined herself knocking arrow to bowstring, aiming its point at Serill, letting loose and driving the arrow straight and true into his traitorous flesh. As often as she'd daydreamed something similar, Serill Hart had more invisible arrows sticking out of his body than spines from a hedgehog.

Serill handed the book over to Janey. "Billy's too young for such a treasure. And you *will* have an escort."

Janey's lips tightened. Without replying, she tossed *Mon Coeur* on the part of the bench she'd recently vacated and stalked away.

CHAPTER 2

JULY 1397, ON THE ROAD TO TINTAGEL

*W*hat had caused Lady Elizabeth Ravenne, Matthew Hart's older sister and Serill Hart's aunt, to undertake an excruciatingly unpleasant journey of two hundred fifty miles? From East Anglia all the way south to Cornwall? To ride, at her advanced age, inside a bone jarring carriage over roads that were sometimes little more than sheep trails?

One reason and one reason only: her sixth son, Lancelot of Glastonbury.

To find Lancelot a proper bride.

Now, Elizabeth Ravenne was the first to admit that naming her sons after Arthurian characters—from Arthur to Galahad and Perceval and Lancelot— had been a witless act. For her red-haired ruffians were about as far removed from the Knights of the Round Table as swans from toads. But Elizabeth had been young, her head bursting with romantic verses and fancies that caused her to thus name them, one after the other. By the time she'd given birth to Kay, her youngest, she'd persisted largely out of a desperate stubbornness in the face of the far more brutal reality of offspring possessing the manners of goats and the coarseness of Irishmen. (Elizabeth actually knew very little about Ireland other than the doomed tale of Tristan and Isolde. Beyond that, the entire island was apparently overrun with hairy barbarians.) Surely, God and the saints, *someone* would honor her faithfulness and imbue at least one of her sons with the chivalric virtues so omnipresent in King Arthur's knights.

Lancelot had come closest. Beneath that rough exterior, her child shared a portion of her poet's heart which he'd revealed when in the throes of his unrequited—or so Elizabeth believed—passion for Jane le Babbe.

Their Janey, who Elizabeth also loved like a daughter. But Jane le Babbe was married to her brother's son and forbidden to Lancelot. Thus, Elizabeth Ravenne did the only thing a mother could do. Went on a hunt for Lancelot's Guinevere. For certes, not Guinevere since Guinevere had already been married, and their forbidden love had crumbled Camelot. Rather an unmarried and less dangerous version.

The search had been difficult, not because of Lancelot's position as sixth son for his martial prowess and the financial success that accompanied it were well known. But because Lancelot himself was so very...uncooperative. He would either ignore Elizabeth's suggestions or hie himself off to one of his isolated properties after telling her—none too gently—to cease meddling.

However, recently Elizabeth Ravenne had detected a softening in Lancelot's attitude.

A mother, after all, can read the signs.

Around May Day, Lancelot had written informing her that he would be at Tintagel through Michaelmas, that he treasured his solitude and hoped to visit her at Edmundsbury Castle before winter's snows.

Elizabeth Ravenne's interpretation: "I am ready to marry. Begin negotiations!" And she had. But now she must make certain her instincts were correct, that Olivet of Camelford, whose family holdings were only a few miles from Tintagel, was worthy of her boy's attentions. Then she would introduce them, and by this time next year, God willing, her Lance would be joyously awaiting the arrival of his first child.

Jane le Babbe had also interpreted Lancelot's missive, though very differently. He was letting her know, in an admittedly circuitous fashion, of his whereabouts over the next four months. Following this year's Cherry Fair, which was always celebrated when Kent's cherry blossoms shimmered their loveliest, Janey had decided that before she reached middle age, she would experience love, *real* love, not the pretense that had been her infatuation with Serill Hart. Thus, she would toss caution aside and throw herself at Lancelot.

So Janey had sent him her own secret message, first copying verses from *Lancelot of the Cart*, which she considered their story.

30

"...Of what was I thinking when my lover stood before me and I should have welcomed him, that I would not listen to his words? Was I not a fool, when I refused to look at or speak to him?"

Then she'd drawn a unicorn with its head bent most tenderly toward a heart placed atop a gold cushion nestling beneath its hooves. (She'd pondered adding a lance somewhere appropriate, but decided the symbolism was obvious enough without it.) She, the unicorn, was offering her heart to Lancelot of Glastonbury.

Unbeknownst to Janey, Lancelot had been both touched and befuddled upon receiving her correspondence. He understood that she lamented her previous indifference and also understood—experiencing happiness and terror in equal measure—that Lady Jane reciprocated his feelings. However, this changed nothing. That was the truth of courtly love, wasn't it, that one was allowed to look but never to touch?

And the drawing was so confusing. Lancelot considered Janey's drawings to be charming works of art, though he could seldom decipher the identity of whatever it was she chose to sketch. (But her colors were wondrously brilliant, were they not?) Lancelot simply assumed that he was too unsophisticated to understand such talent. As in her current offering: what exactly was the creature? A whale spouting water from its blowhole? But a whale with legs? It must be a metaphor for something, though he could not think what. Nor the blob that the creature appeared to have disgorged. A cluster of grapes, mayhap? A hedgehog? Lancelot had spent days leafing through his bestiary, trying to decipher a connection to some mythical animal, to puzzle out a hidden meaning. Janey was so clever; it must be a clue of some sort, and he despaired as to how to respond. Nay, not respond, for he could never act upon his devotion beyond the presents he periodically sent her and her babes. He'd done his best to be faithful to his friend and cousin, Serill Hart, his church, his conscience and his creed. Which meant he would continue worshipping his lady from afar.

Thus, Lancelot did the only thing he dared.

Every morning he kissed Janey's drawing before placing it somewhere upon his person.

And went about his daily duties as before.

Janey had not really expected her bashful lover to reply. She'd not even seen Lancelot in three years. When they'd all attended the Cherry Fair and

Janey, fed up with her husband's adultery, had broken her lute over Serill's head and tossed an ewer of wine upon his current whore.

That year, as always, a tournament had been held during the festivities. How Janey had enjoyed watching Lancelot joust, knowing that he had placed her embroidered favor next to his heart. Her secret satisfaction when Lancelot had knocked Serill from his destrier, understanding that he'd struck that blow for her. (Even as she'd prayed her husband wouldn't be too badly hurt.) How Janey's wounded pride had been soothed knowing that someone, at least, loved her, had loved her from the time she'd arrived at Edmundsbury Castle as a frightened girl. Over the years, Janey had been too besotted by Serill Hart to even notice Lancelot of Glastonbury, lumping him in with Lady Ravenne's other boorish brood.

How wrong I was!

It had been Lancelot who had sent her love poems after she'd caught Serill kissing one of his chits. Who had sworn that during Serill and Lancelot's forthcoming crusade he would keep her husband faithful. (A promise he had valiantly—though unsuccessfully—tried to keep. This was Serill Hart, after all. Of such charm and immorality that not even a pilgrimage to the Holy Land had curbed his licentiousness. At this very moment Satan must be stoking the fires of hell in anticipation of his arrival!)

And now, Janey planned to fall into the arms of a man who cherished her in a way Serill Hart never had. A man sought after by some of England's most beautiful ladies. How women chattered on and on about Lancelot of Glastonbury—his grace and success in the lists; his perfectly chiseled profile; his long hair the color of sunset; that "mysterious" or "irresistible" half-smile he donned whenever he was approached by those who sought to win him for their own.

Yet Lancelot of Glastonbury had pledged his heart to *her*.

Three years since you've seen him, mocked her pesky inner voice. *Who do you think you are that Sir Lancelot—that any man—would love you? Plain Jane le Babbe. How high you think to reach above yourself!*

Largely confined to her miniature palace on wheels, Elizabeth Ravenne and her fellow travelers sometimes managed only ten miles a day.

At this rate, Janey fretted, *it will take us three weeks to reach our destination.*

However, she was increasingly grateful that her husband had insisted upon an armed escort. Their small caravan shared the road with more than the usual merchants, pilgrims and travelling noble households. Sergeants-at-arms bearing letters seeking loans (extortion!) from various magnates and towns to further King Richard's business; mailed troops rushing past with pennons flying, stirring up fears along with dust; drovers driving their animals to markets; processions of townsfolk publicly praying that their king's heart, which seemed to have shriveled beneath his exquisitely brocaded doublet, might bloom from hatred to love.

Of course, everyone they met passed along rumors as fact or swore the most outrageous of lies—"Thomas of Woodstock has been murdered!" "The Duke of Lancaster/his son/their children have all been thrown in London's Tower."

Finally understanding that Henry Bolingbroke in peril meant Serill and Lancelot and her father-in-law in peril, Janey tied Lunette to the back of Lady Ravenne's carriage and sat with Elizabeth and her two maids seeking reassurance.

They had been near Bath then, and Janey had found it so very difficult to sort out the tittle-tattle, largely from the pilgrims who flowed across England in a never-ending wave. Even the court poet, Geoffrey Chaucer, had penned tales of those bound for Canterbury Cathedral, though Janey trusted he had made his characters more interesting than those with whom they traveled. So much of their conversation was the same, causing her to close her ears. The endless litany of aches and pains! Of apocalyptic portents so, really, we must repent and rend our garments! King Richard is the Anti-Christ! John of Gaunt is the Anti-Christ! Boniface IX is the Anti-Christ! Nay, Avignon's pope is the Anti-Christ! Lollards are true Christians! Lollards are heretics!

But, amidst the prattle, lay nuggets of fact that Janey was helpless to interpret. The most prominent narrative ran something like this: since the death of his beloved Queen Anne three years past, Richard had gone mad. He forbade anyone to address him in terms other than "Your Majesty" or "Your Highness," and did not allow those approaching him to look him directly in the eye. Or turn their back on him. Or behave as if he were king, but rather a god. To do so risked imprisonment or worse, depending on his whim. Richard of Bordeaux had begun to rule through terror. Even the most favored of magnates who were showered with titles and lands and largesse knew the king could yank it all away in a fit of pique.

Janey began to worry that England might soon be caught up in an insurrection as had happened seventy years past against the bad king, Edward Caernarvon. Or, with all the armed men on the roads, had it already happened? Even now Swaffham Manor might be burning and her husband and babes harmed; Lancelot might have donned his armor and ridden north to take up arms against King Richard or—oh, she didn't know—*someone*. Her father-in-law, Matthew Hart, might have combined forces with his liege, the Duke of Lancaster, and was even now storming Westminster.

An increasingly distraught Janey had entered the wagon to lay bare her fears.

"Nonsense, "Lady Elizabeth replied with a negligent wave of the hand. "Even King Richard knows better than to do anything more than poke the bear. John of Gaunt's claws yet remain far too sharp for that popinjay to really engage him or his kin. Or the duke's liegemen," she added meaningfully.

Elizabeth paused. "I will admit that something does disturb me." She lowered her voice, as if that might somehow keep her maids, seated right next to them, from overhearing. "The king recently adopted his cousin, Edward, Earl of Rutland, as his "brother.""

Janey had no idea what that could mean. "Tell me," she urged.

Elizabeth Ravenne clutched her gnarled hands over the embroidery hoop that had been barely stitched throughout their journey. A songbird in its cage hanging from the ceiling flapped its wings and shifted position. "When King Richard was out of the country, he twice made the Earl of Rutland's father keeper of the realm."

"And—" Janey prodded. While she could concoct stories and memorize passages and poems, she knew so very little about political matters—a condition she vowed to rectify.

"By calling young Edmund "brother" some say that, should Richard die without an heir, he wants England's crown to pass to the house of York. Bypassing the house of Lancaster."

Janey slumped against the cushions. "Henry Bolingbroke," she murmured. John of Gaunt did not covet England's throne for himself, but as the third King Edward's eldest living son, he could make a strong case that his first-born should ascend it.

So this was politics? It was all too devious for her. "How can this be? Our king's actions seem deliberately designed to stir up more enmity among his most powerful subjects. What is he thinking?"

Elizabeth Ravenne sighed and absently soothed the fabric stretched across her hoop. "We will continue to pray very hard for peace at each shrine we pass along the way. And when you reach St Michael's Mount, you must bequeath an extra generous donation for the monks to offer up constant masses."

Janey nodded, as if she had any intention of continuing her journey on to that place of mermaids and sirens and Jack the Giant Killer. Even had she been so inclined—for it might be interesting to glimpse a mermaid—Janey was beginning to fear the machinations of Richard of Bordeaux might be too twisted for even God to sort out.

Elizabeth Ravenne's carriage and its escort crept on, ever closer to Camelford. When the weather was good, Lady Ravenne watched out her window and increasingly thought about the past—how so little other than herself had changed. Even in the fullness of summer, this part of England was becoming bleaker with windswept moors and great slabs of granite. Just as she remembered. She'd not been this far south in many years, when she'd undertaken her own pilgrimage to St Michael's Mount. Once she'd been a great one for pilgrimages, which had not only served a religious purpose but had allowed her surcease from her boor of a husband.

Now, here she was an old woman, who could look out at a countryside scarcely altered from when she'd been a mother of two rather than eight. Her last trip to Cornwall had been a decade or so after the Black Death, when more villages had been abandoned than inhabited, and it seemed God had turned his back upon mankind. So many scars in one's life, not only of a personal nature but those of a cosmic nature over which no human had control. Odd, that after almost fifty years she would be remembering the Death—the fields of dead sheep along with piles of corpses corrupting villages, monasteries, abbeys and cities. The red crosses painted on plague doors. The aftermath when so many simply wept or stared or went mad or gave themselves over to debauchery and other vices. Elizabeth yet thanked God that not a one of her family had been snatched away. She liked to believe that was because of her piety. But how then to explain why monasteries and other religious houses had been especially decimated?

One of Lady Ravenne's maids laid aside the lute she'd been strumming, and as if catching her mistress's gloomy thoughts, said, "Yestereve I heard some pilgrims saying the world will end in 1400."

"Less than three years," said Elizabeth's second maid, crossing herself.

Before Lady Ravenne could respond, Janey, who was once more sharing the chariot, leapt in. "Pilgrims' prophecies are more common than the badges upon their sweaty old hats." Privately, she thought, *I've no intention of allowing the world to end just when I've decided to live!*

Finally, they reached the crossroads to Camelford. Janey said good-bye to Lady Ravenne, who rolled away east. To Sir Frederic, who headed her escort, she said, as she had previously planned, "Continue on to the Mount." She handed him the purse he was to present to St Michael's monks with instructions for perpetual masses. "I will soon catch up with Lady Ravenne." How easily the lies slid from her tongue! "Meet me at this crossroad on the Feast of the Beheading of John the Baptist."

And then Janey was alone, seeing only the back of the Hart meinie and inhaling the dust from Lady Ravenne's slowly disappearing wagon.

Sir Frederic would not return for three weeks. Three weeks. What would she do if Lancelot of Glastonbury refused her?

Sweet Christ, I've not thought this through.

Mind whirling, Janey turned Lunette toward Tintagel, with Fearless padding placidly beside her, as he had throughout. She knew the outcome she desired and that it was sinful; that she was using Lancelot, that she had once again created a phantasm to love. Just as she'd done with Serill.

And that she was asking Lancelot to betray a boon companion.

Though she wasn't exactly asking that.

I am not sure what I am asking.

While Lunette and Fearless picked over the barely discernible path, Janey began formulating questions she should have pondered before ever striking out on what might be a sleeveless errand.

Will you be able to carry on a coherent conversation? Will your sheepish nature cause me to find you unattractive? Will I be too frightened to allow you to seduce me? Will you be a clumsy lover? Will I? What will happen afterward? Will we be able to quietly continue our lives? Might we stir some tawdry scandal?

Ha! Ha! cried that inner voice, harsh as a raven's caw. *What if 'tis you, not*

Elizabeth Ravenne, who is delusional? What if Lancelot has already met this Olivet of Camelford and burns with a white-hot desire to wed her?

Janey only knew for certes that she wanted a man to love her.

Or at least that she wanted a man who was capable of thawing the block of ice that had once been her heart.

CHAPTER 3

*I*t was late afternoon by the time Jane le Babbe reached Tintagel. What a wild place it was, with waves crashing all around and that giant slab of rock protruding from the equally wild coastline. If this spoke to Lancelot of Glastonbury's soul, perhaps Janey was in store for quite an adventure.

Janey crossed a forbidding isthmus which provided the only entrance to the castle. The trackway was wide enough, but if she veered, if Lunette started, they could easily tumble to the water below. Seagulls called a warning. She felt a sickness rise in her stomach and gripped her roan mare's reins more tightly. Once she'd heard Serill and Lancelot discussing how, because of Tintagel's natural terrain, a handful of knights could forever hold it, even against an entire enemy army.

Janey didn't know whether to be terrified or mesmerized. Why would Lancelot choose such a place? She remembered the ancient tale of Uther Pendragon, who'd been driven mad with lust for Igraine, wife to Gorlais. Janey shivered. She was trodding the exact path over which Pendragon and his mount had thundered when, aided by Merlin's magic potion which had transformed his likeness into that of Igraine's husband, Uther Pendragon had

38

crossed into Tintagel Castle. Once inside, he'd ravaged Igraine. To plant the seed that would become Arthur, King of Britain.

Janey could visualize the entire scene. Here it seemed, if not normal, inevitable. Here, in this savage place with the waves beating against the headland which jutted like a giant's jaw out into the vastness of the Celtic Sea. Here, in this place where legends had once walked, where God Himself had surely looked down, like pagan gods from Olympus, to shape the fate of England.

Janey passed through a gatehouse which sported open gates and no sign of a guard to deliver a challenge. An ever alert Fearless, great head swiveling from side to side, walked beside her. She didn't spot anyone in the lower ward, though smoke curled from what was probably a kitchen. And from an area to her left and above, most likely where Lancelot's men lodged, emerged the clashing of swords, the clack of wood as quarter staffs slammed against each other; shouting, ribaldry and laughter.

So, I am not alone.

Janey continued on, the patter of her heart increasing with each clop of Lunette's hooves.

"I have made a terrible mistake," she whispered to Fearless, who turned his dark eyes to her as if in acknowledgement.

Deeper into the heart of Tintagel.

The original castle had been built more than a century past, by one of bad King John's sons who had been enamored of the Arthurian legends. Since then it had obviously fallen into serious disrepair. In a way, the ruin suited Janey's perception of her would-be lover.

"Magic," she whispered. Tintagel was either a magical place or a diabolically wicked one. Not only did legend claim this on behalf of Arthur, but Tristan and Isolde had herein played out their illicit love affair, which also dealt with magic potions, betrayal and, *naturellement*, tragic death.

Janey drew rein at a stable within the gatehouse courtyard. She was relieved to see a groom leading a huge black destrier she recognized as Lancelot's Manslayer. The groom tied the stallion to a nearby post before beginning careful inspection of his hooves.

Which meant Lancelot of Glastonbury was in residence! Janey sat up straighter, anticipating that her intended lover would momentarily emerge from the stables. Or might he be one of the knights she spotted in the distance crossing the inner courtyard?

The groom's back was to her. Janey directed Lunette to a mounting block and eased herself down, biting back a groan from her time in the saddle. Fearless waited patiently beside her.

When she called out, the groom turned in surprise. "My lady?" he asked, after approaching her and acknowledging her station with a bow. He eyed Fearless warily and behind her for the expected maid and escort.

"Might you tell me the whereabouts of Sir Lancelot?"

"I believe he is in the great hall, my lady." The groom nodded toward a portcullis above which rose the tiled roof of Tintagel's primary residence.

Janey's breath puffed out in an audible sigh. She felt suddenly so alone and tired. So small and lost. Now that their meeting was at hand, she realized the enormity of her miscalculation.

Now that inner voice sounded like the scoldings of a flock of seagulls. *Witless, witless girl! Thinking that Lancelot of Glastonbury has been pining for you. Just who do you think you are?*

"Please attend to my horse."

After the groom led Lunette away, Janey squared her shoulders, took a determined breath and began walking. Once she reached the great hall, she immediately saw that, while lights bloomed from its interior, the room was only partially habitable. An entire section had crumbled into ruin, though a handful of workmen were making repairs.

From the kitchen and bakehouse wafted mouthwatering aromas, reminding Janey she'd not eaten since a breakfast of brown bread and cheese. Spotting a group of men throwing dice, she called out, "Sir knights? Please tell me where I might find your lord."

The knights stared at her, open-mouthed. Obviously, this was not a place that regularly entertained the female sex. Which was reassuring, was it not, since Olivet of Camelford was a woman?

The knights bowed; a younger one stepped forward. "Lady Hart? I have seen thee at Lord Bolingbroke's, have I not? In happier days?"

Janey felt her cheeks flush. There would be no hiding her presence. She would be disgraced.

Is that not what you wanted? And by disgracing yourself, you will also heap disgrace upon your husband?

"How kind to remember. Now, will you escort me to your liege?"

A pack of hounds, lounging in the shadows of the ruined hall, began barking and bounded toward Fearless. A growl sent them slinking back to their corner. Somewhere a goat bleated; she heard the cooing of doves from an invisible dovecote.

The young knight led her, not to the great hall, but beyond the crumbling parapet toward the sea.

Tintagel was unlike any place Janey had ever been, wilder even than Cumbria, for it seemed to have grown organically out of the rock itself. The lights from the great hall cast a golden glow that, with each step, dissipated in the gloom, like a candle spent down to its nub. While they walked, the young knight offered pleasantries to which she responded by rote. All the while knowing that he must be scandalized and, if a gossip, eager to hasten her shame.

"Sir Lancelot spends most evens out here. He even constructed a hut. It gives him peace, he says."

Sunset had painted the sky, at the point where it met the endless waters, the bloodiest of reds. Janey shivered, though not from the crisp air, but because she'd never seen anything so desolately beautiful. The wind whipped at her cloak. With each step the roar of the waves grew louder. How far was she from the ledge? She felt a prickling of fear for her depth perception was somehow skewed and the drop off seemed dangerously near.

Janey dismissed her escort when she saw *him*, with his back to her, huge and dark against the gloaming, his feet planted apart and the wind whipping his hair. Something twisted inside her. She'd always been so wrong about men, about everything really, creating a world out of an imagination that refused to see things as they were, but as she would have them.

Was this another of her fantasies? Thinking that Lancelot of Glastonbury would rescue her, somehow take her away from the pain that was Serill Hart, provide simple answers so she need not mourn a husband who had become husband in name only?

Could he, as she did with her children, kiss away the hurts and make them all better?

"Lancelot?"

He turned. It was too dark to see his face, whether it registered surprise or displeasure. Fearless stood still at her side, as if he too were curious as to Lancelot's reaction, though his tail swept back and forth in welcoming fashion.

Janey's limbs were suddenly impossibly weary, for the long days in the saddle seemed to have settled upon her with bone-aching force, making her too paralyzed to move. But it wasn't that, at all. Fear it was that held her in its paralyzing grip.

What would she do if Lancelot were cruel to her? Said hateful things? Perhaps he didn't love her, had never loved her. Like the precepts of courtly love, his attentions might all have been a pretty tale to pass the time between jousts and crusades and the day-to-day tedium of manor life. Had he been toying with her the way Serill toyed with his conquests? The way Serill had toyed with her?

Lancelot slowly approached, his body language offering no clue as to his state of mind. Janey could hear the crashing of the waves, the distant call of gulls winging out into the darkness. It was all so lonely, so achingly beautiful that she swallowed back a sob.

Then Lancelot stood before her. They stared at each other. He was not Serill, he was not like any man she'd ever known. But she did not know him now, did she?

Oh, dear, oh, dear, oh, dear…

"You are here." He said, his voice filled with wonder. For indeed, Lancelot felt as if he'd stepped into a dream. Jane le Babbe could not possibly be at Tintagel. Yet…

"How can this be?" he asked softly. What would he do? What *should* he do? He knew from Serill's laments that they no longer interacted as man and wife. But that did not make Janey a free woman. That did not make her presence proper.

Janey could hear her heart above the hammering surf. As Lancelot continued to stare, she knew with blinding certainty that her fears had been justified. Just like Serill, he would reject her; just like Serill, he was about to crush her very soul. Unconsciously, a hand went to Fearless for support.

Abruptly, as he had done in the scriptorium at Edmundsbury Castle during a bygone Christmas, Lancelot knelt before her. His head remained bowed while stretching his arm to her.

Janey clasped his hand in her own. "Rise, Sir Lancelot," she whispered.

How very odd. She felt as if they had been concocted out of all the stories she'd read about Lancelot and Guinevere. About forbidden longing and forbidden love and how small acts, one upon the other, led to larger acts with larger consequences until one was tangled in such a web that one's destiny was no longer one's own, but inevitably led to destruction—even the destruction of an entire kingdom.

Such nonsense. She and Lancelot of Glastonbury were simply a man and a woman, one kneeling, one standing with hand outstretched, invisible to all save God, if He had chosen this moment to gaze down upon Tintagel.

Lancelot rose to hover over her. He seemed so very tall, as if he were something more than human. Something created out of the rock, the waves, the tears, triumphs and tragedies of all those legends that had shaped this hallowed place.

But while Lancelot might seem like something mythical, Janey knew that she remained simple Jane le Babbe, cuckquean of Serill Hart. A plain woman with dreams far too big for her.

"Oh," she breathed. She felt it, the urge to plunge into the darkness like a crazed animal, to fling herself into the sea rather than endure more rejection, more heartbreak from one she'd convinced herself might care.

Lancelot reached out and drew her to him. He hugged her tentatively at first and then with the fierceness of a lifetime of denial.

Against the rough wool of his tunic, Janey choked, "Please love me."

Though even as she uttered the plea Janey realized it was a request too big for any man to fulfill.

CHAPTER 4

*J*aney had often imagined their lovemaking or seduction or sin or whatever the proper terminology. A solar, plain but neat, with the usual curtained bed, also plain but clean. Sometimes she pictured them drawing the draperies so that they would be sheltered from the rest of the world in an erotic cocoon; other times they seemed to be outside castle walls with a balmy breeze caressing their naked flesh while they forever pledged themselves to each other via their forbidden acts...

However, their first night was unfolding rather differently. They did not return to dine in Tintagel's great hall. Nor did she enjoy a leisurely bath after which Lancelot would draw her to his private chamber—for surely this rough hut was not his main abode—and once inside make such passionate love to her that she would forget all about her devil of a husband.

Instead, Lancelot gestured for her to enter his hut, which consisted of a pallet, table and bench and cupboard. From the crude cupboard he withdrew bread, cheese, and a wooden bowl filled with fresh apples.

He prepared their meal with slow, deliberate movements, as if thinking while he worked. He said very little, for wasn't that ever the way with Lancelot of Glastonbury? Janey rather enjoyed watching him slice their apples and cheese and bread, finding the silence comfortable rather than awkward. Besides, conversation would mean she must explain desires she wasn't sure she could even articulate. Her journey had been long and arduous; her emotions bounced between nervousness, exhaustion, fear, excitement and the urge to take a very long nap.

Janey turned her attention to Lancelot's pallet. The blanket looked of a fine quality, but the mattress was most likely made of chaff, after the manner of peasants. Not so comfortable to sleep upon, even if there had been room for the two of them. And certainly not the seductive site of her imaginings.

"I've stew left over from dinner." Lancelot extended a bowl. "For Fearless?"

Janey fed her dog before she and Lancelot sat down to their fare. Afterward, he shook his mane of hair so that it caught on his shoulders and out of his face. "Come sit with me," he said, holding out his hand. This was the first time Lancelot had voluntarily touched her in an intimate fashion.

Janey allowed him to lead her outside to a bench in front of his hut, which looked barely big enough for one. Lancelot pulled her onto his lap. The man who trembled to touch her? Obviously, he was braver in the dark.

Or perhaps he'd simply come to a decision.

Janey shyly slipped her arms around her would-be lover's neck. She felt so small against the vastness of this man and the surrounding wilderness. Even in the dark she could discern the edge of the cliff, so close that disaster awaited one who stumbled home drunk, or sleepwalked.

Beside them, Fearless placed his head between his paws and watched them lazily.

"I do adore thee, Lady Jane," Lancelot began. "I canna remember when I did not. But I could not speak. I could only watch and worship from afar, knowing more was forbidden to me."

The wind blew chill off the ocean, cooling her suddenly fevered body. Lancelot was addressing her in the language of the Romances, haltingly but articulately, and how it thrilled her!

"Tell me," Janey whispered. She was acutely aware of the scratchy linsey-woolsey of Lancelot's tunic against her cheek, the thud of his heart, the scent of sweat, wool, and earth. She suspected he spent far more time with nature as his bed and the heavens as his roof than in civilized surroundings.

Lancelot's eyes shone upon her. "There are things more important than a man's desires," he continued in his deliberate manner. She was discovering that was his way. Speaking as if words were so precious, they must be measured out in the manner of exquisite jewels. "I've learned that much in my thirty-one years. Though I would have it otherwise, you and I can never be together. I can never make love to you, lay with you in my arms, run my hands over the silkiness of your flesh...."

Oh, my. Lancelot's words inflamed Janey even as she realized he was rejecting her. Beneath the evocative phrases, he was saying, "No!"

Why? Why??

Was she too plain, her body too much like a boy's? Was she too fat or thin or uninteresting? Was it because he feared breaking God's sixth commandment?

"'Tis my name, you see. And the cursed legacy that comes with it."

Janey drew back in surprise. "What do you mean?"

"You are a student of history, my heart." His gaze was focused on her lips, increasing the heat of her body. If this was a rejection, it was a most peculiar one.

"You know that Lancelot and Guinevere destroyed a kingdom."

"Aye. But that was so very long ago. There have been other knights named Lancelot. And I'm, for certes, no Guinevere."

Lancelot pulled her close so that his lips rested against her neck. He held her as if she were the world, as if there was nothing more tender, more exquisite, more precious than that which rested between his massive arms. Janey closed her eyes to better experience a moment so profound it defied description. Was this what mystics experienced in the bliss of their visions?

"Even as a wee lad, I pondered what would have happened to Lancelot du Lac if he'd not lain with Lady Guinevere. 'Twas more than the mere act of adultery. It was as if they set in motion some cosmic fortune's wheel that destroyed both King Arthur and Camelot."

A shiver passed the length of Janey's body at words she herself had recently contemplated. Could part of Tintagel's magic be that here they were capable of roaming each other's minds? "We are not important enough to make a difference to the fate of anything beyond ourselves," she said, her voice shaky with emotion.

"I cannot risk it," Lancelot said against Janey's neck. He drew back again to seek her gaze. "Always I've felt as if the fate of England is on my shoulders, foolish as that seems. Therefore, I did what I must."

"Which was?"

"I made a vow."

"Oh." While Janey was disappointed, she would never call his disclosures foolish. All her life people had labeled her own thoughts and beliefs and stories thus, but they were not foolish to her.

"How brave you are!" she murmured.

"I have something more to confess."

Fascinated by the unexpected turnings of Lancelot's mind, she waited. She felt as if they'd entered an enchanted realm, albeit a barbaric one, where anything might happen.

"I…I've never even lain with a woman."

Janey tried to gauge his expression in the dark, searching for the lie. "But all those strumpets…how you haunt the stews." Was Lancelot thinking to tell her a tale, as her husband so often had? "Everyone says so."

"People see what they wish to see. As they assume certain things which somehow become truth, even though they are not."

"I do not understand." Not even clergy could be counted on to be celibate. What was Lancelot saying?

"When I was poor, no lady would look at me, so everyone believed I was haunting local brothels in the usual fashion. But 'twas never so. My companions *assumed*. We are all too immersed in our own adventures to pay much attention to others. 'Tis simple to tell tales or allow others to tell tales for us."

"But I've seen how ladies vie for your favor—"

"Aye, seeking marriage. So 'tis easy to treat them with *courtesie* because I am not supposed to bed a lady, am I?"

Of course not. In theory. But reality was very different. Reality was why she was here.

"You've never lain with a woman?" Janey repeated stupidly.

"I have dreamed of it many times. Dreamed of you," he amended. "But, when I was landless, I had to make my fortune, and a knight who refrains from carnal behaviors enjoys increased prowess at the jousts. We are so easily distracted by fleshly weaknesses. While I could not control my thoughts, I *can* control my actions."

Janey considered this. Such oaths were commonplace in Romances. She'd even heard whispers involving a few flesh and blood knights, but she'd not taken them literally since men were ever born to boast. So, what was she to make of Lancelot?

"I've not even kissed a woman," he confessed.

"Oh." She cupped Lancelot's cheek with a hand. He was so artless, so sincere she knew he was telling the truth.

"My dear sweet Lancelot," she whispered. What a fine jest. She had chosen one of the few honorable men in Christendom with whom to commit adultery! "Please tell me about your vow. Where did you swear it?"

"Before the spring in Glastonbury where Joseph of Arimathea hid the Holy Grail. The water runs through the grail cup so that when it reaches the surface—"

"'Tis stained red with Christ's blood," Janey finished, nearly making the sign of the cross. While she'd never visited the Chalice Well, everyone agreed upon its holiness. Like all the greatest knights—though primarily those portrayed in literature —Lancelot of Glastonbury had given his word. She would never disrespect him or risk the wrath of God by tempting him to break a solemn vow.

"This is unexpected," she managed, feeling awe and disappointment equally.

"But I would kiss thee, Lady Jane, just this once, if 'twould please you."

As if granting a sacred request, she nodded solemnly. "I would like that."

Lancelot gathered her into his arms; she raised her face to his. He brushed her mouth, which was slightly open, and the touch ignited her to her soul. His lips settled over hers, first lightly, then with more urgency. Her mouth parted to allow him entrance, and his kiss deepened until Janey's head was spinning.

It was something larger than a mere kiss, something both divine and erotic. She could feel his desire and knew that it was within her power to make him break his vow, to lay with a man who, she was certain she desired more than she'd ever desired anyone, including her traitorous husband. But to what purpose? If Janey loved Lancelot—and she was beginning to believe she might —why risk a lifetime of torment for a few moments of physical pleasure?

Still, how tempting the contemplation!

Finally, Lancelot ended his kiss and buried his head in her hair, which had fallen partially free from its caul.

"Dearest Lancelot," she whispered, her voice husky, for she was overwhelmed with the enormity of what seemed to be unfolding between them. "What a pair we are!"

CHAPTER 5

TINTAGEL

The only time Lancelot left Janey was when he returned to the great hall to speak to his knights.

"Mother has already sent a message," he said, the first morning. "It appears Olivet of Camelford is beautiful, charming and has been longing to meet me since she first saw me joust at Smithfield."

Janey gazed at him with alarm. A rival? And so close!

He waved a hand dismissively. "I already had word sent back that I long ago departed to SnoDun, my property in Wales."

During their three weeks together, food and drink and other necessities were brought to them, but Janey only occasionally glimpsed Lancelot's men. They two were the only inhabitants of this part of the promontory, save for the occasional bleating goat or sheep or wandering cow. And, of course, the seagulls, which, if one looked deeper than their screeching and shitting, were believed to fly between the earth and heavens so they might bring messages to mortals.

While Lancelot shared the magic of Tintagel, he had no idea that Janey found herself more enthralled with the magic that was Lancelot of Glastonbury himself. How, all those years, could she have been so ignorant of the nature of this man?

The first day out, he showed her a private cove in which to swim. When Janey confessed she didn't know how, Lancelot replied, "I will carry you on my back."

They stripped naked, and he indeed carried her while Fearless, ears pricked forward, eyes watchful, guarded them from the shoreline. Janey enjoyed the experience so much they made it a daily affair. Never had she felt so free. They were like children; like Adam and Eve, locked away in some primeval Paradise. Here, in this isolated cove where the water was as blue as Lancelot's eyes, nakedness seemed the most natural thing. And while Lancelot of Glastonbury was long of limb and muscular of chest and so very beautiful to look upon, Janey curbed her lascivious impulses. Gazing upon him through lustful eyes would sully their relationship, and that she must never do.

After they did their version of swimming, they would lay beside each other, fingers touching, letting the sun dry them. There was something so pure about Lancelot that it spoke to the wounds in Janey's soul—the mockery of childhood companions, the assaults of her first husband, the condescending forbearance so many showed when she mentioned her fabulisms, and most of all, the husband who had been so indifferent to the love she'd once offered with such naïve innocence.

Lancelot could have been fashioned from any literary hero. Noble. Kind. His broad shoulders indeed capable of carrying the weight of a kingdom upon them. It was easy to believe that they two *might* cradle England's fate in their hands, that their virtuous behavior would make all the things right that had been wronged by Tintagel's other lovers. Her Lancelot was a worthy successor to Lancelot du Lac. And amazingly, because of the way he looked at her, Janey could sometimes believe she might measure up to Guinevere.

When not at the cove, they explored the rest of Tintagel. Some of the ruins, Lancelot told her, dated back to Roman times. There was a chapel and a garden with crumbling walls where they would oft sit, facing the horizon. There they would speak of many things. The history of the Arthurian lovers, *naturellement,* though their interests ranged much wider than literature.

"On our journey, there was much talk about Lollardy. Several friars were preaching its merits. What are your thoughts?" Janey was sure Lancelot would have an informed opinion of everything.

"They do not believe in purgatory and say that priestly celibacy is an invention of the Antichrist."

"Mother Mary," gasped Janey, delighted when Lancelot drew her closer as it to protect her from the Antichrist.

"Nor do they believe that baptism and confession are necessary for salvation, and that honoring saints' images is a form of idolatry."

"How do you know such things?"

"For a while our Duke of Lancaster was sympathetic to their teachings, but no longer."

They spoke of so many other things that Janey found herself silently begging Lancelot's forgiveness. For how could she ever have dismissed this scholar and poet as a bumbling oaf?

Lancelot showed her a long manmade vault which Janey decided must be the Cave of Lovers, where Tristan and Isolde had hidden from Isolde's husband, King Mark, who was aggrieved that Tristan had taken his wife. (But it was that pesky love potion they'd drunk. Which rendered them blameless.) Lancelot and Janey shouted their names into the cave's vastness and laughed at the echoes, but when they then called the names of Tintagel's legendary lovers, she felt humbled. Here Janey could believe that she was, perhaps not so much an ordinary woman after all, but one of destiny.

Lancelot showed her the rose tree that grew from Isolde's grave which was met by a vine from Tristan's, a vine that would wrap itself around the trunk of the rose and could never be cut down, no matter how many tried.

Meaning the doomed lovers would never more be parted.

"Why must love always be so sad?" Janey mused. Lancelot wrapped her in his arms. "Why cannot someone have a happy ending?"

"We will have one," Lancelot said, kissing the top of her head.

"How so?"

"Because we will choose where we will begin and end our story."

Sitting with their backs to a dilapidated chapel wall, shoulder to shoulder, they gazed out across the Celtic Sea. Storm clouds were beginning to stack, one upon the other, far out on the horizon. The weather had been so perfect, but it, like their time together, was coming to an end

"Tell me a story. About us," Lancelot said. His tangled locks glowed like fire in the gathering sunset.

Janey found his fingers and entwined them in her own. After gathering her thoughts, she began.

"Once there was a dragon." There was almost always a dragon. "This dragon lived in a cave overlooking a meadow rimmed by trees. Conifers, I think, like those around Lake Winandermere. Everyone was afraid of the dragon who breathed fire, even when he tried to speak so softly and only wanted to say, 'Good morrow.' Which meant the dragon was very lonely."

Janey paused to touch the bracelet on her wrist, which she'd braided with both her hair and Lancelot's. He wore an identical one on his own.

"One day the dragon spotted a doe picking her way carefully through the meadow. She looked so very frightened emerging from the forest. The dragon continued watching her and over time, fell in love with her."

"Because she was so brave," said Lancelot, raising her hand and exposing the palm in order to brush it with his lips. "And bright and innocent. And lovely."

"One day the doe wandered so close to the dragon that he tried to speak, but flames erupted from his mouth, causing the doe to flee in terror. The dragon was inconsolable. What would he do?" Here Janey hesitated for she had no idea how to solve the poor creature's problem.

"Might there be a nearby stream from which he drank that helped tamp the flames? So that, if he spoke very softly, he and his beloved could communicate?"

"Exactly." Janey slipped her arm around Lancelot's naked waist and snuggled against his chest. "Over time the frightened deer and the lonely dragon grew to love each other. But when she tried to draw too close, 'twas not only his fiery breath that kept them apart. His scales burned like lighted coals. Because of this, no one had ever gotten close enough to touch the dragon."

"Which was the reason he was so hungry for his doe's caress."

Janey felt tears well. The tale was rather like the two of them, wasn't it?

"So, what could be done?" Janey considered, then continued. "The deer decided she could not live without the dragon, so she approached him very, very carefully. 'If I must die,' she told him, 'this I will do. For love.'"

Remembering something he had seen in Jerusalem, Lancelot picked up the narrative. "Thus, the doe dared touch the dragon's scales."

Janey gasped at the image of it. "And what happened?"

"The most wondrous thing."

"Tell me," Janey cried, enraptured.

"They both burst into flame!"

"Nay. What a terrible fate! 'Twill never do!"

"A flame that burns eternally," Lancelot said. "Here at Tintagel, overlooking the sea, so that even in the darkest night, travelers can find their way."

"Or lovers," Janey breathed. "Two flames becoming one." It was all too beautiful and all too tragic to be endured. She burst into tears.

Lancelot did not berate or question or tease. He merely held her till the storm clouds, limned in red from the sunset, crept close enough that they could smell rain.

"I love you, Lancelot of Glastonbury," Janey whispered.

Lancelot kissed the crown of her head. "And I love you, Jane le Babbe."

Coincidentally, on Janey's last day, one of Lancelot's men interrupted their privacy. She saw the pair, standing far enough away from where she sat on the bench in front of Lancelot's hut that their voices were lost to her. But she could tell by their expressions and body language that something serious had happened.

When Lancelot returned, he said, "Our king has issued a letters patent ordering that my lord Bolingbroke bring an army to parliament. 'For the king's protection,' so Richard said. Two hundred men-at-arms and four hundred archers. Which means my men and I must ready to ride for London and Henry."

"Why does our king think he needs protection?"

"'Tis not just Henry, but the Duke of Lancaster, and two thousand of Richard's Cheshire archers."

Janey knew that the finest archers in England came from Cheshire and that these had become personal bodyguards to the king—meaning woe to anyone who crossed them. "What has happened?"

Lancelot shrugged, as if to say something was always happening in Richard of Bordeaux's England. "'Tis to prevent supporters of the Lords Appellant who have been arrested to rise up. And, I suspect, with that many of his archers, the king is planning for a most unpleasant parliament."

Janey's voice was small. "I wish we could pretend all of this away."

Lancelot pulled her against him. "For one more day we can."

~

On the morning of John the Baptist's feast day, Janey bound her hair and put her veil in place. Lancelot helped her into Lunette's saddle. His men would escort her to the crossroads where they reported her troupe was already waiting.

In a fortnight at most, she would resume her life as lady and mother. And wife, if Serill too had not already answered his lord Bolingbroke's call. 'Twas odd. After her time with Lancelot, the bitterness in her heart seemed such a puny thing, even unworthy of her.

"I will see you again," Lancelot said, his hand upon her calf.

"Aye. But not like this."

He reached up to kiss each of her fingertips. "This we will always have."

"Think you we saved a kingdom?" Janey's voice wavered. It sounded so ridiculous. And she would miss him so much. To pretend this never happened, to forever keep it her own private secret? A treasure that must remain hidden? But they had no choice.

Lancelot's smile was sad. "We did our part. But I think we have a king who is intent on penning his own demise." He released her hand and stepped back.

"Go home to Serill, Lady Jane. He would be a good husband. And he does love you."

"But not like you," she wanted to cry. "No one can ever love me like you."

Instead, Janey whistled low to Fearless and turned Lunette away from this magical place and her beautiful Lancelot.

CHAPTER 6

SEPTEMBER-OCTOBER 1397, WESTMINSTER

There were jousts in the meadows beyond London; Henry Bolingbroke entertained His Majesty in his Fleet Street lodgings, and on Sunday, September 16, 1397, King Richard himself rode into the city surrounded by five thousand men-at-arms. London's inns were overrun by the king's Cheshire archers who, drunk as much with the power bestowed upon them by the white harts on their breasts as the ale they guzzled, harassed the populace.

Historians would label this the Revenge Parliament. On St Lambert's Day, September 17, 1397, lords and commoners assembled in a great marquee which had been set up in Palace Yard. Westminster's old hall was being rebuilt, so the men gathered in a huge pavilion possessing a tiled roof and side walls but with both ends open. At the open ends, Richard's archers arrayed themselves in clear view of those inside. When displeased with the events occurring within, they sometimes drew back their bows and nocked their arrows. Parliament was officially opened with a sermon extolling the blessings of monarchy. Which could be boiled down to: Richard's subjects must be obedient to him and his laws. Parliament must punish all who, in the past, had restrained the king's authority.

The Revenge Parliament was simply a mirror to 1388's Merciless Parliament. Richard might recite a litany of more recent wrongs, but his animosity had been hardened on the day the five Lords Appellant had entered, arms linked and wearing cloth of gold, to usurp his authority. Now, nine years later, six Counter-Appellants appeared, dressed in red silk robes banded with white and powdered with gold letters. In a mocking echo of the Merciless Parliament, they "appealed" all those original Lords Appellant—King Richard's royal uncle, Thomas of Woodstock, Duke of Gloucester; Richard FitzAlan, Earl of Arundel and of Surrey; Thomas Beauchamp, Earl of Warwick; Thomas Mowbray, Earl of Nottingham, and Henry Bolingbroke.

Charging all five with treason.

On the first day, King Richard demanded that every single act that had been passed at the Merciless Parliament be annulled. All the lords or clergymen Richard had been forced to tolerate this past decade, were declared traitors.

Richard had made certain that the Commons, which could be contrary, was packed with supporters. Its speaker, John Bussy, often extended his arms and steepled his hands as if praying to the king. Then, in the most obsequious of terms, he would entreat his "High, Excellent and Most Praiseworthy Majesty" to listen or to agree or to grant this favor or that.

Rather than finding such groveling offensive, the king accepted it as his due. It was as if he, they all, had decided that by some alchemical miracle Richard of Bordeaux had been transmuted from king to god.

The first time Matthew Hart, Earl of Cumbria, saw John Bussy so debase himself, he'd suppressed a laugh. But amusement was soon replaced by puzzlement...and then something altogether more discomfiting. Never had he seen the like.

Matthew Hart had known England during its golden age, engaged in some of the century's greatest battles and grueling *chevauchees* against the French. Matthew had also witnessed the subsequent descent of fortune's wheel—the senility of their warrior king, Edward III; the illness and death of England's beloved Black Prince; the raising of the prince's ten-year-old son, Richard of Bordeaux, to the throne. The Great Rising when fourteen-year-old Richard had bravely met his rebellious commons and singlehandedly saved the monarchy.

But afterward?

A kingship that, over two decades, had gone from feckless to unhinged. But, while Matthew had experienced much in his sixty years, never had he witnessed anything like what was taking place here in Palace Yard. Even fellow knights who had proven themselves fearless on the battlefield had no idea how to handle this makeshift Parliament. How can one keep a king in check when he has so brazenly careened into despotism? All the warriors' weapons—which had literally been taken from them on the first day of Parliament—and battle tactics were useless in these circumstances.

Can it be? Matthew thought, stunned by the sudden turn of events. *Will we all crawl before him on our bellies? Has the king made cowards of us all?*

John of Gaunt, seated beside Richard, certainly feared for the safety of his family, particularly his first born. And Henry Bolingbroke, one of the original Lords Appellant, had been granted a pardon from his "crimes," so he dared not do anything to jeopardize that pardon. Matthew suspected the only reason Richard had tossed Henry that particular bone was because the king feared rousing the old lion if he attacked his cub.

What about the rest of us? Are we all cringing at what we might lose the very moment Richard turns his baleful glare on us?

One man, Richard FitzAlan, Earl of Arundel, did stand up to the king. FitzAlan was another member of the original Lords Appellant. He had passed judgment on His Majesty's favorites during the Merciless Parliament and had refused the first queen's pleas of mercy on behalf of Simon Burley, the king's beloved mentor. FitzAlan had further disrespected King Richard during Queen Anne's funeral ceremony, causing England's sovereign to beat the earl senseless on the steps of Westminster's chapel.

Richard FitzAlan might be many things, but coward he was not. He knew he was about to lose his head, not because of the specious charges currently laid before him, but because he'd long ago disrespected Richard of Bordeaux's dead wife.

To every accusation, Richard FitzAlan calmly responded,

"All those who accuse me of treason, you are liars. Never was I a traitor.'

The Earl of Arundel was immediately sentenced to be hanged, beheaded and quartered. Matthew, at least, was impressed by FitzAlan's brave façade. Arrogant, the earl might be. Ambitious. Over-reaching. But, while Matthew had seen men weep like babes when similar sentences had been passed, Richard FitzAlan did not flinch.

Citing FitzAlan's exalted rank, King Richard later amended his sentence to a simple beheading.

On the day of his execution, Richard FitzAlan, his step jaunty, was escorted to Tower Hill. Along the way, he smiled and bantered with the sympathetic crowds lining the streets. Upon reaching his destination, the earl forgave his executioner before testing the edge of the man's sword and approving its sharpness.

"Torment me not long, strike off my head in one blow," he said, to the delight of spectators who would long repeat his insouciant command. The executioner struck true. (Though in one more troubling portent, FitzAlan's headless corpse remained eerily upright for as long as it took to pray the Pater Noster.)

After his execution, there was the business of Thomas of Woodstock, Duke of Gloucester and Richard's detested royal uncle. Gloucester had been summoned to appear before Parliament—an interesting command since so many rumors were circulating that he had already been murdered.

Apparently so.

Thomas Mowbray was the Governor of Calais, the port city where the Duke of Gloucester had been placed in custody to await his trial for treason. This day Mowbray appeared before Richard and Parliament to report, "Thomas of Woodstock is dead. Of natural causes."

At the news, so baldly delivered, Matthew felt something akin to despair. To have the rumors confirmed, to know that Richard of Bordeaux had so ignored the bonds of blood, the rule of law to have his royal uncle murdered?

Around Matthew, the other lords stirred, turning their heads one to the other, whispering their alarm. Watching his liege, Matthew Hart noticed a tightening around John of Gaunt's eyes when his youngest brother's death was announced, as if someone had pricked him. Otherwise, the Duke of Lancaster remained expressionless, his gaze fastened at the end of the marquee, where Richard's Cheshire archers maintained their menacing presence. Edmund Langley, a year younger than Gaunt, ran both hands over his face and bowed his head.

What were they thinking? That only they two, of their seven brothers, remained alive? That the son of their beloved brother, the Black Prince, had committed avunculicide, and they must pretend their youngest brother had died of natural causes?

So then, were the facts behind Thomas of Woodstock's abduction also true? Had the king indeed ordered the Duke of Gloucester pulled from his bed and when his wife pleaded for mercy, replied, "I will show my royal uncle as much mercy as my royal uncle showed Simon Burley."?

The story went that, upon King Richard's orders, Woodstock had then been whisked away to Calais. There, in a dirty room tucked away in a dirty inn, he'd been wrestled into submission and smothered neath a piss-stained mattress.

Matthew's eyes cut to the king, whose face remained a blank. Richard would later blandly assure John of Gaunt and Edmund Langley that he'd had naught to do with their younger brother's death. And, because they could not do otherwise, both men would pretend to believe him.

Questions were asked that day of Thomas Mowbray, bearer of the grim tidings, though it was ceremony rather than an actual inquiry.

"The Duke of Gloucester had been ill through the summer, do you not remember?" said Thomas Mowbray. "After confessing to his treason, Gloucester's soul was unburdened, allowing him to die a natural death."

No one dug into contradictory details lest that lead the questioners into areas that would expose the king's culpability and earn them a stay in London's Tower. Safer to pretend to believe.

While Thomas of Woodstock's "confession" was presented to the king and read aloud, John of Gaunt continued staring into nothingness. Edmund Langley, who suffered from arthritis that hampered his ability to war, had sunk to a bench and was curled into himself. Eyes on the hard-packed earth at his feet.

As a last vengeful act, King Richard condemned all of Thomas of Woodstock's male heirs as traitors. Which meant that every Woodstock male into perpetuity was stripped of his inheritance, as well as from all councils and parliaments. Effectively consigning descendants with royal blood to lives on a par with a villein's.

John of Gaunt's face appeared to be carved from alabaster. No wonder he dared not cross Richard or his puppets. The great Duke of Lancaster could suffer the same fate as a brother who'd once had marginally realistic ambitions of becoming king of England.

Edmund of Langley buried his face in his hands and stayed that way until Parliament moved on to other business.

The days passed. Sometimes a wind blew through the assemblage; sometimes the afternoon was as still and hot as if summer yet lingered; sometimes rain beat upon the roof tiles and slithered down to create muddy ditches around the marquee. Following FitzAlan's execution and Woodstock's trial *in absentia*, members sat a bit more hunched, as if expecting further blows from their master. Matthew experienced something which he could not name but which daily grew stronger in him and judging from the faces of his fellow lords, in them as well. Something inchoate that caused Matthew's throat to tighten as if being squeezed by an invisible hand and his stomach to roil as if he were crossing the Strait of Dover and suffering from sea sickness.

Finally, he was able to give the emotion a name.

Terror.

Certainly, Matthew had experienced it before. At the Battle of Poitiers, when France's forces had seemed poised to annihilate them all. After the Siege of Limoges, when he'd been ordered to slay its townspeople. During the March to Oblivion, when he and his younger brother Harry and the rest of John of Gaunt's army had been trapped in Auvergne's wintry mountains.

But not like this.

This was like ivy creeping inch by inch up the trunk of a tree to gradually smother its life. Matthew was terrified, as one is so often terrified of things we do not understand.

We all sit here, behaving as if someone has cracked us over the head with a mace. Because that's how Matthew felt. Bewildered. Disoriented.

After puzzling it through, he finally began to understand why not anyone, including himself, raised a voice in objection to actions previous parliaments would never have tolerated. How can you challenge someone whose power is absolute? Richard had gone from monarch to despot so quickly that Matthew still could not quite figure how. Maybe it was a simple thing. Since Parliament had acquiesced, there was no one to enforce any laws Richard chose to disregard. Which meant, in practice, England existed in a state of anarchy. Tradition, precedent, all the rules previously guiding Englishmen had been reduced to scribbles on parchment. Now the only laws were Richard's laws, enforced by his Cheshire archers.

Who would next be accused of treason? Who would next be sent to Tower Hill? It was like trying to read sheep entrails in order to divine the future.

His Majesty toppled his enemies as skillfully as Richard FitzAlan's executioner had wielded his sword. Deaths. Banishments. Forfeiture of lands and goods which, as a side benefit, swelled England/Richard's treasury. The king asserted that he had a list of fifty men who would be impeached, though he refused to release their names. Moreover, should anyone seek that information they would immediately be declared a traitor, with the attendant consequences.

Watching all this unfold, Matthew decided there was no such list. He was beginning to understand Richard's tactics, the same as he might those of an enemy commander, which lessened his fear.

"The list is simply another tactic designed to create the maximum amount of terror," he said to John of Gaunt, who gazed into the distance, as if viewing the final shattering of their hopes for this, the son of their beloved Black Prince.

John's eldest son, Henry Bolingbroke, began wearing a necklace with a medicine stone to ward off poison. His health suffered. Matthew's muscles were as taut as if he'd just participated in a joust, though he'd done little save sit on his arse or pace or stand about with fellow lords trying to convey with a vague gesture or look what they were all too cowed to utter.

In October 1397, Richard began parceling out the forfeited properties of the dead "traitors" to those upon whom he smiled. He bestowed five dukedoms, more than any in history. How to interpret this unexpected largesse? On the same day Henry Bolingbroke became Duke of Hereford, one of the king's archers murdered one of Henry's men, even as the man was waiting to meet with his lord Bolingbroke. (To advise him of a plot to end Henry's life? So it was rumored.)

What did this mean? What would King Richard do next? He was like Janus. Which face would he show? When would he single someone out for favors? When would he withdraw his approval? And over what? When would he follow established law? When would he assert laws he'd just plucked out of the air? Was he serious when he declared that his priority was to be crowned Holy Roman Emperor? Was he mad?

Matthew started running again, outside London's walls, with the opening of the city gates before each day's Parliament and before the gates closed at night. He craved physical exercise in order to clear his head, to restore his body to pre-Parliament shape. Aye, he could feel his years as he ran, the slowing of his reflexes, the twinges and pains, more pronounced now that his wife wasn't near to massage them away. But it was all Matthew had, the only thing over which he felt he had control. While running, he thought of Parliament, of the king's machinations and how they might be thwarted. He thought of his father who had died of a failing heart, though William Hart had lingered long enough for Matthew to return from the March to Oblivion to sit at William's deathbed. And confess his failure. For Matthew had left his younger brother's body on the plains beyond Auvergne where Harry had perished. After shepherding Harry through blizzards and starvation and privations which even twenty-five years later, Matthew could not bear to ponder...

'Twas was not enough. You died all the same. Matthew's feet pounded on the dirt paths, on the grassy byways snaking through various woodlands. Trying to outrun the memories that came with a life long-lived. *I am older than you, Father, when you passed. What if my heart seizes up and it will all be over?*

Despite his despair, Matthew knew must persevere.

I have obligations. Meg. Family. Cumbria. Legacy.

And as he ran, Matthew knew, oh, he knew that fortune's wheel would continue its turning. He pictured the wheel as two giant gears and Richard of Bordeaux being ground between their teeth where they joined. It was the only thing that allowed him sleep.

On Sunday, October 30, lords and commons attended high mass at Westminster Abbey. Afterward, they participated in a ceremony which was another mirror of that which had ended the Merciless Parliament. Richard, wearing his crown and seated upon his throne, watched as each of England's lords appeared before the shrine of St Edward the Confessor. There they swore to observe, into perpetuity, the laws and judgements passed in the present Parliament and to hold as traitors anyone who sought to annul or repeal them. As did knights of the shire. As did the clergy, who added the threat of excommunication to anyone who might dare decide otherwise.

Richard of Bordeaux had won it all. He assured himself he was greater than any of the Edwards who'd preceded him for he had snatched power away from parliament, something they'd never been able to do. And, as he informed the assemblage, "I am absolute Emperor of my kingdom of England." Parliament was no more effective than the tiny dogs ladies cradled in their arms, capable of occasionally yapping but who could be silenced with one well-placed kick.

As was traditional at the close of parliament, Richard presented a sumptuous feast. Heralds received large gifts from attendant lords and ladies, who danced and sang and received prizes for their performances.

All to please the king.

At Hart's Place, Matthew Hart scrawled a one-word message to his son, who was staying with his liege, Henry Bolingbroke.

"Home," the note said.

CHAPTER 7

LONDON

*M*atthew was taking his leave of John of Gaunt when one of the duke's men entered, followed by a pair of King Richard's archers.

Matthew immediately stiffened on the bench he was sharing with the duke. The Cheshire bastards were everywhere and too stupid to be anything but insolent.

"His Majesty wishes to meet with you, Your Grace," said one to John of Gaunt after a perfunctory bow.

Matthew gazed into the eyes of each, trying to read something there. Their presence was always an ominous sign. And a summons? Might this portend yet another assassination attempt? Richard's hatred of his uncle Lancaster, accompanied by the inevitable murder plots, ebbed and flowed with whatever grievances had most recently taken root in his imaginings.

John of Gaunt placed the wine goblet he'd been holding on a folding table and rose to his feet. As did Matthew.

"Alone," growled one of the archers.

Matthew remained standing.

"Where is the king?" asked John, his voice resigned.

"Westminster Abbey gardens."

A curious choice. When Matthew moved to follow Lancaster, the larger of the archers stepped in front of him. As if meaning to threaten Matthew? All the frustrations of these past months narrowed to this broken-toothed, smirking man. Before the archer could react, Matthew had one hand around the man's throat and had slammed him up against the chamber wall. "Listen, you son of a dog. I have had all of your kind I am going to take. Understand?"

When the man did not respond, Matthew jerked up a knee so it was connected with his groin. Not enough to maim, but to offer painful warning. "Understand?"

"Aye, my lord," the man croaked.

His Majesty was sitting in Westminster's secluded garden with his eight-year-old wife perched upon his knee. A pretty picture they made. Queen Isabella with jewels in her shining unbound hair and looking like an exquisite doll come to life. Generally oblivious to fashion, Matthew did notice with a twinge of disgust that both husband and wife were dressed in matching white satin.

Around them lounged several of the queen's ladies, one of whom strummed her lute. *No assassins with mattresses*, Matthew thought, gaze sweeping the area. *A good sign, that.*

Richard whispered something in Isabella's ear, which caused the girl to turn to study the intruders. After standing and sweeping her in his arms, the king kissed his wife on both cheeks and made to put her down. Isabella clung to his neck and returned his kisses with charming giggles.

"Enough, poppet," Richard said fondly. Soon, surrounded by her ladies-in-waiting, the tiny queen exited the garden. Afterward, the space appeared oddly forlorn with the orchard bare, fallen leaves in the fishponds, and the monks' herbs and vegetables all plucked from the soil.

Matthew and John bowed to the king, then waited respectfully for him to speak.

"Strange things are happening," Richard said, his merry air having disappeared with his wife.

As if everything that had happened these past months was not strange? Matthew bit back a sarcastic quip and studied the now agitated king, who'd begun wringing his beringed hands together. More like some mewling maid, for sweet bloody Christ, than the emperor he fancied himself to be.

"Sire?" the duke queried, addressing the king simply rather than using one of the honorifics he'd come to demand.

"The people are saying that Richard FitzAlan's head has miraculously reattached itself to his body."

John of Gaunt raised his eyebrows.

Matthew could not quite stifle an exasperated groan.

"'Tis so!" Richard ceased wringing his hands to pace before them, his poulaines crunching among the fallen leaves. He was taller than his father with spindly legs and arms and the beginnings of the paunch so common among priests and scholars.

"My men say 'tis all people speak of in the alehouses and markets. And that FitzAlan is performing miracles."

"Folk look for omens everywhere," countered Matthew. "You know how superstitious they are." He nodded toward several bee boles in the abbey wall. "If a swarm of bees settles on a roof, they cry that the house will burn down." A subtle jab at Richard, who was every bit as superstitious, ceaselessly looking for signs of ill favor, as well as good.

"Hundreds have been congregating around FitzAlan's tomb. They say it might become as famous as Thomas Becket's."

John of Gaunt kept his silence, though such a comparison existed only in the king's fevered brain. Nor did this have anything to do with religion, John knew, for he himself was well acquainted with Londoners' hatred. Rather, it was an act of rebellion. Richard's subjects were demonstrating their opposition by elevating a man who'd given his life resisting their sovereign's tyranny.

Matthew and John shared a glance as Richard continued his pacing, hands behind his back, eyes downcast.

"Come with me to FitzAlan's tomb, my lord uncle," said Richard, abruptly halting before them. "You also, Lord Hart, for you have well served me and my father. All of our family, for certes. I must see for myself that the rumors are false."

Both men stared at him. Richard was indeed mad.

"What do you mean, see for yourself?" Matthew asked rudely. "What do you think to do?"

"We will have FitzAlan's tomb chest opened."

The duke glanced at Matthew, who suppressed the urge to cross himself.

This was ghoulish beyond belief. And even the bravest of knights would tremble if faced by the walking dead in the blackness of a deserted church.

Seeing the cast of their faces, Richard's expression settled into its obstinate oh-so-familiar lines.

Which is how the great Duke of Lancaster and the Earl of Cumbria found themselves, accompanied by the king and two nervous workmen, on Bread Street long after London's curfew had been rung. Entering a tucked away church belonging to Augustinian friars.

Once in the choir, near the high altar, the workmen forced open the Earl of Arundel's tomb. One of them held a lanthorn and when he swung it into the tomb, stepped back with a frightened oath.

"What is it?" called Richard from the safety of the shadows behind the high altar.

The man dropped his lanthorn. Both workmen spun on their heels and ran from the church.

Matthew's heart hammered. He remembered all those lonely nights during his retreat to Lake Winandermere, when he'd imagined Satan and his minions emerging from its inky depths...

Matthew had been holding a rushlight. Lancaster retrieved the lanthorn, whose flame danced wildly. Both men warily approached the tomb to shine their lights upon the corpse.

First, was the smell, only partially masked by the mutton fat in which rushlights were steeped. But neither man was a stranger to decaying flesh.

"What do you see?" prodded the king, his voice quavering. "Tell me."

Matthew held the light closer to the corpse. Richard FitzAlan's body indeed appeared intact. He heard the duke's sharp intake of breath. Matthew forced himself to move the flame directly above the corpse's neck so as to better examine it.

"The head's been stitched to the body," he said, loud enough for the king to hear.

"Aye," echoed John, relief evident in his tone. "Some friar's trick thinking to attract pilgrims' coin." He nudged Matthew in private merriment before addressing his nephew the king. "Come see for yourself, sire."

"Nay. I mislike the sight of corpses." This from the man who had ordered the embalmed body of his favorite, Robert de Vere, returned to England three years after his death for a "reburial ceremony." Matthew had been one of many who had refused to attend the macabre event in which His Majesty had the coffin opened so that he might kiss de Vere's hand and gaze one last time into his face.

"Have the corpse carted away," Richard ordered, "and we'll speak no more of it."

Matthew and Lancaster did as told, rousing several Augustinians and overseeing their removal of the Earl of Arundel.

Afterward, when they knew they were alone and safe, Matthew said to the duke, "Hiding Arundel's body will not stop the rumors."

John nodded in agreement. "This has naught to do with some stitched together horror. And everything to do with Londoners' hatred of their king."

With that both men departed London.

CHAPTER 8

PENDRAGON CASTLE, CUMBERLAND

*V*iviane Halle had been a bossy child. Since her mother, Lady Clare, was so often tucked away in their solar—servants whispered of lost babies (where might they have gone off to?)— Viviane was virtually allowed the run of Pendragon Castle.

Which very much pleased Viviane. She could wander the heath, moors and bogs almost at will and follow the path of the River Eden that circled the castle, though at an early age she'd discovered her true passion. Food. Primarily the preparation of it. Thus, she became a permanent fixture in Pendragon Castle's kitchen. Traditionally, girls—save for perhaps an occasional scullery maid—were denied entre to its environs, but who was going to gainsay the closest thing Pendragon often had for a mistress?

Besides, Viviane Halle was undeniably fetching with her carelessly braided hair swinging down her back as she bounced in and out of the kitchen on her way to and from the great hall; eyes, dark as currants, ever seeking mischief; chubby body in perpetual motion. While domestic servants kept the castle running—Viviane was not above criticizing if the floors had not been properly swept or the linens poorly bleached—she'd been irresistibly drawn to the comforting smells and bustle of Pendragon's kitchen.

Such a magical place! Cook—Viviane thought his real name was Alfred Something, but everyone addressed him thus—was a remarkably thin man, which in and of itself was a wonder. For, surrounded by all this deliciousness, how could one not be plump as a partridge? Better still, Cook never seemed to hurry or raise his voice or become flustered, even during the infrequent times Pendragon received important guests. (While the demesne was only a half-day's ride from Cumbria Castle, it was quite isolated.)

How old had Viviane been when she'd first wandered into the kitchen? Five perhaps? "Nay, Pickle," Cook had said, scooping her up and depositing her outside the door. Viviane liked the way he called her "Pickle," though he'd had to explain to her exactly what a pickle was. And she'd never actually seen a cucumber. But the nickname set her apart in a fashion that pleased her.

"Why can I not help, Cook? 'Tis unfair for you to have far more fun than you'll grant me."

"Too dangerous. Sharp knives, fires, boiling pots. 'Tis no place for a wee miss." To convince her, Cook had related a tale about a spit boy who'd fallen asleep and toppled into the fire where he'd burned to death.

"But I'll be very careful," she'd insisted. "I no longer even take naps."

Cook's offering of toy pots and pans had done nothing to assuage her.

Viviane had stuck out her lower lip while vigorously shaking her head. "'Twill not do," she'd said. "'Twill not do at all."

Of course, Viviane had won out.

Daily, she would fetch a stool and plunk it next to Cook, peppering him with questions—"why does this herb go with that sauce? why is bread used for thickening? why do you brush chicken with egg whites?" Chatter, chatter.

Patiently, he would explain:

"When a pot boils over, throw in a dash of cold water and carefully, carefully remove a few fire brands."

"To melt cheese on bread, hold a red-hot shovel above it."

"To properly cook eggs without their shells, break them into boiling water."

Viviane had been a willing—and determined—student. In the beginning, when Cook banked the kitchen fire for the night, he would often find her asleep beside it. Gathering the mite in his arms, he would carry her to the small chamber adjacent to Lord Halle's solar where all those lost Halle babes should have been resting in their cradles.

"Good night, Pickle," Cook would say, kissing her cheek. Wondering what would happen to a girl who was developing the skills of a master cook but could scarce write her name.

Lady Clare never sent Viviane away to be schooled. And, alternating between bouts of ennui and genuine illness, Lady Clare could seldom manage more than haphazard lessons. Who was left to guide Viviane Halle? Certainly not her father who was always about "the king's business," according to her mother, though she never elaborated on what the king's business might be. Nor Viviane's older brother, Gerald, who had been sent to Alnwick Castle where he would serve as a page to Henry Percy the Younger, also known as Harry Hotspur.

The important Halle offspring had been taken care of.

The Halle daughter was left on her own.

Until the summer of 1395, when Viviane had turned seventeen, and Gerald sent word of his pending knighthood ceremony.

"I suppose it's time to think about marriage," Lady Clare had said, a weary sigh escaping her lips. Viviane heard her mother's disappointment in that sigh. Viviane was clear-eyed about her physical limitations. The kindest description of her physical form was "bountiful," though she had been blessed with a small waist and current fashions disguised the worst of her gluttony. (Which she was forever confessing to Father Crispin.) She suspected that as she aged, she would look more like her brother and father, who were short and stout and resembled tree stumps with limbs.

Still, Lady Clare had been cognizant enough of her maternal duty to undertake what would prove to be her final journey.

At the feast following the dubbing ceremony at Alnwick Castle, Gerald Halle had introduced Viviane to Reginald Luci, also newly knighted. Next to her squat brother, Sir Reginald had appeared impossibly elegant. Upon sight of the young baron, Viviane, who was accustomed to bossing most everyone, found herself incapable of speech. Reginald Luci was as exquisite as the *soltelte* currently adorning the Percys' high table. Skin pale as snow; face as flawlessly constructed as that of a marble effigy. Luci wasn't actually delicate —for what knight could be?—but he was slender and moved more with the grace of a dancer than a warrior. The thought of such perfection being put through the rigors of a campaign—or even a joust—seemed a defilement.

Human confectionery, Viviane thought, unconsciously licking her lips. *Too perfect to even touch.*

"*Demoiselle.*" Reginald Luci had bowed, his gaze lingering on her ample bosom. Generally, in the company of Cook and others who had long-ago ceased to actually "see" her, Viviane had first found this reaction among Alnwick's male guests puzzling. Then annoying. Now her cheeks flushed as though she'd been standing over a fire, and she'd felt the oddest tingling sensation.

While the gallant Luci had tried to engage her in the usual flirtations, Viviane could only respond with an occasional strangled "Aarrp," or "Hmmff."

What is wrong with me? Cook was forever chiding her to curb her saucy tongue. Yet here she was, dumb as a dog.

The tournament following the knighthood ceremony had been an agony. Not only because Viviane kept remembering her embarrassing behavior of the previous night, but because she feared for Reginald Luci's life. He couldn't be expected to be as accomplished as knights like Harry Hotspur, but Reginald could most charitably be described as...unseasoned. Viviane lived in agony, imagining that during a tumble he would snap his neck as easily as she might snap the neck of a pigeon.

Most terrifying was when her beautiful knight had faced Lancelot of Glastonbury, who had knocked Reginald from his destrier with almost contemptuous ease.

I hate you, she thought, glaring at this threat to her champion, who even sprawled upon the earth appeared impossibly graceful. Oh, there was no doubt Sir Lancelot was a crowd-pleaser. His stallion, black as a storm cloud; his armor seemingly limned in similar black. And, after removing his helm to rapturous applause, Lancelot of Glastonbury was an undeniably compelling sight—so fierce and dark and elemental. As if Alnwick Castle, thought to be the real home of Lancelot du Lac, should be this knight's by right, rather than the Percys.

All this Viviane Halle later contemplated. In the summer of 1395, her maiden's heart had no room for premonitions or anything else beyond Reginald Luci.

No need to detail how Viviane and her young knight became lovers. There was nothing unique about their mating except perhaps the setting. Viviane lost her maidenhead inside a circle of giant stones within riding distance of Pendragon Castle. A dazzling carpet of bluebells, frothing in all directions, had surrounded the circle.

As if the sky has fallen to the earth, Viviane thought in uncharacteristically poetical fashion, while she and Reginald strolled, hand in hand across the field to the stones where, once inside, he would deflower her.

After that, Viviane Halle waited breathlessly, determinedly, then irritably for a marriage proposal that never arrived.

CHAPTER 9

DECEMBER 1397 TO FALL 1398, LONDON

Oft times events that totally alter our lives seem inconsequential when unfolding. It's only upon looking back that we say, "This is the moment when everything changed." Other times we immediately realize nothing will ever again be the same.

Henry Bolingbroke's chance meeting with Thomas Mowbray on the road from Brentford to London lies somewhere in between. However, in importance it would do much more than alter the course of two men's lives. It would alter the history of a nation.

Henry, his household staff and knights, met Thomas Mowbray—he who, as governor of Calais, had reported the demise of Thomas, Duke of Gloucester —riding in the opposite direction. The two newly created dukes called out to each other while they and their accompanying meinies drew rein.

The December afternoon was cold; the River Thames, which snaked through the area on its way to the North Sea, was glutted with ice. Mowbray and Bolingbroke nudged their mounts closer so they could speak privately.

Henry Bolingbroke had not seen Thomas Mowbray since Parliament's end. In six weeks it would reconvene in Shrewsbury, but until that time Henry had thought it prudent to stay away from King Richard and his court.

Mowbray addressed Bolingbroke without preamble. "We are about to be undone."

The man who had killed his royal uncle. An ambitious second son. And…a former Lord Appellant like himself, simply scrambling to stay alive?

"Why?" Henry asked cautiously.

"Because of what was done at Radcot Bridge."

Radcot Bridge had been rather a farce, when Richard's ill-favored favorite, Robert de Vere, and an army of five thousand had thought to take on the original Lords Appellant led by Henry Bolingbroke. The king's force had been quickly overcome, some of the Lords Appellant had marched on London threatening Richard's deposition, and there their cornered sovereign had been forced into humiliating concessions.

Henry Bolingbroke continued studying Thomas Mowbray, trying to ferret out possible trickery. Who now could trust anyone? Mowbray had proven himself far more ruthless, at least as far as Henry was concerned. Yet, what had Lancastrian loyalty to King Richard gained Henry and his father beyond a few extra days of freedom and increasingly sleepless nights?

"The king has given us a pardon," Henry Bolingbroke countered. "He even declared his will to uphold that pardon in parliament. As he publicly declared we had been true and loyal to him."

Mowbray shook his head. "Richard will do with us what he has done with the others." Mowbray had obeyed the king's orders in the murder of Thomas, Duke of Gloucester, but those who committed dark deeds could quickly outlive their usefulness.

The two men's breaths puffed in the cold, as did their horses. Henry's stallion pawed the ground. Behind Mowbray, his banner—gules, a lion rampant argent—stirred with the shifting of the standard-bearer's palfrey, an occasional blast of cold from the Thames. Involuntarily, Henry shivered beneath his warm gambeson and pulled his mantle closer.

Mowbray continued, "Richard wants to wipe clean any trace of our opposition."

Henry inhaled sharply. "It would be a great wonder if the king went back on what he said last Parliament."

Mowbray laughed mirthlessly. "It is a wondrous world, and a false one." He paused, as if considering his next words. "This much I know. Following Parliament's end, you and your father would have been murdered on the way to Windsor had several of us not taken action to prevent it."

"God's nails! Will this madness never end?" But shouldn't Henry know better by now? Both his and Thomas Mowbray's fate—as well as that of his lord father or any other magnate—might be altered by whoever whispered in the king's ear. Or whatever grievance upon which Richard was currently chewing.

Henry later repeated Mowbray's conversation to his father, John of Gaunt —with whom he shared everything.

"And it grows worse, my lord father. Mowbray said the king is once again brooding over Thomas of Lancaster. He's revisiting ancient charges and accusing Lancaster of being a traitor."

Of course. For, nearly eighty years ago their ancestor had nearly deposed the bad king, Edward Caernarvon, who some referred to as the Sodomite King. The Sodomite King Richard championed; the Sodomite King Richard was determined to have beatified. Thomas Lancaster had lost his head when his rebellion against Edward Caernarvon had failed, and his lands had been forfeited, though they'd been restored two years later.

"Will the dead never stay buried?" John asked, more in weariness than anger.

He and Henry need not articulate what a re-visiting of Lancaster's "loyalty" meant. Should Thomas, 2nd Earl of Lancaster, once more be labelled a traitor, it followed that the Lancastrian titles and estates should not have been passed down to future Lancasters. All the way down to John of Gaunt and by extension, John's first born. Meaning that, since 1322, the year of Thomas Lancaster's death, no one but the king should have enjoyed the benefit of the Lancastrian riches. And, as a convenient byproduct, Henry Bolingbroke would be permanently removed from royal succession.

The more John of Gaunt and his son conversed, the angrier the duke became. Loyal, John had been, and yet he still walked a knife's blade between being one of history's richest men and ending up on Tower Hill or with a dagger to his gullet in another of Richard's witless schemes.

Enough was enough. If the king planned to disinherit them, if he planned to weave more plots, John of Gaunt would at least confront him. While they'd given His Majesty everything he could want in the Revenge Parliament, Richard yet acted like a glutton gorging himself on sweets. He would never be sated.

While representatives began gathering in Shrewsbury, which was conveniently closer to Chester where Richard's private army resided, the duke and his son confronted the king. (After yet another assassination attempt along the way.)

Richard tersely ordered Henry Bolingbroke to put his accusations in writing before opening Parliament.

More accusations. A show trial. A sentence of death that was revoked. More reiterations that none of the parliamentary decisions granted to King Richard could EVER be reversed.

This was too much for Matthew Hart, who'd had nearly three months to ponder the precedents being set and had decided that the best way to lose all was to remain silent. When several prelates dared contradict Richard, saying, "You cannot oblige future kings to abide by your will," Matthew added his voice. As did a handful of other lords, whose spines had been re-attached during recess.

Abruptly, King Richard turned to the matter of Henry Bolingbroke's accusations against Thomas Mowbray.

Here begins the series of events that, while appearing to further consolidate Richard's power, actually led to his downfall.

In the stillness of Shrewsbury Abbey, Henry Bolingbroke approached Richard's throne. Reading from a parchment, Bolingbroke recounted the conversation in which Thomas Mowbray had apprised him of Richard's assassination plot.

Even couched in Henry's measured terms, Richard of Bordeaux was being accused of orchestrating the murder of him and his father.

Richard's response? He declared that Thomas Mowbray, who had gone into hiding, had slandered *him*.

Before the matter could be satisfactorily resolved, Richard abruptly adjourned Parliament, though not before being granted permission to levy various profitable subsidies for the remainder of his rule. Meaning that, so long as England did not go to war, Richard could rule without ever again having to call parliament. No more would His Majesty be forced to consent to the wishes of his subjects. No more would lords and commoners be able to hold his ministers and favorites to account.

My rule will be absolute. As God intended.

However, Richard dared not leave the matter of Thomas Mowbray hanging. Should certain facts emerge, His Majesty could be held accountable, not only for the assassination plot against his royal uncle and his royal cousin, but for the death of that pesky second royal, Thomas, Duke of Gloucester.

If Mowbray dares publicly point the finger at me...

Richard immediately stripped Thomas Mowbray of his lands and title. After which, he ordered the arrests of both Mowbray and Henry Bolingbroke.

Four dukes, all relatives led by John of Gaunt, stood bail for Bolingbroke so he might remain free.

Thomas Mowbray protested, "I am not a traitor." And Thomas, Duke of Gloucester? "He died of natural causes."

Richard knew he must tread very carefully, lest the actual truth emerge.

What to do?

A joust of war, with lances uncapped, was decided upon. Thomas Mowbray and Henry Bolingbroke would fight to the death. Whoever survived would be deemed the truth-teller.

The joust would take place at Coventry, in the fall of the year.

If God is merciful, Richard thought, *you'll both be killed.*

And, if not?

I will think of something.

CHAPTER 10

SUMMER 1398, CUMBRIA CASTLE

*W*atching. That's how the former Margery Watson, current Countess of Cumbria, spent the months following her husband's return. Watching her beloved Matthew as he struck out on his punishing runs; as he practiced with sword and lance and mace and quarter staff or grappled with fellow knights. As he and his horseman trained his newest destrier to properly maneuver the quintain and run at the rings; to kick and bite and step high so that in battle he could maneuver over dead bodies. To remain still when startled by a loud noise. To overcome his head shyness.

All in preparation for war?

Talk to me, Margery silently pleaded. It was not as it had been in the bad old days following Matthew's return from the Black Prince's last campaign when he had been haunted by the atrocities following the Siege of Limoges, atrocities he himself had committed. That distance had led to Matthew and Margery's parting, which had lasted two years.

However, in the sixteen years since their marriage—*Could it really be that long?*—Matthew had been as open as a quiet man could be. As he still was. They spoke of the usual everyday things along with the usual whispered

78

intimacies, but Margery was not fooled. Something was different. Jesu, they'd known each other since childhood; how could she not notice the change?

Matthew spent more time than usual in Cumbria's chapel, with the tomb chests of his parents. He did not travel to his other demesnes, but rather summoned his stewards to go over accounts at Cumbria. Around May Day, he said, "I have sent for Serill and his family. 'Tis time our son learns the duties entailed upon becoming Earl of Cumbria."

"Why? You've not had premonitions, have you?" Margery's heart suddenly knocked wildly against her chest. Death often forewarned its victims with dreams or other signs. Was this what Matthew was trying to tell her? Nightly Margery massaged his knots and pains, fingers probing for unusual weaknesses or alarming changes. She'd not observed more stiffness in the way he moved or any diminution of strength. But if he was training his son to succeed him …

"No premonitions, sweet Meg." Matthew kissed her forehead. "Except, mayhap, about England."

He'd not further burden Margery with the fear he already spent far too much time feeding. Though there were signs aplenty that his particular beast had already grown grotesquely obese. Recently, there had been skirmishes against King Richard, though they'd been far to the south. Mainly yeomen and artisans. The rebellions had been easily crushed, but such would not always be the case. Hadn't the king—any of them—learned from the Great Rising near two decades past?

"No good will come from Henry Bolingbroke's forthcoming duel," was all Matthew could bring himself to share. "If Henry is killed none of us will be safe. Not even the king. For Henry is more popular than His Majesty, particularly with Londoners who would riot if anything happened to their hero."

Once Serill and his family arrived, Matthew's mood lightened. He and Serill took three-year-old Billy most everywhere, settling the boy atop a post in order to watch their daily martial practice and providing him with a pony so that he might accompany them on short rides. The twins, shadowed by their summer-shorn dogs, spent most days at Cumbria's Enchanted Cottage, the one-room hut Matthew had constructed for Margery as a wedding present.

Margery noted with relief that Serill and Janey were acting more like a regular married couple than a pair of snarling badgers. Janey would sometimes even reach out to touch Serill's hand, and their conversations were pleasant enough, at least on the surface.

What was most different was Serill's temperate drinking and his refusal to even glance at anything in skirts. Margery and Matthew both remarked upon it. At twenty-seven had their son finally embraced duty? The Hart motto: 'All is lost save honor'?

Serill also attended Cumbria's Lordship Court so that Matthew might demonstrate the proper way to settle disputes in a part of the kingdom where a lord's word was absolute. The great Marcher barons, whether here or in Wales, were largely a law unto themselves. Some likened them to kings with a king's power, at least in these border lands. All too easy to rule as a tyrant, which in time would lead to rebellions. Not so very different from what was now happening in the whole of England.

As Matthew explained to Serill, more by his interactions with all those who knelt before him than through lectures.

"But why now?" Margery persisted, doggedly returning to Matthew's grooming of their son. "Why is the Lordship Court and all the rest suddenly so urgent?"

"When I was Serill's age, I was too busy warring to pay much attention to Cumbria's needs. Times are different now." Matthew paused. His next words were spoken so softly Margery didn't immediately register their meaning. "We've different wars to fight."

The hairs rose along her arms. Margery felt, as she had before 1381's Great Rising, that calamity was about to befall them all.

"Surely there is no need to rush matters," she said, fear causing her voice to catch. "You are still young and Serill has long administered Swaffham Manor. Unless there is something you're not telling me..."

"I am past sixty." Matthew's voice was calm. He reached out to loop his arm around Margery's waist, to draw her close so that their thighs touched. "You see me through the eyes of love, as the man I used to be."

The man you still are, she wanted to cry. *What do you know that you refuse to share? Has the king committed more atrocities? Are you ill?"*

"If Serill is to keep Cumbria safe, he must learn to rule with a firm but fair hand. Otherwise, he will be looked upon as a tyrant. And we know the inevitable fate of tyrants."

Like our king?

The unspoken words hung between them. As words so often did these days. So much was left unsaid that Margery sometimes wondered whether they'd all been rendered mute. Like a hunter scanning the forest floor for signs of his prey, she was reduced to interpreting actions. She divined that Matthew feared their king would strip him of lands and title; that Serill was working to erase his father's scorn and seeking forgiveness from his wife for his infidelities; while Janey, in turn, had accepted his silent apology with silent actions of her own.

And me? How to interpret my actions? How to calm my fears? What can I do other than bend my knees before the Virgin and the rood and plead to keep my loved ones safe?

CHAPTER 11

"The greatest chivalric event of the age" was a term applied to many entertainments. The duel between Henry Bolingbroke and Thomas Mowbray was similarly described. What could be more exciting than two jousting champions fighting to the death over a matter of honor? From across England and beyond, lord and commoner descended upon Coventry to finish what was thought to be a fight to the death.

Once again, Richard of Bordeaux, who oversaw the joust, did the unexpected.

There would no clashing of lances at Coventry, no physical determination of which man had been telling the truth. At the last minute, Richard halted the duel. He well knew that the death of one man, regardless of whether it be Mowbray or Bolingbroke, would not serve his ends. Should Henry Bolingbroke slay his opponent, suspicious subjects and blathering churchmen would interpret it as confirmation that Henry had spoken the truth, that he, Richard, had indeed been involved in murder. Conversely, if Thomas Mowbray prevailed, the resultant enmity would further fray the shaky alliance between him, John of Gaunt and Gaunt's allies.

Unfortunately, since Richard could not manipulate the death of both combatants, he simply cancelled the event. At the last minute, in order to heighten the drama, while the two combatants were lined up on opposite sides the field.

After which, he banished both men.

Henry of Lancaster, Duke of Hereford, was ordered to quit England for ten years.

Thomas Mowbray was banished for life.

Each man had one month to obey.

There.

Should they disobey they would be charged with treason.

Recently, Richard had boasted that he had ground down his opponents "not to the bark only, but even to the root."

Thomas Mowbray and Henry Bolingbroke were the last two original Lords Appellant. Now Richard of Bordeaux had ground them down as well.

While far weightier events took place at Coventry, Margery Watson was reunited, in a sense, with the only man she'd not loved, exactly—for Matthew was her beloved. But Fulco the Smithy was the only other man who had ever stirred her.

It happened before the phantom joust. The stands and the slopes around them were packed. Though there were the usual refreshment stalls, musicians, acrobats, stilt-walkers and other amusements, the atmosphere was desultory. Modern tournaments might result in death, but that was not the usual intent. Today it was.

Margery and Matthew were seated next to Serill and Janey. Margery had a clear view of Henry Bolingbroke's beautiful pavilion, which was decorated with red roses. Since there was yet little activity around it, Margery found herself discreetly swiveling around to watch the royal couple. The treacherous king and his exquisite little queen. Isabella possessed such a charming mixture of dignity and gravity that one might forget her age until she dissolved in giggles or bounced upon her throne. Margery tried to imagine her own granddaughters, a scant few years younger, in a similar situation. Alice, perhaps; Guinevere would be slipping between the wooden planks and running off to wheedle treats from a food seller.

A sudden roar. Margery returned her attention to the lists where Henry

Bolingbroke had appeared, clad in dazzling Italian armor and astride a powerful white destrier draped in blue and green velvet embroidered with gold swans and antelopes. Spectators threw flowers, tippets and other pieces of clothing onto the field and, as one, chanted his name.

After Henry's arms were formally acknowledged, the duke rode straight for his huge pavilion. From Margery's position she had full view of the men who now swarmed the area—heralds, squires, barbers, grooms, Bolingbroke's Italian armorers....

And then she saw him.

Margery narrowed her eyes, as if her vision had played her false. Nay, it could not be! Matthew had once mentioned that Henry had hired Italian armorers, for they and the German were the world's finest, but he'd also mentioned something about English armorers. She'd barely listened... she'd not even thought...Henry Bolingbroke and Fulco the Smithy?

Margery felt suddenly lightheaded. After all these years, could it be her May Day lover? Aye, there was no mistake. Fulco's long hair was streaked with gray and tied behind, as always. He was standing beside one of the Italians with his arms across a chest that had lost nothing of its breadth, observing Bolingbroke's approach. In a stance she well remembered.

I would know you anywhere, Margery thought. Though that was no great feat since he was little changed. Even the way he held himself, the way he positioned himself amid the armorers—yet somehow apart. As had ever been his way.

Nay, Fulco had not changed, for he'd been a good decade younger than Margery. But she had.

I am an old woman, for certes.

Margery was glad she could watch Fulco privately without fear of being caught out, that he would remember her the way she'd once been. Her surroundings fell away until only he existed—as it had been when she'd first seen him inside St. Dunstan's smithing shop on the outskirts of Canterbury. Fulco's great muscles gleaming while he'd hammered his metal into submission. Silhouetted against the flames from the nearby forge, the young blacksmith had appeared as dark and dangerous as one of Satan's fallen angels.

Fulco the Smithy had driven Margery near to madness with desire.

Twenty years. Two decades since they'd lain together beyond the banks of the River Stour. How had Margery lived so contentedly when the very sight of

Fulco gave rise to those ancient emotions, endangered all the subsequent peaceful years with the man beside her, the man she truly loved?

The crowd was still roaring. Or was that simply her heart in her ears? A part of her registered that Matthew had leaned away to speak with Serill—a reminder that she was blessed, that for her, there had only been Matthew Hart.

Save for those long-ago summer days...

It is enough, she thought, silently addressing Fulco, *to know that you are well, that your skill has gained favor, and with such a lord as Henry Bolingbroke. The rest I do not need.*

She prayed that Fulco was happy. Perhaps he'd married and had a baker's dozen of children, but even as Margery thought it, her wayward mind rebelled. She'd always simply assumed that Fulco the Smithy had been faithful in his fashion. Over the years, a traveling pedlar or a merchant from York would pull her aside to hand her a cloth pouch. Inside she'd find a piece of jewelry—an intricately wrought bracelet with two intertwined hearts; a brooch, once again fashioned like a heart with a pin in the shape of smithy's hammer; a pair or ankle-rings which even now encircled her ankles. At one time she'd felt a certain smugness, telling herself that he would never marry, that he would keep a promise she'd never asked him to make.

But the gifts had ended years ago. Whatever connection she'd fancied was surely gone. Such arrogance to think otherwise!

Still, just as they'd once been able to sense each other's presence, Fulco suddenly lifted his head. He scanned the stands and effortlessly, as if the tiers contained a handful of faces rather than hundreds, locked his gaze to her. Margery saw his expression of surprise. And recognition.

Did he smile? She thought he might, or at least imagined a lifting of one side of his mouth. Again, it was as if time had stilled, as if they'd never had any other lives or loves or obligations. With his eyes still upon her, Fulco slowly raised his arm and slipped a hand inside his tunic, to remove the necklace that yet rested there. Attached to a pendant that he'd fashioned of her naked body, tracing it from the memory of his fingertips gliding across her flesh beneath that long-ago summer moon. The pendant he swore he would always wear.

Fulco brought the metal figure of her, hair spilling over her breasts, long legs wantonly exposed, to his lips. There his kiss lingered. Then Fulco bowed his head, in secret acknowledgement.

Some things do not change, Margery thought, *no matter the passing of years. How curious; how wonderful...*

Margery crossed both arms over her heart before raising a hand to kiss her fingertips and extend them toward her former lover.

CHAPTER 12

*T*he year 1399 arrived, brimming with ill omens. Chroniclers wrote of laurel trees that withered and then revived. A river in Bedfordshire dramatically changed its course, symbolizing England's political divisions and continuing defections from King Richard. Most dramatically, a comet appeared for eight days in a row, its tail pointed westward, causing astrologers to predict the death of kings. Or revolution.

Perhaps not exactly the death of kings, though John of Gaunt had titled himself King of Castile. And he *was* dying.

"I'll not lay eyes on Henry again in this life," John said to Matthew Hart, during their last meeting following Twelfth Night. They were at Leicester Castle, in the duke's bedroom where he was propped up on a raft of pillows. "How that saddens me."

"He's been a dutiful son."

"You will guide Henry, will you not?" John reached out to take Matthew's hand. His grip was still strong, but the knuckles on his hand were more prominent, starting to shrink around the phalanges.

Matthew managed a twist of a smile. "On his dullest day, Henry is far the smarter. And wiser too, I think. Your son has no need of me."

"But I do."

John's grip tightened until Matthew nearly winced. The duke's rings dug into his flesh. "This cannot stand," John said, his voice suddenly fierce. He gazed deeply into Matthew's eyes, as if he might relay his intention without words. What was the duke intimating? Any speech would have to be coded, for Richard of Bordeaux had spies everywhere.

Before their conversation could continue, they were interrupted by a commotion outside the chamber. As if conjured from hell, King Richard himself suddenly stood before them, flanked by several courtiers. Matthew hadn't heard trumpets or any announcement of the king's arrival. Yet here he was. They'd known Richard and his court were nearby, celebrating his thirty-second birthday on the Feast of Epiphany with the usual merriments, which included jousting that went from day to night and back again. (Though Richard himself had certainly not broken any lances.)

As the king swept forward, Gaunt's courtiers and attending doctors and clergy all bent their knees. As did Matthew. Beneath the king's expression of concern, Matthew glimpsed the triumph in his eyes as he approached the duke.

After gaining Richard's permission, Matthew discreetly retreated to stand with the others in the shadows.

The king and his uncle traded the usual banalities. As if there was no deeper meaning in Richard of Bordeaux's visit. When His Majesty had come to judge for himself the condition of the old lion. How he must be gloating! But then death came to all men, didn't it? What had been carved on the Edward the Black Prince's tomb?

On earth I had great riches
Land, houses, great treasure, horses, money and gold.
But now a wretched captive am I...

While observing the interchange—Richard with his straight back, his extravagant gestures—Matthew thought, *Do not gloat overmuch, Richard of Bordeaux. Death might soon be on the prowl for you, as well.*

Afterwards, much would be written about the final meeting between John of Gaunt and his royal nephew. Some said that Lancaster was "lying thus diseased in bed," and that he showed the putrefaction of his corrupted genitals and other parts to King Richard in order to warn him against a licentious life. They wrote that John of Gaunt was dying from a sickness caused by the frequenting of women "for he was a great fornicator."

Matthew didn't recall that particular scene at all. For certes, John of Gaunt had enjoyed many women, even in addition to his mistress and current wife, Katherine Swynford, though there was no doubt of their love. Infidelity was simply the way of the court.

Furthermore, the idea that John would warn this fop against carnal intercourse was laughable. Here was a king married to a child, and whose first queen had failed to produce a child because, it was rumored, Richard had taken an oath of celibacy. Believable enough, for there was his outsized worship of Saint Edward the Confessor, who had also declined to produce an heir. Since, of course, a monarch should think of his own wants and needs and religious quirks rather than his duty to his kingdom, shouldn't he?

And there was that other matter, the matter of Richard's fondness for Edward Caernarvon, whose kingdom had been brought down by his loyalty to his male lovers. Similar rumors had long circulated about Richard. Did he not surround himself with kerchief waving half-men in this oft-called Court of Venus? Not to mention the king's hysterical reaction to his favorite, Robert de Vere's death. Surely, that had been beyond the normal bounds of grief...

Beside Matthew, two of the doctors whispered, heads close together. A priest was diligently working his paternoster while Richard's courtiers, rosy-cheeked and pretty as girls, watched from the doorway.

Feeling protective of John of Gaunt, Matthew edged marginally closer, hoping to better hear the conversation, the real reason Richard was looming over his dying uncle.

Matthew's ears pricked when he heard the duke ask his sovereign to remove his oldest son's banishment. "If not that, I would ask that you allow Henry to return to England so that we might gaze upon each other one last time."

Such glee when Richard denied his uncle with an expression of false concern and a voice dripping with reluctance, every bit as false. Matthew's stomach roiled; his temper flashed. He imagined burying his dagger between Richard's elegant shoulder blades.

"My cousin brought this on himself," said Richard primly. "Some wrongs are not easily righted."

How false was Richard of Bordeaux, as false at age thirty-two as he'd been at fourteen, when he'd promised safe passage and the addressing of grievances to all those who'd participated in the Great Rising. Apparently, King Richard had learned duplicity early on, mayhap even when suckling at the breast of his wet nurse.

A few more words were exchanged with His Majesty slipping back into banal expressions of comfort. Then in one of his mercurial mood changes, Richard withdrew papers from inside his tunic and threw them atop the counterpane covering the duke's wasted frame.

"Regardless of circumstances, a man must always pay his bills. These are righteous debts which must immediately be discharged, my lord uncle."

A collective intake of breath from those around Matthew .

With that, Richard of Bordeaux spun on his ridiculous poulaines and exited John of Gaunt's chamber.

As false to his faithful uncle in the end as he'd been throughout his life.

CHAPTER 13

MARCH 1399, WESTMINSTER ABBEY AND ST PAUL'S
CATHEDRAL

*D*espite the fact that today was Passion Sunday, Westminster Abbey was nearly deserted. All the prelates and members of the nobility would be inside St. Paul's Cathedral awaiting John of Gaunt's requiem mass, while Londoners outside would be waiting respectfully to say good-bye to a man they'd hated more often than they'd loved.

Gone, Matthew thought, swallowing back the urge to throw himself upon the paving stones and weep like one of his grandchildren. He knew how their great King Edward had felt when so many of his offspring, his wife, his fellow knights and members of the Order of the Garter, had all been relegated to ghosts in his memory.

Matthew approached Edward Windsor inside the chapel of St Edward the Confessor, resting within his tomb chest of Purbeck marble, sleeping near his queen. Alone, as he'd been on his death bed. Such an unworthy demise for a monarch who had given so much to his kingdom.

Atop the tomb was Edward of Windsor's bronze effigy, but Matthew knew the truth of the image, which was what lay beneath.

I am so weary of worshipping bones, he thought, his sigh loud in the stillness.

How often had he stood beside his Black Prince at Canterbury Cathedral, running his hands over the tented gloved hands, contemplating the epitaph, which reminded visitors that the grave was their ultimate destination?

Matthew prostrated himself on the paving stones with his arms outstretched in the shape of a cross. "My liege," he whispered, and tears slid along the bridge of his nose. Matthew was sure his father had not cried before tomb chests; had not unmanned himself with such melancholia.

And now I am older than my father. And I am the one to whom the fearful turn, seeking a leader. If they only knew...

How cold the stones, cold as the grave, surely. Matthew couldn't remember the last time he'd spread himself thus. On the eve of his knighthood, near a half century past? He settled his cheek against the biting stones. With his eyes closed, Matthew mentally recited his great king's epitaph, which he knew by heart.

Here is the glory of the English, the paragon of past kings, the model of future kings, a merciful king, the peace of the peoples, Edward the third fulfilling the jubilee of his reign, the unconquered leopard, powerful in war like a Maccabee. While he lived prosperously, his realm lived again in honesty. He ruled mighty in arms; now in Heaven let him be a king.

Matthew's outstretched hands clenched into fists. *How can I bear this, my liege?*

How relentless was fortune's wheel. Matthew resented it at times, resented God's plan, which in the case of their great Edward seemed more of a tragedy laced with cruel irony. To have outlived such greatness. Edward Windsor, who captivated with his charm and grace even those who swore they would not be captivated. Who possessed the courage of the lions of England he represented. For a true king cannot lead troops into battle from behind. Edward had stood on the decks of England's ships at the battles of Sluys and Winchelsea, refusing to back down when facing insurmountable odds, to retreat to a place of safety. At Crecy, ten thousand against thirty, and he'd not once shown a flicker of fear. Even the Rheims Campaign, when Edward had experienced the wrath of God and ever the obedient servant, renounced his claim to France's throne. Always Edward led. No wonder his men went through hell for him and, of course, for his son, the Black Prince. Courage in the face of battle, in the face of losses, even in the loss of health.

Distant echo of footsteps, lonely voices echoing in Westminster's vastness. The relentless ice of the stones.

Is this how it will feel when I die?

Matthew was grateful that toward the end, Edward little knew where he was. On the level of the physical body it was a sadness, but 'twas a mercy if their great king could live in another realm where he was still young and virile and surrounded by his boisterous pups and his loving wife. To think that he could thank God and the Virgin for his many great accomplishments, foreign and homespun, rather than the truth, which was Edward Windsor was in the grips of a greedy mistress and a court riven by quarrelsome nobodies. To live in the jumbled world of glorious remembrances, for somewhere, somehow, those deeds still existed, the greatness was ongoing, beyond time—just as everything that had happened was beyond time.

Matthew silently addressed his liege. *And now I must say good-bye to your fourth son.* He struggled to his knees, then aright. *The aches from all the years, from all this living. How it settles in one's bones.*

One more sweep of his gaze across his king and his tomb. Dressed in his coronation robes and clutching two scepters. Small buttons on his cuffs and decoration on his shoes. With the joke of it being they weren't clothes or wands at all, but simply bronze renderings.

And marching across the sides of the tomb, twelve statuettes of Edward and Phillipa's offspring.

Matthew imagined the royal brood, the nine who had lived past infancy, running through Westminster Abbey as they'd once run through Windsor Castle. John and Edward and Thomas and all the rest…Matthew could almost hear their shouts and squeals echoing off the enormous vaulted ceilings; glimpse them hiding among all the Roman arches and chantries and tomb chests; chasing the colored patterns from stained glass windows upon the paving stones. Exuberant and so full of life, their laughter drifting heavenward like incense from a censer.

And now my lord the great duke lies in another tomb chest in another cathedral, awaiting my farewell.

∾

Rather than listen to his duke's requiem mass, Matthew stood beside his wife, deliberately distracting himself from this bleakest of facts—*My lord is dead,*

dead, another loss to stack one atop the other—by mentally acting as though he were conducting a tour.

For Matthew knew what lay ahead, a bit more pleasure leached from his life with the death of John, his liege, but most importantly, his friend.

Let's look about, here in St Paul's. Aye, there's the king, not even trying to hide his triumph; his little queen who comports herself with more dignity than her husband. Edmund Langley, the last living member of our great King Edward's brood. Look to your life, Edmund, for you could be next... The duke's former mistress and current wife, Katherine Swynford, dressed all in black, as are Henry Bolingbroke's children. Oh, aye, and where is our Lord Henry himself?

The Archbishop intoned the mass, often pausing to swing an incense censer at the worshippers or the duke's magnificent tomb chest, located in a chantry chapel of St. Paul's. Twenty-five enormous candles lighted the alabaster effigies of John of Gaunt and his first wife, Blanche of Lancaster— ten for the Ten Commandments John had broken, seven for the Seven Works of Charity he'd neglected, as well as the seven deadly sins; five for the Five Wounds of Christ, and three for the Holy Trinity.

Of course, Henry Bolingbroke would never view this scene, or any similar. Richard had made certain of that. The king had expressed his royal desire to keep John of Gaunt's death from his eldest son as long as possible, even though the duke had dictated that his funeral be conducted forty days after his death with the—now vain—hope Henry would have time enough to attend.

Away as he was in France and as chary as the French court was of King Richard's wrath, Henry Bolingbroke might yet remain ignorant of his father's death.

Once again, Matthew's gaze rested on England's monarch. Perhaps 'twas a blessing their Edward the Black Prince had not lived long enough to view the contrast between his son and Henry Bolingbroke.

As if sensing Matthew's turmoil, Margery reached out to lace her fingers through his. Matthew tried to focus on his lord the duke's tomb chest. The effigies had been carved when John had been a young man, mourning the loss of his wife Blanche in childbirth, she all of twenty-three years old. The flickering candlelight caused the ivory figures, hands clasped together for eternity, to shimmer as if surrounded by a halo of holy light.

Christ on a cross, Matthew thought, feeling sadness alongside the anger that was his dominant emotion in King Richard's presence. Matthew's friend and liege, the duke, was gone.

"*Credo in unum Deum.*"

Matthew joined in the reciting of the Creed of the Apostles.

"*Factorem caeli et terrae...*"

Matthew's gaze once more swung to Richard of Bordeaux, to the long delicate fingers covered with rings instead of a warrior's callouses.

As they are covered with blood. Matthew pushed down a wave of disgust.

It all came down to this, didn't it?

Over the last several days, while participating in the emotionally and physically exhausting round of mourning, Matthew had worried the puzzle that was Richard of Bordeaux. How the son could be so inferior to the father.

There was only one plausible answer. It had come to Matthew as he'd ridden from Westminster Abbey to St Paul's.

As if God had reached down to enlighten him.

Richard of Bordeaux was not Edward of Woodstock's blood. All those ancient rumors were true. Joan of Kent, never the most chaste of women, had lain with a commoner. The Black Prince had mostly been away on campaign—how well Matthew remembered the glories of Najera—and had returned to his newborn son. A son obviously conceived by some anonymous lover. Nothing else could explain the unexplainable.

Which made Matthew's decision that much easier. Rather than allow melancholia to grip him as it had after the slaughter of Limoges, he would shape events—not allow events to shape him. "It is better to eat the dog than be eaten by the dog," their great Edward had been told before he'd taken down the traitor, Roger Mortimer, as a very young king.

I must remember that I have everything to lose, as does my family.

Even so, the time had come for Matthew Hart to follow his conscience. In memory of his lord, John of Gaunt, in hopes of saving England itself.

CHAPTER 14

*M*atthew paced the spacious chamber, his leather boots whispering upon the rushes, releasing a pleasant lavender smell. Here inside the manor house of his nephew, Ralph Hart, Count of Vanves, on the edge of the village of Pierre-Peulise, his ears strained for other noises. Hoofbeats, shouts, the arrival of an army to arrest him. Or a quiet tread upon the stairs.

'Tis the most dangerous day of my life, Matthew thought. Even more so than his many battles. Then one expected death. Here in this secluded French village, near the tomb chest of his brother, Harry, guarded over by his brother's wife walled within her anchorhold, it seemed absurd—if not impossible—that treasonous plots might soon be hatched.

It was nearing sunset before Matthew heard a whisper on the stairs. He could discern two different sets of footsteps. Matthew eased himself up from his bench, stepped back into the shadows where he could see without being seen and slipped his dagger from its sheath. Just in case.

When Henry Bolingbroke stepped inside, Matthew re-sheathed his dagger and softly called his name.

"Lord Hart!" Henry's smile was genuine, though the sadness behind it was apparent. The stress of these last months had aged him far past his thirty-two years.

They embraced. "To see someone from home...my father's friend," Henry said, before again embracing Matthew. Matthew sensed the boy inside the man, the son longing for his papa, the child wishing that, with a few soothing words, his life might be made right again.

If only it were that simple.

Henry's retainer retreated to stand guard outside the door, while Matthew served Henry a simple meal, poured them wine and settled across the table from the young duke. Matthew enjoyed watching Henry dine, for after nearly a week in the saddle, the usually fastidious duke tucked into his food with gusto.

After presenting Bolingbroke's knight with a trencher of food and jack of wine, Matthew returned to his seat across from Henry and waited for him to finish. All the while pondering how he might most articulately present his case.

He knew that he wouldn't be the first to urge a course of action. Surely, Henry had spies aplenty. But Matthew had an advantage; Henry would consider him to be uttering the wishes of Henry's father. Therefore, his counsel would carry more weight.

Where to begin? Matthew might say he knew Henry had lost everything because of Richard. That Henry had always tried to placate his royal cousin, as had his father. That such a talented man as Henry Bolingbroke could have accomplished so much more—as an international diplomat or scholar or even knight errant if he'd not had to worry about overshadowing his cousin the king. Henry had endured plots against him and his father; Richard's fickleness; the murder of his royal uncle, and the execution of friends.

To what end? Perpetual banishment? Virtual penury?

Matthew might go on to say, "You have been deprived of everything, including your children. All Englishmen, from the lowest clerk or villain, can rely on the king's protection and some level of justice. But not you. Because your enemy IS England's law."

Instead, Matthew sat in silence until Henry pushed away his trencher with a satisfied sigh. Focusing his intense gaze upon Matthew, Henry said, "Tell me about my father's passing."

"Peaceful," Matthew began, though that most likely wasn't true. It had not been him, but the duke's wife and other of his children who had clustered round John's bedside. Matthew spoke of John of Gaunt's concern for Henry and his love for his eldest son. He described the ceremonies surrounding the duke's final entombment in enough detail that Henry could at least form a mental picture of all he'd missed.

The young duke placed his head in his hands and, near the end, wept. As did Matthew for he was an old man, so he chided himself, and given to such things.

Bolingbroke finally wiped his eyes. He squared his shoulders, his manner signaling it was time to throw off his grief in order to address matters of state.

"The entire French court joined with me in attending a mass to pray for Father's soul. They have been kind. Upon my arrival they pretended I was an honored guest and even set me about trying to mend the problem of the two popes." Henry laughed ruefully. "There was talk of marriage to a member of the royal family. But that was before I was labeled traitor." With an edge to his voice, he added, "I am pitied, of course, but France's political interests must rest with our king, not someone without title or prospects."

What could Matthew say? Henry spoke true. A sentence of perpetual banishment and forfeiture was considered an admission of guilt. What was Henry Bolingbroke to do, spend the rest of his days traveling from court to court, wringing his hands and lamenting his fate, until even his dignity was forfeit?

"Describe the scene at Westminster that took place following Father's funeral," said Henry. "After my cousin the king officially designated me the equivalent of the Wandering Jew."

Matthew reached for the flagon in order to refill their jacks. A slight noise from outside, probably Henry's knight placing his trencher upon the floor.

"There it was," Matthew said, handing Bolingbroke his wine. "Richard upon his throne, where worthy kings have sat, arrayed in even more jewels than usual. As if their brilliance might somehow blind those of us in the hall to the truth."

Matthew paused, collecting his emotions, for everything about the scene struck him as blasphemous. "Richard glowered at us, as if we were responsible for his problems. Which in his mind we are. He reminded us that we must address him only as His Majesty..."

"'Tis better than 'Prince of the Coxcombs,'" Henry interrupted, referring to one of Richard's less flattering nicknames.

Matthew hid his surprise. He'd never before heard Henry jape at his cousin's expense. "And his close friends must be addressed as 'Magnificent.'"

Henry choked on a mouthful of wine. "Christ have mercy," he managed after he'd regained use of his voice.

"Your cousin, the Duke of Aumale, has been made Constable of England and, Richard said, must be referred to as his 'brother.'"

The Duke of Aumale was Edmund of Langley's son. He'd probably had a hand in the murder of Thomas of Woodstock, as well as in Henry's exile. Another fist to the gut. It was almost as if, while appearing to address his barons, Richard's performance had been staged for Bolingbroke alone.

"Ah. He continues to dangle the crown in front of Aumale, does he?"

Matthew shrugged. "Richard will change his mind tomorrow, depending on his whim."

Henry's gaze was hard upon Matthew's face. "I'm told he has dictated a new will."

Matthew's suspicion about spies was confirmed. Letters were prohibited from being sent abroad before first being vetted by the privy council in order to stop the flow of such information as Henry obviously enjoyed. "You are well informed."

"That the will hints at Richard's successor," Henry prodded.

"The king made it very clear you have no right to any place in the line of succession. And should Richard die, it is his expressed command that your banishment be upheld."

Henry nodded. "As traitor to the realm."

"Aye."

Silence stretched between them. Pierre-Précieuse's chapel bell rang out Vespers. How lonely it sounded. Matthew drew his mantle closer, as if the previously cozy room had developed a chill. He thought of his younger brother, Harry, in his tomb within its narthex and wished for the sound of his voice. More than that, he wished for their father's wise counsel.

But I am the Hart patriarch now. I must make my own decisions. Hopefully, those that will not ruin us all.

"With the sequestration of your lands, Richard has amassed more wealth than Croesus. He has been sending wagonloads of treasure for safekeeping to his new stronghold, Holt Castle, where it is guarded by his Cheshire archers. And, as he readies for his foray into Ireland, he extorts money, horses and wagons without a care to legal means. He has seized grain, meat and fish without bothering to pay. His actions have only increased the common folks' enmity toward him, especially Londoners.

"Then there are the prophecies," Matthew continued. The eaglet that Merlin had prophesied. The greyhound that would put to flight all the white harts. Everyone, including Richard, knew those stories, which was why he was so frantic to find others more to his liking.

"I saw the comet myself," said Henry, referring to the star that had blazed across Europe's skies following All Soul's Day. "For eight days it appeared. I watched it from the window at the Hotel de Clisson, and at the court."

"Astrologers said it portends the death of kings. Or revolution." Matthew's gaze held Henry's. Perhaps here was his opening. "Or both."

Bolingbroke shrugged. "Sometimes we fulfill our own prophecies. We shape our actions to their words and then express wonderment when the prophecies come to pass."

Once again, the room was pregnant with unspoken words. In the increasingly uncertain light, it was hard to read Henry's expression. Matthew suppressed a sudden urge to remove his sword, plant it among the rushes so that it replicated Christ's cross and kneel before it in order to pledge his fealty to his liege lord's son.

"His High, Excellent and Most Praiseworthy Majesty," Matthew uttered the title sarcastically, "is like an unbridled horse who need not worry about ever being reined in. Since the rider—your father—is dead."

Henry spread his hands upon the table, as if in supplication. "So, here we are."

"You must reclaim your patrimony," Matthew blurted. While he privately believed the only way Henry, they all, would be safe, was for Henry to claim England's crown for himself, he dare not yet say that. "Richard will embark for Ireland in June, leaving in power those who might be turned. Or who are poor fighters."

Bolingbroke nodded. "He took my eldest for hostage when he decided on his campaign. Just as he's taken hostages from other families he fears might rise against him. You are lucky Serill is grown."

"We northern lords will support you," Matthew said bluntly. "Westmorland and Northumberland have already pledged so. And between us three, we will raise larger armies than the Duke of York. Edmund Langley may be guardian of the realm, but he is feeble. Besides, he mourns your father. Nor has he forgotten that Richard engineered the murder of their brother. Think you Langley will be a stalwart champion to such a viper?"

Henry's gaze upon Matthew did not waver. "Invade?"

Such a brutal word. Such ordinary surroundings in which to be contemplating the overthrow of one's divinely appointed sovereign.

Folding his arms across his chest, Henry looked thoughtfully into the distance—for Henry Bolingbroke was nothing if not a thoughtful man. "Presuming I can also raise an army, what would I achieve? If I force Richard to restore my inheritance, he will lay in wait until he feels safe enough to step like an assassin from the shadows. Should my rightful inheritance be returned, 'twill be the equivalent of handing me a slow-acting poison. Richard will eventually annihilate me as he did all those he hates."

"The people are embittered by your banishment. They will support you."

"Other would-be invaders have been assured of similar support. Only to have those promised armies melt away at the first sign of trouble."

Matthew remembered sitting in the great hall at St. Albans when King Richard, then an angelic-looking fourteen-year-old, had nodded in approval as sentence was pronounced against the hedge-priest John Ball. For daring to speak out against the treatment of his fellow commoners, Ball had been hanged, drawn and quartered and his head stuck on London Bridge—killed along with thousands of others.

"Many have not forgotten Richard's perfidy during the Great Rising," said Matthew. "The ghosts of the dead still whisper in the ears of their family members, seeking vengeance."

"You border lords ever go your own way. What about other magnates? Will they join us?"

"If only out of self-interest. If the king can deny the son of the Duke of Lancaster his rightful inheritance, they know no one's lands are safe."

Henry's gaze sought the shadows. "I am only reclaiming what is right," he finally said, as if trying out his rationale on an invisible audience.

"Aye," agreed Matthew. Though he could not see how Henry Bolingbroke could ever safely reclaim his inheritance while his royal cousin remained on the throne. But the first step was to successfully raise an army; the second to successfully invade.

Matthew reached across the table to clasp Henry's hand. "You have my loyalty. As did your father, my prince and our great King Edward."

Matthew felt a shiver, not so much of fear, for he was more awed by the enormity of their undertaking. He could not—would not—fail. And from now on, he would put aside his doubts. He would think only of victory.

"If we fail—"

"Our cause is just. God will not forsake us. Of that I am sure."

"I wish Father were here," said Henry wistfully, and once again Matthew saw the child he had been. "He would have found a way to temper King Richard's wrath."

"But he is not. Which means we are on our own."

CHAPTER 15

JUNE 1399, CUMBRIA CASTLE

*U*p ahead walked the twins, Alice carrying a bouquet of wildflowers while Guinevere, with her gown tied above her knees, alternated walking on her hands and executing cartwheels. Billy had tied a rope around Happiness, who followed him docilely, as if he were the three-year-old's rouncey; Fearless padded beside Janey. The family had spent the afternoon at Cumbria's Enchanted Cottage, this last day before Serill Hart, his father and the other rebels who had gathered at Cumbria Castle would depart.

'*The path to paradise begins in hell,*' Janey thought, for she'd been reading Dante. Though in this case the path to hell might begin in hell. *But I believe*, she told herself. *Nay, I* know *Henry Bolingbroke will prevail.*

Janey deliberately reached out to slip her hand through Serill's. In the two years since her tryst at Tintagel, Janey had done her best to resurrect her marital relationship. Because Lancelot had directed: "Go home to Serill. He loves you."

She had discovered, however, it was far easier to destroy a relationship than to rebuild one. Still, she'd done her best, working it as slowly, as methodically as she stitched embroidered scenes in her hoop. And in the process, had she once again fallen in love with her husband? Perhaps. But more than that, she'd come to believe that kindness was the noblest of virtues.

Serill tightened his hand in hers. "Billy, do not jerk on Happiness. You'll choke the poor beast to death." Then to Janey, "Lancelot and three of his brothers arrived yester eve. Did you know?"

"I did not," Janey said. Though of course she did. As soon as she'd heard the clatter in Cumbria's bailey, she'd had to force herself to remain in the bakehouse, where the children had been begging treats from Cook. She wanted to rush out past Cumbria's jumble of outbuildings, if only to view her secret beloved dismounting following a grueling week-long journey. She felt that invisible pull of him, one she'd often experienced across hundreds of miles when she knew Lancelot was thinking of her.

"Do not fear for me," Serill said, mistaking her quiet for concern over his forthcoming departure. "We will not fail. Not with Father as one of our leaders."

"All will go well," Janey agreed serenely. It wasn't just the new life inside her that gave her such placidity. In that most private part of her being, she believed that she and Lancelot, by refusing to sin—at least in the carnal sense —HAD saved the kingdom. Whatever happened, with Lancelot on the side of Matthew Hart and Henry Bolingbroke, the rebels would win.

Our destiny, she thought. *And it does not matter that only we will know.* She felt a bit like Merlin, who orchestrated the affairs of Camelot through magic and prophecies. Well Janey knew she possessed no magic, and this was her only actual prophecy. (Daydreams and wishes did not count.) With Henry Bolingbroke, now Duke of Lancaster, sailing across the North Sea, and King Richard chasing wild men around Ireland, prophecies—most of them contradictory—were common currency.

But I believe Lancelot. And he believes that the fate of England depends upon our actions. We passed the test. We did not repeat the tragedy of Lancelot and Guinevere. We have set right their ancient wrong.

She imagined God marking down their sins and their good deeds on opposite sides of a giant ledger, tapping his equally giant finger against the parchment—for she always pictured herself in relation to God as a human to an ant—and nodding his approval.

While the children meandered vaguely in the direction of Cumbria Castle's postern, Serill abruptly stopped, turned and hugged Janey tight against him. Her husband bore only passing resemblance to the carefree, charming—and oft shallow—man of earlier years. Daily, he reminded her more of his father, though she sometimes found herself swallowing the words, "It's about time!" Janey was glad she could feel his body's tension. That meant Serill was taking the forthcoming events as seriously as they merited. To lash out against a king by force of arms—if only to regain one's rightful inheritance—was like backtalking to God. It could not be done without risking the harshest of punishments.

Janey returned Serill's embrace, breathing in his familiar mix of scents. She'd also grown up these past years, certainly past the mindless adoration, the breathless confessions she'd once made, the personality she'd donned in the vain hope that she could force Serill Hart to love her. And not hate him for his frailties, his inability to be who she wished rather than who he was. Also, she'd come to realize that there were more important things in life than love between a man and woman. So, if her marital relationship was imperfect, if her intimacy with Lancelot of Glastonbury could only live in her memory, she accepted that.

"You may not have your wars of a long season," she said, leaning back in her husband's arms. "But the tales we will tell our children about this time. Such a hero you'll be!"

"Aye," said Serill, his hands tightening around her expanding waist. He did not add, "If we survive," though he thought it.

As he continually wrestled with waking nightmares of his and his father's heads impaled high atop London Bridge. Imagined their eyeless sockets pointed in the direction of the Tower of London where Janey, his children, his mother—all those bearing the Hart lineage—would be imprisoned.

All for daring to cross a king.

CHAPTER 16

PENDRAGON CASTLE AND CUMBRIA CASTLE

$\mathcal{I}$solated as she was at Pendragon Castle, Viviane Halle knew very little about events beyond the Marcher lands. While she'd heard of Henry Bolingbroke's banishment, the activities of great lords had little to do with a young woman of middling heritage, middling looks and middling prospects. A rare visit from Viviane's father during last year's Advent season —when she'd created delectable fasting-appropriate dishes she hoped would leave him speechless with wonderment—had left her thoroughly confused.

For while John Halle *was* often speechless, it had naught to do with her cooking.

When her father deigned to address Viviane at all, he spoke in riddles. She understood that he was in service to Thomas Mowbray. That King Richard had ordered a tournament during which Mowbray had been banished. (Why? What had one to do with the other?) Then something about Thomas Woodstock, Duke of Gloucester, but beyond the fact that Gloucester was dead, Viviane could not puzzle through a connection.

I will ask Gerald to explain when I see him, she thought, but when her brother rode across Pendragon's drawbridge a half-year later, John Halle had long departed, and Viviane was distracted by far more worrisome news.

"We are here to escort you to Cumbria Castle," Gerald Halle said, following the usual greetings. "You will be safe there should there really be…" he substituted the word "trouble" for "an invasion."

Viviane had already received an offer of protection from the Earl of Cumbria, (read to her by her bailiff), though wasn't it a happy coincidence that her brother and her beloved Reginald had arrived to provide additional escort to the trio of Halle retainers?

"Why must I leave?" Viviane asked, for there were sheep to be sheared and fallow fields to be ploughed.

"If the Earl of Cumbria thinks you will be safer behind Cumbria Castle's walls, you'll not gainsay him."

Beyond that, Gerald would not try to explain complexities he himself scarcely grasped. From gossip at Alnwick Castle, he had deduced that the Henry Percys, both elder and younger, were ambivalent about Henry Bolingbroke's rebellion against England's rightful sovereign.

While the rest of Pendragon was packing up, Reginald Luci maneuvered Viviane into a secluded nook for a quick tupping. "I could not have gone off to battle without seeing you," he said afterward, trailing kisses along her jawline and above the hem of her bodice.

"We will be riding off to great danger, death even," Reginald Luci continued, when she did not react.

"Seeing" me? Viviane thought. *Is that what sarding is now called?* As always around her lover, Viviane tempered her razor tongue. What she actually wanted to say was, "And with your martial skills death is a distinct possibility."

It had been four years since Reginald Luci had taken her maidenhead, and all Viviane had received in return was his prick and a handful of sweet words. Neither of which she could build a future upon.

"How brave you are," she said, hoping to keep the sarcasm from her voice.

"Surely, we will soon be together forever," Reginal Luci whispered, not for the first time.

"Soon?" Viviane echoed.

"Promise, *mon pigeon succulent,*" Reginald whispered, moving his lips against the hollow above her collarbone.

Throughout the hours-long journey to Cumbria Castle, Viviane repeatedly glanced across at her suitor, riding so elegantly next to her, thinking, *If promises were sweets, yours, Reginald Luci, would be stacked halfway to the moon.*

By the end of her first week at Cumbria Castle, Viviane Halle was firmly ensconced in its enormous kitchen. While cooks were notoriously proprietary, they also routinely engaged caterers (if of the male sex). Daily, more knights arrived, along with members of the Hart family, which caused the population to swell until Viviane, Cook and Pendragon's helpers toiled comfortably alongside Cumbria's staff from Matins to Compline.

Viviane was pleased that she could be of use, so that the Countess of Cumbria would not consider her and her household a burden. Besides, amidst the heat and noise and controlled chaos of Cumbria's kitchen, Viviane need not fret over what might be happening beyond its walls. Her Reginald and her brother had already left to rendezvous with the Henry Percys, who were gathering their own army and heading south in anticipation of Bolingbroke's arrival. So long as Viviane stayed busy, she wouldn't worry about the repercussions that Reginald, Gerald and all those armed men flocking to Cumbria Castle would suffer if they failed in what even she understood would be considered treason.

Viviane sensed that underneath the Countess of Cumbria's placid surface ran a current of fear, as it did in all the women with whom Viviane interacted. Jane le Babbe bore a distracted air, as if waiting for something, while her children shadowed her like anxious chicks. Elizabeth Ravenne haunted Cumbria's ramparts where, paternoster in hand, she gazed south, straining for the first glimpse of her last two sons, who had not yet arrived.

Matthew Hart seemed to be everywhere, consulting with his marshal, his knights, squires, farriers, armorers and all those so necessary for a successful campaign; his steward, constable, chamberlain and the trusted retainers he would leave behind to guard Cumbria.

Viviane found Lord Hart impossibly intimidating, but drew comfort from the knowledge that such a man would never take notice of her. Thus, she was both surprised and alarmed when he called her to him.

"Your father is John Halle, is he not?" Matthew asked. They were standing near the kitchen, where he was overseeing the untrussing of the boars he and his hunting party had killed that afternoon.

Viviane, who had thought to supervise the animals move to the hooks upon which they would be impaled, dropped into an awkward curtsy.

"Aye, my lord."

Lord Hart studied her with the most disconcertingly direct gaze. Viviane didn't fancy anyone would dare lie to this man.

"Was John Halle not recently at Calais? In service to Thomas Mowbray?" Matthew Hart pressed. "Duke of Norfolk?"

"I do believe so," Viviane managed, though she wasn't sure of the man's title. When a tightening around the earl's eyes warned her she'd given the wrong answer, she rushed to clarify. "Papa's actually not visited Pendragon since last Christmas so I'm not sure where he might be."

Jesu. If Viviane were a man, she would not want to meet Lord Hart in battle. She was suddenly reminded of the great crags beyond Pendragon Castle, where storms were like to congregate.

"Maman used to say my father was about the king's business," she added, hoping to please Cumbria's lord.

"The king's business." Matthew Hart repeated the phrase as if it were distasteful. Viviane sensed another misstep. But then his expression softened. "My lady wife tells me you have been a great help to her. For which we extend our gratitude."

With that Lord Hart returned to the business of the boars, and a relieved Viviane retreated to the bakehouse next to the kitchen.

"Someone else can supervise those bloody animals," she muttered. She'd braved enough danger for one day.

The morning of departure arrived. Cumbria's bailey teemed with mounted knights, their various identifying pennons attached to their lances; squires carrying shields and lances; grooms soothing nervous destriers; packhorses bearing weapons, supplies and armor—even a priest to tend to souls should the worst happen.

It was only in hindsight, when Viviane Hall's fate was intrinsically woven with two of those in the bailey, that she would remember one seemingly inconsequential event. And which would one day emerge from the past, like figures from a fog, to torment her.

This is what Viviane Halle observed, that morning the Earl of Cumbria and his men rode out to greet Henry Bolingbroke.

Jane le Babbe, back ramrod straight, crossing the crowded bailey following a final embrace with her husband. Toward Lancelot of Glastonbury, wearing simple mail topped by a jupon bearing both the raven and the hart, and astride his black destrier.

Lancelot, watching her approach.

Coming to a stop beside him. Looking so slight next to his mount, which was nervously prancing in place.

Gazing up at her dark knight.

The slightest exchange of smiles, though Viviane, who has full view of their faces, understands something unusual is happening.

Jane le Babbe raises her hand to Lancelot. He leans down from his saddle to take it in his own ungauntleted one. The subtlest altering of facial expressions, but Viviane knows, for 'twould be impossible to miss, that the knight is in love with Jane le Babbe. Viviane looks in alarm to Serill Hart, who is handing his squire his shield and sees nothing.

Lancelot of Glastonbury bends further forward to press his lips, not to Jane le Babbe's exposed palm, as Viviane would have thought, but upon her wrist, at the ending of her sleeve.

Viviane moves closer. Even amid the surrounding noise, the baying of excited hounds, she hears Lady Jane say, "Sir Lancelot. You and I, I believe we have saved a kingdom."

As if pieces sliding together from a puzzle box—one, two three—Viviane understands. Forbidden love. Such as hers and Reginald's? But that particular thought causes her vision to blur and her attention to drift to her own troubles, forgetting Jane le Babbe and Lancelot of Glastonbury.

Until much later, when she will repeatedly dredge up this particular memory.

And each time it will pierce the misery that is her heart.

CHAPTER 17

*M*atthew Hart watched Henry Bolingbroke's cogs appear on the horizon. He waited on Ravenspur's dunes with Serill, Lancelot and a small group of Hart retainers. The rest of Matthew's soldiers were camped near Bridlington, alongside Henry Percy the Elder, Earl of Northumberland, and his son, Harry Hotspur/Henry Percy the Younger. The Percys had promised an army of thirty thousand by the time they rendezvoused with the young Duke of Lancaster.

Matthew Hart had been granted the honor of being the first face the duke would see upon returning to English soil.

Honor or curse? Matthew wondered. For if the insurrection died aborning, he and his men would also be the first to lose their heads.

Still, Matthew would not have had it otherwise. *I am here because my liege lord cannot be*, he thought, while Bolingbroke's ships, sails puffed like the breasts of great birds, neared Ravenspur's shore. Part of a whispered promise made while kneeling before John of Gaunt's tomb chest. Matthew's gaze drifted heavenward. He imagined his liege looking down, more giant than mortal man and as powerful an intercessor as St George or Michael the Archangel.

The blue of the North Sea was as dazzling as the July sky. A steady wind blew off the water, tugging at Matthew's uncoiffed hair, cooling his body, still clad in a hauberk and sweating from the long ride and afternoon's heat.

To his left, Serill shaded his eyes, turned and said something to Lancelot before calling, "Father!" and pointing to a scattering of herons circling Henry's cog.

Odd. Herons were solitary birds except during mating season, which was well past.

Lancelot crossed himself. "An auspicious omen," he said, for herons not only symbolized wisdom but were God's messengers.

All along their journey knights had looked to nature for signs of favor, just as Henry and his scholars had scoured the chronicles for encouraging prophecies throughout his banishment. A goat wandering across the roadway was good; hearing or seeing an owl might be good or bad; a black cat was definitely an evil omen.

While Matthew believed in such things, he also knew they must make their own luck.

After Henry's cog anchored, the young duke was the first to disembark. (How pitifully few boats accompanied him!) Matthew noted approvingly that Henry was dressed in full plate armor, with his surcoat proudly displaying the family coat of arms. A wise man to understand the importance of both appearance and ritual. For, the first thing Henry Bolingbroke did after planting himself on English soil, was to kneel and kiss the ground.

Matthew swung from his destrier to await the approach of his liege. On the shoulders of this compact, self-assured man all their fates depended. Who Matthew had known since he'd been in swaddling bands, since he'd clutched at his father's knees and begged for a pick-a-back ride. Jesu! Were they all arrogant or mad or England's saviors? Or something else altogether?

Allowing the young duke his moment alone, Henry's men remained respectfully aboard ship. Henry rose. Turning, he scanned the great expanse of sea as if reminding himself from whence he'd come, squared his shoulders and turned back to Matthew. Lips curved in a half-smile that at least appeared to be genuine, Bolingbroke approached. The blue background from the fleurs-de-lys upon his surcoat matched that of the sky; the gold of England's lions bright as the shiniest of nobles.

"My lord," Matthew knelt before Henry. Lancelot, Serill and his other men dismounted and followed suit.

Thus began the usurpation of Richard of Bordeaux.

All along the route, so many supporters from Yorkshire and Lancashire joined —gentlemen, knights and esquires accompanied by well-armed retinues—that one chronicler later pegged their number at one hundred thousand. Crowds lining their roadway called Henry Bolingbroke "Savior" and compared him to Christ. Others cried, "Blessed is he who comes in the name of the Lord, our King of England!" Poets likened him to the Emperor Augustus, while Geoffrey Chaucer, friend to both John of Gaunt and the current regent, wrote that Henry Bolingbroke had come "to mend all harm."

Though Richard of Bordeaux believed his right to rule descended directly from God, the majority of his subjects— certainly those gathered in the summer heat to cheer his enemy— didn't care a fig about such complexities. They were more impressed with Henry Bolingbroke's pilgrimage to Jerusalem, which had brought honor to the entire kingdom; his international reputation with lance and sword; his crusading and battlefield experiences. Englishmen revered their warrior kings, which their current coxcomb most certainly was not.

In addition, there were the prophecies, more frantically circulated than ever before, claiming that the line of Lancaster would inherit the throne. It was God's will, according to scholars' new interpretations of old chronicles, that Henry Bolingbroke should end Richard's rule.

Even while Richard of Bordeaux might or might not be reconnoitering ships to transport him across the Irish Sea, success appeared inevitable.

The Henry Percys were true "Kings of the North." Henry the Elder was shrewd and ambitious, as were so many of his fellow magnates. Henry's son, Harry Hotspur, had been knighted with both the young king and the young Bolingbroke, and had subsequently gained a reputation as a fearless fighter. The Percy household had been unswervingly loyal to Richard of Bordeaux—at least until he committed two serious blunders. First, Richard elevated the Percys' rival, Henry Neville, to the title Earl of Westmoreland, thus putting the two greatest border lords in competition. Secondly, thinking only to spite John of Gaunt and his cub, Richard had threatened to reverse those ancient pardons granted to Thomas Lancaster after Lancaster had rebelled against the Sodomite King. Forgetting that the Percys were related by marriage to Thomas of Lancaster. Meaning that with one signature, England's current Majesty could make Percy titles and lands forfeit.

Henry the Elder and Henry Percy the Younger felt they had no choice but to join the insurrection. But could they trust Henry Bolingbroke? The Percys had their own claim to the monarchy, though that claim rested on the shoulders of an eight-year-old. Henry Bolingbroke, Matthew Hart—all of those who looked askance at the Percys' motivation—could be forgiven if they winced at the thought of a second boy ascending England's throne.

Before the Percys formally pledged their fealty to Bolingbroke, before they risked their heads and their heritage simply to elevate another to England's throne, they demanded Henry swear a sacred oath. He would not "seize" the throne but would stand aside for anyone "more worthy of the crown."

Henry Bolingbroke so swore on a plethora of holy relics. The Percys were placated. While the rebels made plans to head south to London, the Percys agreed to ride beside Bolingbroke.

Unfortunately for the usually clever Percys, they'd ignored a basic caution. That even the greatest of lords should employ the services of shrewd lawyers. In this case, in order to determine the meaning of every word of Henry's oath. Particularly the definition of one: "worthy."

CHAPTER 18

BERKELEY CASTLE, THE MARCHER LANDS

*E*dward Caernarvon, the current king's idol, had been murdered in Berkeley Castle, near the Welsh border. Common belief was that Edward, a lover of men, had been murdered by having a red-hot poker jammed up his anus. How odd—or how fitting—that Berkeley Castle would play a part in the downfall of Richard of Bordeaux. For it was here that Edmund Langley, their great King Edward's surviving child and current regent of England, would await either the arrival of King Richard, perhaps even now docking at the port of Bristol, or the arrival of the Usurper.

Hoping to avoid civil war.

Henry Bolingbroke arrived first.

In the church of St. Mary's, amid the tomb chests of the Berkeley family, Edmund Langley forsook his king and officially gave Henry Bolingbroke his blessing.

Events now moved at a faster pace.

Henry dispatched Edmund Langley to take Richard's nine-year-old queen into custody. Then, prepared for battle, he marched toward Bristol. Though he did not find the king, in nearby Bristol Castle he found three of Richard's lords who had approved the confiscation of Henry's lands, as well as his banishment.

Henry ordered the trio executed and dispatched their severed heads to York, London and Bristol.

King Richard had learned almost immediately of the traitor's invasion, which made him turn "pale with anger."

So be it, he assured himself. *I will put a stop to my cousin's treason soon enough.*

Richard need not fear desertions. The soldiers who'd traveled with him to Ireland were among his most loyal. The king's frustration lay in the time it would take to collect his troops and set sail from Waterford—weeks rather than days. During that wait the king's anger burned hot as fired metal, as did his desire for revenge.

Before summer's end, he silently vowed, *I will finally, brutally remove the festering thorn that is Henry Bolingbroke from my flesh.*

First time around, during the Great Rising of 1381, the commons had thought to rise up against him. And now lords of the realm? The result would be the same. England's ground would be soaked with their blood, while he, Richard of Bordeaux would emerge stronger than ever!

At July's end, Richard landed at Milford Haven in southwest Wales. The accounts he'd heard of Henry Bolingbroke's advancement were all contradictory, though universally alarming. Depending on his mood, the king dismissed the worst with a torrent of oaths or shrug of the shoulders. Richard considered himself to be an enlightened monarch. He had enriched England with building projects, while overseeing a court as cultured as any in Europe. Only a handful of malcontents could say otherwise.

Which I will deal with soon enough.

After docking, Richard began marching toward Carmarthen, Wales' oldest city and the birthplace of the wizard Merlin. The trickle of news became a deluge—all of it incomprehensible.

My kingdom has turned against me? Hundreds of thousands are following Bolingbroke's banner?

Richard had a mental image of malcontents spreading across the landscape like a squawking, flapping brood of chickens scurrying after seed corn. Laughable. And yet...

Richard raged and paced while considering various actions. Though vehemently denying the seriousness of his plight, privately the king felt such a fear. One so ancient he could not even pinpoint its origin. But it had suppurated and then metastasized until it was crowding out every emotion save dread. More than dread.

Terror.

When Richard had penned his new will; when he'd consulted his augurs, who'd assured him that the signs remained auspicious for him to become Emperor of the World. Even when he had discovered that golden eagle in the Tower of London—a stone ampulla nestled inside the eagle containing the holy oil Christ's mother had bestowed upon Thomas Becket. Not only should the oil be used to anoint kings, but its wearers would achieve wealth and prosperity—along with the re-conquest of the Holy Land.

A powerful relic indeed.

Yet, despite all that, Richard still felt that terror—if only as faintly as the scent of a distant fire borne upon the wind.

Throughout his frenetic pacing, Richard's fist remained clamped around the eagle resting on a chain around his neck.

The prophets cannot be wrong, he assured himself a dozen times a day. *Neither can my beliefs.*

England's king was a virtual god. This was not Richard of Bordeaux's assertion; it was fact. England's long-term peace depended on its sovereign's absolute control over his unruly magnates and their ever-increasing armies. That in turn required that the king preside over the greatest court and the greatest army and that his very person be respected as holy. Which was the reason symbolism, pageantry, ceremony—all the trappings of regality—were so necessary. It might be mummery, but it was divine mummery.

But, in return for so successfully discharging his duties, it came down to...this??

No wonder sleep eludes me. No wonder my mind constructs fearsome night-mares.

While Richard had never honed his tactical skills on the battlefield, as had his father and grandfather, he was shrewd and crafty—so he assured himself— and more than a match for his royal cousin or anyone else.

The truth was something else again.

Richard of Bordeaux was woefully inadequate to cope with this, the greatest crisis of his reign. All coherent thought had taken flight from his brain like a flock of panicked starlings. At Carmarthen, the king actually abandoned his army. With only two dozen of his most loyal lords and three of his bishops, Richard scurried further north.

What was the purpose in this? What was the king thinking?

More than a century past, Edward Longshanks, Hammer of the Scots, had built an "Iron Ring" of castles along the Welsh border to subjugate its inhabitants. Richard now fled toward these great border fortresses, which also brought him closer to the loyal city of Chester where his royal treasury was hidden at Holt Castle. Throughout, he tried unsuccessfully to raise an army. Worse, previously devoted lords—didn't he have their oaths of loyalty to prove it?—abandoned him.

While Richard ran to and fro like a demented terrier, Henry Bolingbroke headed north. Relentlessly shadowing his royal cousin.

Through Ross-on-Wye.

Hereford.

Leominster.

Ludlow.

The paradox of the first King Edward's Iron Ring is that, while castles appear indestructible, they actually require as much maintenance as an aging courtesan. In the century since their construction, most had fallen into disrepair. A king who had demanded to have his throne set above all, who had commissioned a wedding outfit costing the annual maintenance of his entire household revenue of £30,000, who traveled with thousands of retainers and mile long baggage carts, now slept on straw in rooms devoid of furniture, with crumbling floors and ceilings and only his knights to wait on him.

Pale and trembling, cheeks sunken and hands shaking as if from a palsy, Richard started at every sound in the night. During the day he stalked the battlements for a glimpse of his cousin Lancaster's army. Even though the landscape remained empty, he would order his men to mount up for another mad dash to another ruined fortress in order to flee his so-far phantom pursuer.

CHAPTER 19

*H*enry Bolingbroke reached Chester. Continuing his demented peregrinations, King Richard fluttered to temporary rest at Caernarvon Castle, birthplace of the first Prince of Wales, Edward Caernarvon, the Sodomite King. The beleaguered king's present destination could be read either as another ominous portent or, to Richard's way of thinking, a reminder that his sainted ancestor had endured similar indignities.

While the city of Chester was loyal to Richard, it offered no resistance to Henry Bolingbroke, who easily established himself at Chester Castle. From there, Bolingbroke set about exacting his revenge upon the county palatine of Chester.

Rebel captains and their men were allowed to pillage and plunder without mercy. Fields were wasted; houses destroyed; a church at Coddington was stripped until only the walls, a door and a scattering of empty chests remained. One of His Majesty's favorites was executed without trial, his head set on a stake by the east gate of the city.

Unless a miracle occurred, Richard of Bordeaux's days as England's sovereign could be measured by the handfuls.

Unfortunately for Richard, he appeared to have used up his allotment of miracles.

~

A certain rhyme kept running through King Richard's head as he raced from castle to castle, as he surveyed the countryside from various battlements for the first sign of his enemy. The rhyme had first been told him by his grandfather, the old king. It began:

For want of a nail a shoe was lost.

For want of a shoe the horse was lost.

Richard thought he remembered someone—his father?—holding his hand and swinging their arms in unison while recounting the ditty. Did Richard also remember nestling against the prince's chest, listening to the way his father's voice vibrated against his ear as he recited those lines, soft as a lullaby?

For want of a horse the rider was lost...

Am I misremembering?

Richard's thoughts had such a tendency to hop around, like those of a mad hare.

His father the Black Prince. Richard's most vivid memories were of an ashen face twisted with pain, of an invalid, and his tiny self thinking, *You are the greatest knight in Christendom? Why can you not even rise from your pillows to attend to yourself?*

Still, there had been times, at least in the early years, when Richard was certain he recalled his father tossing him in the air and catching him in his mighty arms. Was that so?

Or had that been his grandfather?

For want of a rider the message was lost...

What Richard remembered was that England's king had been a doddering fool in thrall to his whores. *I will never be like him.* Many times, Richard had had that and similar thoughts. *This is what happens to warriors. They grow old and sick and trapped in past glories of no current consequence.*

Richard preferred to remember his father and grandfather as broken-down carts, good for nothing but being tossed on a rubble heap. And yet, other images had begun to intrude, nudging aside his decades-old narrative.

Edward the Black Prince being buckled and laced into his armor by his squire. For a battle, tourney, what? When the prince had placed a helm topped by his lion crest upon his head, he'd appeared inhumanly tall. And so frightening that Richard had run to someone, who? His mother? His grandfather?

For want of a message the battle was lost...

Richard had been but three years old when his older brother, heir to England's throne, had died. What memories could he conjure from that time? His parents' grief, *naturallement,* for the first-born Edward of Angouleme had been a golden child. But was there not something else? An encounter at Windsor Castle with King Edward before his visage had slackened into senility? His grandfather bending down to him, handing him something—a sweet perhaps, a toy, what? Aye, Edward Windsor had been ancient, but he'd had the kindest eyes, and he'd been so gentle with Richard, as if assigning to him a sorrow Richard was really too young to feel. With his flowing grey hair and beard, King Edward had looked just like God. But not the God who punished naughty boys; rather the one who cuddled them in His arms.

For want of a battle a kingdom was lost...

Did Grandpère teach me that rhyme?

Mayhap when they'd been seated on the lip of a fountain with their hands trailing in the water and tiny fish darting through their fingers? That seemed familiar. And why wouldn't the rhyme be popular? The old king had created it as a reminder that he, his archers, his knights, all of England must attend to the smallest details of combat in order to remain victorious.

All for the want of a horseshoe nail.

War, war, war. War had shaped his grandfather's reign as the lack of it had shaped Richard's own. Well, he'd not had to unsheath his sword to have the commons follow him on that long-ago summer's day which ended their insurrection. Edward of Windsor and Edward of Woodstock embodied old-fashioned, worn-out legacies better buried beside them in their tomb chests. Richard was sick unto death of being measured against legends, which were never about truth, and ever about fantasy.

Yet...

Now Richard worried whether he should cross swords with Henry, an actual warrior.

But, how can I? Where is my army? Where are my archers? Even my ancestors could not have fought without troops.

Anxiety trailed Richard the way his exhausted men trailed him across Wales.

Still, Richard had sent two of his most trusted men to demand that Henry surrender to him in exchange for the return of all forfeited lands. Richard imagined his humbled cousin on bended knee, pleading for his life. "Mercy, Your High Royal Presence."

I will enact such sweet revenge, he thought, as he kept watch. *And I'll not rest until every last traitor suffers the full weight of my justice.*

CHAPTER 20

NORTH WALES

*M*id-August. Lammastide was past and 1399's harvest in full swing. While Matthew Hart, Henry Percy and their men rode toward Conway Castle, Matthew recalled a line from Ecclesiastes: *"A time to plant and a time to pluck up that which is planted."*

Matthew imagined plucking King Richard from England's soil like the diseased tare he was. For there was another verse that perfectly described the knights' mission: *"A time to love, and a time to hate; a time of war, and a time of peace."*

Now was a time of hate, for certes, and unless God willed otherwise, for civil war.

During their expedition from Henry Bolingbroke's headquarters at Chester Castle, they witnessed the disintegration of Richard's-army-that-never-was. Stragglers, deserters, some laden with booty stolen from the king's own wagons; others who were survivors of the Welsh's fierce loyalty to England's sovereign. Many recounted being ambushed and robbed by bandits hiding in the countryside's narrow, winding ravines; of being stripped of all save their doublets and forced to travel barefoot with only a staff for protection.

Bolingbroke's men-at-arms were dressed in full armor and remained alert throughout the forty-five-mile journey. When passing peasants in their fields, the knights pretended not to notice those who ceased their scything to glare. One even dared sing "Sweet Richard," a popular song lauding the king. He was soon joined by others.

A deliberate act of provocation.

Henry Percy the Elder, who was of an age with Matthew, glanced at him. Matthew shook his head in warning. It might prove temporarily satisfying to run down the malcontents and destroy their harvest, as other rebels were doing throughout Wales, but they must not be distracted from their current task. Upon reaching Conway Castle, Percy had been charged to lure King Richard from its safety with the promise of a rendezvous with Bolingbroke. Matthew and the main army would be hidden in a nearby mountain pass through which Richard must ride, and once trapped within, the king would immediately be arrested.

A simple plan to snare a simple man, Matthew told himself. He caught his first glimpse of Conway Castle, high and forbidding above the hilly countryside. It was yet too far away to ascertain whether Richard's standard flew from its towers.

Serill, who rode beside his father, said, "Wales reminds me of Cumbria. Fierce. Savage."

"Aye," agreed Matthew. He may not be a friend of the Welsh people, but their mountains, crags and tumbling streams spoke to an answering wildness in his own heart.

"At home they'll also be gathering the harvest."

"Aye."

"Cumbria isn't so very far away. Do you ever ponder slipping away, to visit Mother?"

In the midst of sedition? Matthew hoped his expression didn't reflect his shock. It would be just like Serill to concoct some blockheaded scheme to visit his own family. "Your mother can well care for our lands without my help."

"But do you not miss her?" Serill prodded.

Matthew sighed inwardly. A nonsensical conversation to be having with their quarry in sight. "If we do not capture Richard, I'll not be missing anything other than my head."

Far to their left, the River Conwy sparkled in the afternoon light. From a nearby enclosure, peasants, naked save for their braies, beat loose stalks of hay with great wooden flails in order to separate grain from chaff. Some paused to watch them pass, expressions guarded.

Resuming their largely one-sided conversation, Serill said, "I worry about Janey. She has passed her sixth month."

"Aye." Matthew scanned the countryside, seeking the most appropriate place for him and the army to camp while Percy continued on.

"I miss the twins and Billy. I know not how you lasted years away."

Matthew bit back the response that a proper soldier did not allow himself to be distracted by domestic affairs. "War is our profession. And all that goes with it. We may not always enjoy it, but we endure it." Relenting of his harshness, he added more lightly, "Never fear. We'll have that kerchief waving man-child trussed up like a capon and you home ere the tithe barns are full."

Silence.

"I have so many regrets…about… " Serill gestured vaguely with his gauntleted hand.

Nay, not much of a soldier at all.

Matthew's gaze lifted to Lancelot of Glastonbury, who rode in front of them. Lancelot's long hair caught the rays form the waning sun, turning it the color of drying blood.

All those deaths, all those wars of a long season… And I would wish that on my son?

"If the greatest regret of your life is infidelity, you are blessed indeed." Then, Matthew added, "And, aye, I do miss your mother."

Richard of Bordeaux was captured in a narrow pass on the way to Chester Castle. After fake negotiations with the wily Henry Percy the Elder, where both lied about their intentions, Richard and Percy entered the narrow mountain pass where Matthew Hart and his soldiers awaited. A stunned king did not immediately grasp the meaning of those knights swarming from their hiding places, all wearing Henry Bolingbroke's blue and silver badge.

"I am betrayed!" he cried. "There are pennons and banners in the valley!"

Matthew Hart's trap had been successfully sprung.

Richard of Bordeaux had drawn his last breath as a free man.

Flint Castle was the first-built of Edward Longshank's Iron Ring. Since it was located halfway between Conway and Chester, Henry Bolingbroke's men decided to house Richard there while awaiting the young duke's arrival.

At daybreak of August 16, 1399, after receiving the news of Richard's capture, Bolingbroke rode out to claim their prize.

Every afternoon King Richard haunted the ramparts, straining for a first glimpse of his enemy. Plumes of smoke mixed with the grey of a sultry afternoon, a graphic reminder that rebels had laid waste to much of the area. With banners streaming and armor gleaming, Henry Bolingbroke's army finally crossed the open fields in orderly columns, joyously blowing horns and trumpets all the while. Riding in front was the young duke himself, bareheaded but dressed as always in armor. Bolingbroke sat effortlessly astride a high-stepping white charger, which upon command, reared before kicking its hind legs in salute to those cheering from Flint's crenels.

Overcome with despair, King Richard abruptly bent forward, as if recovering from a blow. 'Twas all over then? Was he to suffer the same fate as his great-grandfather?

Richard began to pray in a high, strained voice. "Good Lord God! I commend myself into Your holy keeping and cry Your mercy, that You may pardon all my sins since it is Your pleasure that I should be delivered into the hands of my enemies. And if they cause me to die, I will take death patiently as You took it for us all."

Serill and Lancelot, who'd been assigned to guard Richard upon the ramparts, stepped forward.

"Your Majesty," said Lancelot politely, though he dared to place his hands upon the king, an action unthinkable before the invasion.

Serill flanked his other side. "My lord father said we will await Lord Bolingbroke in the great hall."

Richard looked around wildly, as if he meant to bolt, but where? Lancelot's grip on his elbow tightened, while Serill shook his head in warning.

With an audible sigh, Richard of Bordeaux allowed himself to be guided down Flint's vice, to the great hall. Where he would await his dreaded encounter with the cousin who would be king.

∼

Rather than make a swaggering entrance, Henry Bolingbroke waited outside Flint Castle for Richard to be brought to him. From this day forward Bolingbroke's every movement would be recorded. He dared not risk a misstep that might stir unwarranted sympathy. Henry would—he must—treat Richard with more dignity than the king had ever afforded him.

When word was sent that Richard needed to eat, Henry agreed, allowing the king and his loyalists to be seated at a dais as if they were honored guests. Fearing poison, the king declined to eat or drink anything save bread and wine, which he demanded be delivered by Matthew Hart's own hand.

While tearing Richard's food, Matthew thought, *You are not my prince's blood. You are a brass coin masquerading as silver.*

"Eat well," mocked some of the rebel knights positioned nearby. "For soon your heads will be off."

Matthew was pleased that neither Serill nor Lancelot had engaged in the taunting. When the prey had been downed, it was too easy for those who could only circle the wolves who had brought it down to jump in. Cowardly. Unworthy of a true knight.

This was not a celebration, but a tragedy. Particularly remembering Richard's father, remembering his vow to the dying prince that he would be loyal to his son.

Throughout the meal, Matthew engaged in an internal argument with Edward the Black Prince.

I would never betray you... You ever acted with courage and dignity... England can no longer be ruled by a permanent child.

Matthew remembered John of Gaunt discussing St Augustine's *City of God* —Sweet Christ, Matthew could never sit still long enough to complete such a tome—in which heaven consisted of lots of tall buildings and angels and naked people who God had returned to their natural state. He imagined, somewhere high in the clouds, a bare-arsed Prince Edward and his equally bare-arsed wife fulminating over their progeny's fate. Matthew focused on those images rather than the reality of the pathetic creature seated next to him.

Finally, after the passage of hours, Henry Bolingbroke ordered his herald to enter the dining hall and have the king's supporters removed. Then, helmless but still dressed in full armor, the young duke entered Flint's great hall.

Here it was: the two men, their circumstances totally reversed, facing each other. Matthew heard the king's sharp intake of breath, witnessed the sudden tremor of his hands.

Carefully, Matthew rose and moved away, back toward Serill, Lancelot and other of Bolingbroke's retainers. All stood at alert, hands on the pommels of their swords, watching the interplay.

Henry bowed low before the king. Then he stepped closer and bowed once again.

Richard removed his hat as a sign of respect. Having spent his entire life being scrutinized, he had regained his equanimity and, with composed expression, faced England's Usurper.

"Cousin Lancaster, you are right welcome."

"I am come before my time." Bolingbroke addressed Richard in English, boldly holding his gaze in a manner that would have once earned the king's sharp rebuke.

Richard fixed him with a baleful stare.

"I will show you the reasons your people complain that you have ruled them harshly. However, if it please God, I will help you to rule them better." Henry went on to insult his royal cousin in the bluntest of terms. Richard's subjects no longer considered him their rightful king, said Henry, because they were convinced he was no son of Edward the Black Prince.

Beside Matthew, Serill gasped. Some things were simply not said aloud. And Serill had suffered from his own matters of legitimacy.

"How could you be the prince's kin when you lack so completely his fine spirit and that of our great King Edward before him?"

The once girlish blush of Richard's cheeks flushed to a mottled red. He reached for a goblet of wine which he grasped so tightly that had it been clay it would have broken in his fingers.

The usually tactful Henry bluntly continued. "It is well known that your mother was desperate to present her husband the prince with a second heir. And that in her household there were several handsome young churchmen. And the prince was away on campaign."

Matthew noticed the bobbing of the king's Adam's apple, as if swallowing back an angry retort. All the times Richard had humiliated his cousin, all the cruel words and deeds heaped upon the Lancasters, father and son, were now being returned tenfold.

Throughout his reign, Richard had mocked courtiers to their faces; had carelessly ordered men, both common and noble, to their deaths—sometimes on a whim. Now he could but glare at Henry whose words were beyond insulting, beyond endurable.

"Fair cousin," Richard finally managed, "since it pleases you, it pleases us as well."

With that King Richard, surrounded by an armed guard, was removed to Chester Castle. From Chester, Henry Bolingbroke sent out missives summoning Parliament to be held forty days hence, the day after Michaelmas.

CHAPTER 21

AUGUST-SEPTEMBER, 1399, LONDON

On the first night following Richard's capture, a handful of loyalists tried unsuccessfully to free him. A few nights later, the king escaped from a slitted window and down the fifty-foot wall of a tower at Lichfield Castle. Only to find himself entrapped in a totally enclosed garden. After that, Henry placed his royal cousin under twenty-four-hour armed guard.

Once in London, where Londoners greeted Henry Bolingbroke with rapturous cries of "Long live the good Duke of Lancaster!' "God bless Henry of Lancaster!", Henry dismounted in front of St Paul's Cathedral. Once inside, he approached the tombs of his parents, knelt on the side where his father the duke was buried, bent his head and wept.

Richard of Bordeaux was housed in Lanthorn Tower, his official apartments within the Tower of London. There he was informed by two lawyers, flanked by the most influential royalists, that he must resign. Immediately. Before the opening of Parliament, in order to nullify certain relevant statutes.

All of this was tricky business. None of those assembled, including

Matthew Hart, dared speak what they'd secretly known must happen the moment Henry Bolingbroke had stepped ashore at Ravenspur.

One king must be cast down.

A second raised up.

Legally.

Somehow the lawyers had to find a way around the inconvenient truth that only a very weak case could be made for Henry Bolingbroke being Richard of Bordeaux's legal heir. Such would never do. John of Gaunt's eldest son had not led a rebellion only to have someone else don England's crown.

Royal lawyers had scoured voluminous legal reports until finding a century old loophole restoring a law declaring that only males could inherit England's throne. Thus, various female ancestors who had given birth to various males in the Plantagenet bloodline were rendered illegitimate. Ergo, Henry Bolingbroke was first in line to become king.

Matthew observed everything, while saying little. He knew this particular legality would hold weight only so long as Henry Bolingbroke remained popular.

Afterward...

God help us all when fortune's wheel turns against us.

Yet another in an endless line of humiliations. After being officially asked to resign, Richard demanded to see a copy of the terms.

That was done. Once the horde of treasonous Black Robes and the king's former barons retreated, he stared sightlessly at the parchment.

"I have been appointed by God," he reminded the room, now empty save for a servant who was exchanging old rushlights for new. "This is beyond sinful. Surely, Our Lord and Savior will smite them all. He must." Richard paused, staring down at the document. "Mustn't He?"

When the rebel delegation returned the following morning, the king was in a combative mood.

"Why should I, a rightfully anointed king, resign my throne?" he asked. "And to whom? To my designated heir, Edmund Langley? Or to my conqueror, Henry Bolingbroke?"

The lawyers had to tread carefully. If they agreed that the king must resign to his "conqueror," they were creating a dangerous precedent. Some future someone might also lay claim to England's throne by conquest.

Instead they told Richard, "You are illegitimate," and counted off their arguments. Richard's parents had been cousins, after all, and had secretly wed before receiving clerical permission. And, of course, there was the matter of his mother's promiscuity, which all and sundry were forever throwing in his face when Richard remembered Joan of Kent as a loving parent and doting wife. Thank God she'd not lived long enough to endure the besmirching of her reputation and the fall of her son!

The lords presented Richard with further arguments, which only increased the king's agitation.

"My God," he finally cried. "A wonderful land is this, and a fickle; which hath exiled, slain, destroyed or ruined so many kings, rulers and great men! And is ever tainted with strife and variance and envy!"

The lawyers looked on, impassive before the king's wrath. Finally, slumping back in his chair, he waved a weary hand.

"Bring me Lord Bolingbroke. I am willing, upon certain conditions which I will explain to my cousin, to relinquish my throne."

But that evening when Henry arrived, he was in no mood to discuss conditions.

"You must abdicate," Henry said bluntly. "Without argument."

A myriad of expressions flitted across Richard's face before finally settling into what chroniclers would later term a "cheerful" countenance. Something would…must happen to circumvent this most blasphemous of events. His great-grandfather, the second Edward, had suffered similar. But no one had arrived to save the Sodomite King.

Sitting at a table in front of the hooded fireplace, Richard read aloud the entire abdication document. "I confess, acknowledge and recognize and from my own certain knowledge truly admit that I have been and am entirely inadequate and unequal to the task of ruling and governing the kingdom …"

Richard's voice did not waver. They were simply words. He had read and agreed to many such blatherings during his reign with no intention of upholding most of them. Once Richard reached the end of the document, he carefully affixed his signature. Immediately, clerks recorded the names of the witnesses, though once again the king demurred.

"I cannot renounce my anointment or the other special dignities of a spiritual nature which were bestowed upon me at my coronation."

One of the justices reminded Richard that by signing the document he'd done precisely that. "You also agreed to the language saying you are 'not worthy or adequate of government.' Did you not understand?"

"'Tis not so, Richard cried. "I was simply unloved by my people."

Matthew Hart had to look away, beyond all the figures hovering menacingly around Richard to tapestries that shimmered in the uncertain light of the hearth fire. Those who had all too willingly carried out Richard's most outrageous orders now treated him with singular viciousness.

Is life ever about expediency? Is anyone capable of acting out of other than self-interest?

The long and short of it was that Richard of Bordeaux was a broken and pathetic figure, and it was no longer possible for Matthew to maintain a hardened heart. Edward the Black Prince had dearly loved his son, and Matthew, all of them, had sworn to Edward on his death bed that they would accept Richard of Bordeaux as England's king...

Richard asked that he be allowed sufficient income to maintain himself honorably. After that was agreed to, Henry Bolingbroke and the rest of the delegation made ready to leave.

Thus, a king is unmade, Matthew thought, his heart feeling like a boulder in his chest. He was among the last to depart, hanging back, trying to think of something comforting to say. But, of course, he had not words.

The deed had been done. And they would all live with its consequences.

On the afternoon of September 30, 1399, Henry Bolingbroke appeared before a packed assembly in the Palace of Westminster. Quickly, lawfully Richard of Bordeaux was deposed "by the authority of the clergy and people."

After much ritual and ceremony, Henry was designated as deliverer of England. Rising from his seat to face members of Parliament, he made the sign of the cross on his forehead and breast.

In English, Henry said, "I, Henry of Lancaster, claim this realm of England, and the Crown with all its members and appurtenances..."

When asked to deliver their judgement on his right to be king, parliament's lords collectively shouted, "Yes! Yes! Yes!" Individually, they then declared they would have Henry Bolingbroke as their sovereign and "no other."

Henry approached the vacant throne, draped in cloth of gold, bent his knee and prayed. After performing more rituals, two bishops, flanking Henry on either side, led him to the throne.

Henry sat.

Crowds inside and outside Westminster roared their approval.

A sermon was preached. The subject matter could be condensed to one line: England must be ruled by a man rather than a boy.

With that, the chronicler Froissart's forty-year-old prophecy foretelling the house of Lancaster's triumph was fulfilled.

CHAPTER 22

SEPTEMBER 1399, SWAFFHAM MANOR

"*J* was so fearful for you," Margery said. Arm in arm, she and Matthew strolled along the waterway beyond Swaffham Manor. Sunset painted the sky, turning the sluggish water the color of rubies.

"I had more to fear from blisters on my backside than Richard and his phantom army. Long hours in the saddle reminded me that I now officially number among the ancients."

She laughed. "As we both do. But you will always be my faerie knight."

As they continued their walk, Matthew slipped an arm around Margery's waist. He and Serill had left London following Henry's enthronement ceremony, though they would soon have to return for the coronation, followed by the new king's first parliament. Here they were guaranteed a measure of privacy from the activity inside Swaffham Manor, where Lady Jane was ensconced in her lying-in chamber. All about was low-level chaos. Since men were denied entrance, Serill spent his time surrounded by his children or distracting himself with hawking or hunting or pacing beyond his wife's door.

"I have a bad feeling about this," he'd confessed to Matthew after Janey had retreated to her chamber. "That God will punish me for my sins by..." There was no need for Serill to complete his thought. Whenever a woman went

135

into childbirth, death waited in the shadows to snatch either mother or babe and sometimes both.

"You've confessed your transgressions a hundred times over, I'll wager," Matthew had reminded him. "Do not snare God's attention with melancholic thoughts."

"How quickly our lives pass," Margery mused. "It seems only yesterday when I was in my own chamber and our son was impatiently awaiting his entrance into the world."

Matthew had been away on campaign, as he'd always been away. Now he paused to enfold Margery in his arms and whisper against her ear, "I wish I did not have to return to London. I would much prefer the mundanities of the Lordship Court and the company of my sweet Meg."

Margery closed her eyes, breathing in her husband's dear, familiar scent. "All will be well as soon as King Henry is officially on the throne—"

"So long as we pretend that the last unseating of a king did not end in that king's murder."

Edward Caernarvon. A part of England's history that could not be pretended out of existence. But Richard of Bordeaux's few followers would have the good sense not to try to restore the deposed king to power. Such would seal His former Majesty's fate, just as it had his great-grandfather's.

"We'll not think of that now," said Margery. "We will concentrate on Christmas in Cumbria. And after that, I'll not let you go, ever again."

Matthew nodded, as if his wife had some say over the warp and woof of his life—of their lives. He tipped Margery's chin so that he could brush his lips over hers.

"Who would have thought all those years ago when I first glimpsed you as a frightened lass hiding in East Anglia's fens that we would end up here?"

"'Tis passing strange," Margery agreed, before returning his kiss. "But I am so grateful to Our Lord and the saints that we did."

Janey's labor pains had begun on Michaelmas, just a twinge which she'd chosen to ignore, but three days' later she was in her final stages. And exhausted. A matter of concern for Margery, two midwives and various household servants.

Sitting beside Janey's bed, Elizabeth Ravenne held her former ward's hand

and prayed to all the saints associated with pregnancy and childbirth. She also promised a pilgrimage of thanksgiving to Walsingham, which was about as far as her old bones could carry her.

When Janey's contractions worsened, Margery draped cool, scented cloths across her daughter-in-law's brow. One midwife rubbed rose oil on Janey's belly and flanks while a second gave her regular sips of a sugar and vinegar concoction. In order to expedite Janey's labor, servants kept a fire roaring, closed all the windows and covered them with heavy tapestries in order to block out unhealthy natural light.

Janey's son entered the world with a lusty bellow that caused the gathered women to laugh with a mixture of amusement and relief. Labor had been long but ultimately easy; no complications, thanks to Saint Margaret of Antioch, patron saint of pregnant women and childbirth. After the newborn was washed in wine, swaddled and laid in her arms, Janey murmured to his fuzzy head, "We will name you Edward after all the Edwards your grandfather has loved."

"Lord Hart will be pleased," Margery said, voice thickened with emotion.

"And someday you will be as great a warrior," Janey said to her son, whose initial bellow had softened to a mewing, more kitten than bull.

"But for now, we will call you Neddy," said Elizabeth Ravenne, alarmed that martial allusions had invaded even this most feminine of spaces.

"Neddy," Janey agreed. Her eyes drooped and she snuggled deeper into the pillows. "Does Serill know?" she managed between yawns. She'd not seen her husband, save for a short stopover following the second Richard's capture, in three months. And, as was traditional, not since her lying in.

"He is ecstatic," Margery said. "He is readying everything for Neddy's baptism tomorrow. And a wonderful celebration it will be, with half of East Anglia already invited."

Janey was glad that she would not participate, that it would be weeks before she would be allowed in church or any other holy place. *Sleep*, she thought. *I could sleep a fortnight.*

Janey had no idea of time's passing. She could not be sure when her babe was taken from her and placed in his cradle, or when the bustle of the chamber faded to stillness. Was she yet dreaming when all of Swaffham Manor seemed still and silent as a painting? When the chamber's stifling heat had mercifully cooled to a manageable temperature? When her husband stood beside her bed, gazing down at her?

Serill, in her chamber where men were expressly forbidden? Where was the wet nurse, the other servants to shoo him away?

Janey struggled to open her eyes, but it was an impossible task. Did she ask her husband what he was doing here? She thought not. She was too weary to scold anyone, certainly not Serill. If she could stay awake long enough to assure him that she did not care about custom, she would ask if he was pleased by Edward, if he approved of Neddy as a nickname, if he would please remain close so that he might guard her and their son while she slept.

Janey was almost certain Serill bent over and whispered in her ear, "God has granted us another miracle, has He not?" As he also whispered, "Might you now write a happy ending for us, *mon coeur*?"

Did she nod? Did she say, "I will try?" Or did she simply echo the word "happy" before sinking back into her dreams?

CHAPTER 23

OCTOBER 1399, LONDON

"*I* can scarce believe I am in London," Viviane Halle gushed to her brother, whose chaperon was pulled up to protect his face from a persistent mizzle. She and Gerald were part of the raucous swarm watching the newly crowned Henry's procession wend its way from London's Tower to Westminster Palace.

Despite the weather, Henry Bolingbroke rode bareheaded on a white charger. He was arrayed in the most exquisite short doublet of cloth of gold with a blue garter on his left leg. Around his neck rested the badge of the King of France—a reminder that, he, all of the Plantagenet kings—possessed legitimate claim to the French throne.

How regal you are, Viviane thought, straining on tiptoe for a better view. Despite her certainty that her lover, Reginald Luci, would have looked far prettier bedecked in identical clothing, Henry Bolingbroke appeared every inch a proper warrior king. Unlike Richard of Bordeaux (though Viviane had never actually seen their deposed monarch). But she could imagine him—more girl than man, caring only about his fripperies and his favorites, issuing outlandish commands in an impossibly screechy voice, similar to a raven's caw. No wonder Londoners, many of whom had actually glimpsed Richard on his way to Westminster or Smithfield or Windsor, clamored for his execution.

Around this fourth King Henry strode several lords, resplendent in red satin or velvet, carrying ceremonial swords. Viviane spotted Matthew Hart and the Henry Percys, though she couldn't identify the rest. So many, all looking so very…important.

Her gaze swept the crowd, seeking her beloved, though Reginald Luci would be far to the rear of the lords and ladies, positioned among the younger knights but before the clerks and household servants. And all of them a riot of color, which helped beat back the dismal grey of the day.

"Where has Sir Reginald been? I've not seen him in nearly a sennight. Has he lost his way to the Cock and Bull?"

Gerald ignored his sister's sarcasm. This morning he had arrived soon after the opening of city gates, sweeping Viviane and her maid, Kate, into the celebrants while their father, John Halle, had remained closeted in an adjoining room with several mysterious men.

Gerald had been evasive in his answers, and not only about Reginald. Viviane assured herself she was imagining the apprehension that sometimes furrowed her brother's brow and deepened the lines around his eyes. Nor had it yet occurred to her to ask why Gerald was beside her rather than with his fellow knights wending their way to Westminster Palace.

Cheers as row after row of England's finest passed. London's streets were decked out with gorgeous hangings, seasonal flowers and beautiful maids tossing petals into the throng. All the shouting and huzzahs had been intensified by the ale flowing freely from various conduits.

Clop, clop, clop. Thousands of hooves sinking into rain-softened ground. The closeness of unwashed bodies, of wet wool, of garbage missed by the street sweepers, of manure and horses, caused Viviane to swallow down a sudden sourness in her stomach.

Once again, she stood on tiptoe, straining unsuccessfully for a glimpse of Reginald, who had promised, *promised* they would meet for something more than the usual tupping.

Viviane felt an elbow to her ribs and instinctively jabbed back.

"Mind your purse," Gerald hissed against her ear. "Pick-purses."

She finally identified Elizabeth Ravenne, who, along with Lady Margery, had so kindly accompanied her from Cumbria Castle. Viviane suspected that Lady Ravenne had ulterior motives, i.e., betrothal to her sixth son. (Viviane had already spotted Lancelot of Glastonbury, bareheaded among so many hatted or hooded barons, his long hair caught behind his neck in a careless knot.) Viviane had learned more than she cared to about Sir Lancelot. Beginning with his birth—surprisingly easy since Lady Ravenne had begun labor while on pilgrimage to Glastonbury Abbey, Saints be praised—followed by Lancelot's departure as a page to the Duke of Lancaster, (He had cried when denied the company of his favorite hound) and ending with his martial prowess.

"And did I mention Lance's trip to the Holy Land?" Lady Ravenne had asked. Aye, repeatedly. Elizabeth Ravenne would then recite from memory long passages of Lancelot's letters, detailing various and sundry adventures in places with such peculiar names Viviane suspected they were figments of Lancelot of Glastonbury's imagination.

Viviane *was* grateful to both Lady Ravenne and Lady Hart for their hospitality and the Earl of Cumbria's protection, so she forced herself to politely listen. 'Twas true that Elizabeth Ravenne's son would be a coup for a nobody like herself, but even at the age of twenty-one, Viviane Halle understood that Lancelot of Glastonbury was like thunder being called down from the hills. Viviane liked to be in control, and how could one harness such a force of nature? Nay, her gentle, beautiful, passionate, adorable, manageable Reginald Luci offered a far more compatible pairing...

Besides...

If Reginald keeps ignoring me, I will do... something. Every day that passes... Well, Viviane could not think about that.

Viviane and Gerald followed the pageant until they were in the vicinity of one of the Eleanor crosses. "We'll be able to see better from there," Gerald said, taking her elbow and pushing against the crowd back to the towering monument. Viviane's cheeks felt clammy with the drizzle; she blinked against the drops which increasingly clung to her lashes. Once at Eleanor's Cross, they ascended several steps, trailed by Viviane's maid. Gerald was right. She had a clear view of London's mayor and aldermen in their fur-trimmed scarlet liveries.

Gerald abruptly pulled her to the very top step, away from other spectators. Viviane frowned. "What are you doing?"

"I must tell you something troublesome. Once I do, do not cry or make a scene." Gerald's dark eyes, so similar in color to her own, were suffused with concern.

"Don't be foolish. I seldom cry, and my scenes only revolve around the kitchen." Though Gerald might not know that. He'd left for Alnwick Castle when she'd been barely five.

"Still, it could be dangerous to draw attention to ourselves."

"What is happening? What is wrong?" Viviane quickly checked for her purse, which remained securely in its proper place. Once again, her gaze drifted to the parade, this time to dozens of young men newly knighted and dressed in identical long green robes.

An explosion of cheers. Several knights doffed hats trimmed with miniver and cords and tassels of white silk.

"Look at me!" Gerald shook Viviane's arm. "This is important, sister. Our lives may depend on you taking seriously what I am about to say."

Gerald now had her full attention. "What do you mean?"

His fingertips dug into her arm. "Have you not wondered at Father's absence today?"

Actually, no. John Halle's presence would be more unusual than the other way around. "What are you trying to say?"

"Father has been arrested."

Viviane was sure she must have misheard, that the noise of the crowd had distorted Gerald's words. "But, but... why would anyone arrest Father?"

"For his part in the murder of Thomas, Duke of Gloucester."

Viviane did not even immediately recognize the name. Aye, the king's royal uncle. Who had died in Calais. Her father had been in service at Calais...

"Murder? What do you mean? And what do such doings have to do with someone as insignificant as John Halle?" *Terrible things are happening, and you've been too simple-minded to even notice.* "You have my full attention, brother. Tell me."

"Father was there when the deed was done. Guarding the door while others..." Gerald shrugged as if that would convey all the necessary details.

"I cannot interpret shoulder twitches! Explain!"

"Father was thrown into Newgate. Soon after we left. He's been expecting it for days. I think that's why he decided to summon you to London. So that he might see us one last time if..." Once again Gerald did not finish.

Viviane reached out to steady herself on the base of the Eleanor Cross. The cheering faded until it was merely background noise for the roaring in her head.

"I canna tell you more," her brother said. Gerald Halle was short and stout and already nearly bald, the kind of man one would never notice. As was their father. Yet John Halle had somehow incurred powerful enemies?

"We must soldier on as if nothing has happened," Gerald continued. "And take comfort that, should the worst come to pass, Father and others still to be arrested will receive a fair trial."

Viviane felt as if someone had reached into her chest and clamped a fist round her heart. "Aye. Our new king is surely more merciful than our old one, is he not?"

Something flickered across Gerald's face, an expression she could not read. "That we must count on. Today is a reminder that things can change in an instant." He snapped two gloved fingers together, as if in emphasis, and the corners of his mouth turned up in the facsimile of a smile.

"Sweet Jesu, protect us," Viviane murmured. And because she did not know what else to do, she chose to remove from her mind her father's arrest, with all its attendant repercussions. "King Henry has a kind face. He will set matters to right, I am certain."

Gerald's lips parted, as if he might speak further but instead simply grunted.

Then both, by unspoken agreement, returned their attention to the parade.

Monday, October 13, 1399: An important date for three reasons—first, it was the Translation of Edward the Confessor, England's talisman. Secondly, it was exactly one year since Henry Bolingbroke had departed England for France and his forced exile. Third, it was the day the fourth Henry would be crowned King of England.

Matthew Hart had been given the honor of carrying what was being called the Lancastrian sword, which Henry had worn when he'd landed at Ravenspur. Henry's oldest son, Henry of Monmouth, now a strapping thirteen-year-old, bore Curtana—the coronation sword which Bolingbroke himself had borne at Richard of Bordeaux's banquet twenty-two years earlier.

There it is, Matthew thought, feeling uncomfortably pretentious in his resplendent scarlet robes. *Past and present. No wonder we grow confused with age when so many events mirror each the other.*

Though Matthew had great hopes for this king he'd grown to love, he'd had enough of the accompanying pomp and pageantry. His thoughts repeatedly returned to Margery, who remained at Swaffham Manor tending to baby Neddy, his mother and the rest of the Hart brood. Matthew had grown increasingly impatient to retreat to Cumbria before the settling of winter, to re-embrace a routine that included only mundanities... blessed mundanities.

But a coronation must be about tradition in all its extravagance, mustn't it? In this case to reinforce this Henry's legitimacy. One thing Matthew had learned during his sixty-two years: forces would inevitably align themselves against the kingdom's new monarch. That was simply the way of the barons.

A blur of coronation images...

Cloth of gold upon England's throne, upon the paving stones leading to Westminster's high altar... rebated spurs, sword, bracelets and pallium, all of which had also been worn by the previous king. Though the red velvet slippers, of course, were new.

For at his coronation, young Richard of Bordeaux had lost a shoe...

A new crown, designed, ironically, by Richard himself; the signet ring that had been stripped from his finger in the Tower of London... "Do you want Henry Bolingbroke as your king?"... "Yes, Yes," the congregation responds, arms outstretched to signify their faith and allegiance... The new king stripped to the waist... anointed with Thomas Becket's holy oil, given to the saint by the Blessed Virgin...

Accompanied by the inevitable prophecy: the first king to be crowned using Becket's oil would be Mother Church's champion; would recover all forfeited French lands; would drive the infidel from the Holy Land.

Thus, the chroniclers—or at least the monk, Thomas Walsingham—had interpreted this anointing to mean that God had chosen Henry Bolingbroke to accomplish greater deeds than any previous king.

Throughout the ceremonies, Matthew's thoughts kept drifting back to the coronation of the deposed Richard. *Still in mourning over the loss of England's Arthur, incapable of imagining how he, any of them, could survive without their great king Edward... Richard, a delicate ten-year-old upon whose fragile shoulders rested the hopes of a fractured England.*

We all wished him well, Matthew thought. *We all willingly pledged our fealty.*

Afterward, Simon Burley, the young king's faithful mentor—now dead via an executioner's axe—had swept the white-faced, exhausted boy into his arms. In the process Richard had lost a slipper—a slipper dating back more than three centuries to Edward the Confessor.

So obvious, wasn't it?

How could any of us have believed England could prosper following such a troubling omen... the king who'd lost a shoe?

What about Henry's coronation? Matthew wondered, after the rituals finally, finally ended, and yet another mass had begun. *What is the meaning of this interminable drizzle, which descended yesterday and continues draping itself like a smothering cloak upon London? Upon us all?*

When future chroniclers pondered the fourth Henry's coronation ceremonies, would they point to the weather, nod their heads sagely, and declare, "There it was, for all of us to see."

The baneful omen that ushered in the reign of Henry the fourth.

CHAPTER 24

WESTMINSTER HALL

*V*iviane Halle had never seen the like! Pendragon's entire keep would have fit inside Westminster Hall. Tonight was Henry Bolingbroke's coronation feast, in the building that his disgraced predecessor had spent six years remodeling. Was this God's irony? His judgment? That the first business following the completion of this architectural masterpiece had been its creator's deposition?

What little Viviane learned about affairs of state was largely due to Elizabeth Ravenne, who she'd not really spoken to since the scandal involving her father. Viviane wished she had someone with whom to share her fears. Perhaps she and her brother were the only ones who even knew of John Halle's imprisonment. Or, mayhap this was simply the way of the royal court. One day Newgate or the Tower, the next receiving a coveted assignment or position.

How am I to know? Looking around the room, Viviane vowed she'd not let personal problems spoil this most momentous of nights, a night she would describe in detail to Cook—and perhaps someday to her own children. Westminster Hall, so breathtakingly magnificent with its hammerbeam roof and its statues of England's kings, from Edward Confessor to the current

Richard, nestled in their tabernacles, stone eyes gazing down upon England's newest monarch.

Henry Bolingbroke, Earl of Northhampton and Hereford, Duke of Hereford and Lancaster. And now England's fourth King Henry.

England's sovereign, wearing an elaborate crown topped by a cross that had been designed by the deposed Richard—another irony—sat at the opposite end of the long hall. With prelates flanking either side of his throne, Henry was seated upon a dais so that all could more easily view him. Viviane recognized the king's first-born son, Prince Harry, and the elder Henry Percy, each holding ceremonial swords, positioned behind him. As she recognized Matthew Hart, one of a pair clasping King Henry's scepter and his staff.

So much ceremony. Hundreds of guests, all seated by precedent, which meant nonentities like herself were relegated near the exits.

Viviane tried to gauge Henry Bolingbroke's expression, but he was so very far away, and she caught only glimpses of him among the great lords attending him. She spotted Harry Hotspur and several others presenting meat, meat, and more meat—heaping platters of roasts, larded capons, pheasants, herons, baby swans and sturgeon.

What are you thinking, King Henry? Do you even remember that you had my father thrown in Newgate? If Gerald and I went to you begging for mercy, would you listen? Would you remember how you felt when Richard refused yours and your father's pleas?

How exactly did royal justice work? Viviane had no idea. All the whispered intrigues and half-caught political rumors were completely beyond her ken.

Deciding to take a cue from her brother, seated near her Reginald and acting as if he hadn't a care, Viviane determinedly banished all thought beyond those of the wonders around her. While they were only halfway through the first of three courses, Viviane allowed herself to be overwhelmed—delightfully so—by the bountiful parade.

Great pies were now being brought in, some even to the lower tables.

Oh, if their crusts are cut and birds fly out! What a glorious sight that would be!

Once, when her mother had still been alive and her father had graced them with an infrequent visit, Viviane had helped Cook create such a pie with the bird box beneath. After the crust had been sliced open and the captive birds released, Lady Claire had clapped her hands in delight. Even John Halle had saluted them with a raised goblet.

Tonight's offerings remained disappointingly free of a similar surprise.

Picking up a spoon, Viviane began her personal sampling with the *Viaund Ryal*—a soup of almond milk, wine, and such exquisitely blended spices she struggled to confine herself to a few measured sips. Otherwise, she would be too stuffed to properly describe the rest of the night's culinary wonders to Cook upon her return to Pendragon.

Once finished, Viviane sighed her contentment, though not too deeply since she'd increasingly had to loosen the loops of her girdle. And her kirtle felt uncomfortably tight.

Viviane experienced that familiar coil of dread whenever she thought... No! Earlier she'd managed a few minutes alone with her Reginald, and he'd promised a proper visit on the morrow.

My dilemma will resolve itself. Once my beloved truly understands. Viviane's mind ran on, as it so often did, to the hurried wedding ceremony, her resultant life of bliss. *Reginald will not fail me.*

Determinedly, Viviane concentrated on more pleasant matters——the bright colors of various cotehardies and houppelandes, the chaperons and crespines; the jeweled crowns, rings, necklaces and headpieces twinkling in the rushlights and overhead candle wheels. Westminster Hall itself. She counted the stone trim on the walls displaying the deposed king's harts and the wooden angels attached to the ceiling beams. (Twenty-four or twenty-six. She would have to complete a third recount to be certain.) All this their deposed king had planned and executed. All now a wood and stone mockery of the man in the Tower.

Not for the first time that evening, Viviane noticed Elizabeth Ravenne and her sixth son watching her from a vantage point far closer to the royal dais. Were they discussing her father's imprisonment? Saying cruel things? Would they snub her? Perhaps, though she could find no condemnation in their faces. In fact, Lancelot of Glastonbury seemed quite interested in something about her. Was her dress too shabby? Should she have braided her hair? Lightened her complexion with wheaten flour? What fashion *faux pas* had she unwittingly committed?

Viviane retrieved a generous slice from a stuffed suckling pig, closing her eyes while identifying each individual flavor. Then she sampled the larded capon.

I will tell Cook his recipe is every bit as savory. And some of the roasts were just a wee bit bland. But the pheasants, complete with tails, were as much a delight to the palate as the eye. And the *Crustade Lumbarde*! The custard melted around the dried fruit in delectable combination.

Immersed in all things delicious, Viviane happily contemplated the arrival of the Venison with Frumenty, which signaled the beginning of the second course. Soon, however, she felt a resurgence of her stomach discomfort.

Eat slowly and carefully, and you will be fine.

A wave of loneliness washed over Viviane—she, an ill-favored peahen among peacocks who would not care whether she lived or died had they even known her name—and she blinked away tears.

For unless a miracle occurred in the form of her beloved—And it must!—Viviane Halle knew with a sudden blinding certainty she was NOT going to be fine.

~

"She'll never do, you know," Elizabeth Ravenne said, following her son's gaze, which repeatedly strayed to Viviane Halle.

Lancelot's mouth curved in the half-smile so many female admirers labeled "mysterious," "enthralling," or "irresistible." "You have been singing the praises of the *demoiselle* Halle since my return from campaign. And now you warn me away?"

Lady Elizabeth, who had confined herself to aspic and brawn cooked in sweet butter until the two teeth she'd recently had wired were properly set, patted his arm.

"Do not be difficult, Lance. I've became quite fond of Viviane. An unorthodox young woman with her culinary fascinations, but her tarts and breads are heavenly." Lady Ravenne looked longingly at yet another forbidden dish being placed atop the fine linen cloth gracing their table. "But we must heed the signs. Obviously, God has decided Viviane Halle is wrong for you."

Lancelot refilled her goblet. "You are too concerned with gossip, Lady Mother. By the morrow John Halle might be released from Newgate and returned to royal favor."

Lady Ravenne shook her head mournfully. "I had such high hopes this time." Lancelot grunted, leaving her to interpret his meaning. "The Countess of Cumbria and I both agreed that the poor dear is healthy enough to have provided you with a baker's dozen of sons."

That she is, Lancelot silently agreed, and, in a way so unusual for him, he found himself imagining what act precipitated the making of such a baker's dozen. Ah, his thoughts. Just as Avalon in all its glory would sometimes rise from the mist, Lancelot's senses had recently emerged from his self-imposed fog of piety. The results had proven most vexing.

Because Viviane Halle was unmarried, her dark hair was held back by a simple fillet. Lancelot found himself fascinated by a shining lock of hair that had curved over her bountiful breasts—for, while the demoiselle's gown was modestly cut, the bodice could do little to hide its contents—and the manner in which Viviane carelessly brushed it back. Only to have the wayward strand creep forward again to nestle, sometimes in the center of her cleavage.

Lancelot absently tore off a slice of *Leche lumbarde*. Though he generally found the mix of dates, wine, and spices too rich, he might have been eating sawdust for all he'd actually tasted of any of the coronation dishes.

So much had changed since they'd met Henry Bolingbroke at Ravenspur. Camelot had been saved! Lancelot and his Janey's sacrifice had broken the curse. Logically, Lancelot knew that the success of the subsequent rebellion, of the former king's almost embarrassingly easy defeat, had naught to do with the oath of one unimportant knight. Regardless, Lancelot chose to believe God had smiled upon his private vows of celibacy and perennial bachelorhood. Lancelot had behaved honorably. He had refrained from laying with his beloved. The proof of their sacrifice was right here in Westminster Hall, seated upon England's throne. The House of Lancaster, Lancelot's private version of Camelot, had prevailed. All would be well in England.

"I am too old to deal with yet another family scandal," Elizabeth Ravenne was saying. "A husband who sired enough bastards to field a football mob, two sons who kidnapped their brides, and Matthew—well, I dearly love his wife but one canna ignore the fact that my brother wed someone so lowborn 'tis a wonder we weren't forever banished from court."

"Lady Mother—"

"I am not implying any of this is Mistress Halle's fault, Lance, but—"

"Punishing the child for the sins of the father," Lancelot interrupted, his gaze returning to the object of their attention. "It hardly seems fair, does it?" Viviane Halle's complexion was far from lily-pale, which he did not mind, for she seemed to glow with health. And he'd never seen anyone eat like that—as if each bite was an occasion of rapture. "Besides, John Halle was a minor player in Gloucester's death, was he not?'

Viviane Halle reached out to caress a spread of pheasant's tail arranged upon a nearby platter. Lancelot wondered how such gentle fingertips would feel upon his...face. He tore his attention away, back to his mother, who was studying him with lifted eyebrows.

"Now I recall the details," Lancelot continued. "John Halle was Thomas Mowbray's man." The duke who had faced Henry Bolingbroke in that ill-fated joust that never was and who had been forever banished from England.

"Unfortunately, Lord Mowbray died a fortnight past. Surely you heard, Lance, unless you were off riding Slayer or whatever you seem to do rather than mingle where you can meet interesting *people.*"

Lancelot cut a slice from a gilded capon and placed it on his mother's plate.

Elizabeth considered whether she dared risk tackling the meat. Perhaps just a sliver. "Any secrets Mowbray possessed that could exonerate John Halle or anyone else have been buried with him."

Viviane Halle's eyes were so bright she reminded Lancelot of Fearless (though he had the good sense to understand that no woman would find such a comparison flattering). Did the *demoiselle* have any idea of the political danger she might soon be facing?

"Meaning that John Halle might be a convenient scapegoat for the actions of all the plotters? Particularly when so many *important* magnates appear to be involved?" Without waiting for her answer, Lancelot finished, "If John Halle is punished, his lands will be forfeit."

Elizabeth reluctantly decided she dared not risk dislodging her dentatore's recent work. What a trial old age could be! "Which proves my point. Viviane Halle is out of the question. You must look elsewhere for a bride."

A bride! With the lifting of his oath, Lancelot had found himself mesmerized by sights he'd once studiously ignored. Slender arms and necks and curving waists and breasts so artfully concealed by necklines and stitchery that one could not help but stare. Even the glimpse of an ankle or wrist set Lancelot's imagination afire. For thirty-four years he'd been more celibate than many priests. But now that his self-imposed chastity could be cast aside, all Lancelot could think of was laying with a woman.

Not any woman. *A wife.* He would wed and then bed. To refrain from sin only to commit it? Nay, that he would not do.

Viviane Halle's enraptured gaze was on an enormous *soltelte* on the dais depicting two jousting knights. Holy Mother, if she ever looked at a man the way she looked at food…

Lancelot wished he could talk to someone about this and similar intimate matters. But who? While he would ever love his Janey, that part of his past must remain behind him. No one else had any idea that he and many of the church's favorite saints held one very large virtue in common. But, just as Lancelot had once clung to his virginity, he was now equally determined to relinquish it.

Viviane Halle had placed a finger in the filling of a small tart on her trencher, then brought it to her lips. Lancelot's gaze was riveted to that finger. 'Twas the way it was during battle when he could view only a narrow bar through his helm. Right now, he could not see past Viviane Halle's finger being raised to what he'd decided must be an eminently kissable mouth. (Though in truth Lancelot was too far away to actually determine its shape. A lifetime of reading or listening to Romances was wreaking havoc on his imagination.)

As if privy to Lancelot's thoughts, his mother said, "Do not further mar our family's reputation by marrying someone whose father has been executed for treason. Which very well might happen."

Too late Elizabeth noted the stubborn set to her son's jaw. What was happening? Lancelot could be so contrary, blowing hot and cold with his moods and confusing quirks. Why the sudden change? What about Jane le Babbe? Hadn't he pledged his undying fealty to her? Was this another doomed affair of the heart? Another dangerous quest, not for the grail, but for a lady's love?

"Should Viviane Halle be alone in the world she will need someone," said Lancelot. Then there was the other matter, which provided secret confirmation of her worthiness. Viviane was the name of the Lady of the Lake, she who had presented Arthur with Excalibur. And this particular Viviane lived at Pendragon Castle. What other signs were necessary?

Elizabeth Ravenne once again studied her son. She was familiar with that obdurate expression, which he'd borne from earliest childhood. Once Lancelot made up his mind, God himself could not dissuade him. And to combine such stubbornness with the plight of a demoiselle in distress…

The truth of it hit Elizabeth with the force of a thunderclap. Her son was a romantic! Lancelot of Glastonbury yet believed in the truth of the tales she'd once read or whispered into her sons' ears when they clamored for a bedtime tale. Truths inevitably shattered by life's harsh realities.

But, apparently, not in Lancelot's mind.

CHAPTER 25

*V*iviane Halle lay sprawled atop the bed in her room at the Cock and Bull. Once again, her maid had gone out to gather more information about the ongoing horror. Viviane often had difficulty discerning actual fact, not so much from the many contradictory rumors, but from her fears and nightmares. Where was her brother? Gerald had faithfully reported the proceedings against John Halle and the rest of the conspirators—until King Henry's pronouncement of death against their father. Then Gerald had come to her railing and crying and cursing Henry Bolingbroke, vowing nonsense about vengeance. After which he'd simply vanished, the way Viviane's dreams had vanished. Or more precisely, been smashed into oblivion.

How many days had passed since the coronation feast? Since a manacled and shackled John Halle had stood before King Henry, confessing his part in the conspiracy against Thomas, Duke of Gloucester? So hard to tell for the room's shutters remained drawn, making it impossible to distinguish between day and night, and she alternated between sleeping as if she were drugged and staring up into the gloom, too numbed to think.

Though details had such a way of sliding past Viviane, she could grasp some things. John Halle had appeared in front of the king and Parliament, along with all those who'd been accused of plotting and executing Thomas Woodstock's death. Halle had been an unwilling participant in the murder, simply standing guard at the door while others held the duke down and smothered him beneath a mattress. The great lords from some of England's most influential houses had been responsible, though they'd sent their valets to actually do the deed. But since King Henry needed those lords, John Halle was the one who had been singled out to pay for their sins.

John Halle must die a traitor's death. This very morning, if Viviane's shaky grasp of time was correct. Perhaps right now her father was at Tyburn, his sentence being carried out in the most barbaric fashion. Hanged—cut down before he could actually expire from strangulation—and disemboweled with his intestines being burned in front of him. The act took great skill; how much pain to inflict, when to ease off so that the condemned would not die before full measure of vengeance was enacted.

Is that where Gerald is? Witnessing Father's execution?

Viviane curled in a ball on her narrow bed. She must have dozed for when she awakened, her maid was standing at a nearby table, pouring a jack of ale.

Approaching her mistress, Kate extended the leather cup. When Viviane shook her head, she said, "You must drink. And later I'll order a bath. You're a sight, Mistress Halle, I grant you that."

"What have you heard?" Viviane croaked. "Has my father been executed yet? Where is Gerald? Has he also been arrested?"

Kate shook her head, but Viviane couldn't interpret her maid's meaning. She didn't know? Or the truth was too horrendous to utter? Viviane heard a distant cheering. London's citizens applauding her father's disembowelment?

The very thought caused Viviane to reach for the chamber pot. Afterward, she slumped back on her straw mattress. Kate placed a wet cloth on her forehead.

Viviane groaned. "If only I could concoct an elixir to help me forget."

But it was not simply her father's fate that so devastated her. When had it been, how many days since Reginald Luci had betrayed her?

The event itself...the most potent elixir could never erase *that* from her memory.

Another fit of weeping. Viviane had wept until there were no more tears, and she was a hollowed-out husk.

Did Kate tell her to sleep and afterward, she would press the innkeeper for a tub and enough hot water for a decent bath?

What was the purpose? Let Viviane lie here in her own filth. Let her father die the most excruciating death imaginable. Let Viviane expire of a broken heart. That would be the best of all outcomes. For then she would not have to face the fact that she was with child.

A child whose father refuses to acknowledge it.

Having only the most basic knowledge of such things, Viviane had taken nearly three months to come to terms with the meaning behind the lack of courses, the nausea, the sleepiness, the odd food cravings—or their converse, antipathy toward once favored dishes. After living in a state of confusion and denial, she'd arrived in London knowing the truth. To scientifically confirm her condition, she'd captured her urine in a vial and dropped a needle in it. Praying that it would not turn rust red or black; knowing all the while it would. Making the matter of the utmost urgency since she must be nearly four months along. Pregnant brides were common enough, and she'd had years of promises from Reginald. The sooner she told him the sooner they could marry.

Miserable creature! How could you have been so foolish?

Reginald Luci had last visited… when? Not the day after the coronation as he'd promised. Viviane had stayed in her room nervously awaiting him until St. Martin's-le-Grand's giant bell had tolled Vespers. Perhaps the day after? It was all so mixed up.

Finally, she'd faced him, here in this room while her father's fate was being determined at Westminster Hall.

As my fate was dependent on the reaction of the man who fathered my child. My Bastard! How did my life veer so off course? What did our family do to so displease God?

Reginald Luci's reaction had certainly not been what Viviane had anticipated. (Or had she always known it on some level? Is that why she'd procrastinated?)

"But, *ma poulet,* I canna marry you," said Reginald, so elegant in his patterned gold-colored costume complete with fashionable high collar and matching chaperon. "You have been disgraced. Do you not know? Your family lands are already forfeit."

Viviane recoiled. No, she had not known. Gerald had not told her. And, certainly, her maid would not have found out such details in the tavern below or in the streets beyond.

Amazingly, Reginald had nuzzled against her and grabbed for her breasts, as if her dilemma was simply a prelude to lovemaking. "Let us lie together, my sweet, so that I might comfort you."

Viviane pushed against his chest. "I am pregnant with your child and you are saying you'll not marry me? What about all those times when you assured me—"

"I told you," Reginald said, with a trace of annoyance. "All that has changed. I did not ask your father to commit treason, to disgrace the Halle name into perpetuity."

Viviane gaped at him. He reached out again to grasp her shoulders. She twisted away.

Reginald sighed, as if dealing with an exasperating child. "I will talk to my relatives, mayhap someone close to the Earl of Northumberland himself, see what might be done."

Even as he said it, Viviane knew he lied.

"Perhaps a position might be found for you with a lady somewhere..." Reginald's voice trailed off. He took a step back from her, closer to the door. "Mayhap you can retreat to a nunnery. Or there are wards here in London— perhaps even in York—where unmarried women can stay until their babes are born."

Viviane's knees, her entire body, felt weak. Her head roared, not from the headaches that came from lack of food and her wayward stomach, but from words so cruel her mind could scarce comprehend them.

"This is your babe," she managed, anger overriding her vulnerability. "If you'll not marry me then you will support me. The church makes that very clear, that such is the father's duty."

Reginald recoiled. His face paled. "Viviane, *ma perdrix*—"

"I am not some stupid bird so quit insulting me with your ridiculous nicknames!" She balled her fists. "You must support me *now* and after the child is born. I canna stay in London without funds. I canna stay anywhere. How will I return to Pendragon?" But if the Halle lands had been forfeited, she would have no home to return to.

I will be poor as a cottar. My babe and me. Our babe.

Reginald raised his chin and reared his head back, as though to better study her. His eyes narrowed and suddenly Reginald Luci did not look so appealing.

Like a fox.

After which her adored Reginald said what so many others in similar positions have said back into the mists of time. "How do I know 'tis even mine?"

Viviane imagined burying Cook's cleaver, the one she'd used so many times to chop off chickens' heads after their necks had been wrung, into her former lover's skull. Imagined how deftly Cook took his longest, sharpest knife to slit a boar from gullet to groin; how many times she'd watched the animal's intestines tumble out. Would doing something similar to Reginald Luci give her satisfaction?

As the executioner would soon do to her father?

Viviane had gagged at the images. Hand to mouth, she'd scurried to the chamber pot where she'd retched and coughed up the nothing that remained in her stomach.

By the time she'd straightened, rinsed her mouth from a nearby pitcher of water, wiped her lips on her sleeve and turned, Reginald Luci was gone.

~

A nest of vipers, was Lancelot of Glastonbury's first thought after Viviane Halle answered his knock. While he'd never actually seen more than a handful of snakes, and most of those had been in the hills surrounding Jerusalem, how else could one describe the lady's hair?

"Mistress Halle?" He was not even certain he'd found the proper address. This creature with eyes so puffy they were slits in a face the color of whey, bore no resemblance to the woman who had assumed the status of enchantress in his memory, a veritable Lady of the Lake.

Viviane blinked. He noticed she was dressed in a chemise that would reveal far too much if he allowed his eyes to so explore. But, Jesu, the smell emanating from her! Where was that rosy-cheeked maid with the sleek dark hair and charming expressions, the delicate but sensual way she approached the business of eating?

Viviane wiped her nose on a sleeve and finally motioned for him to enter. "Sir Lancelot of Glastonbury?"

She didn't bother to curtsy or make any effort to rearrange herself, which was good for such an attempt would have been futile. He stepped into the room. A wooden tub was positioned in the middle of the floor, which meant she was preparing to rectify her unfortunate condition.

Thank the saints!

Without asking permission, Lancelot crossed to the window to open the shutters. The animal horn covering the window frame at least allowed a modicum of light. Later he'd have it removed to air out the place.

"Where is your maid?" Lancelot asked. "Who have you to tend your needs?"

Viviane reached up to touch the mess atop her head with one hand and with the other pulled at her bodice. As if that might make a difference. "Gone to fetch water. Bath." Then, "Why are you here?"

"I am sorry for your father," Lancelot said. Feeling a perverse obligation to a woman he'd never spoken to beyond a "Good morrow," he had attended John Halle's execution. Stayed to watch Viviane's father being beheaded and cut into quarters with the instruction that each piece be publicly displayed while the head be sent to Calais.

Such was the fate of traitors.

Viviane's face had contorted in a most peculiar way. "My father is dead then?" Why had not Gerald returned to tell her, to comfort her? Or had he too been arrested?

Before Lancelot could respond, Viviane Halle began wailing. So, she had not known. What a mess, that Lancelot should be the one to carry such bad news.

Viviane sobbed into her hands. For an alarming moment, Lancelot feared she would reach out and cry against him. That she didn't was equally disconcerting.

He felt so awkward, so completely out of his depth. Thinking to offer some sort of condolence, he cleared his throat, but thankfully Viviane's maid arrived, trailed by several servants carrying cauldrons of steaming water.

After a flurry of curtseying, Kate continued with the task of readying her mistress's bath. As she began arranging the curtains that would allow Viviane privacy, Lancelot said, "I will wait outside until your mistress is done."

He could stay. Custom allowed it. Lancelot hesitated, considering. If he left the room he might simply keep on walking, away from a situation that was becoming increasingly complicated. England was filled with women—many of them beautiful and certainly with more to offer than the dispossessed daughter of a traitor. He could have his pick. And all with a dowry that would further enrich him.

But if Lancelot forsook Viviane Halle, she would have no one to champion her.

And that Lancelot could not abide.

~

At least Viviane Halle was recognizable. Kate had plaited her hair and only drying strands curled round a face that bore a passing resemblance to the woman who had so recently captivated Lancelot. Unaccountably, Kate had dressed her mistress in another chemise. Lancelot had to force himself to keep his eyes away from the curves lurking beneath its alarmingly thin fabric.

Kate had retreated to the far end of the small room. Lancelot turned away from Viviane to pour them both a drink from a flagon of ale.

Viviane accepted Lancelot's outstretched offering. Both eased themselves down upon narrow benches, facing each other. She considered pressing him for details of her father's death. Was that the reason he was here? Might God have spared John Halle by having him expire of a heart attack before the executioner had carried out his gruesome deed? Had her father somehow singled out Lancelot to send her a message? She imagined John Halle calling to the knight from the gallows platform, choking out words of comfort to be shared with his daughter. Of course, that didn't make any sense. In all her twenty-one years, John Halle had never paid Viviane any attention. Why would he start now? And by singling out a complete stranger?

Why then was Lancelot of Glastonbury here?

"You are kind, Sir Lancelot," Viviane said tentatively, bringing the jack to her lips. She studied him. Her father and brother were small men and Reginald Luci, though taller, was so slender as to border on delicate. This man was far too large to inhabit such a small space. She imagined that when he stood his head might actually brush the ceiling beams.

Silence stretched between them. Still trying to decipher his reason for appearing, Viviane reverted to politeness. "How fares your mother?" Had Lady Ravenne decided to rescue her by sending her son to offer Viviane a position in Edmundsbury Castle's kitchen? How propitious that would be.

"Well. Readying to return home. Before the worst of winter sets in."

They stared at each other.

Lancelot was trying to formulate the best way, not to propose exactly, for a proposal wasn't necessary. To explain their union? How would she react? Even though Viviane Halle was currently the most cursed of women, she might still decide to reject him. A woman could be more contrary than an unbroken horse. Best to approach with caution.

When Viviane replaced her bowl on the nearby table, she shifted her position, causing her chemise to stretch taut across her stomach. Lancelot saw the swell beneath the flimsy fabric and immediately knew... Viviane Halle was pregnant! Coming from a fecund family—six married brothers with wives who were more often with child than not—Lancelot could hardly misread the signs.

Lancelot felt a chill of dismay.

How can this be? You are unmarried. I must be mistaken. A second glance assured him otherwise. *What did I miss? Are you already betrothed? Wed?*

Detailed inquiries, however, had failed to unearth any hidden suitors. The closest was a friendship with Reginald Luci, but Luci had "friendships" with many women.

Lancelot stood abruptly and spun around the room, as if seeking an exit. If Viviane Halle were with child, then she was no bride for him. All his plans immediately blown away, like dust upon the wind. He felt equal mixtures of disappointment and relief. Now he could turn his attention to someone else and forget this foolishness.

Yet, if Viviane Halle was pregnant and without a dowry, no man would marry her.

Lancelot stood above her. "Who is the father of your babe?" he blurted.

Viviane's mouth gaped. She blinked up at him, her hands unconsciously pressing against her stomach. Lancelot braced himself for a resumption of her earlier hysterics.

Which did not happen. In fact, Viviane Halle's reaction left him completely undone.

Lifting her chin, she met his eyes. Even as tears slid down her face, Viviane whispered, "Reginald Luci."

"And he'll not...?" Lancelot let the implication hang between them.

She shook her head; her lower lip trembled. She inhaled deeply, maintaining her self-control.

Pregnant, landless and friendless. Had there ever been a *demoiselle* more in need of protection? Though, if Lancelot did wed Viviane Halle, his fantasies of bedding her—here he risked another glance at her bosom—were ignominiously, laughably shattered. Intercourse was forbidden during pregnancy, but even after that, did he want the discards of another man?

Still, Viviane Halle's innocence was obvious. And, having heard of Reginald Luci's reputation, Lancelot could sketch the arc of their sordid tale. But more to the point, *his* point, was Lancelot destined to die a virgin?

Sweet bloody Christ, after all this time and I pick a woman bearing another man's child? 'Tis not how I imagined my wedding. Or my bride.

Yet, the girl looked so irresistibly pathetic. Should he reach out and pull Viviane to her feet, press her against him, seek to comfort her? Would she think him too forward? How laughable that was. A woman who had already surrendered her virginity—more than her virginity, her *honor*—to a fop like Reginald Luci?

"You have very poor taste," he wanted to say. But Viviane Halle's choice simply highlighted her naivete.

My duty, my destiny, he thought. He would embrace it, just as he'd once embraced his celibacy. He must rescue this pitiful creature.

"Viviane." He breathed her name. "Viviane of the Lake." Though it was ridiculous to compare this particular Viviane to the enchantress who had captured history's most powerful wizard. To update the ancient tale, Merlin would have to be nearly blind to be so captivated by this contemporary Lady of the Lake that he would allow her to weave a spell keeping him forever bound.

Viviane brushed away the tears on her cheeks. "Sir Lancelot?"

He held out his hands to her. She hesitated before clasping them. Slowly, her puzzled gaze never leaving his, she rose from the bench to stand mere inches away from him.

Lancelot raised his voice to address Kate, who'd been watching from the corner of the room.

"Gather your mistress's things. We are retiring to Hart's Place."

"My lord?" Viviane asked. She knew Elizabeth Ravenne was staying at the family townhouse. But what did this mean?

Lancelot looked down at her. Foolish though he might be, he would embrace this particular future. Reaching out, he lifted her chin with two fingers. How small she appeared in front of him, how desperately in need of a champion.

"You and I, Viviane Halle, are going to be wed," he said. Only lack of experience kept Lancelot from brushing his lips against hers, as if to seal his words. "As soon as possible."

~

King Henry granted Lancelot a boon, the return of the Halle lands, as well as permission to marry Viviane Halle. He and his family owed much to the lords of Cumbria and their relatives. This knight, who had accompanied him on campaign and on pilgrimage—a time Henry was already looking back upon with as much fondness as a childhood reminiscence—asked for very little.

Before parting, Henry threw a companionable arm around Lancelot's shoulders and said, "I wish you many years of happiness. As well as a house full of healthy sons."

And laughed when Lancelot of Glastonbury blushed.

CHAPTER 26

ADVENT SEASON 1399, ENGLAND

*C*hristmas plays and mumming; caroling and wassailing. Yule logs burning in hearthfires from Alnwick Castle to St Michael's Mount. Outside trees decked with apples; decorations of mistletoe, ivy, and holly, its red berries a reminder of Christ's blood after being pierced by his crown of thorns. Advent images of Mary and Jesus, tucked inside a box and carried from door to door, where a ha'penny would reveal them and bring luck to the household. Three Christmas masses—the Angel's Mass, the Shepherd's Mass and, in the fullness of Christmas morn, the King's Mass. Boxing Day, when the rich gave the poor clay pots containing coins. All accompanied by feasting, where even the most beggarly would sit down to a meal of humble pie.

At Windsor Castle, Henry Bolingbroke celebrated his first Christmas as England's ruler. Ever thoughtful, Henry had carefully mapped out his kingship in his mind. He would emulate his grandfather, their great Edward the Third, whose reign was looking even more glorious in contrast to his deposed grandson's.

"Merciful" will be my byword. I will maintain domestic peace and increase prosperity, even as I confront foreign enemies abroad. Henry's thoughts drifted to the Scots, as pesky and inevitable as bedbugs. Even now

164

they were raiding Marcher lands, but he would soon take care of that. *I will maintain the loyalty of my barons and respectfully work with Parliament. I'll not raise taxes save in time of war. I will create a new chivalric order, which will emulate Grandfather's Order of the Garter. And, just as he did, I will deliver all my speeches in English.*

In short, everything that Richard of Bordeaux had done, Henry would do its exact opposite. Their Edward Windsor had provided him the blueprint as to how to be a great king; Richard of Bordeaux how to be a failed one.

~

Simply because the Usurper hadn't thrown England's rightful monarch in a dungeon, did he really believe Richard's current quarters were other than a sin against God? In the weeks since he'd been unlawfully deposed, Richard had been bounced around from castle to castle. Now he was in the north, in Lancaster country, though comfortably ensconced in one of the royal castles. But he remained closely guarded and forbidden to go beyond the gatehouse.

Thus, Richard of Bordeaux spent the Advent season brooding over his current state and vowing revenge once his supporters rescued him and cast aside the Usurper.

There had already been one attempt, only days following Richard's arrest. Owen Glendower, a Welsh soldier with an impressive pedigree (for a Welshman), had been unsuccessful. However, Richard had no doubt that Glendower, an intelligent man who had received a prestigious education at London's Inns of Court, would succeed. Which, this time, he must. For Glendower knew, as did Richard, that should a second attempt fail, his life would be worth less than the trinkets given out on Boxing Day.

~

Tucked away in Cumbria Castle with all the necessities to sustain them against the north's brutal weather, Matthew Hart enjoyed doing...nothing. Margery had the most peculiar feeling that their lives had come to an end, though not in a bad way. But with a good man on the throne, healthy grandchildren, a son and a spouse who appeared to be genuinely happy, it was as if their history were frozen. Margery could think of nothing to worry about—no wars; no illnesses or deaths (though she knew that could change in an instant), and a husband she could reach out and touch any time she so pleased. When she tried to explain this feeling of contentment, even of security, Matthew murmured agreement. He chose not to share that the Scots had invaded Wark Castle and taken hostages and with the spring, Henry would be raising an army. Nor would he mention the problem imprisoned two days' ride from them. Just as two bulls could not share a pen, two kings could not share a kingdom. Still, Matthew appreciated how rare was happiness, as well as the peace that accompanied it.

This I will cherish, along with Meg, he told himself, *for as long as God grants me.*

~

At Swaffham Manor, Jane le Babbe, holding Neddy and with her bairns gathered around her, often listened to her husband read from her fables. As she'd once imagined.

'Tis all too perfect, she worried, imagining all the ways their happiness might be shattered.

~

Aside from the fact that Elizabeth Ravenne was certain another cold spell would cause every one of her bones to snap like a bundle of dry twigs, she was quite pleased with the state of things. Edmundsbury Castle was chock full of her sons and her grandchildren—and while there was far too much drinking, gambling and quarreling among siblings, spouses and offspring, she was so very relieved that the year 1400 was days away with the world showing no signs of ending. The one concern—and it was a minor one—was that she'd not heard from Lancelot and his bride. Following a scandalously rushed wedding, they'd embarked for Pendragon Castle.

Without a word since.

For certes, they were newlyweds. And Viviane Halle could not help but be ecstatic over having snared Lancelot of Glastonbury as a husband.

A better catch than you deserve, she warned, silently addressing her new daughter-in-law, *so you'd best treat him well.*

CHAPTER 27

*J*esu, Lancelot of Glastonbury silently swore, pushing himself back from the table. Another month of his wife's cooking and his stomach would protrude as far as hers. And she was past her sixth month.

At first, he'd tried to very gently hint to the lady Viviane that she need not concoct feasts for a household that consisted of less than two dozen people.

Priding himself on his subtlety, Lancelot had made the mistake of commenting, "Are we not supposed to fast during Advent season? With baked fish and..." he fumbled, for he'd never paid much attention to food. "Bread, I suppose."

Lancelot found it hard to believe that baked, grilled, simmered, and fried fish lathered in dozens of different sauces, could qualify as fasting. And since when could one credibly count geese as fish? Or beaver tail? Or all those tarts that contained real cheese and milk?

"Are you saying you are displeased with my cooking?" How could a woman appear simultaneously enraged and devastated? Viviane folded her arms beneath her breasts and atop her stomach. (How healthy she looked! Lancelot rather liked the extra weight, the healthy flush of her cheeks.) "I am simply trying to keep you and your men strong and healthy. For all the work you must do."

True enough. When they'd first arrived, Lancelot had been appalled to find Pendragon guarded by a few lax retainers, an ancient steward and servants who wandered as aimlessly as the chickens in the bailey. Only Cook and his staff maintained a degree of professionalism. Lancelot and his men had spent these past weeks mucking out and mending the stables, cowsheds, chicken coops and pig pens; splitting and stacking wood to supplement the supplies of peat; patching holes in Pendragon's roof and crumbling mortar in the walls, and constructing shutters to better protect windows covered only by thin animal skins. Lancelot's own properties might be crude, but they were well maintained. (*Best of all*, he increasingly thought, *my demesnes do not contain my wife*.)

"I know you were disappointed to find Pendragon in such a sorry state," Viviane was saying. "But in my condition, I canna wield a mallet or climb a ladder—

"You would not be expected—"

"I am simply contributing how I know best." The last was said in a tone that alerted Lancelot to the possibility that, should he not carefully choose his words, Viviane Halle would become hysterical. Or at least tearful, which was much the same thing.

"We…I appreciate all your efforts. I regret that I have been remiss with my compliments." Lancelot was relieved when her expression relaxed, and her arms returned to their sides.

"Well, see that you mind your tongue," Viviane said, reverting to her usual bossy self.

So, it went. Ever an abstemious eater, Lancelot quickly learned 'twas impossible for him to leave a meal without sampling everything. More than sample. Should he stop at one or two bites, Viviane would question him.

"Does the pudding…venison…pies…custard…cottage…Roquefort…brie…gorgonzola cheese… *mounchelet* not meet your liking?"

"Don't sumptuary laws forbid serving too many dishes?" he'd ventured after a particularly elaborate supper. Unless one was entertaining or a feast day was being celebrated, supper was customarily a light meal. At least that had been his dining experience in every household he'd inhabited. Until Viviane Halle informed him otherwise.

"Who is here to fine us?" She thrust out her lower lip. God's toenails, as if she was the age of one of his nieces.

Lancelot braced himself.

"Cows? Chickens? Goats? Will they tell us, "No!" Eat, husband. Cook and I have worked all the day just for you."

Lancelot had no idea how to respond. With Jane le Babbe, hopeless, helpless, forbidden love had tied his tongue. With Viviane, confusion and frustration largely rendered him mute.

What had Viviane Halle *not* forced on him this Christmas season? Stuffed goose, gingerbread, apple and plum puddings, sweetmeats and spiced cakes; marzipan sheep, donkeys, cows and camels representing the animals who had watched over the Christ child in Bethlehem's manger.

"Look how cunningly they are made," she said, holding up each cookie for his inspection. "So lifelike, are they not?"

Lancelot obediently nodded, more concerned with how many she would make him eat rather than their actual resemblance to biblical animals.

Then there were the mince pies, twelve days of them representing the twelve days of Christmas. Each was shaped like Jesus's crib and filled with cinnamon, cloves and nutmeg to symbolize the gifts presented by the Magi. So Lancelot later learned. When his wife had first placed several on his trencher, he'd mistaken them for tiny coffins.

Lancelot nearly blurted, "Who has died?" but he was quickly learning the less said the safer. Instead, he'd smiled into Viviane's eyes, which were shining in anticipation of his approval. Reminding him of Fearless when the Bear Dog had been a bright-eyed ball of fluff.

"Eat, husband," Viviane urged. "I've more mince pies for you to taste."

Lancelot could not quite suppress a groan. He imagined himself falling from his bench the way an over-sated leech fell from a wound. How much could one man endure? Either his stomach would burst or by the time King Henry summoned them for their spring campaign against the Scots, he'd be too fat to fit his armor. Poor Slayer.

If I do manage to heave myself into the saddle, I'll break his back.

With the approach of Christmas Day—which would technically last until the Feast of the Epiphany—Lancelot shuddered to think how many more succulent horrors awaited him.

"Cook and I have created a boar's head for Christmas dinner," Viviane informed him. "We have invited all the villagers."

(*What villagers?* Lancelot wondered. A handful of huts beyond Pendragon's curtain, at best.)

"I've made loaves for each of the tenants and bundled the most cunning faggots of firewood, and we will drink wassail and carol and play games." Viviane clapped her hands. "I canna remember when Pendragon has been so merry!"

Lancelot tried one last time to rein in his wife. "Should we not have a care to the larder? Lest all the staples be used 'ere spring?"

Viviane's eyes narrowed dangerously. Once again, she folded her arms. "Did we not just receive word that the Earl and Countess of Cumbria will be visiting us before Twelfth Night?"

"Aye, but—"

"Would you have them think us miserly?" Before Lancelot could reply, she ordered him. "Hunt. Fish. Hawk. Whatever you must do so that we do not insult the earl and countess with salted meat. Cook and I will take care of the rest."

While Lancelot prepared to slink away like a scolded hound, Viviane suddenly balled her hands into fists, opened her mouth and emitted an earsplitting wail. His first thought was that she looked like one of his Janey's twins throwing a tantrum—though not past the age of four.

"What is wrong? Are you in pain? Is something happening with your babe?"

Viviane's response was to wail all the louder. She looked so pathetic, standing in the door to the kitchen while behind her Cook and other servants dropped their utensils and foodstuffs to gawk.

Lancelot didn't know whether to flee or take Viviane in his arms in an attempt to comfort her.

He stepped forward. "Please, wife. Stop crying and tell me what is wrong."

Hurrying awkwardly to him, Viviane flung her arms around his neck. Her stomach was like a boulder against him. Tentatively, Lancelot curved himself around her bulk to settle his hands upon her waist. "What?"

Viviane murmured something indecipherable against his tunic.

Thinking she could more easily speak without a mouthful of wool, Lancelot slackened his embrace and tried to step back. Instead, Viviane clung to him like barnacles to a ship. Awkwardly, he patted her back, then began running his hands the length of her spine in soothing fashion. To his surprise, Lancelot discovered he rather liked the feel of his lady wife. Her curves were pleasantly distracting, and her hair, covered by only the flimsiest of coifs, smelled pleasantly of bread and roses.

"Tell me, Viviane of the Lake, what is so distressing," he murmured against her ear.

A final shudder. Viviane raised her tear-streaked face to his. "We have only been wed since the time of All Hallow's Eve."

"Aye?" His wife's nose had already turned red, and her eyes were starting to swell. Viviane Halle would never be a pretty crier.

"Look at me. Lady Hart will immediately know that I was with child when we wed. She and her husband will be so scandalized you will be forever disgraced."

Lancelot considered. While many women were similarly wed, the groom was generally the father. Hatred of Reginald Luci coiled inside him like a poisonous snake, though he forced himself to maintain eye contact, even to brush a stray strand of hair clinging to his wife's wet cheek.

"As far as anyone will ever know I am the rightful sire." Obviously, Viviane had no idea of his uncle and his wife's scandalous past, and Lancelot would not enlighten her. "The Earl and Countess of Cumbria will also believe it," he soothed. "And they'll not be judging you."

Viviane managed a nod. "'Twill be all right then?"

Lancelot kissed his wife on the forehead. "Aye, wife. Everything will be fine."

That evening Lady Viviane lay alone in her curtained bed, its moth-eaten curtains drawn against the night's chill. Since the castle only contained one sleeping room other than the great hall where most of the servants and retainers bedded down, Lancelot had erected a divider and slept on a trundle bed at the opposite end of the solar, while her maid, Kate, slept right outside the door. When first she realized her husband did not mean to join her, Viviane had been relieved, insulted and hurt in equal measure. 'Twas common enough for married couples to sleep separately, and she couldn't imagine having intimacies with him—well, she could if the Church had not forbidden them during pregnancy—but his lack of interest merely added to her certainty that Lancelot of Glastonbury hated her.

I am so diligently trying to be a good wife, she thought, feeling very sorry for herself. Daily, she and Cook would concoct another marvel to dazzle Lancelot's senses. As obedient as a dog, he ate everything put in front of him. But he seldom complimented her or acknowledged the exquisite nature of each dish. He might have been schooled in the chivalric arts, but he certainly wasn't applying them when it came to his wife.

I always praise YOU, Viviane thought, having one of her nightly one-sided conversations with the man curled not twenty feet away from her. But when he failed to respond with more than a nod or that enigmatic half-smile, her frustration would boil over and she found herself saying or doing *anything* to goad him.

Here, as usual, Viviane turned her back so that it faced the direction of her husband's trundle bed and began to cry. Quietly, of course, for Viviane prided herself on being in charge of her emotions when in public. By morning, all evidence of her unhappiness would be wiped away, and she would rise, determined to calmly, efficiently embrace another day.

After a while, Viviane wiped her eyes, shifted position yet again in an effort to get comfortable and contemplated her woeful existence.

If only you weren't so insufferably aloof.

Lancelot of Glastonbury was polite, aye, so polite she wanted to hit him alongside the head with a skillet in order to elicit some reaction other than strained courtesy. She tried, how she tried, to draw him into conversation, but she wasn't clever like Jane le Babbe, and she couldn't think of anything Lady Ravenne had shared from Lancelot's childhood that might engage him.

"Did you really pry open a tun of wine and toss in rats to watch them drown?" she imagined herself asking. "Insist on sleeping in the stables so that you might grow up to be a horse? Put knucklebones in a stew so that your father broke a tooth biting into one?"

Would he even respond, or simply fix her with that maddening smirk which could mean anything? Or nothing at all.

Still... this afternoon...

Viviane remembered Lancelot's powerful biceps bunching around her; how wonderful his hands felt caressing her back. She replayed his whispered endearment, "Viviane of the Lake," and decided he would not have given her a pet name if he despised her. Would he?

Outside, a gale force wind howled against castle stones. Reminding Viviane of the barguests that prowled the north.

Huge black hounds... bloody teeth and claws... harbingers of death...

Do not think about it. You'll harm the babe.

But Viviane couldn't help it. Alone in her draperied cocoon, her mind roamed the way the whole of her had once roamed the surrounding fells and dales. From barguests to *mnathan nighe*, spirits of women who had died in childbirth. Whose fate was to kneel beside lonely streams and pools where they would wash the blood from the linens and grave clothes of those who'd been marked for death.

Viviane imagined a *bean nighe* seeking a place to wash Viviane's grave clothes. The River Eden? Or would the creature slither inside the bailey to be closer to her prey? She sincerely hoped Pendragon's horse and washing troughs were either empty or frozen over.

"Move along," she whispered to the imaginary hag.

Viviane suddenly pictured Lancelot rising from his current perch to slip into bed beside her. He would wrap those incomparably strong arms around her and whisper, "I will protect you, my own Lady of the Lake."

It wasn't that Viviane cared about her husband as an individual, mind you. It was simply that Lancelot of Glastonbury had been on crusade and on campaign and had fearlessly faced the doughtiest of jousting opponents. Supernatural creatures would be no match for his courage.

Oh, and the feel of those enormous arms, the gentleness of his lips on her forehead...

...In fact, the only time Viviane had ever seen Lancelot unnerved was when she'd placed her most delectable dessert, a cream custard tart, in front of him. She most certainly had misread his horrified expression, for what could be alarming about a bit of egg and milk and cream and savory spices? Lancelot had assured her the tart was "very sweet," though now that she thought about it, that wasn't an actual compliment, was it?

Perhaps another dessert would better please you, she decided. *Using marzipan as icing. I will discuss it with Cook.*

Viviane tossed on her mattresses, trying unsuccessfully to accommodate her increasing stomach. Only three more months until her lying-in. *But you, husband, what do you care? Women die in childbirth, you know. In a handful of days my life might be snuffed out as casually as a candle's flame.*

Viviane swallowed a sob as she imagined herself, so still and pale and... beautiful...stretched out on this very bed. The bed upon which her own mother had expired.

Viviane would be more beautiful in death than she'd ever been in life.

While Lancelot wailed over her, lamenting the various cruelties he'd inflicted upon his long-suffering wife. (Who'd surrendered to death's clutches so bravely, and once again, so beautifully.) Well, to be fair, Lancelot of Glastonbury wasn't actually cruel. Indifferent was more the truth. Increasingly, Viviane wished Lancelot would look at her the way he...the way he'd looked at Jane le Babbe that day in Cumbria Castle's bailey before the Hart rebels had departed for Ravenspur.

There is was, the secret knowledge of where Lancelot of Glastonbury's affections truly lay. With each passing hour, the truth of it became more impossible to ignore. No wonder he'd merely kissed Viviane on the cheek following their wedding ceremony. No wonder he so seldom physically touched her, unless to help her maneuver a vice or to keep her from stumbling. As he did his mother, who was older than the stones. As he would anyone!

But today...he kissed you. He held you. But he loves Jane le Babbe. I know it. I KNOW it!

Viviane had not realized what she'd witnessed that fateful summer's day until many weeks later. She'd been too wrapped up in the strange faces and milling chaos, in the gravity of witnessing history, in her fears for the safety of her Reginald, wherever he might be.

Still, she'd seen it all. And never, until the day she died, would she be able to erase the memory...

Jane le Babbe crossing the yard, weaving among the press of mounting knights and nervous, sidestepping horses, to gaze up at Lancelot of Glastonbury. To stretch her impossibly slender arm out to him, seated as he was upon his huge black destrier. He'd been eager enough to lean over and grasp Lady Jane's hand, had he not? To linger over it as if he could not bear to release it? To press a kiss to her palm or sleeve or whatever it was? And to fix Lady Jane with an expression that, now that Viviane was more familiar with her husband, would be forever seared in her brain?

I love you, *Lancelot of Glastonbury's gaze had said to Jane le Babbe.* I will never love anyone else. Certainly not plain, plump, immoral Viviane Halle, who, if she does die in childbirth, will probably die unshriven. And if she doesn't, she will still go straight to hell. And I'll not care.

Viviane pushed the soles of her feet more firmly against the heated bricks wrapped in cloth her maid Kate had placed at the bottom of her bed. At least she was warm beneath blankets and furs and counterpane.

At least I am cozy in my misery.

What would Viviane do if Lancelot—who was surely freezing on his trundle bed mere inches above the solar floor—opened the curtains and crept in beside her, murmuring, "I am cold, dear wife."

How graciously she would murmur, "I will warm you, husband."

And then...

But none of that was going to happen. Not with two people in love with two *other* people...

Viviane's baby kicked again. Once, twice. Reginald Luci's baby. Tears leaked from the corners of her eyes. Despite Reginald's treachery, she still loved him. As she would never love Lancelot of Glastonbury.

Love you, hah! I do not even like you!

But then today... *"Viviane of the Lake..."*

Oh, most wretched of women, she groaned, pulling a pillow atop her face to muffle her sobs.

And, as Viviane did every night, cry herself to sleep.

CHAPTER 28

"*I* spotted a wild boar near the waterfall yesterday," said Lancelot of Glastonbury.

"There are no wild boars in Cumberland," Viviane said, looking up from the table where she'd been cutting cabbage. "Not in all of England, so I'm told."

"Feral pig then," Lancelot countered, struggling to control his temper. Everything was an argument with Viviane Halle. "Whatever it was, it was big as a highland pony. Which means pork will grace the table when my uncle and his countess arrive."

Viviane was momentarily distracted with a vision of all the dishes she would create—roasts bathed in various sauces, depending on which of Lancelot's humors were in need of balancing; pork balls in aspic, fritters from the entrails, mortrews, *Leche Lombard*....

"Mayhap it was a pony," she said, forcing her attention back to her annoying husband. "The Scots raided Pendragon once. Though that was before I was born."

Lancelot bit back the words, "Why are you so contrary?" He'd wager she never argued with Reginald bloody Luci. "Whatever it is, we will be tracking it on the morrow."

For three days, Lancelot and a small hunting party followed Pendragon's hounds over the bleak countryside in pursuit of their quarry. The usual process was to drive the boar with dogs and beaters toward waiting hunters. But that would be too simple...too effective. Lancelot was in no hurry to return to Pendragon Castle and the critical eye of his lady wife. With luck, the boar would lead them on a merry chase that lasted until Candlemas.

The animal was as huge as Lancelot had remembered. While a spear was the most effective way of bringing down a boar, they'd used bows and arrows in an effort to slow its progress. The arrows had penetrated its hide but little more. Over the next two days, the dogs maintained their chase, noses to the ground, constantly baying their excitement or frustration. Though Lancelot did not need hounds to mark the boar's course. Its blood upon the heather was sign enough.

The land through which they rode was as beautiful as it was bleak, as beautiful as Tintagel in its own way. Mile after mile of bog and fells; unexpected streams and waterfalls, as well as the River Eden; huge cairns standing like sentinels atop skylines overlooking breathtaking dales. Peel towers, where signal fires would be lit within to warn of the Scots; abandoned kirks and clusters of stone huts, remnants of the time of the Black Death. All of this Lancelot had saved for Viviane, which pleased him. Though she would no doubt correct him.

"No, lord husband, you saved it for yourself," she would retort.

Lancelot reveled in it all: the days of tracking, the nights beneath a cloak of clouds or icy chips of stars watched over by a gibbous moon. The sudden fogs that rolled across the fells and settled in the valleys, the squalls that came and went as capriciously as his lady wife's moods. The bite of cold and wind upon his face; his blessedly empty belly; riding mile after mile and seeing no movement beyond the scattered hounds, the occasional dark flash of their quarry or the dash of small game and flush of birds.

On the fourth day, near an old Roman road they'd crossed and recrossed, Lancelot finally downed their quarry. It was late morning, which, along with evening, was when boars were most active. The hounds had circled the animal who was penned against a cliff. The dogs snarled and howled and raced in and out to snap at its legs. Now one must be especially careful. Boars were notoriously dangerous animals—as ill-tempered as they were intelligent—and harassing hounds could soon turn to dead hounds. However, this particular boar was confused by all the noise and weakened by blood loss. Lancelot dispatched the old giant with one well-placed spear thrust behind the shoulder, which penetrated its lungs.

Afterward, he removed its sexual organs in one piece in order to keep the meat as tender as possible. Then he bled the boar out before he and his men trussed it to a pole for the return trip.

"His meat'll be tough as saddle leather," observed Lancelot's squire. "But I'll wager Lady Viviane will be able to make all sorts of delectables out of it."

"That's what I am afraid of," Lancelot muttered. Dear God, more food. No doubt his wife would also greet him with a bevy of questions and criticisms: "Why did you choose this boar and not another?" "Why did you slash his throat rather than strangle him with your bare hands?" "Why are you wearing leather gloves rather than the wool ones I so cleverly knitted?"

When Lancelot and his men approached Pendragon Castle, he saw that the Earl and Countess of Cumbria had arrived. Increasingly attuned to his wife, Lancelot first noticed, amid the dismounting visitors and their sumpter horses, Viviane looking so distraught Lancelot feared he would have to wrestle her to the ground in order to stay her fluttering arms and demented pacing. After swinging from his palfrey, he hurried to her. Viviane was gazing at Matthew Hart and Lady Margery and their modest train as if the royal court had unexpectedly descended on Pendragon.

"Breathe," Lancelot said. "There is naught to be afraid of. You know Lady Hart—"

"But the earl is so fierce. Will he say cruel things to me when he sees my condition?" Viviane had drawn her mantle across her belly, which only emphasized her stomach. "Will he criticize my table? Will he mock me for spending all my time in the kitchen? Will he—"

"Hush." Lancelot looped his arm around her shoulder and pulled her so that they stood thigh to thigh. Already he missed the peace of the moors, but he must soothe her, the way one would a child. A very volatile child. "My uncle is the last one to judge such matters." He kept his voice gentle. "And the countess has already offered to be by your side when your time is at hand."

After the customary greetings and instructions to various grooms and servants, Lancelot—always with Viviane at his side—and the Earl and Countess of Cumbria drifted toward the entrance to Pendragon's great hall when a lone rider thundered across the drawbridge. Matthew and Lancelot abruptly ended their conversation. All heads turned to the man, who wore the red rose of Lancaster on his muddied gambeson.

"What is this?" Viviane asked, eyes wide with fear. "What is happening?"

"A royal messenger." Lancelot frowned. Judging from the man's mud-spattered attire and lathered horse, he'd ridden long and hard. And not to meet with a sixth son, for certes.

Flinging himself from his obviously exhausted mount, the rider wove among the sumpter horses, Hart and Halle servants and retainers, the hunters and their trophy, in the direction of the Earl of Cumbria.

"I mislike the look of this," Matthew said to Margery. He gestured to Lancelot, who was obviously comforting his wife. "Have a care to Lady Viviane. She looks as if she's about to vomit on the cobblestones."

After Margery hurried to obey, Lancelot and Matthew met the messenger, who had half-staggered, half-strode to them.

"I meant to find you at Cumbria, my lord," the man said, addressing Matthew. He executed a stiff bow. "I was told you were here."

Matthew nodded, his gaze probing the man's dirt-streaked face, as if to find reassurance or tragedy written thereupon. "How fares our king?" For that was uppermost always, the health of their Henry, which ensured the health of them all.

"Insurrection, my lord. Several earls—" the messenger named what seemed to be every earl whose lands had been forfeited by Henry—"plotted to assassinate His Majesty. They thought to capture him while he was at Windsor for the Feast of the Epiphany."

Unless the messenger had sprouted wings, he could not be relaying fresh information. Matthew nodded for him to continue.

"They hoped to seize King Henry during a tournament, kill him—"

"And restore Richard of Bordeaux to the throne," Matthew finished. No need be a soothsayer to predict that one.

The messenger nodded. "Jesu!" Lancelot swore.

"What size army have the traitors raised?" Matthew prodded. He did not appear alarmed, but simply focused, which calmed Lancelot. As if his uncle were saying, "This will be of little consequence. I have endured far worse."

"The earls arrived at Windsor with four hundred men-at-arms and archers.

They also intended to capture and kill His Majesty's sons. All four. But our Henry had already raised a London army and was marching north."

"Where do matters now stand?" No doubt he and Lancelot and an armed troupe would be spending January in the saddle.

"King Henry has closed all the ports and lodged his sons safely in the Tower. He issued writs for the arrest of the rebel leaders and a proclamation to Londoners promising that whoever rode with him would be well paid. In silver coin, which increased the enthusiasm, for certes. Our liege's quick action saved us all. I am hearing—rumors, mind you, but encouraging all the same— that the rebel armies have already disbanded."

Matthew nodded. The earls had been too blinded by the loss of their lands and titles to think strategically. To take on a new king at the height of his popularity? *Too stupid to live*, he thought. *Which is just as well, for live you will not.*

The messenger continued. "There is a man, Richard Maudeleyn, who closely resembles the old king."

"Aye," Matthew said. A young clerk who did indeed look like the deposed Richard. Some said he was a bastard son of John of Gaunt. "What about him?"

"Maudeleyn was to dress in armor and act the part of the disgraced king so that Londoners would flock to the royal banner. Then they planned to march against Henry's supporters, until they could ride north and free Richard of Bordeaux."

Matthew exchanged a glance with Lancelot. He did not ask why an imposter would play King Richard in order to *free* King Richard. Rebellions had their own logic.

"That is all that I know, my lord." The messenger handed Matthew a letter stamped with the royal seal. Duty completed, his shoulders slumped, his face clearly showing the strain of the past several days.

"Well done." Matthew removed several coins from his purse. "Lady Viviane will see that you get food and drink and proper rest." He did not signal Viviane, who had the look of a cornered coney, but Margery, who whispered instructions to the younger woman.

The messenger, flanked by both ladies, retreated to the great hall; stable hands led his mount away. Servants resumed unloading the sumpter horses, while the returning hunters headed for Pendragon's kitchen with their boar. Matthew's knights moved closer, awaiting instructions. Lancelot anxiously watched his uncle break the scarlet seal.

Matthew read slowly, carefully, his face betraying nothing. After refolding the parchment and running a thumb across its seal, he stared beyond Pendragon's battlements, to the ashen sky. Stray flakes of snow danced in the air. Their breaths had begun to cloud, the cold to settle upon the bailey and everyone therein.

"What does King Henry say?" Lancelot finally prompted. "What does all this mean, lord uncle?"

Matthew shook himself free from his musings and dragged his gaze to Lancelot. "It means, nephew, that Richard of Bordeaux is a dead man."

CHAPTER 29

JANUARY-FEBRUARY 1400, PONTEFRACT CASTLE

The Epiphany Uprising was quickly quashed. All those earls had badly miscalculated the mood of the people so that Henry Bolingbroke, leading a quickly assembled army, easily crushed them. Beheadings; hangings. Six men, including the imposter, Richard Maudeleyn, received the full traitor's death. Meaning they were drawn, hanged, disemboweled, and forced to watch their own entrails burned before being beheaded and quartered. Some had their heads sent in a basket to King Henry.

Twenty-six were executed in all, though Henry showed mercy by pardoning a few.

Still, that did not solve the increasingly vexing problem of England's deposed monarch.

Richard of Bordeaux was removed to Pontefract Castle, nicknamed the Jewel of Yorkshire. Built upon an Anglo-Saxon burial ground, Pontefract was a great sprawling mass with towers everywhere; two outer-walled baileys; a kitchen

182

boasting four fireplaces; a bakery with two ovens and a great hall with a ceiling that soared as grandly as York Minster.

Richard remained isolated, alone, and terrified. Following the Epiphany Uprising, he could read his fate as easily as astrologers read the stars. He had just turned thirty-three, the same age as when Christ had been crucified. No coincidence that. Surely, future chroniclers would remark upon that connection. As they would the connection between himself and his favorite king, Edward Caernarvon, who'd been murdered in the foulest of manners. Richard feared—nay, he knew—he was doomed to repeat the second Edward's fate. Here, in one of the accursed John of Gaunt's favorite castles. His uncle the duke's malign presence was everywhere—from the counterpane atop Richard's bed to the silver plate upon which he ate. And, oh, irony of ironies, Pontefract was home to yet a second ghost, Thomas, 2nd Earl of Lancaster. Nearly eighty years past, Edward Caernarvon had ordered Thomas Lancaster executed following a trial right here in Pontefract's great hall. After which Lancaster was marched off to a nearby hill where he was beheaded. Decades past, yet that particular ghost had helped engineer Richard's own downfall. For, by threatening to reverse that ancient pardon given a few years later to this Lancaster-who-had-lost-his-head, the Henry Percys and Henry Bolingbroke had acted out of their narrow self-interest and rebelled against him.

Richard lost track of time. He had no idea when he was removed from his luxurious quarters and taken down, down, some thirty-five feet, to be placed in one of a labyrinth of dungeons that had been hollowed out of Pontefract's great slab of rock. He'd heard of the fate of prisoners kept here in caves black as pitch where they groped about like giant moles; where they cried and screamed and scratched their names into the walls before dying in forgotten despair.

Those prisoners, their fates had meant nothing to him. They had been simply words to be shrugged at or momentarily commented on before moving on to more pleasant topics.

Yet now I am of those moles.

~

Richard of Bordeaux died somewhere between February 9 and February 17, 1400. No one knows the precise date. Or the cause. Many believe that Henry Bolingbroke commissioned the deed. One tale, which sounded like an all too coincidental replaying of Thomas Becket's murder, has a knight, Piers Exton, acting upon this current King Henry's lament, "Have I no friend who will rid me of this living fear?"

With that, Exton, accompanied by eight fellow assassins, rides for Pontefract Castle where they intrude upon the deposed king eating a meal. Richard bravely stands and shoves the table back to allow room to defend himself, after which he kills one of the intruders with the man's own weapon. Then a second. Before Piers Exton kills him with one blow of his pollaxe.

Since Richard was not known for his warrior prowess and no wounds of any nature were found upon his corpse, most dismiss this as pro-royalist propaganda.

Others wrote that Richard was suffocated. Or starved to death. The official version was that Richard starved himself.

What was never recorded is the following:

One man, an expert blacksmith, was tasked with making sure that the manacles clasping Richard's wrists and ankles remained unbreakable. Whether they were comfortable or bit so fiercely into the former king's flesh as to shred it, was left to the blacksmith's discretion.

Fulco the Smithy. The blacksmith who loved the former Margery Watson. Who hated King Richard with a hate as black as the impenetrable blackness inside Pontefract's dungeons. Who had vowed vengeance against a king who had betrayed Fulco and all the rebels who had believed his lies during the Great Rising, two decades past.

And died for their naivete.

Now Fulco the Smithy had it in his power to loosen Richard's manacles enough to make his days bearable. Or turn them so tightly that every movement would be agony. Even to dispatch the king himself. Here in this cold blackness, where few save Fulco even ventured.

Who would know?

Who would care?

Richard of Bordeaux, their pretty young ruler, had ordered rebels hanged by the hundreds. Ordered countless rebels tortured. The leader of the rebellion and Fulco's friend, the hedge-priest, John Ball, had been hanged, drawn and quartered following a sham trial over which Richard had presided. When all John Ball, all any of them had asked for was to be treated as men rather than animals.

But with the turning of fortune's wheel, Richard of Bordeaux was at Fulco the Smithy's mercy. As Fulco had so long fantasized.

Each day Fulco descended the black stone steps to check Richard's chains. Each day Fulco forced himself to conjure the faces of all those who had died because of the former king's perfidy. But Fulco could not call up the hatred along with the faces and the names. He'd grown too old to feast upon revenge.

Thus, Fulco inspected Richard's manacles and adjusted them. Where they gouged his skin, Fulco provided a salve that he himself had concocted.

After which, Fulco would ascend the stairs, carrying a tray with the king's untouched food.

Each time uttered the same explanation to the woman he loved. "I chose compassion over hatred."

CHAPTER 30

*I*n the spring of 1400, Viviane Hall welcomed Clairemonde into the world. As promised, the Countess of Cumbria was in attendance, as well as a skilled midwife, who remarked that Viviane popped out her bairn easier than a sow a piglet. Viviane made it plain that such a comparison was unflattering and quite uncalled for. Viviane's confinement hadn't been *that* easy.

Viviane doted on Clairemonde and assured herself that Lancelot would soon take to the wee bairn, though each time her husband looked at Viviane's impossibly enchanting infant, she imagined him imagining Reginald Luci. Perhaps that accounted for the small frown Lancelot often bore when he studied Clairemonde in her cradle or nestled in Viviane's arms.

How could he not adore Clairemonde's bald head, which reminded Viviane of an exquisitely proportioned egg, or those darling fingers and toes and those huge eyes, which already showed promise of being blue? Like Reginald Luci's. But also like Lancelot's.

No one would ever know that Lancelot was not Clairemonde's true father.

So quit pouting. And love her. Love me, Viviane silently admonished her husband a dozen times a day.

Perhaps Lancelot was simply upset because the Scots were acting up again. King Henry was already mustering troops for a northern campaign, which meant Lancelot would soon be leaving.

How unfair! A husband with a new babe? One would think the king could find someone else to chase barbarians.

Why didn't Lancelot simply tell Henry Bolingbroke that he had better things to do than get saddle blisters and sleep on the ground and eat horrible food that would cause him to return to Pendragon thin as a pike?

We are your duty, after all, Viviane thought sourly, though she dared not voice her unhappiness.

She did want to please her husband.

She only wished she knew how.

The smoke from Midsummer's bonfires was still in the air when King Henry's army mustered at York. Henry's army was impressive—more than seventeen hundred men-at arms and eleven thousand archers. Henry's two eldest sons, thirteen-year-old Henry of Monmouth and twelve-year-old Thomas of Lancaster, also travelled with the army, for a prince was never too young to be taught the way of war. Matthew Hart, who had forced his aging bones once again into compliance, was privately horrified by the cannons that accompanied the train. Which, along with eight hundred pounds of gunpowder, further slowed progress against the far more agile Scots.

As if I need any reminders that my day is past, he thought, though he did enjoy riding with his son and Lancelot.

Though Matthew was too loyal to blame his admittedly inexperienced sovereign, he had a bad feeling about this campaign. The king had not had enough time to summon parliament and ask the commons for a grant to pay for the expedition. In other words, Henry was broke. He asked—nay, demanded—his magnates directly supply men for his expedition. Should they refuse, they would lose their lands. A necessary move, but one sure to stoke resentment.

While riding, Matthew Hart oft studied his king, the way Henry sat his stallion, the manner in which he interacted with his troops, even his gestures. And he remembered... Henry's father; his grandfather, their great King Edward; and Henry's uncle, the Black Prince.

He saw echoes of those giants in Henry Bolingbroke. Still, an echo was a shadow of the real thing. Mayhap it was simply that times had changed, and Matthew's memories of his youth and middle age were increasingly seen through a sentimental haze.

My generation is passing, as those days have passed. So, now must we all be lost and cast adrift?

Though Henry had been king less than a year, he had greatly aged. Apparently, the sacred oil that had been applied during his coronation ceremony had caused Henry's scalp to be so infected with lice that his hair had fallen out. Adding to that, stress lines had appeared around his eyes and mouth —though those might have been etched there by the duplicitous Scots, whose ambassadors were far too wily for Henry. While Matthew expressed his opinion that Scotland's current king, Robert III, was simply stalling, Henry, in his usual deliberative way, countered, "Talking is preferable to war."

In the meantime, Henry had to feed and clothe his enormous army, which soon depleted his monetary reserves and left him begging more loans. England's army was left encamped with little to do save eat, exercise themselves and their horses.

And quarrel.

I am going to kill Reginald Luci, Lancelot of Glastonbury decided.

Lancelot found himself perversely fascinated by his wife's former lover, who had arrived with a small contingent of Percy retainers. Lancelot did not understand how his wife could ever have procreated with such a half-man. Jesu, in armor Reginald Luci was no bigger than Henry of Monmouth, the king's thirteen-year-old son.

Lancelot silently addressed his wife. *If this is what you love, then 'tis obvious you canna desire me.* Yet Viviane was his by right of holy matrimony. Why should Reginald Luci have intimate knowledge of Viviane's body when Lancelot did not? How could she remain enamored of a man who'd abandoned her and their unborn child?

However, Lancelot assured himself, what he most misliked about Luci was simply his inadequacies as a knight. No one could deny that the Percys were accomplished fighters. What, then, had happened to the Percys' cousin?

Daily, Lancelot challenged Luci to the joust. After Luci reluctantly agreed, Lancelot had knocked Luci off his destrier on the first pass. Then he'd gone after the half-man with a sword—well, its tip had been blunted! Several of Lancelot's fellow knights had chastised Lancelot for his unchivalric behavior. Afterward, no matter how Lancelot taunted him, Luci refused to engage.

"What is bothering you, *mon ami*?" asked Serill, after witnessing his cousin's perpetual brooding. "Have you taken a dislike to the Percys?"

Increasingly, Serill had sensed his father's unease with the Percys—especially the elder, who was a sly old fox. But Serill couldn't fathom Lancelot's hatred of such an insignificant relative.

"Luci is an arrogant little bastard. And the way he minces about! Paint his face and slap him in a gown and he could pass for one of the camp whores."

Serill's eyebrows lifted in surprise. He'd never heard Lancelot speak in such a fashion. Not knowing how to respond, he merely said, "'Tis the waiting, is it not? Once we engage the Scots, your humor will improve."

To outside eyes, Lancelot's animosity made no sense. He couldn't tell Serill or anyone the identity of Clairemonde's father. Only he and the Little Bastard knew. And it ate at Lancelot, increasing his determination to avenge Viviane's honor, whether she would or no.

July slipped into August. Henry's army remained encamped. Provisions dwindled. Costs soared. The two sides continued their dithering, until few, save Henry himself, who had assigned himself as lead negotiator, believed the Scots were acting in good faith.

While Reginald Luci continued to deny Lancelot satisfaction on the field, Luci taunted him after another fashion. One of the many ways to while away the days besides jousting, hawking, gambling and drinking, was music. Reginald Luci had a particularly fine voice.

Mayhap, Lancelot thought, *since God denied you a warrior's prowess, He bestowed upon your scrawny arse unusual musical skills.*

Reginald would strum his lute and sing for hours, preferring songs of a ribald nature, particularly pleasing his audience. Since Lancelot spent most of his days jousting, on long runs with his uncle and cousin, or practicing various martial skills, he did not immediately realize that the subject of the Little Bastard's songs often involved a dark-haired, dark-eyed mistress, plump as a partridge and as eager in Luci's bed as any whore. Reginald Luci got quite carried away with his euphemisms for sarding—tent-pegs being driven into yielding ground; swords thrusting into their sheaths; terrains being razed for planting; javelins rising towards shields; pens dipped into inkwells.

It was enough to drive a man mad.

While singing, Reginald Luci would stroke his lute and watch Lancelot through half-lidded eyes. The Little Bastard was obviously goading him. Since Luci could not know that Lancelot had not bedded Viviane, he must be saying,

"It makes no difference whether your wife opens her legs for you. 'Tis me she desires."

Too much time to think, to contemplate certain...mistakes. Such as why Lancelot had decided he would not bed his lady wife. Others came to their marriage missing their maidenheads. There were many ways to fake virginal blood on the wedding sheets with no bridegroom the wiser. Furthermore, half the peasants in any village were pregnant by the time they wed. So, why did he think to punish himself—certainly not the lady Viviane—by denying himself his marital rights?

I did not marry to be celibate as a priest. More celibate. Since so many clergymen took women to bed.

When I return to Pendragon...

But first Lancelot would kill Reginald Luci. He imagined his wife's wails, her grief when word came of her lover's death. And if she found out that Lancelot had been the instrument of Luci's demise? She would never forgive him.

Lancelot imagined years of stony silence.

Which would not be so great a torment, would it?

Since Luci refused to cross swords, Lancelot decided he would kill the Little Bastard during their first encounter with the Scots. In the chaos of battle, he would smash in Luci's head with a pollaxe, run him through with his sword, or dispatch him in all manner of gruesomely satisfying ways that occupied far too much space in Lancelot's thoughts.

By mid-August, King Henry finally realized that the Scots had made a fool of him. There would be no treaty, meaningful or otherwise. He gave the order to march for Edinburgh where Robert III was supposed to do homage to him. That did not happen. From centuries of experience, the Scots knew that if they could draw the far superior English armies into their lands without actual engagement, the English would run out of provisions, patience and money.

Thus, there were no battles, let alone skirmishes, wherein Lancelot of Glastonbury's revenge fantasies might be realized. Near Edinburgh the two sides did meet for more negotiations. The inexperienced Henry believed he'd received assurances that Robert III owed homage and service to him, and that Scotland's king could and would be summoned to attend England's parliament.

The Scots' ambassadors made vague promises they never intended to keep.

Thus, as the first scents of fall sharpened the air, the armies disbanded.

While Matthew Hart held his tongue, he knew how little had been accomplished. Their great king Edward would have kept a force in Scotland to keep pressure upon their enemy, to make certain they kept whatever promises Henry believed had been made.

Henry will learn, he assured himself, as he and Lancelot and Serill and their men rode south. Matthew was eager to reach Cumbria where harvesting would be in full swing, hopefully in advance of the cold and rain which would ruin crops and set Cumbria up for a lean winter.

Lancelot of Glastonbury no longer brooded over the fact that he'd not had an opportunity to murder Reginald Luci. Rather, he turned his attention to his Viviane du Lac and all the ways he planned to plunge his sword into his wife's hopefully willing sheath.

CHAPTER 31

FALL 1400, PENDRAGON

*L*ady Viviane jumped and looked up from the apples she was paring for applesauce when she heard the clatter of approaching footsteps. Followed by an enormous figure rushing into the kitchen.

Lancelot! Wearing a dust-streaked gambeson and brigandine, his coif pushed back from his disheveled hair.

"Husband!" Viviane gasped, overcome with equal measures of astonishment and joy. "You're home? Why did you not send word?"

Only now did Viviane become aware of the continually ringing gong announcing her husband's arrival and the accompanying noises from the courtyard. Around her, the kitchen servants—even Cook—seemed to have frozen in mid-movement, gaping at their returning lord.

Rather than reply, Lancelot strode to Viviane, yanked her by her wrist, causing her paring knife and a half-cored apple to tumble to the table, and pulled her toward the kitchen door. Viviane heard a sudden yelp from Clairemonde, nestled in a cradle located in a tucked away corner, followed by the soothing tones of her wet nurse.

"What?" Viviane cried, while Lancelot dragged her out of the kitchen, across a corner of the bailey to the great hall. "Is something wrong?"

Lancelot made a growling noise, like that of an irritated bear. He was moving so quickly Viviane had to run or risk stumbling. Once they reached the stairs leading to their solar, Lancelot swept her up in his arms.

Viviane's heart was racing so frantically she feared she might faint. What was happening? This from a man who seldom touched her unless by accident? Who now pressed her so tightly against him that the rivets from his brigandine dug through her kirtle into her flesh?

Not that she minded!

Once they reached the solar, Lancelot kicked wide the already partially opened door. Crossing to Viviane's bed, he tossed his wife atop the counterpane as if she were a sack of flour.

Mon Dieu!

Viviane found breathing difficult—though not from Lancelot's rough handling. Lancelot of Glastonbury had ridden away a man who scarcely tolerated her and Clairemonde's presence. Only to return with the force of those wind columns she'd seen toss and turn the landscape?

Lancelot leapt on top of Viviane. His buckles dug into her chest. He smelled of sweat and dust and an earlier rain shower, and she was certain she'd never inhaled a fruit tart or a pork roast or... any food so intoxicating.

"Oh!" Viviane moaned. While she might have been overcome with a rush of heady emotions, she was not so overcome as to forgot to bury her fingers in Lancelot's hair— something she had long dreamed of doing.

Lancelot yanked Viviane's skirt and chemise up to expose her thighs. He was obviously maneuvering his braies and hose and whatever else for she couldn't really think coherently, logically beyond knowing he was removing or adjusting something. Several things.

She felt a sudden violent thrust and knew that Lancelot was inside of her.

"You are mine, Viviane of the Lake," he growled against her ear.

Before Viviane could wrap her legs around his waist, before she could claim so much as a kiss, Lancelot thrust again. And again.

And then he was spent.

Lancelot remained on top of her, his body only slightly relaxing. The tension in his muscles reminded her that whatever had agitated him had yet to be slaked. Might he take her again? At the thought, Viviane grew so flushed she imagined her entire flesh having turned strawberry red. She was experienced enough to recognize that emotion as lust, which she had experienced with Reginald Luci. But her former lover was more like a...

kitten, while Lancelot was one of the lions in the Tower of London's menagerie.

"I want more of that," she whispered against her husband's mouth. If Lancelot were a poached peach tart—her favorite dessert—she would consume him whole rather than confining herself to one dainty slice. "Again and again."

Viviane encircled Lancelot's back and pulled him so tightly to her that, if 'twere possible, he would have melted into her own flesh. Despite the pain of the rivets against her chest, of the chain mail encasing his arms.

"You are so delicious," she said, fierce against his lips. "Like my favorite dishes combined into one." All those nights when she'd lain alone and lonely in this very bed, trying to delude herself into believing she was indifferent...

Lancelot uttered a half laugh before catching Viviane's bottom lip and biting with such force she imagined a drop of blood emerging, delicate as a red currant...

"Now!" Viviane demanded, sliding her hands down to the curve of his exposed buttocks where she dug her fingers into hardened flesh.

Another chuckle. "Patience. After I've scrubbed the stink of the journey from me."

Viviane felt the oddest disappointment, as if he'd delivered a rebuke. Lancelot might have claimed her, but now she wanted to feast upon him the whole day and night and he was concerned about a bit of sweat?

Rather than express her unhappiness, Viviane said, "I will order your bath drawn." She cupped either side of his face and gazed into those incomparable eyes. Her beautiful, beautiful Lancelot. *My Lancelot.* "And then we will both enjoy it together."

After their bath, after a second bout of lovemaking, Lancelot had collapsed atop their bed. Now on his stomach, he was snoring softly and sleeping so deeply Viviane feared not even cannon fire would wake him. She should know. She had tried hard enough to arouse him via other means.

Viviane was half-seated, leaning back against a bolster, while Lancelot was spread-eagled atop the rest of the mattress. Viviane stroked the arm that was closest to her, occasionally plucking a hair on his forearm. Just in case the resultant sting might penetrate his stupor.

How selfish you are, she thought sourly. *Preferring sleeping to mating with your wife?*

Viviane had given Clairemonde's nurse and the rest of Pendragon's servants strict orders not to disturb them. She and Lancelot had enough food and drink to lock themselves away in the solar for at least two more days and nights.

Yet here she was. Viviane tugged at the bracelet of hair that was on the wrist nearest her.

Why do you always wear the thing? Does it have some sentimental meaning?

Whatever it was, he'd worn it before she'd met him. And Viviane didn't like it, the idea of her husband cherishing something that had naught to do with her. She imagined retrieving her scissors from her sewing box and snipping it off. He wouldn't miss it anyway.

Viviane sighed quite loudly. Twice.

Twilight had descended and the bed curtains had been drawn up, allowing September's breeze to easily enter through unshuttered windows. The last several days had been wet, and Pendragon's harvest was proving poor, but this even was a reminder of how exquisite a northern fall could be.

Lancelot snored through it all.

Still, when Viviane thought back to the violent way he had taken her the first time, goosebumps pricked her flesh. So deliciously wanton, unlike Reginald Luci's predictably elegant couplings. Now that she knew what it was like to be bedded by Lancelot of Glastonbury, she would have no other man.

As he would have no other woman.

Viviane thought suddenly, smugly of plain-as-mud Jane le Babbe, with her earnest expressions and silly talk about subjects of no importance.

How foolish to believe my Lancelot ever felt anything for her beyond politeness. Or more likely, pity.

Lancelot had said, "You are mine!" *To me. Not that irritating creature. Not to any woman. He chose me, his Viviane of the Lake.*

Lancelot and Viviane's second pairing had lasted much longer than their first, or any with Reginald Luci, for that matter. By the time Lancelot had spent himself inside her, Viviane felt she might explode from all the sensations he'd aroused. So many she could not sort them through. And all of them so deliciously erotic and exotic she wanted to hold on to them forever.

Now Lancelot sprawled naked upon their bed, for all the good it did her.

Though Viviane did enjoy ogling those well-defined back muscles, running a foot along those thick thighs and powerful calves, and touching the silky hair spilling around his face.

How did this happen? Viviane wondered, feeling an unfamiliar aching in her chest. How had she fallen in love with Lancelot of Glastonbury?

If love it is.

Certainly, she did not love Lancelot in the same way she had loved Reginald Luci, though increasingly she realized she'd constructed that particular dream out of very little. Rather like falling a bit in love with the fine-boned minstrels who'd entertained at King Henry's coronation feast. Luci was pretty and non-threatening, which might have appealed to a girl.

Which I no longer am.

Viviane sighed loudly enough that it might, hopefully, penetrate Lancelot's semi-comatose state. When her thoughts ran in this direction, when she contemplated all the dark delights they might soon share, she found it impossible to be patient. She craved Lancelot of Glastonbury the way a drunk craved his ale. Viviane closed her eyes, running over the various ways he'd earlier touched her, the feel of his calloused hands upon the most sensitive parts of her flesh. While she had not yet returned to her pre-pregnancy weight or shape, Lancelot obviously didn't mind. Rather he'd explored her as minutely, as lovingly as if he were mapping out a previously unknown—but quite enchanting—landscape.

Viviane did wish he'd speak to her a bit more during those explorations. It would be nice to hear, as well as feel, what her husband was thinking. She was nearly as hungry for his words as his caress.

You have called me your Viviane du Lac. Which is quite sweet, is it not?

Though the actual Lady of the Lake had carried off the original Lancelot as an infant and raised him, tucked away in some mysterious kingdom. Hardly the stuff of romance.

Well, no one would say you were blessed with a silver tongue.

Viviane scooted herself rather roughly against the bolster, jarring Lancelot's arm as she did so. When he did not react, Viviane rucked her chemise up past her knees. She raised one leg, then the other, examining her calves. *Well-formed*, she decided, nudging Lancelot's body when she returned them to their original position. When he did not respond, she lifted her bare arms to the frayed canopy.

Pleasingly stout, she thought.

Viviane dropped her arms. One accidentally hit the back of Lancelot's head.

This time Lancelot murmured something. She waited for him to fully awaken. He did not.

Nearly dark now. It was too warm for a fire and the windows provided enough moonlight that she need not worry about candles.

I wonder if I should have the floor rushes changed. I must check the buttery to see whether we are running low on wine. And question the chandler about the quality of the latest batch of candles. After running through her chores, Viviane pondered which of Lancelot's favorite dishes she should cook for him once they left the solar.

Wondered whether her darling Clairemonde was asleep and whether Clairemonde's nurse, who could be derelict without Viviane's instruction, had properly wrapped her swaddling bands.

Fidgeted.

Contemplated singing something but could only think of lullabies.

Am I hungry? Perhaps a slice of bread and some cheese or fruit laid out on the side table?

However, Viviane had no appetite for anything other than her husband. As related memories flooded her senses, she licked her lips.

This is really, really too much to bear!

Viviane decided not even a saint could have exercised more patience. Reaching out, she tugged a strand of Lancelot's hair. No reaction. She tugged harder. He responded by turning his face to the opposite side, away from her, burrowing his cheek more deeply into the mattress.

Once again, his breathing evened out.

Viviane brushed her fingers across his trapezius. When he didn't so much as twitch, she dug them into the flesh of his nearest deltoid.

"Wake up, husband," she said, far louder than was necessary. "Time to play."

Lancelot finally shifted. Finally, finally he stretched. With his eyes still closed, he reached out to touch the whisper thin material of her chemise.

"I like you better unclothed," he murmured, sliding his hand beneath the fabric and edging past her knee up toward her thigh. With such reverence, as if he'd never caressed a woman before.

Aye, this was what she needed.

The flame in her belly immediately re-ignited. Viviane moaned. "Do more!"

Lancelot's caresses made her feel as if she were an exquisite maid when, beneath the bluster, Viviane knew she was big and clumsy, that her stomach would never again be flat nor her waist tiny, her breasts high and firm.

Lancelot scooted upward and turned on his side toward her, one hand propped against the side of his head, the other continuing its exploration.

"Remove your chemise," he commanded. "I would see you in the moonlight."

Viviane shivered.

Looking into his eyes, half-lidded from desire rather than sleep, Viviane wanted to tell him, "Always look at me this way. If you do not, I will die."

Instead, she reached down, between his legs, and squeezed him. "Lance. An apt name for you, my husband."

Lancelot jerked, for she had handled him so roughly he risked maiming.

But rather than hurt his wife's feelings, Lancelot shifted enough to ease the pressure and continued to caress and kiss her until she was once again writhing like a mad woman.

Not that Lancelot minded.

Not that he minded at all.

~

In the beginning, Lancelot had been quite enamored with the act of lovemaking. Now that he'd had a taste, nay, had gorged himself upon his wife's charms, he wondered how he'd been chaste these thirty-five years.

He enjoyed the softness of Viviane's body, learning all its secrets. It reminded him of when he put Slayer, son of Manslayer, through his paces. He was proud that he could read Slayer's moods—interpret the tensing of his muscles, the cock of his head, the flicking of his ears. Intuit when Slayer had begun to tire or was nervous or distracted. Sense how best to soothe his destrier with a word or a few touches of the hand.

He knew better than to tell Viviane she reminded him of a horse, even though he didn't mean it in an insulting fashion. Unlike his Janey, Viviane Halle simply did not stir his poetic nature.

Though she quite stirred his carnality.

Lancelot enjoyed responding to signals that were far less subtle than his destrier's. In fact, Viviane Halle was the opposite of subtle. Sometimes, during lovemaking she was so vocal he had to shut her up by otherwise occupying her mouth. She could be demanding to the point that, after he fell off of her, he would immediately fall into an exhausted sleep. Only to be elbowed in the ribs with demands to be held. Or to service her yet again.

As fall slipped toward winter, Lancelot grew increasingly befuddled, and truth to tell, unhappy. Sometimes, Viviane could be sweet and shy and address him as if he were some sort of god come to life. Other times she bossed him about as if *she* were lord of Pendragon Castle.

Lancelot had two choices—placate her or confront her. Initially, he tried the former, which only made Viviane more insufferable. When she criticized him about *what*—too many consultations with his bailiff and reeve; too much time training at the Pells, where he and his men would attack the poles with wooden swords, spears and shields; too little time on castle repairs; his reluctance to pick up Clairemonde; his feeble compliments concerning a particular meal, *anything,* he would think, *Termagant.*

When Lancelot's patience was stretched past endurance, he would fix her with a look or warn her with a sharp "Viviane!" When that didn't work, he would throw her over his shoulder and retreat to the solar where he fucked her into compliance.

Which, Lancelot soon decided, was precisely what Viviane wanted.

So, he stopped.

The sharper his lady wife's tongue, the less he wanted to bed her.

Which increased her frustration. And bad behavior.

If only the French would invade, Lancelot thought. *Or Henry call a parliament. Or Viviane lose the art of speech.*

Anything to give Lancelot a measure of peace.

CHAPTER 32

LATE DECEMBER, EARLY JANUARY 1401, LONDON

*J*t was during this time that an exotic visitor arrived, Manuel II Palaiologos, Emperor of Byzantium. He, of the ubiquitous red shoes and odd hats and equally odd speech, was hoping that King Henry would live up to his chivalric reputation and provide men or money, along with other Western European rulers, to free a blockaded Constantinople from the Turks.

Henry was flattered by the presence of such an exalted guest. Never before had an emperor set foot upon English soil. Manuel's presence reminded Henry of his youthful trips to Eastern Europe and the Holy Land, which time had burnished to a nostalgic sheen. Life had been less complicated then, crowded with dreams and longings that, now largely realized, were proving bittersweet in the tasting. Particularly because Henry still missed his father, and the death of his royal cousin weighed heavy. Furthermore, Henry worried that his health might be proving a fickle friend. It was not only the loss of his hair, which had occurred following his coronation feast. (How might prognosticators interpret that odd occurrence?) Henry sometimes hearkened back to the waning days of the Black Prince's life. His memories of Edward of Woodstock consisted largely of a bedridden figure propped against a cloud of pillows, though the prince had still possessed a commanding voice and manner that warned his royal nephew to be on his best behavior.

Might I have inherited my uncle's sickness?

For the Prince of Wales had enjoyed superhuman strength and endurance—until he had not. (And at a more advanced age than Henry.) Such concerns, however, did not keep the king awake. With the cares of the kingdom heavy on his shoulders, after the dousing of chamber lights Henry invariably fell into an exhausted sleep. Still, being ever conscientious, he could not ignore a potential problem simply because it was uncomfortable.

I will make certain I do not share my uncle's fate.

England had endured a ruler sick of heart and soul; physical illness would provide another kind of danger. Henry vowed to be even more abstemious in his eating and faithful in his exercises. He would wear the necessary stones to protect him from various maladies and endure the regular bleedings and prescribed remedies his physicians recommended in order to balance his humors.

After an elaborate procession through London, Henry and the Emperor Manuel, accompanied by a court and guests numbering in the thousands, retreated to Eltham Palace. Eltham, a royal favorite for more than a century, had been lavishly prepared for the emperor's arrival. Pennons and standards bearing England's royal arms were everywhere, as were Christmas greenery and appropriately festive decorations. In his role as chivalrous host, Henry relinquished Eltham's luxuriously appointed royal apartments to his foreign guests.

However, one thing Henry Bolingbroke knew, for certes. He would be as gracious as his revered grandfather, but Manuel II Palaiologos was on a fool's errand if he thought to leave England with anything more than an abundance of pretty words and a handful of coins.

Not now. Not while St Edward's crown rested so uneasily upon Henry Bolingbroke's brow.

When the former Viviane Halle thought back to last year's Christmas, she felt like raising her arms in thanksgiving to God and the saints. Then she'd been pregnant and frightened and feeling so alone. Add to that mixture the misery of trying to please the cranky stranger who'd become her husband. Now she and her undeniably irresistible Lancelot were here at Eltham Palace as King Henry's guests!

Eltham Palace was every bit as magnificent as the Palace of Westminster where Viviane had attended Henry Bolingbroke's coronation feast. She and her husband had been invited, as had the Earl and Countess of Cumbria, their son and *her*, to participate in festivities honoring the Emperor of Byzantium, whose name was so unpronounceable Viviane simply referred to the potentate as "His Majesty's Emperor."

Magical. Beyond anything Viviane could have imagined. Feasts with dishes so delicious or exotic Viviane itched to rush to the nearest kitchen in order to recreate similar marvels. (Without all the cinnamon, nutmeg and saffron, which were generally too costly for the purse of a middling baron.) Jousts, mummeries, music and dancing. Mystery plays in Eltham's courtyard recreating the Nativity and other Advent related events. Hunting parties streaming across the snow-dusted parkland beyond Eltham's moat on the trail of royal stags.

While Viviane delighted in all the merriment, she knew from overheard discussions between the Earl of Cumbria, Serill Hart and Lancelot that weightier matters were afoot. His Majesty's Emperor was seeking a commitment from Henry to go on crusade against some sultan. England's treasury was hemorrhaging in order to entertain their guest in a manner befitting his position. His Majesty's Emperor had presented Henry with a piece of the seamless tunic that the Virgin Mary had personally woven for her son. These and other topics were discussed following their return from Eltham Palace to Hart's Place where the three couples generally slept. Unlike *that other woman*, however, Viviane had very little understanding of or interest in state affairs.

Why should I pretend otherwise? No one could criticize my talents as mistress of Pendragon. I deserve some frivolity.

And even though she missed Clairemonde, who remained at Edmundsbury Castle with her wet nurse, doting grandmother and plenty of others willing to cater to an adorable eight-month-old's every need, Viviane felt happier and... freer than she had since perhaps her mother's long-ago death.

Ah, but since life was a vale of sorrows, happiness must be fleeting. For, amid all the pageantry, feasts and distractions, Viviane had become increasingly alarmed over the female attentions bestowed upon her husband. From wealthy merchants' wives to baronesses and higher, heads turned whenever Lancelot entered Eltham Palace's great hall or dance chamber, participated in the mumming and caroling or faced an opponent during daily jousts. At first, Viviane had assumed Lancelot's dress was to blame for such improper interest. After the Countess of Cumbria had so generously insisted on purchasing new gowns that—if Viviane said so herself, showed a tantalizing glimpse of shoulders and cleavage, while mercifully skimming the lumpier parts of her body—Viviane had insisted that tailors array Lancelot in the latest fashions.

"These fripperies reveal so much of my arse and pillicock I might as well be naked," Lancelot had complained, growing surlier with each fitting of the popular short doublets and revealing hosen.

Viviane had laughed and smacked his arse, which was undeniably fine. Best of all, that arse and all the rest of him belonged to **her**.

Viviane's complacency had evaporated the first time he'd stepped out in his finery.

How bold the women at Eltham Palace! Viviane thought, dark brows drawing together and lower lip jutting out in a perpetual pout. *Falsely parading yourselves as ladies when you're as wanton as any Southwark whore. No amount of indulgences will keep YOU out of purgatory.*

After a particularly outrageous bout of caroling, with women pushing one another aside to clasp her husband's hand, Lancelot had complained he felt like a prized stallion on display.

A fuming Viviane had snapped, "Wear your houppelande then." Ignoring Lancelot's raised eyebrows, she'd continued, "'Twill cover all that *magnificence* of yours."

Stalking to his clothing chest in their chamber at Hart's Place, she'd rummaged through the neatly folded garments until she retrieved a voluminous green woolen velvet. When worn it would be belted at the waist and end below the knee. No need to worry about revealing parts of flesh, save for a flash of muscular calf and practical ankle boots that were hardly fashionable.

However, more modest clothing had not been the solution. High-born harlots continued to flit about her husband like hawk-moths around summer flowers.

"You do know he is a sixth son," Viviane said, fed up with one particularly persistent woman who'd been stalking Lancelot for days. "A *married* sixth son?"

He was supposed to marry me," said Olivet of Camelford. "His mother had it all arranged." She shrugged her elegant shoulders, clad in a neckline with jewels. "Such a pity we did not meet when Camelford is only a few miles from Tintagel—"

Viviane glared at her.

"Sir Lancelot's mother traveled all the way from her manor to set up a match. She and her former charge, Serill Hart's wife, though I never got to meet her then for—"

"Leave my husband be or I will—" Before Viviane could threaten this Olivet of Camelford with something appropriately violent, the wanton had retreated to a group playing Bee in the Middle. It was only later when she would think back on this Olivet of Camelford's conversation, as well as her alarming reference to Jane le Babbe's presence near Tintagel. For now, she was more obsessed with the licentiousness of Henry Bolingbroke's court, which appeared to be as immoral as the dead King Richard's. Sluts, all these duchesses and countesses and baronesses and aldermen's' wives! Viviane felt like a sheepdog guarding her flock of one against circling wolves.

Jousts were agony. When Lancelot unseated Harry Hotspur, Viviane could scarce refrain from racing out on the field in order to scoop up all the flowers, gloves, tippets and other favors being showered upon her husband.

"Mine!" she wanted to yell, flinging everything back at the cheering women. "Leave him be!"

Viviane had broken off mistletoe from the wealth of greenery adorning manifold surfaces to tuck away in her purse and wrap around her wrist. Not only was mistletoe known to increase fertility, it was a powerful aphrodisiac.

However, though she waited for Lancelot to be driven mad with desire for her, there'd been precious little lovemaking during their time in London.

'Tis simply the late nights of revelry, the relative lack of privacy in the townhouse.

Though Viviane feared it was something far more serious...

I am not so dim-witted I do not realize from whence the real danger arises, she thought, fighting down that increasingly familiar sense of panic. Not from palace bawds, but right here, right in the cozy confines of Hart's Place.

In the form of *that other woman.*

Carefully Viviane observed the interaction between Lancelot and *her.* (She could scarce choke out Jane le Babbe's name, let alone allow it to take up residence in her mind.) Everything between Lancelot and *her* seemed perfectly respectable. (And surely Viviane's husband must nod off from boredom whenever *she* spoke of books or ruminated on the merits of Lollardy.) Viviane saw no jealousy or alarm on Serill Hart's face when Lancelot and his wife were thus engaged. Viviane caught no lingering glances between the pair. Jade the other woman might be, but she was clever enough never to vie to stand next to Lancelot during caroling. (Though that might merely be an act of self-preservation since Lancelot's warrior grace disappeared when dancing.) And sometimes the creature looked at her own husband so adoringly that Viviane vacillated between dismissing this as yet another ruse to throw everyone off the scent and believing the creature really did love her husband.

How well the other woman had perfected her expression—so irritatingly placid save for the tilting of the mouth and the eyes that shone into Serill Hart's, as though she were Dover's pharos lighting ships to shore.

Viviane imagined the creature practicing the affectation before every piece of polished metal upon which she could lay her tiny hands. And therein resided another source of Viviane's frustration. The woman was so slight, so dignified in her bearing that Viviane felt like a sow next to a…oh, she didn't know; she was so poor at analogies. A duck? A starling? Whatever the appropriate comparison, Viviane always felt so self-conscious hovering nearby. Yet Viviane must monitor the pair's interactions so she could immediately nip any waggery between her and Lancelot.

Only one time did they slip, and of course Viviane had been there to observe it all

It had been during some seasonal play, though this one had included knights riding into the hall, the caparisons on their destriers having been threaded in gold so that they shimmered with every movement.

The banqueting tables, save for the king's upon the dais, had all been removed. Perhaps that was why she and Lancelot and Lady Jane, who outranked them, found themselves together watching the spectacle.

"Oh, Lancelot!" Viviane heard the creature say, pretending to be overcome with emotion.

Viviane's spine prickled. Speaking to her husband with such familiarity, in that tone of voice?

"'Tis just like in *Sir Gawain and the Green Knight*. 'The most famous knights save only Christ,' " Janey quoted. "'The loveliest ladies that even had life, and he, the comeliest of kings.' "

Lancelot bent down to her and, gazing into her shining eyes, seemed to forget all propriety. *"Sir Gawain and the Green Knight?"* he echoed, his voice unmistakably tender.

"Aye. I've been devouring its verses with every free moment I can snatch."

"Of course you have," Lancelot said, studying Jane le Babbe with such adoration that, had anyone been looking, they would have wondered at the pair's true relationship.

Viviane Halle had looked. She'd heard. She did not wonder. Rather, she remembered that moment in Cumbria's Castle's bailey, when the knights of the north had ridden out to depose a king. The first time Viviane had realized that Lancelot of Glastonbury was in love with a lady not his wife.

~

Sitting right below the high table in full view of King Henry and Manuel II Palaiologos, Emperor of Byzantium, Matthew Hart was remembering other visits to Eltham Palace. Eltham had been one of their great king's favorite residences, though much had changed since Edward of Windsor's reign. Richard of Bordeaux had added a walled garden, stone bridge, bathhouse and other buildings, all under the watchful eye of his clerk of works and highly-overrated versifier, Geoffrey Chaucer. Well, both Richard of Bordeaux and Geoffrey Chaucer were dead now…and Eltham Palace endured.

The transitoriness of life. As transitory as the Cherry Fair.

Matthew had first visited Eltham following the Black Prince's return from the Poitiers campaign. Here in Eltham's great hall, their great King Edward and his son had feted the captured French king, Jean le Bon. Their Edward Windsor had loved masked balls, entertainments and tournaments, throwing so many that London's bishops had publicly thundered their disapproval. But their King Edward's extravagances had been strategically designed to bind his magnates to him so that when crises occurred, they would remain loyal. Richard of Bordeaux might have overseen a similar court, but the debauchery had been both the means *and* the end.

Yet another misstep that had contributed to his downfall.

And you, my liege? What is your strategy?

Matthew raised his eyes to the high table where Henry sat in his scarlet robe topped by a cape of white ermine trimmed with black tail tips. While his attire was appropriately regal, several guests had contrasted it to Richard of Bordeaux's at his last Christmas debauch. Only two years past, when Richard had been at the height of his powers. Adorning himself in a robe of gold cloth decorated with pearls and precious stones which must have cost twice as much as Henry's.

Will I ever feel pity for you? Matthew wondered, silently addressing the dead king. *Even in the end, you chose the coward's way out by starving yourself.*

Henry had turned to Manuel II, respectfully cocking his head to better hear the emperor's conversation.

Following Matthew's gaze, his wife, who sat beside him, said, "Doesn't Serill look handsome?" Their son, taking Matthew's place at the dais, and several other of England's lords were personally serving the king and his guests.

Jane le Babbe, who sat to Matthew's right, gushed, "Most handsome!" while Matthew absently nodded. His attention was focused on Manuel II and his long-bearded priests, all of whom wore identical flowing white tabards. Surely Byzantium's Emperor was not so unschooled in human nature as to believe a newly crowned king would abandon his kingdom in order to fight another man's battles. The possible fall of Constantinople was of far less consequence than a homegrown insurrection should Henry be foolhardy enough to undertake Manuel II's quixotic quest. And Henry Bolingbroke was no fool. Besides, behind the king's gracious demeanor and lavish entertainments was the brutal fact that England had not the money to pay its troops from the Scottish and Welsh campaigns, let alone to undertake a crusade.

After trumpets announced the night's second course, London's aldermen arrived to perform a seasonal mummery. Wearing masks consisting of donkeys, sheep, camels, cows, and, peculiarly a unicorn and a dragon, the twelve gave a performance tedious in its solemnity.

Afterward, Matthew leaned against Margery's shoulder. "You are the comeliest woman here tonight," he blurted. Reaching out, he ran his fingers over the necklace of sapphires gracing her throat. "Your eyes are far bluer than mere stones."

Startled, for Matthew had ever been close-fisted with his compliments, Margery managed to murmur, "Thank you." Then, recovering from such unexpected praise, she leaned against his shoulder to whisper in his ear, "And even in this great crowd, I would pick you as my champion. The only man I could love."

A look of such sweetness passed between them that Margery felt her heart pitch, as if they were once more young and indulging in a forbidden tryst.

Throughout their time at Eltham, Matthew had been so dear, seldom leaving her side, determined to ward off the slights that inevitably accompanied Margery's public appearances. She also appreciated King Henry's sensitivity to her position. At affairs of state England's earls—few enough to count on both fingers—and other magnates traditionally performed duties that Henry had largely waived on Matthew's behalf. The king need not put into words what he was surely thinking; that his beloved father's second wife had also been base born and mistress before achieving respectability by marrying the Duke of Lancaster. So, Henry would spare the Countess of Cumbria some of the humiliations endured by John of Gaunt's duchess.

What neither the king nor Matthew could know was that their concern was unnecessary.

I do not care what these people think. Not now. Not ever.

Margery was proud of her blood—all of it. And even though she seldom spoke of her peasant sympathies, they'd never changed. John Ball had been right when he'd railed against society's injustices; her stepbrother, Thurold, remained as much a martyr for the common's cause as any saint.

Beside her, Matthew sipped his wine and contemplated, of all people, Fulco the Smithy. His wife's one-time lover, who she swore had never been her lover. Which was the reason behind Matthew's unexpected compliment. Though one could easily follow the course of his thoughts. The alderman in the devil's mask had belonged to the blacksmith's guild. Fulco the Smithy was a blacksmith. From there it was a logical leap to contemplate the black-haired, black-eyed man.

While Matthew did not doubt Margery's fidelity—they'd been estranged during her affair—an occasional compliment was surely in order. And as a man, 'twas only natural that he would be both possessive of and protective toward his lady spouse.

Sliding his hand beneath the linen tablecloth, Matthew rested his hand upon his wife's thigh. Her fingers intertwined with his, and they shared a smile.

All was as it should be.

CHAPTER 33

HART'S PLACE

*N*early a century past, the first King Edward, known as the Hammer of the Scots, had ordered the construction of a trebuchet so enormous that thirty wagons had been required to carry its parts across Scotland's fens and glens to Stirling Castle.

Warwolf, the trebuchet was called. Following its assembly in full view of Stirling's rebels who had been holed up for four months—since Easter of 1304 —the Scots immediately sent forth a truce party.

Edward mocked his enemy's offer of submission.

"You do not deserve any grace but must surrender to my will."

Warwolf was capable of hurling three-hundred-pound boulders. With its first toss, an entire castle wall crumbled. After emerging from the wreckage, the thirty surviving Scots pleaded for mercy.

Viviane Halle likened herself to that castle wall. Reduced to rubble.

Before her current troubles, Viviane had paid little attention to the story of Warwolf or any of the other military-related blatherings so popular among her husband and his knights.

But now, she found herself obsessed with Warwolf. If not the monster trebuchet itself, its aftereffects. For Viviane Halle's entire life had been smashed as quickly and brutally as had Stirling Castle.

Swish. Boom. Crash.

Where to date the fall? January 1, 1401, she decided. Beginning with the tournament meant to be the highlight of His Majesty's Emperor's visit.

By the time Advent celebrations had been nearing their close, Viviane had wearied of Eltham Palace, the revelries, Hart's Place and *her*. Viviane missed her daughter, her kitchen and her husband, who was always so *busy* he fell asleep immediately after collapsing upon their bed.

High in her royal box, Blanche, King Henry's eight-year-old daughter, presided over the jousts. There were lots of trumpets and proclamations referring to King Henry as "the King of Albion" and "Lord of the land of wonders." Gloriously appointed knights parading around the lists, some putting their destriers through a series of prancing and kicking and rearing routines. (Viviane had always been suspicious of horses other than the small, friendly sort who preferred walking and grazing to showing off.) Thirteen ladies, adopting silly names like Venus and Virtue, were to be championed by knights whose names were plucked from Romances—including one challenger calling himself Lancelot. (Hah! And where was her own Lancelot at this particular moment? Mingling with the squires, heralds, knights, and various hangers-on closest to the jousting barriers.)

Leaving me to freeze my arse off on these very uncomfortable boards.

In addition to keeping an eye on her husband, who was easily recognizable by the flame of hair falling wildly and—she had to admit—gloriously free, Viviane's attention increasingly wandered to the food stalls on the edge of the stands. She amused herself by distinguishing various aromas. Increasingly, she found herself distracted by visions of her favorite treat: nice, hot, spicy wafers.

Finally, succumbing to temptation, Viviane elbowed her way through the press of spectators—how rude people could be—to the vendors.

Long lines had formed in front of the wheelbarrows where waferers had set up their charcoal braziers, bowls of batter and individual pairs of wafer-irons. Luckily, since the cooking process was simplicity itself, customers would be quickly served.

Hurry, Viviane silently commanded the waferers, while flipping up the hood of her mantle. *'Tis colder than a man's soul out here.*

Anticipating her first mouth-watering bite, Viviane hunted beneath her mantle to pull a coin from the purse attached to her girdle. So intent was she on her task she did not immediately hear her name called. Upon turning, she found herself gazing into the grinning face of Reginald Luci.

"If you think to cut in front of me, sirrah," she snapped, before recognizing her former lover, "you are sadly mistaken."

"*Ma douce Viviane*!" Reginald Luci cried, stepping forward as if to embrace her.

Though Viviane fixed Luci with a fierce glare, her heart betrayed her with a frantic pounding. While Reginald Luci was shorter and slighter than she remembered, he was still angelically handsome, damn his traitorous heart.

"What are you doing here?"

Luci appraised her as if she were a sweetmeat to be devoured. "How delectable you look, Viviane! Is your mantle trimmed in miniver? Or is that ermine?" Luci reached out to touch her hood. "And your gown so charmingly peeking from beneath your cloak. The artichoke pattern is quite ingenious."

Did he mean to chat with her like some feather-brained maid?

Viviane slapped Luci's hand away. "Of course, it isn't ermine, you goose. A simple baron's wife is forbidden such luxury," she explained icily, as if he were ignorant of sumptuary laws.

"*Chère* Viviane, why are you so angry? Have you not missed me just the slightest?"

She had her own questions for Sir Reginald Luci, such as, "Why do you not ask about your babe?" "Why did you never acknowledge your paternity?" His presence reminded her that if their fates had been left to Sir Reginald Luci, she and Clairemonde might have ended up begging in front of castle gates or merchants' doors.

"What are you doing here?" Viviane repeated. "Is my brother with you? I've neither seen nor heard from Gerald since our king's coronation."

Luci dismissively waved a hand. "Did he not write to you? He assured me he would."

If he had she would have struggled to read it. "Why would he need to write? Where is he?"

Luci shrugged. "On the continent somewhere. He hired himself out as a mercenary. To make his fortune following your family's unfortunate scandal—"

Before Viviane could chastise her former lover for his boorish manners in bringing up unpleasant subjects, they reached the front of the line.

Viviane handed the waferer a coin and retrieved a steaming wafer in return.

After moving free of the crowd, she raised the thin cake to her nose with gloved fingers and inhaled its heavenly aroma. Pointedly ignoring her companion.

"*Mon pinson,*" said Luci, bending close, his voice husky. "When can we meet? We have so much to…discuss."

Yet no mention of their daughter. Or expression of regret for abandoning her. "Never!" Viviane snapped. She considered throwing the wafer in his face but was too hungry for such a pointlessly dramatic gesture.

Instead, she stalked off, imagining Reginald Luci's gaze following her. Remembering how those eyes used to darken when he explored her body; how once she'd ached for the merest caress of those long, beautifully shaped fingers.

Hah! Now that I have a real man, I have no need of a pretty boy. A real man who, Viviane thought with a sudden tightening of her chest, *is obviously avoiding me.*

Warwolf had been wheeled into place and was readied to launch.

~

The day preceding the Feast of the Epiphany. Enjoying a lazy day at Hart's Place in anticipation of tomorrow's revels. Viviane and her maid had walked to Cheapside where she'd purchased a variety of spices to take back to Pendragon or Lancelot's Welsh holdings or wherever he decided they would reside after leaving London. While approaching the townhouse, Viviane was contemplating two things. First, begging a chest from the Harts' cook to store her spices; secondly, raiding the comfit-box she kept on a folding table beside her and Lancelot's bed in order to enjoy her cache of sweetmeats.

Hart's Place was quiet. When Viviane questioned Cook, he professed ignorance concerning everyone's whereabouts. Viviane suspected he was being deliberately obtuse in order to punish her for her earlier remarks about the burnt crust on one of his tarts. Odd how people could be needlessly sensitive over constructive criticism.

While Kate remained in the kitchen packing Viviane's purchases, she climbed the stairs leading to the three chambers where she and Lancelot and the Harts resided.

At the landing Viviane heard voices, one she recognized as her husband's.

Who was he speaking with? A servant? Lord Hart? Serill? Before she could call out, she heard an answering murmur. Female.

Her.

Viviane experienced such a thundering in her ears that for a time she was deaf to anything beyond its roar. Collapsing against a nearby wall, she closed her eyes, fighting to catch her breath.

The sounds were coming from her and Lancelot's chamber.

Viviane willed her hammering pulse to slow, willed herself to form a coherent thought. Bending over, she slipped off her pattens and gripped them in one hand before tiptoeing forward in her slippers. She was careful to keep to the various carpets in order to muffle her steps.

I knew it! You didn't fool me. Neither of you. Never. So right and proper when all along you've been meeting behind my back and—Viviane couldn't follow the thoughts to their natural conclusion, which involved bared flesh and frenzied tupping and pain, so much pain…

The voices were louder now, though below the level of normal conversation. Furtive. As if Lancelot and she were engaged in an assignation and feared discovery. Viviane imagined the pair in a fervid embrace. But they couldn't kiss and talk at the same time. Then they must be nestled in the curtained bed, exchanging endearments following a particularly animalistic bout of illicit passion. (And her faithless Lancelot was certainly capable of behaving like an animal, one of the things she'd most enjoyed about his lovemaking.)

I will kill you both, Viviane silently vowed. *I will poison you with nightshade or wolfsbane. I will gut you as effortlessly as I've gutted boars and deer*. She raised her free hand to her mouth and bit her knuckles to keep from crying out.

The door to their chamber was partially open.

Shameless! You are not even trying to hide your wantonness.

Viviane reached the entrance. From her position she had an excellent view of the philanderers.

Damn you to hell!

She could hear their every word.

Warwolf's monstrous boulder had been launched and was flying toward its target.

⁓

"What have you heard about that Lollard priest who was arrested? Your uncle warned me that Lollardy is out of favor, and I should not discuss their doctrines." Jane le Babbe sat facing Lancelot in the window seat, hands folded primly in her lap. "You know how I respect your opinion. What are your thoughts?"

In the light from the chamber window, Lancelot's eyes were surely bluer than the Virgin Mary's cloak. And his hair...how well Janey remembered the way it had shone in the afternoon sun as they'd strolled among Tintagel's ruins; how it had tickled her face when she'd nestled within his arms while they'd both gazed upon the Celtic Sea.

"I am merely a simple knight," Lancelot said, with the dear, familiar flickering of his smile. "I would not speak of such matters."

Janey laughed. "You are anything but simple, Sir Lancelot," and was gratified when he echoed her laughter. Already, in their first few minutes alone, they'd effortlessly slipped into their former intimacy.

"What is your opinion of Lollardy?" She pressed. It was an effort to keep her hands still rather than extend them in order to entwine her fingers with his. A decade of marriage and children, as well as the healing balm of forgiveness, had strengthened Janey's love for her husband. But she and Lancelot would ever remain a thing apart.

"I well remember your discourses about Lollard doctrines, though I canna remember whether you actually expressed a personal opinion."

Lancelot's voice dipped. "We were distracted by other matters, were we not?"

Tintagel! Their enchanted idyll. The same images flashed before them both —lying naked on the beach in their private cove, bodies drying in the afternoon sun, fingertips touching, their conversation its own form of lovemaking.

Lancelot had leaned so close she caught the scent of him, so close that their lips were mere inches apart. Unconsciously, her fingers stroked the bracelet she'd woven from their hair. And noted that Lancelot yet wore his own.

His next words, however, returned her to reality. "England's dissensions did not disappear with the coronation of our King Henry. Friars are preaching doctrines the Archbishop of Canterbury has labelled heretical. And there are rumors that a Lollard priest, William Sawtrey, might be executed."

Janey shuddered. Based on the wickedness of the dead king's reign, she'd wrongly assumed the mere coronation of Henry Bolingbroke would solve

England's problems. "I think, like you, I am too simple to understand such weighty matters. We'll change the subject then, though please, let us not waste precious moments alone with talk of the weather!"

The atmosphere between them suddenly thickened, becoming as charged as though preceding a lightning storm. Janey knew the hunger in Lancelot's eyes mirrored her own. Tintagel, so wild, so free, so pure, shimmered between them. But Tintagel was a place out of time, as had been their love. As it must ever remain so.

"Dearest Lancelot," Janey murmured, impulsively reaching out to capture his hands. "Are you happy?"

His hands were large and warm and calloused, not so very different from Serill's. Lancelot cocked his head, considering. She'd forgotten how deliberative he was, how carefully chosen his words.

"Content. Mostly."

"Your lady wife is a fine fit for you." Janey had been relieved that Viviane Halle wasn't a beauty, though the young woman was such a bundle of energy she reminded Janey of an over-excited but endearing pup. And Janey truly wanted Lancelot to love his spouse—so long as he never loved any other woman the way he loved her, vain creature that she was!

"After we saved a kingdom, God granted you a wonderful reward."

His harridan of a wife? Lancelot was surprised by such an idea, though he guessed she *could* be a reward. Though he would, for certes, not describe her as "wonderful." At least most of the time.

"I would rather see you with an adoring spouse and beautiful babe than as I more often think of you...like the Green Knight on a quest through a dark woods. We've had enough of that, haven't we?"

Lancelot laughed. "I've found myself in my own share of woods traipsing after Welsh devils. Or gorse and heather pursuing berserker Scotsmen."

In the waning afternoon light, Lancelot's mane was painted with that color she loved so well, the color of sunset. Softly Janey asked, "Have you taken Viviane to Tintagel?"

Lancelot's face twisted. And, as he'd done on that long- ago Christmas Eve in Edmundsbury's scriptorium when he'd confessed his love, Lancelot was suddenly kneeling at Janey's feet.

"I could never do that, my lady. Tintagel is sacred to *us*."

Janey's heart swelled with the sweetness of his sentiment.

"How beautiful you are!" she murmured, allowing herself the intimacy of caressing his cheek.

Lancelot gazed up at her, and because he could tell Janey anything, blurted out what he would never have revealed to another. "Clairemonde is not mine!"

"Oh!" Lancelot bent his head, as if in shame. Janey hesitated. How selfish she'd been, not to have guessed Lancelot's private torment. How well she understood the pain of infidelity. But Serill Hart and Viviane Halle could not be more dissimilar. Viviane was so young and innocent and so clearly worshipped her husband that there must be more to this confession.

Janey rested her palm atop Lancelot's head, hoping her touch might convey what words could not. That she ached for him. Her compassion for them both. While she'd simply assumed Lancelot had lain with his wife before marriage, such an act ran contrary to his nature. As she should have known.

Whatever the truth, however, Viviane Halle was no harlot. Beyond that, Janey would not inquire. Placing her fingers beneath Lancelot's chin, she raised it until their gazes held. "We all stumble, do we not, dearest Lancelot? And how like you to save your Viviane from shame."

Hearing a sound outside the door, as if something had been dropped, Janey removed her fingers. "My lord husband and the others must be home."

They both rose. Janey slipped her arms around his waist. "Do be happy, my Lancelot," she whispered against the chest of her secret lover who was not her lover. "You and your charming Viviane."

Lancelot had not even had a chance to shed his clothes before Viviane confronted him. With the return of Serill, the earl and his countess, she'd complained of a headache and retreated to their chamber. After dismissing her maid, she'd paced before the leaping fire in the fireplace, mentally replaying the scene between Lancelot and *her*. Sometimes Viviane focused on the sight of the both of them together, sometimes simply on their conversation. By the time Lancelot closed the door behind him, the steaming cauldron that was Viviane Halle's temper had boiled over.

Facing her husband, who'd begun unbuttoning his cotehardie, Viviane blurted, "I want to go to Tintagel. I plan to send for Clairemonde. Once she arrives, we will journey there."

Lancelot's fingers paused; he raised his eyebrows in surprise. Suddenly wary, as if he were a stag hearing the first baying of hounds, he studied his wife. Taking note of the heaving bosom, snapping eyes, hair springing haphazardly from beneath its cover.

"In the middle of winter, lady wife? I was debating whether we should stay at Edmundsbury until the border skirmishes are resolved. Or mayhap, if we head north, Cumbria Castle where you'll be safer—"

"Tintagel!" Viviane screamed, stomping her foot. "You. Will. Take. Me. Immediately!"

Totally confused, Lancelot asked, "Why are you so interested in a place I've never heard you mention? Tell me what has happened. Why you are so overwrought."

Wrong choice of adjective. Spared as he'd been these past weeks from the majority of her mercurial moods, Lancelot had let down his guard. Now, hoping to forestall a tantrum, he crossed to her. Tucking a wayward strand of hair behind her ear, he murmured, "Tell me what is so distressing you."

"Tintagel," Viviane repeated, jerking her head away. Saints have mercy, was she going to fly into a tantrum? Shame him with her antics in front of his uncle and his cousin?

"Viviane du Lac," he said softly, in French, hoping to forestall her screaming, which was all too often accompanied by physical violence. "Has someone said something to disturb you? Do you fear for our safety at my other properties?"

Viviane's eyes flashed like lightning over Snowdonia's mountains. "Do not think you can distract me with pretty words and false gestures of concern."

"Distract you from what?" Lancelot said, his patience slipping. "Collect your thoughts, wife, and tell me why you think to indulge in hysterics in front of my family."

Viviane fisted her hands on her hips and thrust out her bottom lip until it was in danger of hiding her chin. How sweet his lady wife could be, though more often she preferred to act the virago. Lancelot braced himself for what would come next, as irksome as it was inevitable.

Something between a wail and a howl escaped Viviane's mouth. "How could you?"

"Keep your voice down," he growled. "How could I what?"

"Tell her?"

"Tell who what?"

"I heard you!" Viviane cried. Abruptly, she turned, swept the comfit-box from beside their bed and bent back her arm.

Lancelot wrenched the box from her hand, tossed it on the bed and shook her. "Stop it. And I told you to lower your voice. Your caterwauling will disturb the entire household."

Viviane's voice emerged in a sibilant hiss. "I saw you and her together! I know all about your love nest. I heard you tell that...that creature that Clairemonde is not yours. I heard everything. You are a horrible husband, and I hate you."

Almost negligently, Lancelot caught her hand before it could connect with his cheek. Sometimes Viviane threw things; sometimes she hit him. Apparently, today she was attempting both.

"Not only are you predictable, Viviane Halle, but I have lost all tolerance for your antics. I'd hoped you'd changed. Or could at least confine your embarrassing behavior to the two of us. I see I was mistaken."

"You do not love me!"

Lancelot considered. At times he indeed enjoyed his Viviane, the eagerness to please beneath her bossiness and wayward temper. And her physical need of him was flattering, though sometimes wearying. But what if she was simply a toddler masquerading in a woman's body? Could he endure a life of this?

Lancelot folded his arms across his chest and studied her, coolly, dispassionately, as if she were a jousting opponent to be dissected. "You are right, lady wife. I do not love you. Not the way I love Janey."

Viviane flinched at the familiar use of her rival's name. As the import of her husband's brutal candor sank in, she experienced equal measures of pain and horror. Mutely, she gazed up at Lancelot of Glastonbury, her warrior husband who kept her and Clairemonde and everyone at Pendragon Castle safe; who responded to her tirades with admirable forbearance; who banished her fears by whispering soothing words and administering gentle caresses; this man who made such tender, such passionate love to her.

This stranger she thought she knew.

Crash.

Warwolf had struck its target.

"Listen well, wife."

Viviane blinked.

Lancelot loomed over her. Viviane had to remind herself that she wasn't afraid of him, that she'd not show weakness by submissively dropping her gaze or physically retreating.

"Lady Jane is a figure from romance, something finer than ordinary life. You are reality and you are my wife. I have treated you honorably, marrying you when you were pregnant with another man's child."

Had Viviane been a cat she would have hissed. She opened her mouth, but Lancelot clapped a hand over it.

"God's blood, I told you to *listen.* I would protect you and laugh with you and bed you and build a life with you. I'll tolerate your tirades and your insecurities, and even eat so much of your bloody food that I'll have to be rolled about in a wheelbarrow. You must decide whether that is enough. If 'tis not so, I'll not spend the rest of my life chasing after you." He almost added, "As Serill did Janey." But Serill Hart *should* have pursued his put-upon wife. Lancelot had done nothing wrong.

"I will continue being a faithful spouse. I will fulfill all my husbandly duties. But what I will not countenance is more screaming and throwing things and ordering me around as if I were some spit boy from the kitchens. Your choice, Viviane Halle. I await your decision."

Lancelot knew precisely what would next occur. The moment Viviane's eyes narrowed, and she angled her head, Lancelot removed his hand before she could bite it.

"I take that as your answer." Lancelot spun and strode to the wall peg where his mantle hung. Retrieving it, he wrapped it around himself, tossed a log on the fire and stretched in front of the fireplace hearth with his back to her.

Viviane considered placing a well-placed kick upon her husband's spine, smashing him with one of the logs from the nearby woodpile or snatching a bellows from its hook and dropping it on his head.

Instead, she retreated to their bed, drew its curtains around her, and amidst much stifled sobbing, spun her scenarios of revenge.

CHAPTER 34

ELTHAM PALACE

*T*welfth night revels. Mummers in grotesque masks had already distributed gifts through Eltham's great hall, and would later execute a final mummery revolving around the Three Wise Man.

All fine and good, thought Viviane Halle, her head bent to hide angry tears. After taking another swig from her bowl of wassail, she attacked the slice of venison resting cold upon her trencher.

As if it were an enemy who must be slaughtered.

I will never, never forgive you, she screamed at her horrible husband, if only in her head. Her horrible husband, who she'd not seen since last night's quarrel.

Where are you, husband? Upon awakening, she'd discovered that Lancelot had vanished. Later, during the seven-mile ride to Eltham Palace, the other women in the Hart chariot had carefully avoided mention of his absence.

Occasionally Viviane would glare at the object of her husband's lust, as if the strumpet might be hiding Lancelot in her purse. Lady Jane had simply stared out the window.

What had Lady Jane said to Lancelot at Cumbria Castle? "Between the two of us we saved a kingdom."

"I do not love you, not the way I love Janey."

It was then that Viviane's gaze had dropped to the creature's hands, nestled in her lap. There she saw it. Atop the tight sleeves. A woven bracelet exactly like the bracelet her husband wore.

Viviane blinked.

Why did I never notice before?

She remembered that scene in Cumbria Castle when Jane le Babbe had approached Lancelot. Viviane had thought it curious that he'd not appeared to kiss his *amour's* palm or wrist.

Nay, he'd pressed his lips—those lips that belong to me—to Jane le Babbe's bracelet!

The treachery, the perfidy! Viviane had been so intent on keeping her tears from falling, she'd scarcely noticed that the Countess of Cumbria repeatedly patted her gloved hand.

So, Lady Hart knows. Along with all of London!

From her window Viviane could see Serill Hart, riding alongside the carriage upon his palfrey, his stupid, stupid expression proclaiming he'd not a care in the world.

When cuckold's horns have sprouted from your head! I should—I will— expose the treachery occurring beneath your very nose.

Except Viviane had felt so exhausted, so emotionally wrung out she didn't really want to do more than flee to Edmundsbury Castle, where she would scoop Clairemonde in her arms, squeeze her precious babe against her chest and cover that chubby face with kisses.

Clairemonde, at least, she thought, swallowing a sob, *will be happy to see me.*

Warwolf had lobbed its missile into Eltham Palace, where it had annihilated Viviane Halle with one tactical strike.

Splat!

Of no more consequence than a bowl of pottage being dropped on kitchen stones.

Lancelot remained missing.

Everyone knew where he was, save her.

Everyone was laughing at her.

Everyone knew Lancelot was in love with Jane le Babbe. Before the evening's end, King Henry might announce it from the dais.

Viviane glared at Lancelot's doxy at a table above her, placidly eating while observing the proceedings.

As if you are innocent!

So many things had become clear. At Cumbria Castle, Viviane would often come across Lancelot's beloved boring her brood with her stupid, stupid tales. Now Viviane understood all too clearly the creature's actual intentions. Knowing she could scarcely read, Jane le Babbe had been mocking her!

After dicing her venison into pieces too miniscule to eat with her fingers, Viviane reached for a tart. She crumbled its crust atop the meat. Then she nudged her dinner companion, whose name she'd not bothered to remember and waved for her bowl of wassail to be refilled.

Viviane raised her eyes to the candle wheels overhead, to the tapestries and banners shimmering in the flickering flames, and warned herself she mustn't cry.

Trumpets announced the end of the banquet. The mummers' various performances would complete Twelfth Night revelries. Already masked beasts, both mythical and real, had gathered in the vicinity of the high table.

More wassail.

So many fantastical faces roaming the hall—unicorns, hawks, bears, goats and wolves—as well as men in women's masks and clothing and vice versa. No wonder bishops railed against Twelfth Night, even when many of their own clergy indulged in similar shameless revels, including rolling dice upon church altars.

Everything is so topsy-turvy.

Viviane waved her bowl to be filled with yet more drink. After which she buried her head in her hands. Tears leaked from her eyes.

Lancelot, my heart, where are you? Why can you not love me?

"*Ma tarte delectable!*"

Viviane raised her head to the angel bending beside her. Or at least the mask of one.

The angel's voice was muffled, but eventually she identified it, and him, the man beneath the mask, which actually consisted of a head and drapery extending well past his shoulders.

"Come dance with me," said Reginald Luci, offering his hand.

Viviane frowned at it. Her head felt muzzy from the wassail. "There is no music."

"Then a walk in the courtyard to enjoy the new moon? Or in the walled garden beyond the moat?"

"Too cold," Viviane muttered. The distorted cherubic face, which she found disturbing, swam before her. Surely, St Michael and Raphael and heaven's other angels looked nothing similar.

"*Beau pigeon,*" cooed Reginald Luci. It was difficult to hear him, even when the grotesquerie covering his face brushed her cheek. "How you wound me!"

Viviane drained the rest of her wassail, lifted the dagger she'd used to cut her food and pointed it at him. "I'll not go anywhere with you until you remove that bloody thing!"

"Then you will agree to accompany me to a quiet place? Eltham has so many cunning nooks and crannies..."

Viviane knew what he was inferring. She hesitated. How had it come to this, wishing the man courting her was not her one-time lover but her husband?

"Aye."

Why not? Lancelot has abandoned me. I will never, ever see him again. I will end my days in some...nunnery... or disgrace...or sleeping in Pendragon's stables. Anything horrible is possible now that I've lost my love. My love who never loved me.

Viviane's attention drifted from Luci, whose voice was largely a garbled bunch of nonsense.

Why not cast aside all caution? Why not snatch a few moments' illicit pleasure? Why not do precisely as I please?

But this was hardly what Viviane pleased. Now that she'd grown accustomed to the magnificence of Lancelot of Glastonbury's body, now that they'd explored so many dark pleasures together, she could not fool herself. Reginald Luci was an anemic—and unwelcome—substitute.

But all men are faithless, are they not? One or the other, what is the difference?

Viviane rose unsteadily, spreading her palms atop the long table to keep herself from swaying.

Lost, lost. I've lost my beloved.

"Show me the moon," she said, fumbling to replace her dagger in its sheath. "Show me your prick for all I care, Reginald Luci."

Luci had divested himself of his mask. Where had it gone? What did it matter? What did anything matter?

"How bold you are, *ma belle Viviane,*" he said, his eyes kindling. "I believe I will very much enjoy sampling the changes a year has wrought!"

Viviane swung first one leg, then the other off the bench, not bothering to apologize for kicking her dinner companion. Once upright, she clutched Reginald's arm for balance. As they made their way toward the exit, she noticed a giant in a dragon's mask behind them. No heraldic markings on his non-descript clothing. When a group of mummers paraded past, energetically playing their instruments to warn of the dousing of lights that ceremoniously occurred at the midnight hour, she promptly forgot the figure. A boar crashed his cymbals, while a man with a soot-blackened face and head topped by a turban, banged on a metal cooking pot.

Viviane yelled after the turban, "Pots are for cooking, you bloody fool." Then to Reginald, "How daft some people can be!"

In response, Reginald Luci slipped an arm around her waist.

Viviane allowed it to stay there.

~

Lancelot was grateful that God in His mercy had created Viviane Halle female. Had she been born a male who had to depend on his observational skills in order to track an animal or an enemy or find something as simple as a trail through a forest, she would never have survived childhood.

Lancelot could understand why she had not recognized him once he'd donned his dragon mask, but he'd been in full view of her throughout the banquet. Mayhap she would have noticed if he'd been the peacock upon its gold platter or the *soltelte* of the Three Magi that the Earls of Westmorland and Northumbria had earlier placed before King Henry.

Lancelot followed his weaving wife and the popinjay beside her. Should Viviane mean to commit adultery, he'd make no move to stop her. He simply meant to see for himself. Unlike her, Lancelot would not make assumptions. Or hurl false accusations. Or any accusations at all.

If you betray me with the Little Bastard, I will view it all. Before walking away. Forever.

Lancelot's entire body felt numb. Worse than numb. Dead.

I've had enough of Viviane Halle, he thought, trailing the pair toward the exit. *I bargained for a wife, not a petulant child. Who, apparently, will spread her legs out of pique. Or hurt. Or even love. Whatever the reason, the end result is the same. Treachery. I'll not have it.*

While the crowd had thinned, Lancelot felt no need for caution. Viviane and her Little Bastard were too engrossed in each other to notice they were being trailed by a dragon.

Suddenly, the rushlights along the walls, and the wheels of overhead candles were snuffed in a synchronized act. Midnight, signaling the climax of the revelries. Lancelot paused, allowing his eyes to adjust. He turned back toward the high table. Slowly, majestically a lighted chandelier glided overhead, the squeaking of its pulleys unnaturally jarring in the sudden silence. After it came to rest, three actors dressed as the three Wise Men stepped forward to begin delivering lines in a play many guests knew by heart. After the Magi defeat King Herod, the celebrations would officially be completed, Eltham Palace's guests would return to their manors scattered across the kingdom, King Henry would bid his foreign guests' goodbye and ready for the second parliament of his reign.

Lancelot turned back to his wife and the Little Bastard, who had paused at one of the alcoves irregularly spaced in the wall.

Stealthily he crept forward.

Reginald Luci pulled at Viviane's hand, obviously meaning to maneuver her within. Viviane resisted. As she resisted when Luci tried to kiss her mouth, offering her cheek instead.

Enjoying his anonymity, Lancelot viewed the unfolding scene through the narrowed eyeholes of his mask. Dispassionately observing the dance between the two—he pressing forward, she hesitating, retreating. So far, while his wife's behavior was improper, it was also so typically his impetuous Viviane. Not so sinful as to earn her more than a handful of Pater Nosters from a bored confessor.

Until she allowed the Little Bastard to draw her into the depths of the alcove. Stone seats flanked either side of a large window, though the only real light came from a lanthorn resting upon a corner shelf. Not the ideal quarters for an assignation, but 'twould do if one were shameless.

Lancelot angled himself to one side of the alcove's steepled opening where he could watch without being seen. His numbness was suddenly replaced by a roiling fury. Or, he thought, his mouth twisting in the darkness of his dragon's head, if his wife described him in the language of her culinary concoctions, she might say, "Filling of rage flavored by a pinch of despair." And topped by a crust of ice that had once been his heart.

I will witness every moment of your betrayal so I'll not forget.

As he'd so foolishly—fatally—forgotten that Viviane Halle was Reginald Luci's whore.

I am glad I did not kill the Little Bastard. He is allowing me to see how unworthy of my title, my care and my bed you really are.

In the flickering light from the lanthorn, Viviane's former lover embraced her. Viviane relaxed into him so naturally, as if her body were a ship returning to its harbor. Lancelot watched Viviane turn her face to nestle her cheek against Luci's shoulder. Before abruptly rearing back and pushing against his chest. "Nay, I should not have done this."

"Kiss me, *ma chère.*" Reginald pressed his lips to her.

Lancelot heard it, saw it all. The music from the minstrels' gallery, announcing the close of revels, was a whisper heard from a far distance. Once he would have strode into the alcove, pushed apart the pair, and thrown that prancing, dancing mockery of a man against one of the stone seats or out the window.

No longer.

I have ceased being Lancelot the Rescuer. And you, Viviane Halle, for certes, are no Guinevere.

Viviane was shaking her head from side to side and had arched her back away from the Little Bastard. "No, Reginald. I've changed my mind. This was a mistake."

"Do not play coy. Not after all we've been to each other."

"I was nothing to you but a toy. A bauble. To fondle and caress until you wearied of it. Then to stomp on and discard." Lancelot was very familiar with that particular tone, which should alert even an addlepate like Luci that Viviane Halle was about to explode. "I must have been mad to have surrendered to such foolishness. Leave me be or I'll..."

Her protest was lost in another kiss.

Viviane stomped on Reginald's foot, stylishly encased in embroidered cracows.

He jerked back in surprise.

"You bloody pismire," she yelled. "I should tell my husband. He would run you through." With that, she headbutted him.

Reginald reeled back. As did Viviane.

"Ow!" she cried, rubbing her fingers against her forehead. "See what you made me do, you rutting pig!"

When Reginald Luci lowered his hand from his own forehead, his expression was a mix of shock and anger.

Now things could get dangerous.

"What is wrong with you? If you think to tease me, I'll show you what happens when—"

Before he could finish, Viviane stepped away from him, toward the window. Reaching behind her, she scooped the lanthorn from its perch.

Lancelot watched with amused fascination. He knew exactly what would happen next. Perhaps he'd been too hasty when chastising his wife for hurling things.

Perhaps…

Since the alcove was too small for effective throwing, Viviane swung the lanthorn, catching Luci alongside his cheek.

"Bloody hell!" he yelled, stumbling back.

"Touch me again—ever—and I'll do worse than that."

Gathering her skirts, Viviane swept past him, flouncing out of the alcove and back toward the merriment.

Never noticing the dragon, shoulders shaking with laughter, who followed behind her.

CHAPTER 35

uring the 1401 Parliament, King Henry ordered a man burned at the stake.

While burning heretics was a common enough punishment on the continent, not so in England.

Many of Henry's subjects, including Matthew Hart, were horrified.

The heretic's name was William Sawtrey. Sawtrey was a Lollard chaplain who'd publicly recanted his heretical beliefs, only to recant the recantation.

As damning, at least from Matthew's more secular outlook, was that William Sawtrey had participated in the Epiphany Uprising. Which meant that Henry was getting rid of the turncoats who'd plotted to restore Richard of Bordeaux on England's throne.

While England's clergy should have been grateful that Henry was stamping out heresy, they were not. At every crossroads and village church, Franciscan and Dominican friars preached their sedition—"Richard of Bordeaux is alive; Henry Bolingbroke is a Usurper."

"My revenant," Henry said to Matthew, during a private conversation. While they both very well knew the king was dead—had Englishmen and women forgotten the public display of Richard's body?—he was apparently capable of rising from the grave.

"My cousin never listened," Henry said. "I promised Richard he would be safe so long as he eschewed any plot to free him. Of course, his promises were as worthless as he was."

Yet revenants were stubborn things, determinedly returning to wreak their havoc upon the living.

"This is one battle I'll not win," Henry mused. "If my enemies finally admit that Richard is dead, they'll simply take up arms in his name and raise someone in his stead to kill me and my sons."

When the friars could not be stopped by persuasion, Henry had some executed. Others were thrown into the Tower. Still, remembering his coronation oath to rule justly for all, the king stressed he'd not punish those who were simple or naïve and who simply repeated calumnies.

"Only those who start them."

~

"Never since my youth do I recall hearing such foreboding in wise men's hearts, because of the disorder and unrest which they fear will shortly befall this kingdom."

So wrote Philip Repingdon, Abbot of Leicester and King Henry's close friend, to Henry himself.

"For law and justice are exiles from the kingdom; robbery, killing, adultery, fornication, persecution of the poor, injury, injustice and outrages of all kinds abound, and instead of the rule of law, the will of the tyrant now suffices.

"Now widows, the fatherless and orphans wring their hands and tears flow down their cheeks, whereas recently, at the time of your entry into the kingdom of England, all the people were clapping their hands and praising God with one voice, and going forth, as did the sons of Israel to meet Christ on Palm Sunday, crying out to heaven for you, their anointed king, as if you were a second Christ, 'Blessed is he that cometh in the name of the Lord, our king of England.'"

How had matters gone so dreadfully awry? The devil appeared at Danbury. An evil spirit tormented the village of Hertford, along with a thunderstorm the like of which locals had never seen. During the spring of 1402, another ominous comet blazed across the European sky, as it had before Richard of Bordeaux's deposition. Was that another signal of God's displeasure with a man people were increasingly deriding as a "Usurper?" Henry's enemies observed that since becoming king, England had barely enjoyed a sennight of seasonable weather. The only logical interpretation? That eleven-year-old Edmund Mortimer, the great-great grandson of their revered great King Edward and conveniently related to the Henry Percys, must be England's rightful king. Therefore, it followed that Owen Glendower must be the rightful Prince of Wales, rather than King Henry's teenaged son, Henry of Monmouth.

For how could any progeny of the Usurper have rightful title to anything?

Over the following months, Henry's unpopularity increased. Chroniclers recounted various attempts on the king's life, including a rather implausible one: a vicious three-toothed iron torture device that had been hidden in his bedstraw. Should he lay atop it, its wicked teeth would instantly skewer him. (The chronicler Walsingham did not relate how Henry escaped his fate.)

However, preventing a spectre from being returned to power turned out not to be Henry Bolingbroke's most persistent challenge. That came in the form of men who were very much flesh and blood. Men who had broken bread with him.

Who had pledged their loyalty.

And who turned out to be traitors.

CHAPTER 36

PENDRAGON CASTLE

he former Viviane Halle had never spoken more than two sentences to Harry Hotspur, the younger Henry Percy, heir to the Earldom of Northumberland. Aye, Hotspur was a fearless soldier and brilliant tactician, which everyone asserted were highly prized qualities. Which was why Harry Hotspur had been charged with crushing the current Scottish and Welsh rebellions. It was Hotspur and his soldiers who roamed the Marcher lands in their role as King Henry's avengers. While the rebels were forever popping up, like thistles in a hay field, at the very worst Hotspur fought them to a draw. Viviane didn't so much care about all of that. She prayed nightly for Hotspur's personal safety, as well as the success of his campaigns, for one simple reason.

So long as Harry Hotspur fought in the name of England's monarch, Henry Bolingbroke would have no need to call up his vassals—meaning Lancelot.

When word came of various bloody skirmishes between Hotspur and the rebels, Viviane supposed she should be more concerned. Her brother Gerald, who'd returned hale and whole and weighed down with booty from France or Italy or wherever he'd been fighting, rode with Hotspur.

Still, if Gerald enjoyed war enough to seek it out on foreign shores, he certainly did not mind risking death. Furthermore, Gerald did not have a family, did he?

Better my brother than my husband.

Better anyone than Lancelot.

Whenever the Earl and Countess of Cumbria visited Pendragon, Viviane was filled with both dread and eagerness. She was certain that Matthew Hart hated her, which made her alternate between such shyness in his presence as to stutter and tangle her words or, alternatively, to mercilessly boss Pendragon's servants in order to impress the earl with her domestic skills.

Which inevitably, following Margery and Matthew's departure, led to torrents of Viviane's weeping against Lancelot's chest. "I do not mean to shame you," she would wail. "Yet I always do."

Lancelot would stroke her back and murmur soothing reassurances, which Viviane always translated as "I do not love you the way I love Janey."

What am I to do? The question was repeated whenever her mind had a quiet space to think. *What? What?*

Viviane had had a glimpse of the desolation awaiting her should Lancelot actually abandon her. She would do anything to bind him close, to make him love her the way she had come to love him.

Love was such a peculiar thing. Once smitten, she saw Lancelot of Glastonbury through completely different eyes.

How could I ever have been enamored of Reginald Luci? Such nonsense, when her Lancelot was a hero worthy of the legendary Lancelot du Lac. No one could approach Lancelot of Glastonbury in strength, beauty, martial skills or... (Viviane might have added conversation, but he remained quiet around her. Not that she would have wanted a husband who blabbed about books and science and pondered religious conundrums that only Jane le *Horreur* would find fascinating.)

I speak enough for both of us, Viviane assured herself, without irony.

Whenever Lancelot rode out to hunt or hawk, Viviane found an excuse to depart the kitchen or hall or wherever her location in order to watch her husband mount ever so gracefully, and in a clatter of hooves and barking hounds and shouts, exit the bailey, long hair streaming behind him like a pennon. At such times the most peculiar feeling gripped her stomach. How could such perfection fix her with that alluring smile—though not nearly so often as she craved; how could he condescend to compliment her as he so courteously did—though less often than she liked; how could he willingly reach for her in the confines of their bed and caress her so sweetly or hungrily? (Though his lovemaking was not enough. Never enough.)

Her Husband.

Her Tormentor.

As he was her Protector.

Even during these days of pitiful harvests, dwindling supplies and near-empty barns, Lancelot never failed to return with meat for the table.

After his outings, Viviane would always rub salves into her husband's over-taxed muscles, order the wooden tub and curtains dragged out and hot water carried for his bath, or, if he had no need for a full cleaning, insist upon washing his hair. Sitting on the edge of their bed, Lancelot would bend over a basin while Viviane carefully wet and soaped that glorious mane, massaging his scalp until he groaned with pleasure. After rinsing her husband's hair, Viviane would stand between his thighs to towel dry it. Each individual strand if he had the patience. When Lancelot pulled her close, kissed her and thanked her, she was struck dumb with gratitude.

Viviane loved Lancelot's scents—roses from his soap, cloves from his perfume, flowers and herbs from her oils and unguents. Lancelot smelled of sweat and fresh air; of heather and windswept moors; of summer's sunshine and autumn mists. All of that and more, Viviane told herself. She lived to tangle her fingers in his silken mane during lovemaking; to brush her fingers through the hair darkening his chest; to stroke the swells and ridges of his muscles—chest and back and thigh and calf, to dig her fingers into the arc of his backside.

And was ever left with an ache that constricted her throat, as if a fit of weeping longed to burst free.

Whenever Viviane tried to speak to him of her infatuation, her fears, anything Lancelot related, her husband gazed at her in puzzlement, or brushed her comments aside, or responded with a kiss to the forehead and pat to her behind.

Which was not what she needed.

Though Viviane wasn't precisely sure what she *did* need.

Worse. She didn't know what Lancelot needed.

A smoothly running household?

More exquisitely flavored dishes?

An obedient daughter? (Admittedly, a struggle. But what two-year-old did not have her moments?)

A willing lover?

A ravenous lover?

A lover who would perform any act he asked of her?

So why didn't Lancelot ask?

Why did he behave as though she should be able to read his mind? Or as though he didn't care if she spoke to him at all?

Why can you not care? she repeatedly asked Lancelot.

Though that particular question, like so many others, never made it past the strangling constriction in Viviane's throat.

The Hart visits were the most effective way for Viviane to hear political news. Which was important primarily because events at Westminster would determine whether Lancelot remained or abandoned her.

Viviane didn't exactly eavesdrop during Lancelot and Matthew Hart's conversations. Rather, following the even meal, she and Lady Margery would sit on a bench near the fire in their solar—Margery with her mending or embroidery or a book while Viviane generally held a drowsing Clairemonde. Listening to Lancelot and his uncle, wine goblets in hand, long legs stretched toward the flames, converse about current events. Trying to make sense of conversations that were so nonsensical Viviane wondered whether the pair were being deliberately obtuse in order to frustrate her.

"Quit speaking in code!" she wanted to scream. "I am a grown woman. Just tell me!"

Afterward, Viviane would spend sleepless nights—which her contentedly snoring husband most certainly did not notice—imagining Lancelot riding around the kingdom in the guise of an errant knight or doing *something* equally dangerous.

When your duty is here at Pendragon.

Finally, Viviane unwound England's political machinations enough to strip them to their essence, which was: Harry Hotspur and King Henry were quarreling. While Hotspur was one of England's finest soldiers and was keeping the Scots and Welsh from burning half the kingdom, apparently King Henry didn't want to pay the baron and his men for their services.

When crowned, Henry had promised no new taxes. But since all these Welsh and Scottish excursions were costing England's treasury some incomprehensible sum—several times Viviane heard mention of £130,000 – Henry complained he had no money.

Bad harvests, he said, which doubled the price of wheat. Low wool prices. It was expensive enough to fight on one front against the Scots, but Henry had not expected to be betrayed by a former friend. This friend's name being Owen Glendower.

Apparently, the Welsh were an extremely quarrelsome people, whose primary occupation was tormenting England. Their current rebellion was led by this Glendower. Owen Glendower was a Welsh prince who had spent decades in England where he'd trained as a lawyer, had married an Englishwoman and had even fought on England's side during various campaigns. For some reason to do with a ridiculous dispute involving a strip of moorland, Glendower had recently burned a nearby castle and proclaimed himself Prince of Wales.

Harry Hotspur had been commissioned to bring Owen Glendower to heel. (Which meant Viviane's brother must be traipsing about that barbaric country. What about Reginald Luci? she wondered. Highly unlikely. He would probably fall off his destrier before crossing Alnwick Castle's drawbridge and break his scrawny neck.)

Anyway, while Hotspur was an excellent commander and tactician, Glendower and his rebels had the most unnerving way of melting back into the mountains. Lancelot and Lord Hart had both laughed over the rumors that Owen Glendower possessed a magical stone, coughed up by a raven, which rendered him invisible.

(The very possibility caused Viviane to shiver with fright and cross herself. Glancing over at Lady Margery, placidly reading a Romance by firelight, she thought, *Are you so deaf in your old age you canna hear the potential danger all around us?*)

"Glendower and his men are familiar with every stream, hill, ruin and ravine in Wales," Lancelot said. "They simply withdraw and disband before Hotspur's scouts can track them."

"And no locals will act as guides since Glendower would kill them on sight. Instead they flee into the backcountries where they hide out with the rebels."

This information Viviane gleaned over several nights. All too often she likened herself to the great mastiffs stretched out near the fire, watching their master's every move. Gauging his moods and his needs because their very existence depended on him.

No better than a dog, Viviane thought, silently addressing her husband. *And you are no more aware of me than your hounds.*

Despite her debasement, Viviane gleaned what she needed: So long as Harry Hotspur, rather than King Henry, fought the rebels, her Lancelot was safe.

After that, Viviane turned her attention to Lady Margery. Subtly, she queried the countess about Serill Hart and Jane le Horreur by discussing the couple's children.

"I have been to Alnwick Castle," she said. "I am sure your..they...the twins...I've quite forgot their names...are learning so much from Lady Mortimer. She seems very...learned in the ways of housewifery."

Seemingly not noticing Viviane's stumbling—for in truth Viviane did not give a whit about the Hart grandchildren, who couldn't possibly be as precious as Clairemonde—Margery happily shared the latest. As well as remodeling projects at Swaffham Manor and her son's other holdings. And, all too often, a clever turn of phrase from Janey's latest missive.

These updates caused Viviane's heart to hurt, but she needed to know. During each visit she braced herself for the news she most dreaded.

"Janey is with child again," she imagined the countess saying. After which Viviane would be forced to express happiness over child number five, which would be beyond endurance.

When I remain barren. Because God hates me.

While Viviane was spared the devastation that would accompany any changes to the state of Jane le Babbe's womb, she was soon confronted with an even worse calamity.

In June of 1402, Lancelot of Glastonbury left Pendragon.

And her.

CHAPTER 37

*I*t was in the first days of summer that Owen Glendower executed his boldest strike yet, into the heart of the Marches. At Bryn Glas, located just inside Wales, Glendower decimated Edmund Mortimer, brother-in-law of Harry Hotspur, and his far larger army. Following the battle, Welsh women cut off the genitals of the English dead and stuffed them into their mouths, sliced off their noses and shoved them up their anuses. Most horrifying of all, the mutilated soldiers were denied a Christian burial.

King Henry's reaction was swift. Heading an army of many thousands, he entered the Marcher lands, ordered the usual hanging, drawing and quartering of a rebel lord, evicted monks from the Welsh abbey of Strata Florida and ordered his men to destroy everything in the region. Strata Florida Abbey itself was robbed of its plate; horses were stabled in its church.

That promising start was halted by an act of God.

After less than a fortnight in the field, King Henry was lashed by rains so fierce they threatened to sweep away his entire army. Gale force winds blew over men and their mounts. Otherwise brave soldiers fell to their knees, imploring God to end the deluge. The king's tent blew down upon him, poles and all. It was a miracle, so said chroniclers, that England's sovereign had been sleeping in his armor. Otherwise he would have been crushed.

Matthew Hart was reminded of the freakish hailstorm during their glorious Edward the Third's Rheims campaign, some forty years past. Then thousands of soldiers and their horses had been felled by lightning. Whereupon, reading God's disapproval in the act, Edward had renounced his claim to the French throne.

Everything is connected, Matthew reminded himself, as he shared his tent with his son and Lancelot. As he'd once been balled up next to his younger brother, when their hair had stood on end, signaling that lightning breathed upon them, and hail had pummeled them until it was like Death's fists, demanding entrance.

On the heels of the storm, King Henry ordered his army to retreat so that squires could roll rusted mail in barrels of sand and oil their lords' plate armor in advance of the next campaign. Soldiers shed themselves of clothes still sodden from those cursed rains, bathed and spread ointment upon armor-chafed limbs. While some, including Matthew Hart, pondered how it was that Owen Glendower continued to thwart Europe's finest army.

King Henry headed off to Westminster to beg more money from the October parliament.

~

After Lancelot abandoned her, Viviane took to her bed. Clairemonde was her only joy. Under her nurse's watchful eye, Clairemonde would scoot up next to Viviane and spread her dolls and clay animals upon the counterpane.

"Play," she demanded, mimicking her mother's tone at its bossiest.

Clairemonde had spinning tops and rattles that she enjoyed shaking near Viviane's ears. Sometimes she banged upon a metal pot retrieved from the kitchen with a pair of spoons until Viviane pleaded a headache.

"Please stop," she cried, covering her ears with her hands.

Which caused Clairemonde to laugh and bang all the harder until her nurse scolded her and took away the spoons.

Finally, Viviane shook off her melancholia. As she shook off visions of Lancelot's skull cleaved in two by some barbarian, or of his running off to fight on the continent, never to return.

After resurrecting her household duties, Viviane mentally prepared herself for her desolate future. So that when Lancelot and his men rumbled across Cumbria's drawbridge astride their dust and sweat-streaked horses, Viviane at first thought it was a vision. After which she brought shame upon herself, as she always did, by bursting into tears and fleeing to their solar.

Where she locked herself inside until she gained control of herself and the torment that was her love.

~

When Serill Hart returned from campaign, Janey threw a feast for him and three of Elizabeth Ravenne's eight sons, who would be traveling to their demesnes farther south. In thanksgiving, she and Elizabeth Ravenne made a short pilgrimage to Ely Cathedral.

There, Janey lit candles in the Lady Chapel and thanked God for the safe return of Lord Hart, Serill, Lancelot and all she loved. She also prayed for King Henry and an end to civil war.

Elizabeth Ravenne, she of eight sons who had survived childhood, plague, war, and unsavory domestic incidents, thanked God for His unusual beneficence. To have all one's children still living into middle age, was a miracle in itself.

It is because of all the pilgrimages I undertook, Elizabeth thought, reminding God that she was feeling grateful rather than smug. "Pride is a sin; gratitude is not," she explained to her maker, in case He might have somehow confused the two.

Elizabeth ended her prayer with "Please keep my boys safe."

No further explanation needed.

God could very well see for Himself that a day's journey to Ely Cathedral was all the pilgrimage Elizabeth Ravenne could endure.

~

When word came that Henry's army had disbanded, the Countess of Cumbria climbed to the battlements of Cumbria Castle, as she had so often in the past, to keep watch until she spied Matthew's banner in the distance.

One more campaign, Margery thought, her heart soaring with relief and gratitude. As Matthew had survived so many campaigns in France and England over the decades.

Let this be Matthew's last, Margery silently implored God, as a wind whipped her veil and tugged her gown, and she awaited her beloved.

CHAPTER 38

*I*t is sometimes easy to point out heroes and villains, but in the case of Henry Bolingbroke and Harry Hotspur, a case can be made for either side. Like examining a multi-faceted jewel, events and motives change with how one turns the jewel in the light.

Yes, the Henry Percys, those great lords of the north, were ambitious. As were all magnates. Yes, they did act out of self-interest. But everyone does. So, what would lead two former friends and allies to meet on the bloody field of Shrewsbury in less than a year?

Ever cognizant that the Percys' support had helped him ascend England's throne, King Henry rewarded them with all manner of lands and titles. Unfortunately, from the Percys' point of view, Henry also rewarded the other northern lords, causing the Percys to complain that their hold on that vast tract of land had actually been weakened.

That, while Harry Hotspur had admirably kept the Scots and Welsh at heel and England safe, he must constantly plead for funds to pay his troops.

The king eventually paid. But Harry Hotspur shouldn't have to beg.

Still, the younger Percy rode out, even when he'd grown weary of fighting and had come to believe that a settlement might be reached—at least with Owen Glendower.

On September 14, 1402, Hotspur defeated the Scots at a place called Homildon Hill in Northumberland, near the Scottish Border. Once again it was England's archers who provided the victory, so decimating the Scots that the remainder either fled, were captured or were slaughtered by soldiers who exchanged longbow and arrow for dagger, mace, spear and morning star.

Hotspur captured nearly one hundred Scots to hold for ransom, including Archibald Douglas, 13th Earl of Douglas. A prize indeed. The resultant money would go a long way toward paying back wages to Hotspur's soldiers and in enriching Hotspur himself.

Or so Harry Hotspur thought.

King Henry thought differently.

Which led to the quarrel that precipitated the two Henrys' final rift.

King Henry was presiding over Parliament when he heard of the victory of Homildon Hill. Henry was delighted. And with one hundred Scots being held for ransom, the king mentally tallied up all the money soon to flow into England's treasury.

Henry commanded that all the prisoners be brought to Westminster. "So that I might view them."

However, it was not Hotspur who brought the prisoners. It was his father. And Henry Percy the Elder presented a handful, rather than the demanded hundred.

While privately angered, Henry received the rebels sternly but graciously. For they, after all, were gold in human form.

However, Henry Percy the Elder, whose fiery temper had only been partially tamped by his advancing years, immediately quarreled with the king. Once again demanding recompense.

"My son and I have spent our all in your service."

What a tired old song that was.

"I have no money," King Henry said, his voice clipped. "And money you shall not have. "

Which caused the elder Percy to let loose his anger.

"When you entered the kingdom, you promised to rule according to your council; you have year by year received large sums from the country, and yet you say that you have nothing and pay nothing, which angers your commons. God grant you better counsel!"

To speak thus to your sovereign!

But Percy the Elder's disrespect simply set the scene for what was to come.

CHAPTER 39

NOVEMBER 1402, WESTMINSTER

*I*n November of 1402, Harry Hotspur traveled from the Marcher lands to Westminster with the intention of directly confronting his sovereign. Henry of Lancaster—for Hotspur had ceased thinking of him as Majesty or King—was many things, but one thing he was not.

Stupid.

Hotspur knew that he and his father had disrespected their liege. Henry of Lancaster had asked that Hotspur personally present one hundred prisoners. He had not.

Harry Hotspur also knew that he had further infuriated King Henry by holding back his most valuable prisoner—the Earl of Douglas.

Not that Hotspur wasn't fully in the right.

"How many letters have I dispatched begging for funds?" he privately complained to his wife when they were in the privacy of their chambers at Alnwick Castle. "How many excuses have I received?"

His wife, Elizabeth Mortimer, whose bloodline also descended from their great king Edward, was inclined to play peacemaker. "But you are always reimbursed, are you not?"

"Slowly. And it's never enough. Does the king think I can pay my men with empty air?"

So, now here he was, outside the door to Westminster's Painted Chamber, where he'd been summoned by the king himself.

Harry Hotspur had swept down from the north along with the winter winds, arriving wearing gambeson and mail and the mud from winter roads, as a reminder, if needs be, of who was England's actual protector.

Ever a restless man and well known for his mercurial temperament, Hotspur paced like a caged leopard outside the Painted Chamber. His favorite crescent handled sword, which he considered his talisman, had been taken from him upon entrance. While such was custom, Hotspur felt unusually vulnerable. A superstitious man, he had always believed that, so long as he had that particular sword at his side, he could not be vanquished.

While Hotspur paced, his spurs jangling with each step, he thought suddenly of a prophecy regarding his death. It had been delivered by a wizard who had warned him that he would be killed at Berwick, and that he would be killed without his talisman.

A problem Harry Hotspur resolved by being careful to stay away from any place called Berwick, and to always keep his sword close.

A simple solution, really.

Finally, Hotspur was allowed inside the Painted Chamber. Here it was where parliament was formally opened and where the king often resided during session. The Chamber was so long and narrow, with the walls crowded by murals of Old Testament battles, that Hotspur felt claustrophobic with the garish colors, rearing horses, slashing warriors wielding swords and pikes and axes leaning in upon him.

Harry Hotspur approached King Henry, his tread and his spurs unusually loud in the sudden silence. Eyes, both human and painted, observed his entrance. After reaching his sovereign, standing before a roaring fire, Hotspur bent his knee. After Henry of Lancaster bade him rise, they exchanged strained greetings.

Following a quick, piercing appraisal of his liege, Hotspur's shifted his gaze to a calendar painted along the fireplace mantel. He need not stare to note that England's crown lay heavy upon the man's brow. Deep grooves bracketed Henry's mouth and eyes. And, even after two years, the sudden loss of hair remained shocking. How could such an unusual happening be interpreted as anything but a sign that God looked with disfavor upon the Usurper?

If you seize the throne through trickery, what do you expect?

After one of several esquires poured the two Henrys' wine, servants retreated to the shadows. Rushlights and candle wheels illuminated the wall murals, catching faces contorted with battle lust and fear, figures so real the chamber seemed alive with maddened warriors, some with mouths open in screams no one would ever hear.

Oddly, Harry Hotspur shivered, though he told himself it was simply the breath of the River Thames pressing against chamber walls. He had the sudden uncomfortable thought that if he spread his hands upon a nearby patch of stone it would feel cold as the grave.

The two Henrys eyed each other. As boys they'd been knighted together; Hotspur had ridden beside the king during his mini-crusades and broken lances at the joust of St Inglevert. How long ago that seemed.

Hotspur tossed off his wine, gestured for an esquire to retrieve the goblet, planted his legs apart, rolled his shoulders within his mail, and faced the king.

"Why did you not allow me to ransom my hundred prisoners? You well know they are spoils of war and belong to me."

So, they would get right into it, would they? Such was Hotspur's way.

That was fine with the king. He could have argued that England's treasury needed the ransoms far worse than the Henry Percys. Instead, he countered, "First, I would have your prisoners brought to me, so that I might view them. A handful, Percy, is not a hundred. As I ordered."

Hotspur fisted his hands in their padded leather gloves. "Spoils of war," he repeated, his voice clipped.

The king shrugged. "After they are ransomed, they'll only take up arms against me again. I count that a poor bargain."

Silence stretched behind him. A pair of Henry's hounds crept closer to the fire; his esquires remained in the background performing various tasks or openly watching the interplay.

"Where is the Earl of Douglas?" the king asked abruptly. Just as he'd asked Hotspur's father. The Earl of Douglas, who would provide the most lucrative ransom of all.

"During Homildon Hill he was wounded in five places and lost an eye. He courts death if he travels."

The king nodded, managing to keep his expression neutral, though inwardly he seethed. The Percys were deliberately withholding the Scottish warlord. Were they thinking to turn Douglas to their cause, and had their cause become that of the Henry Percys rather than Henry, King of England?

More silence. A log, thick as an ox, was thrown on the fire, which attacked it with a mighty roar.

"Edmund Mortimer," Hotspur blurted. Hotspur's brother-in-law, who had been captured at Bryn Glas. "Five months have passed. Yet you've not ransomed him."

Henry stood with his back to the fireplace. Upon its hood had been painted a Jesse tree. The king's head was so positioned that the tree's branches seemed to be twisting upward and outward from his head like the antlers from some malformed stag.

Once again, Hotspur shivered. Later, during his last hours, he would recall this meeting, these reactions, and while putting together the puzzle pieces of his life, wonder whether this was where it all began to go wrong...

"I've good reason not to ransom Edmund Mortimer," said the king. "His ransom would only further fund Glendower's rebellions. Besides, I question whether Mortimer was even captured, whether it was all simply a ruse that resulted in the death of many fine men."

When Hotspur opened his mouth to protest, for the king was disparaging his wife's brother, Henry stopped him with a glare.

"How else to explain the fact that your brother-in-law recently wed Glendower's very daughter?"

Hotspur's face flushed. How quickly news traveled! "Only after you began seizing his estates, his plate and his jewels. What else was he to do?"

"Certainly not deliberately lead his soldiers into a trap."

Hotspur drew himself to his full height. He was taller than his liege and, while both men were fit and Hotspur three years the older, endless campaigning had hardened his muscles to tensile strength.

"Shall a man expose himself to danger for your sake, only to have you refuse to help him in his captivity?"

"I do not ransom traitors," King Henry snapped. "I have done my best to recompense the Percy family. All of you. With offices and lands and—"

Hotspur made a cutting motion, as though taking his invisible sword to Henry's words.

"The treasury is empty," the king continued. As if he'd not repeated that particular phrase as endlessly as he repeated his Pater Nosters upon his rosary beads. "I am not a Welsh magician," he continued, in an oblique reference to the rumors surrounding Owen Glendower. "Look about you." He gestured expansively. "Where are geese to lay my golden eggs? Or do you expect me to somehow miraculously shoot coins from out my arse?"

Usually so measured in his responses, the king began to pace before the fire. "There is no money," he repeated, biting off each word. "You have already been compensated plenty. I count more than £40,000 plus the profits from your lands and—"

"While you are tallying accounts, move the cost of my campaigns to the debit side of your ledger. Campaigns to keep your kingdom safe. Damme, I see more of the King of Scotland and his rebels than I do my wife and children."

Their argument quickly escalated. Somehow—neither could quite remember exactly why afterward—King Henry suddenly wheeled on Hotspur.

"Traitor!" he shouted and punched Hotspur in the face.

Caught off guard by such an unexpected action from his usually temperate sovereign, Hotspur stumbled backward.

There was a shuffling and clanking as Henry's esquires cast aside their role as servants to take up the mantle of men-at-arms.

While his men watched in stunned silence, Henry drew his dagger.

Having righted himself, Hotspur placed his hand to his jaw. "By my faith, this shall be the dearest bought blow that ever was in England." He paused dramatically. "Not here but in the field!"

Hotspur spun on his heels, crossed the long narrow chamber and disappeared out the chamber door.

With that, the Percy-Lancaster *grande alliance* was irrevocably shattered.

As surely as Edward Longshank's Warwolf had once shattered the walls of Stirling Castle.

CHAPTER 40

"*H*is Majesty looks happy, does he not?" Margery asked Matthew. Both King Henry and his bride, Joan of Navarre, were seated in the center of the dais beneath a canopy combining the arms of England with the scarlet and gold of Navarre. What an honor to the Rendell family that the royal couple had graced the Cherry Fair with their presence.

"Henry's had little enough of that, hasn't he?" Matthew wiped his dagger on the linen tablecloth and replaced it in its sheath. Owen Glendower was at it again, and Henry had sent his sixteen-year-old son, the *real* Prince of Wales, to North Wales in another attempt to bring Glendower to heel.

Sipping her cherry wine, Margery contemplated the king. Three years as monarch had aged Henry Bolingbroke. Though Matthew was thirty years older, Margery decided he and his king looked of an age.

Margery looked around the meadow. The area was unusually crowded for the royal court, including Queen Joan's unpopular Breton entourage, accompanied the couple wherever they went. This time on a tour of Kent before returning to Eltham palace for Easter.

"We must help the Rendells pay for the fair," Margery said, calculating the drain on the family's purse.

"Of course."

Perhaps it was the death of her father that had caused Margery to view everything this year through a filter of sadness. Thomas Rendell had lived to a great age so how could one truly mourn his quiet passing? But he was Margery's last link to a mother she no longer remembered. With Thomas' death, her mother had been erased as completely as if she'd never been.

The Cherry Fair of 1403 was certainly not the loveliest Margery had attended. There had been times when the air had been so heavy with the fragrance of cherry blossoms, she imagined she could float away upon their scent. Or when petals cascaded to the ground in a blizzard of perfumed snow. This year the blossoms yet remained upon their branches and the colors were pale echoes of previous scarlet-etched pinks and shimmering whites. As if the flowers themselves were as weary as England's king. And sometimes, beneath the perfume, Margery could detect the faintest whiff of rot.

Following a simple dessert, for it was still the Lenten season, Henry and his queen were enjoying jugglers performing in front of the dais. Joan of Navarre was a widow with eight children and a face one would describe as strong rather than beautiful. Her manner was gracious, but one would never forget she was Queen of England. Since she was a member of France's royal family, she'd been an unpopular choice among subjects like Matthew Hart.

How can one shed a lifetime of animosity?

Oft times Matthew felt as antiquated as the ancient markings etched in stone he sometimes came across—they must have had some meaning once, but what? He wished he were of an age with Lancelot and Serill, or better yet his grandsons, so he'd not have the curse of inconvenient memories. He'd once lamented that his great Edward had been the king who lived too long.

Can the same be said of me?

When they'd received word of Henry Bolingbroke's pending marriage, Matthew had refrained from comment, though Margery could read his displeasure by the tightening of his lips and the narrowing of his eyes.

Still, Matthew's nature was to be loyal.

And when Margery observed, "Our king is not the first to marry for love, is he?" as a reminder of their own circumstances, he'd kissed her on the forehead and managed a smile that had not reached his eyes.

Henry's queen is good for him. Margery silently laid forth the case for Joan of Navarre, who was already being castigated for an alarming drain on the treasury. *A man needs someone with whom he can lay aside his armor, both physical and mental, and simply relate as a man to his helpmeet.*

Odd that men could always find ways to fund wars, while simultaneously complaining about costs that might provide solace to one's soul.

Margery leaned against Matthew, her beloved Matthew. As she'd so often done during their youth, Margery wished they could erase all the duties accompanying their stations, as well as the political squabblings that so worried Matthew, and simply disappear.

Just we two. Being alone with Matthew had always been her wish. *But,* she wondered with an unaccustomed uncertainty, *has it ever been yours?*

She shifted her head until she could discreetly study his profile, the beard that was more grey than brown, the deep lines around his eyes. Eyes that even now swept the diners, strolling couples; the men playing football in the field beyond the cherry orchard; Canterbury Cathedral, barely visible above the tree line, Canterbury Cathedral where his Black Prince was buried. Matthew reminded her of a commander evaluating his troops, nudging below the surface to uncover weaknesses.

Well she knew the toll it took on him, to be protector of her, their families, his villeins and his vassals, his lands and his king. Ever standing guard. As if one man could keep at bay the North Sea.

Margery suddenly remembered that long-ago May when she and Fulco the Smithy had made love not so very far from here. She need but turn her head in the direction of the River Stour to see its ships—their masts like giant fingers raised to heaven—and the copse of trees, the bend in the waterway that had signaled her and Fulco's secret rendezvous.

A less complicated time, surely. But that was not really so. It had simply been the interlude betwixt and between violence and treachery. Like now?

Margery inhaled deeply, the fragrance of the cherries so thick in her lungs it made breathing a struggle. If only one could drift away upon its scent, back into the past so that she might indulge herself in a few more passionate nights with her *fin amor.* To hear the hedge-priest John Ball's rumbling voice, feel his comforting hand upon her head. To return to a tidy white-washed cottage in a village that had subsequently been wiped out by the Pestilence, to wake to a family that contained no more substance in her memory than wisps of smoke. To view her grandmother when Maria Rendell had been little more than a girl sneaking away from Fordwich Castle, across this very field, through the cherry orchard and into her future with her black-haired, blue-eyed knight. And that other love, the love for which Maria had risked everything.

So it goes, Margery thought, draining the last of her wine. *Our lives as brief as the cherry blossoms that will soon blanket the ground.*

"Hold me, Grandmere." Three-year-old Neddy crawled up on her lap. "Maman said you must."

Thirteen years ago, Serill and Janey had been married right here during the Cherry Fair. As someday perhaps Neddy or his siblings might be. Margery's grandson snuggled against her while emitting a huge yawn. Margery stroked his hair. His older brother Billy had recently become a page in the household of Ralph Neville, Earl of Westmorland. As Guinevere and Alice had been sent away last year in order to become proper ladies under the watchful eye of Harry Hotspur's wife. When Matthew and Margery had visited Alnwick Castle, Elizabeth Mortimer had informed them that Alice was as obedient as ever, while Guinevere ... Well, Alnwick Castle had survived for three hundred years. Surely, it could survive a few years with Genny.

Matthew rose and after ruffling Neddy's head, murmured to Margery, "Duty, my love." He left her to join a group of lords whose faces were familiar from Twelfth Night, two years past. Minus Harry Hotspur, of course. Margery's fears did not extend much beyond worrying whether the twins would be safe in the household of someone nursing grievances against the king.

"Hotspur may be impetuous, but he's no fool," Matthew had said when she'd expressed her concerns. "He continues to fight the Scots on Henry's behalf. And the king continues to shower him with titles and money." He paused. "When he has it."

Neddy's breathing was deep and slow. He was heavy against Margery's chest in the comfortable way of young children. God may have only granted her and Matthew one child, but Serill and Janey had more than compensated, with Janey's recent announcement of her fifth pregnancy.

Seeking her son and his wife, Margery saw instead Lancelot, Viviane and Clairemonde in front of a waferer's barrow. Lady Viviane was also with child, her belly enormous though she was scarce six months. Viviane Halle reminded her of some pagan goddess of fertility; the larger her stomach grew the more arresting her face and form. Right now, Viviane was gesticulating wildly, most likely accusing the waferer of inferior cakes. Lancelot eyed her with his usual mixture of indulgence and wariness, while Clairemonde wandered off in the direction of a bear baiting.

Margery smiled and kissed the top of Neddy's head. Poor Lancelot was like a farm animal following the seasons. Sleek and well-fed before heading off on one of the king's campaigns and returning leaner than ever. Which caused Viviane to cluck about like a hen chasing insects, fussing that he would fall ill if he weren't *immediately* fattened up by all her delectable dishes. As farmers fed their livestock in the summer preceding November's inevitable slaughter.

Slaughter.

Margery struggled to ignore the feeling of doom that settled over her. While Matthew tried to shield her at the same time she pretended to be shielded, she saw all too well her husband's increasing weariness following each campaign, his frustrations at the closing of each parliament. As she noted the times he closeted himself with King Henry and his advisors over the matter of Harry Hotspur and the rift with the Percy family.

Slaughter, she thought again.

And this time Margery shivered.

CHAPTER 41

EARLY JULY 1403, PENDRAGON CASTLE

It was near dawn. Viviane left their bed, as was generally the case unless Lancelot caught her in his arms and insisted otherwise. After a quick wash and check on Clairemonde and her nursemaid sleeping at the opposite end of the chamber, Viviane carefully maneuvered the stairs leading to Pendragon's kitchen.

Cook was placing wood on the hearth fire. A scullery maid scoured pots and pans while a second was cutting loaves of bread for sops in wine. Usually, Cook greeted Viviane with a "Good morrow, Pickle. How fares your bairn this day?" This morning, however, he swung his gaze meaningfully toward a shadowed figure standing beside the kitchen doorway.

Gerald Halle. In gambeson and mail, his padded coif still pulled up for protection. Not the usual dress for a pleasure ride.

"Brother!" Viviane had not seen Gerald since the execution of their father. Thinking to embrace him, she rushed to him but, seeing his scowl, stopped short.

"What are you doing here? How did you gain entrance?"

"The postern. Your husband appears remiss at guarding his family."

Her first reaction was to come to Lancelot's defense. But Gerald's terse words went far beyond a casual criticism. "What is wrong? Have the Scots once again gone marauding?"

Without responding, he turned and strode through the door to the bailey beyond. "Walk with me," he tossed over his shoulder.

Viviane followed as best she could, her movements made awkward by her giant belly. "Slow down, brother. Tell me why you suddenly appear when I've not laid eyes on you for three years."

In answer to a question she had not asked, had not even considered, Gerald said, "Do not fear. Your Reginald is safe. He will meet us in Chester."

"Why would I care about Reginald Luci?" she called, gathering her skirts in order to increase her pace.

If Gerald heard, he did not respond.

Only the buttery light from the kitchen illumined their path. A dairymaid, empty pails swinging on either side of the yoke balanced between her shoulders, headed for the milking shed.

Finally, Viviane reached her brother, waiting impatiently at the postern.

"What is this all about?" she huffed. "Tell me."

But he was already striding toward a footbridge that crossed the River Eden. Ducks and geese, resting on the water's surface, stirred before settling back in at their passing.

"Will you wait just a bloody minute?" Viviane discerned the darker shapes of Gerald's horse and his mounted squire on the opposite side of the bridge. "I am moving as fast as I can."

Upon reaching the horses, he turned. After a panting Viviane reached his side, Gerald said, "I rode, miles out of my way, I might add, to warn you. You must convince your husband to retreat to Alnwick Castle. You will be safe there."

"Alnwick? What do you mean 'safe?'" Viviane struggled to catch her breath. "Would you quit speaking in riddles?"

"My lord has called out the Usurper. We will remove Henry Bolingbroke from the throne and set up Edmund Mortimer as England's rightful heir."

Viviane gasped. She thought back to those dreadful days following their father's execution, when Gerald had cursed Henry Bolingbroke. The ensuing years had done nothing to soften his animosity.

"First, we will roust the Usurper's son, the false prince, who has holed himself up inside Shrewsbury. After we down the whelp, we will tear apart the sire."

Gerald reached out to dig his gloved fingers into Viviane's forearm. "Think you I've forgotten the disgrace the Usurper brought to the Halle family?"

"Stop it, Gerald. You're hurting me." She jerked away so fiercely she nearly lost her balance. "King Henry has been generous to Lancelot and me. As he has been with the Percys and you from the look of it—"

"You've not lost your ignorance, have you?" He shrugged. "'Tis your choice. But I am telling you. My lord Percy has gathered a large army, which will further swell when he meets Owen Glendower, with whom he has formed an alliance."

"The Welshman?" Viviane managed. "But he is a traitor!" The air had begun to lose its chill, and the sky had lightened enough so that she could more clearly see Gerald's hate-filled expression.

"I am warning you. Between the Percys and Glendower, our army will crush Henry Bolingbroke. Like a nut between a nutcracker."

"But that would mean civil war!" The implication was too horrible to be borne. The removal of Richard of Bordeaux had been executed with blessedly little bloodshed, but Henry Bolingbroke was cut from a very different bolt of cloth.

"Why would the Percys think to commit treason?" She'd listened so very carefully during Matthew Hart and Lancelot's conversations. How had she missed this?

"Help me understand—"

"Henry Bolingbroke is a liar and a regicide." Gerald's words tumbled out in a fevered rush. "Without Hotspur, the borderlands would have long ago been overrun. Yet the king will not pay him or us, his troops, so much as a ha'penny. After we kill the Usurper, England will be carved up in three parts. Glendower will have Wales and much of west England; the Percys all the north, as well as Northamptonshire, Norfolk, Warwickshire, and Leicestershire; and the Mortimers the rest of southern England, below the river Trent—"

"Tell me you are joking!" Viviane cried, aghast. "They canna just carve up England like some…Christmas goose!"

"Mark my words, sister. 'Tis coming to pass even as we speak."

Gerald's horse shook its head, causing its bridle to jangle, and nudged his back. Gerald's squire shifted impatiently in his saddle, silently reminding the knight they should be on their way.

"I want you and your daughter to be safe. Your lord husband too, if he so chooses to back a winning side for once. Which is why you must ride for Alnwick Castle."

"Alnwick?" Viviane repeated dumbly. "Why? If what you say is true Cumbria would be far closer."

Gerald eyed her as if she were daft. "The Earl of Cumbria supports the Usurper. Once Hotspur crushes their army, all Hart lands will be forfeit and he and his relatives executed."

Viviane gaped. "But that would mean Lancelot," she croaked. "That would mean——-"

"Your husband's only hope is to renounce his allegiance and ride with us."

Could she somehow persuade Lancelot to switch sides? Might they declare a pox on both sides and flee to his Welsh manor or Tintagel? But if Hotspur succeeded in his madness not only Lancelot would be killed. Other people she'd come to love.

"You know he will not betray his king."

"Then he will suffer the consequences." Turning his back to her, Gerald caught the reins from the waiting squire and swung into his saddle. Looking down on her, he said, "In a month's time the Usurper will suffer the same fate as did our father. That I promise you. And I intend to strike the fatal blow myself."

With that Gerald Halle touched spurs to his destrier's belly and rode away.

CHAPTER 42

*D*espite their last heated encounter, King Henry had not actually thought Harry Hotspur and his father would commit treason.

Yet, there it was.

Henry Bolingbroke could do naught but call up his army and ready to defend his crown.

A messenger pigeon had been dispatched to Edmundsbury Castle, warning of Harry Hotspur's insurrection. The reply assured Matthew Hart that the king had been duly warned and that Serill and his men-at-arms were already on their way to rendezvous with King Henry.

So now, Matthew thought, alone as he was in St Bosa's Chapel. *We all ride to our destinies.*

He stood in the aisle between his parents' tomb chests and those he'd had commissioned for himself and Meg. Effigies which, after the manner of John of Gaunt and his first wife, meant Matthew and Margery would clasp hands into eternity.

Matthew walked forward and then to his left until he was positioned between his parents. Their figures were so lifelike that when he gazed into William and Sosannah's faces or traced the cold, cold alabaster of their profiles, the folds of his mother's gown and his father's coif, he could almost believe they were simply sleeping.

Matthew rearranged his sheathed sword so he could more easily kneel on the paving stones, crossed himself and bowed his head.

So much time he'd spent at tomb chests—Edward the Black Prince, John of Gaunt, his King Edward, his brother Harry. So many he'd loved who had left him behind. Matthew experienced that familiar mixture of despair, of sadness, of resignation tinged by longing that always accompanied these private pilgrimages.

His sigh echoed in the chapel's stillness.

Over the past two days, while he and Lancelot and their men-at-arms had readied for their journey south, Matthew had spent his few free moments here. Hoping to hear his father's voice or feel his mother's gentle, comforting touch. Hoping to find in the shadows, in the solitude, in his parents' presence, the strength he needed to embrace what he sensed was imminent.

It was odd. In the past fortnight, well before Lancelot's messenger had arrived with news of Hotspur's perfidy, Matthew had taken to seeing his parents—Sosannah amidst a group of ladies in Cumbria's great hall, William among those watching when he tilted at the quintain or sparred with various opponents to keep himself fighting ready.

Omens, Matthew thought. *Warnings.*

And a promise?

When death was imminent, the departed often physically intruded upon the living.

Is that what is happening now?

After crossing himself, Matthew rose, putting his hands on the carved lip of his father's tomb for leverage.

Not so very spry, old man, are you? Matthew's lips curved in a self-mocking smile. Stepping to his own effigy, he contemplated the face that was his, yet not his. How long would it take for his flesh to match the ice of the marble he now caressed? He remembered the night his brother had died. When Harry had simply slipped away while wrapped in Matthew's arms; when Matthew had not realized he'd been holding a corpse until he'd awakened to feel his brother's flesh cooling through the rags that had once encased his limbs.

While Matthew had seen countless dead bodies, he'd touched far fewer. But enough to understand that that particular coldness was unlike any other.

Matthew heard a whisper of footsteps behind him. Felt a hand on his shoulder,

"Your men are waiting," Margery said before slipping into his arms. Her cheek pressed against the padded leather that provided protection from the rough links of Matthew's mail.

He closed his eyes. *I cannot say it, what I believe in my heart.* Instead, Matthew held Margery in such a way that he might impress upon his senses the feel of her. As if it were their first embrace.

While Margery thought, *If I lose you, I'll not survive.*

After drawing back, she handed him the robin he'd given her upon his return from the Poitiers campaign, nearly fifty years past. The wooden bird had once possessed a bright red breast which was now worn to the nub. She'd had a hole drilled in its center and laced a thong through it.

"Wear it close to your heart." She tucked the talisman through multiple layers of padding and mail until she encountered the warmth of living flesh. "I expect you to bring it back to me." She smiled up at him, knowing how easily he would read the falseness of that smile.

"Cumbria Castle can withstand a siege," Matthew said. "If it comes to that."

Empty words, Margery knew. If King Henry lost his crown, those few who survived would wish themselves dead. Especially her.

A blast of trumpets from the bailey. Hand in hand they exited St Bosa's. Most of the Hart and Glastonbury men-at-arms were already mounted. Though the early July day promised to be hot, Margery shivered and found herself trembling.

After Matthew mounted, she held his stirrup in her hands and looked up at him.

"May God protect you, my love," she whispered.

Matthew leaned over to scoop her up with his right arm until she was pressed against him. Margery wrapped her arms around his neck so fiercely, as if that might force him to stay, and breathed a silent prayer for his safety.

A sudden wail caused Matthew to deposit Margery roughly on the ground. Nearby, Viviane Hall was clinging to her husband, who'd been simultaneously trying to comfort her while easing away so that he might mount his rouncey.

"You canna leave," Viviane sobbed. "What will I do without you?"

An embarrassed Lancelot patted her back, accommodating her enormous belly as best he could. When he tried to remove her arms from his neck, she simply flung herself upon him again. "Do not cry, Viviane du Lac," he soothed. Repeatedly. "I will return in time for your lying in."

"Just like you did with Clairemonde? I could give birth anytime from now to Lammas Day."

"Lady wife—" Lancelot began.

Viviane ignored the irritation in his voice. "I should not have told you about the plot," she moaned. The baby kicked so fiercely she was sure it too protested her decision. "We should have stayed at Pendragon. The king has plenty of men to champion him. He does na need you. Not as I do!"

"Enough!" Lancelot gripped her arms and returned them to her side with such force Viviane dared not move them again.

Hoping to distract his wife, Lancelot picked up Clairemonde, who'd been trying to gain his attention by repeatedly hitting his thigh with a bundle of dried food.

"It won't be enough," Viviane wailed after Lancelot accepted his daughter's offering with an elaborate thank you and a kiss to the forehead. "How can you fight without proper sustenance? You'll be too weak to raise your sword arm!"

Looking from her distraught mother to Lancelot, the three- year-old thrust out a lower lip, as if she might also cry. Then thinking better of it, Clairemonde slid from her stepfather's embrace to clutch Viviane's skirts.

Lancelot took this opportunity to mount, not meeting the eyes of his men, who by now were surely used to the volatility of his spouse.

A second, more insistent calling of trumpets. The bailey teemed with knights and squires soothing nervous destriers; packhorses bearing weapons, supplies and armor; all the usual chaos preceding all the campaigns. Father James, who'd earlier blessed the men and implored God to lead them to victory, followed Margery, who had retreated to stand among servants, family members and villagers huddled near castle wall.

"God is with them," soothed Father James. "And our rightful king. Have faith, my lady."

Rather than respond that Harry Hotspur's priests were certainly uttering the same promises, Margery kept her gaze on Matthew, who was leaning across his pommel to engage one of his squires.

Already you have forgotten me. After all these years I should not be surprised.

Viviane remained where Lancelot had left her. Somehow, she managed to hold Clairemonde against her hip with one hand while waving forlornly at a husband who had already turned his back to her.

Cumbria's portcullis was raised, its drawbridge lowered with a series of unnerving groans, reminiscent of someone being tortured. Matthew guided his stallion to the front, raised his gloved hand and with a clatter of hooves, riders streamed across the bridge and along the village road.

Afterward, everyone began returning to their duties. How empty, how quiet the courtyard. The disapproving cluck of chickens rooting among the straw; dogs returning to their favored places in the sun; Clairemonde slipping free to chase a cat darting toward the mews. Margery stared past the barbican to the drawbridge, as if Matthew might yet remain there, frozen in time.

Approaching Viviane, who remained in her former woebegone position, Margery said, "I am climbing to the battlement to watch."

"I'll come with you."

"'Tis too steep. Stay with Clairemonde."

"I want to see!"

What a child she could be! Well, Margery was no Lancelot who must coax her into behaving.

"As you wish." With a curt nod, Margery left her.

Since her arrival at Cumbria, Margery had watched Matthew's every departure from the battlement. If she followed her usual routine, would he be more likely to safely return?

Once upon the parapet, Margery spotted the Hart banner fronting the column that would increase in size as others answered his summons, as word of the Northumberlands' treachery spread. Margery removed a kerchief from her bosom and positioned herself in front of a crenel so that, when Matthew turned—as he inevitably would—he would see her.

But what if he forgets? she worried.

She thought suddenly of her grandmother, Maria Rendell, imagined how Maria must have felt when she'd accompanied her lover, Richard of Sussex, as he'd tried unsuccessfully to rally support for his despised half-brother, Edward Caernarvon.

Were you as fearful as I am, Grandmere? When you realized the second Edward's reign was bleeding out its final hours and there was naught your lover could do to staunch it? Is that what is happening to our King Henry now? Is he bleeding out his final hours?

She crossed herself and vowed she would light all the votive candles in St Bosa's. Perhaps even undertake an all-night vigil. If only that would keep Matthew, all her loved ones safe.

Please be with me now, Grandmere. Now, when I feel so lost.

Margery was disturbed by a wheezing Viviane who, flanked by two maids, had struggled up beside her. The younger woman leaned against the crenels, eyes closed, forehead shining with sweat, until her breathing slowed.

"I am so frightened, my lady."

At this moment Margery was incapable of playing the role of the ever unruffled, ever gracious matriarch. "No more so than me," she retorted, returning to her watch.

Turn, she silently begged her husband. *Do not forsake me.*

Finally, Matthew swiveled in his saddle and raised a fisted arm in acknowledgement. Margery waved her kerchief and blew him a kiss he would not see.

Oblivious to Margery's curtness, Viviane had moved to stand beside her. Now she frantically waved her arms and yelled Lancelot's name.

To no avail.

Together the two women watched from the battlement.

Watched until they could no longer distinguish the snarling, leaping, prancing beasts gracing the riders' lances.

Until Matthew, Lancelot and Henry Bolingbroke's other champions appeared of no more consequence than a column of bugs crawling across a patch of mud.

CHAPTER 43

On the night of July 20, 1403, King Henry's army was camped in the vicinity of Haughmond Abbey, four miles northeast of the market town of Shrewsbury.

Harry Hotspur had planned to link up with Owen Glendower and proceed to Shrewsbury, where he would overwhelm the small royalist force within—the only substantial enemy force in the Marcher lands. After capturing the town, securing the munitions within and dispatching its commander, King Henry's oldest son, Prince Hal, Hotspur and Glendower would turn their attention to the Usurper himself.

Imagine Harry Hotspur's surprise when he'd arrived at Shrewsbury to find no sign of Glendower—and with the town and its bridge remaining firmly under Prince Hal's command.

Which meant Hotspur was caught between Shrewsbury, the River Severn, and a far superior royal army. While being cut off from any reinforcements that might have been headed his way.

By the blood of Christ! How had that happened? Who could lead ten thousand men—accompanied by lumbering baggage trains and the rest of the royalist war machine—a quarter of the way across England in under three days?

The Usurper had.

Now Hotspur had no choice. With little hope of meeting up with Owen Glendower and the elder Percy, who was in charge of a second force hopefully approaching from the north, Hotspur would be forced to engage an army twice his size.

So be it. I have faced daunting odds before. At least I'll be able to choose my defensive position.

An important advantage in any battle.

After pulling back to the hamlet of Berwick, four miles northwest of Shrewsbury, Hotspur selected a three hundred foot high hillock just south of Berwick, near the Severn River. A perfect position to unleash the might of the longbow on the advancing enemy.

King Henry sent out his own spies and runners. Upon returning, they reported on the strength of the rebel army—possibly five thousand, including one thousand archers.

The archers, in particular, worried Matthew. Against the French, the longbow had been God's gift. But now those wicked bodkins—capable of piercing plate armor as well as mail—would be trained on fellow Englishmen.

Matthew caught King Henry's eye. At Crecy, their great King Edward's army had been of a similar size. Yet, they'd destroyed a French force six times larger.

Matthew suppressed a shudder.

While listening to his spies, King Henry remained calm. As if his crown did not rest on the outcome of this pending conflict. He did not pretend that the Percy rebellion was insignificant; it most definitely was not. Three powerful earls numbered among Harry Hotspur's leaders. And twelve-year-old Edmund Mortimer, who was a great-great-grandson of their great King Edward, had been heir presumptive upon Richard of Bordeaux's death. Many could argue that young Mortimer had a closer claim to the throne than Henry himself. Not coincidentally, his aunt, Elizabeth Mortimer, was married to Harry Hotspur himself.

Which meant that, if Hotspur succeeded, the Percy family would, for all intents and purposes, sit upon England's throne.

Henry Bolingbroke believed in fate, as he believed in God's judgement. *Thus, it boils down to the following*, he reasoned. *If Hotspur speaks the truth, that I've deposed someone divinely appointed, I will lose both my crown and my life.*

If Hotspur was wrong, then the question of Henry's rightness to govern would be forever settled.

And it will be Harry Hotspur's life that is forfeit.

~

What had it meant, Matthew wondered, to glimpse his dead parents at Cumbria Castle?

Lying wrapped in his mantle, with the earth as his pallet, gazing up at a darkness heavy with stars, Matthew pondered the resurrected dead he'd recently observed. And not simply at Cumbria. Yestermorn, when King Henry had swiveled in his saddle, Matthew had seen their great king Edward. Thinking it a trick of uncertain light, he'd blinked several times. But his beloved sovereign had gazed directly in his eyes, favoring him with a smile of recognition.

How could that be? But Edward Windsor had been as solid as Lancelot or Serill, who had been riding on either side of Matthew. As solid as the three-quarter moon now overhead, as the pitched tents around him, as the crushed grass beneath him.

How many other revenants had appeared? Mostly while he rode, long hour after long hour. Had the sun caused Matthew to hallucinate? To see others who had died in battle, or those he'd served, such as John of Gaunt? Matthew's brother Harry, carrying the royal standard and wearing his familiar mischievous expression, as if he was suppressing a burst of laughter. Harry had remained long enough that Matthew had been able to drink in his face and form, not so much with wonder, but with a sense of relieved familiarity.

As if to say, "Ah, there you are."

Was that why his younger brother appeared so amused? As if they'd been engaged in a game of hide and seek wherein Matthew had looked so many places for so very long and had become so very weary? Until his brother had finally, finally stepped out of his hiding place to say, "It took you long enough to find me!"

Matthew had even seen Edward the Black Prince two columns ahead. Astride a favored white charger, where moments before the animal had been a bay. Edward of Woodstock in his prime, with gloved hand, fingers lightly

266

spread, resting on his thigh as he rode, just as Matthew remembered. The flower of chivalry of all the world, untarnished by sickness and the madness that had temporarily consumed him, resulting in the slaughter of Limoges.

Edward Woodstock's presence, the presence of all the dead, seemed so natural. And why not? Despite their absence, they'd remained a part of Matthew. It was just that they had finally chosen to end the game.

Sometimes Matthew wondered whether he might be caught in a dream. But all the apparitions—if that's what they could be called—behaved quite normally. Not at all like dream characters. Nor did one taste dust or smell horse and leather or hear the clink of metal and the thud of hooves in dreams.

Am I somehow being spun back in time?

Nay. Matthew recognized the armor and the pennons and the palfreys and the markings on the shields slung on the backs of the knights he'd ridden beside this past fortnight. The only difference was that one moment he saw Lancelot or Serill or his squire or some of his retainers, and in the next, the face and form of one of those he'd so long mourned.

As alive as I am.

Unless he was dead and didn't know it.

Am I in heaven or hell?

How many indulgences had Matthew purchased over the decades? How many blanket absolutions had priests administered before each martial encounter, assuring immediate entrance to heaven if one died on the battlefield?

Will it be enough?

Matthew knew all too well the blackness of his soul, but who was he to question the dictates of Mother Church?

After placing his hands behind his head, Matthew watched the moon drift westward. The stars had begun to pulse, as if shaken by an invisible hand.

Staccato coughing. The sudden bark of a dog, abruptly squelched. Murmuring voices. The cloaked shadow of a camp follower slipping among the tents. Matthew turned his head toward King Henry's pavilion, topped by the royal standard which drooped, as if unutterably weary.

How do I wish to die? Matthew wondered. Surely, not like his father or his prince or his great king or his liege, John of Gaunt. All had died in bed, rather than on the battlefield.

I would not have Meg see me too weak to void my bowels or even raise my head, to lose the art of speech, to writhe in torment from pains that seize my body while she can do naught but twist her hands as she keeps a death vigil by my bed. I do not want that her last memory of me.

As happened far too often when Matthew thought back on all the Edwards or his father or John of Gaunt. Remembering them in their last sickness rather than in their glory days. As if those final moments were the sum of the man. When they'd simply been the last leaf blown from the oak. Rather than the oak itself.

How do I wish to die?

Simple, really.

In battle.

Odd that, at Matthew's advanced age, he'd never much contemplated the manner of his passing.

However, war had been Matthew's constant, his lover—one that he'd embraced and wearied of and sometimes even hated. Yet, it had remained ever at his side, even more faithful than his Meg. He'd been most alive during battle. Nor had his greatest joys been in the peace of his home life or in the sweetness of coupling or even in his love of his wife.

They'd been in combat.

Tomorrow, if God so willed it, he—all of them—would once again be thus joined.

Quite a proper way to exit this earth, Matthew thought, closing his eyes. *Once again in service to my king.*

CHAPTER 44

JULY 21 EARLY MORNING TO AFTERNOON, CUMBRIA CASTLE, SWAFFHAM MANOR, EDMUNDSBURY CASTLE

A crescent of moon shimmers off the River Wear, flowing dark and sluggish past the English camp. A low string of clouds obscures all but the most belligerent of stars. An intermittent drizzle mists the hundreds of tents huddling near the river and clings to the hauberks and bearded faces of the sentries walking post. The guards' movements are weary, their footsteps careful as they pick their way along the peat bogs.

In the distance comes a rumble like that of thunder. Hoof beats. Tensing, the sentries turn their faces south toward the noise, while simultaneously unsheathing their swords.

A glint of armor, armor splintering in the moonlight, swelling and falling like the River Wear. A troupe of men approach, reaching the outskirts of the sprawling English camp.

"St. George! St. George!" the riders call; the sentries relax. Knights rumble past, into the heart of the camp. Tendrils of cloud reach out to obliterate the fingernail moon. Scraping steel sounds as weapons emerge—not English broadswords, but Scottish claymores. The Scot's leader, black of eye

and beard, motions with the point of his claymore toward a tent larger than the rest, a tent bearing the standard of the King of England.

While other Scotsmen fan to surrounding tents, their leader dismounts and stealthily approaches the royal tent. Removing his dagger, he carefully cuts the tent's canvas to step inside. Sleeping men—knights, pages, a chaplain, all sprawled on the ground in various poses. On a low couch rests a king, a king she doesn't recognize. His golden hair spills across a pillow, his untroubled face almost feminine in its beauty. A knight who looks like Matthew but isn't Matthew is stretched beside his couch; a dark-haired man she doesn't recognize but who somehow seems familiar sleeps near the tent flap. The Black Knight stealthily approaches the sleeping regent. As he pauses before this young king, the knight who looks like Matthew but is not Matthew, stirs and groans.

Outside, a piercing scream. "To arms! Black Douglas!"

Black Douglas grins and raises his powerful arms above his head. The point of his claymore brushes the top of the royal tent. It is aimed at the young king.

Whose eyes snaps open.

"Greetings, Edward Windsor!"

The interior explodes in confusion. A bewildered chaplain rises to his knees; the black-haired knight fumbles for his broadsword. The young king stares at the deadly claymore frozen above him.

The claymore descends. A page yells. The knight who looks like Matthew but is not Matthew hurls himself across the king, taking the blow square across his back. The blade bites through mail, deep into flesh and spinal cord. Blood spurts like a geyser. The knight who is not Matthew does not move or cry out, but merely settles against the king...

Margery screams in her sleep. Bolts upright. Awake. Stares blindly into the darkness. Heart racing as if she is the one who has been fighting this Douglas. Uncomprehending.

Who are these people? What is this nightmare?

It isn't until dawn streaks the darkness beyond Cumbria's solar that Margery remembers. Her grandmother, Maria Rendell, had told her about the dream she'd dreamed before the Scots attacked young king Edward the third. The dream in which Maria's lover, Richard of Sussex, who Maria had said so looked like Matthew Hart, had been killed.

I have dreamed my grandmother's dream, Margery thinks. And such a feeling of desolation overcomes her, so powerful she can barely breathe.

For now Margery knows...

Now she knows...

Viviane awoke in such a restless mood. The babe seemed to have changed position, though for once it rested quiet in her womb. Still, she could not settle. The Countess of Cumbria seemed even more distracted than usual, which pleased Viviane. She would simply spend the day baking in a kitchen that had the finest wheat flour, honey, pepper, saffron and other exotic spices unaffordable to a simple baron.

I will make such exquisite bread and pies and tarts!

Clairemonde perched upon a stool beside her mother—poking dough, popping currants and sneaking honey.

Yet, as Viviane bustled about the kitchen, as she ordered the confectioner, larderer, butler and various scullions about as though she were head cook rather than interloper, the restlessness remained. What was happening with her husband? Had the king and Hotspur come to peaceful terms and were even now signing a treaty?

Will Lancelot return in time for my lying in?

It wasn't until mid-afternoon, right after she'd fed Clairemonde a tart fresh from the oven, that Viviane felt the slightest pop, as if she might have removed a stopper from a jug.

Followed by a gush of clear liquid running down her leg.

Jane le Babbe did not want to be alone. All her babes were gone save Neddy, so she took him to Swaffham's Enchanted Cottage, followed by Happiness and Fearless. There she read to him from one of her stories and thought back to the time when she'd longed for a bench full of children who would listen enraptured to her. Now she had Neddy. She sat up straighter to ease the pain in her lower back. And soon another one.

"Will you live to see your babe?" she whispered to her invisible husband. Rumors, indistinguishable from actual news, filtered to them—that the two armies were squaring off near the Welsh border. That the rebel army had already been joined by the Welshman, Owen Glendower, as well as Hotspur's father, thus vastly outnumbering King Henry's troops.

Even now everyone she loved might be dead.

And I'd not even know. The possibility caused Janey's heart to thunder against her chest, her breath to catch in her throat.

If Janey weren't so near her time, she would ride to Edmundsbury Castle to seek Elizabeth Ravenne's solace. At her great age, Elizabeth had endured so much. She was probably safe inside her scriptorium, deep in verse, not even realizing what might be occurring beyond castle walls.

"Why are you crying, Maman?" Neddy asked, looking up from the fable she'd so lovingly illustrated with a unicorn, lions and some other animal she couldn't quite decipher right now.

Rather than speak, Janey hugged him as closely as she could with her belly.

"Maman's fine," Janey said, running her fingers through Neddy's silken hair. "Shall I tell you again about your namesake, the great Edward Windsor and his son, Edward the Black Prince?"

Edmundsbury's scriptorium was deadly hot. *Naturallement.* At the high point of summer and with a roaring fire, into which Elizabeth Ravenne was feeding a lifetime of her verses and stories and nonsense.

She'd awakened at dawn, feeling an overwhelming compulsion to destroy her work.

How I have deluded myself! Insisting that I was creating something meritorious rather than simply scribbling on a parchment. Erecting a monument to my misguided vanity.

Elizabeth scanned a paper which, judging from its undisciplined penmanship, was a recent effort. Uttering a disgusted "Pah," she tossed it into the flames.

Elizabeth's life, her offspring, her pilgrimages, her experiences—mundane and otherwise—none of that could be captured by words. Certainly not words far removed from her actual life. Though, truth be told, what writer could capture the essence of a life, with all its accompanying emotions?

Will everything die when we die? Does any of it have meaning?

Here are memories: dancing with the Black Prince at his wedding. Attending the tourney when their great king Edward and his sons, dressed as simple merchants, took on England's finest knights and bested them all. Cheering among the London populace when the Black Prince, her father and Matthew and, aye, even her scoundrel of a husband, returned as conquering heroes from the Poitiers campaign.

Personal memories: Watching her brothers racing their ponies in the fields beyond Cumbria. Handing her delighted mother a bouquet she and her father had picked from Cumbria's gardens. Playing hide and seek with her boys. Gazing into each of her son's faces when they were still in swaddling bands and marveling at their beauty.

My boys.

With trembling hands, Elizabeth scooped up a second stack of vellum. She had heard the stories from a place called Shrewsbury. She'd never visited since it had no saints' bones or relics of importance. Unless you counted sheep, which it supposedly had in abundance.

"But I know about battles," Elizabeth whispered to the hungry flames. And not simply from her misguided Romances. How many times had she listened to her father and her brothers and their friends—names now etched in chronicles, which unlike her scribblings, *were* important—recount legendary battles and campaigns?

"I need not actually witness a battle to realize the carnage."

Elizabeth fed her version of the Fisher King into the flames, where it was consumed in seconds.

And, if the rumors are true and a battle is joined...

Oh, my dear children. Being led like lambs to slaughter? Please! She sent off silent pleas to God and all the saints.

Yet Elizabeth Ravenne wondered.

Would her sons be annihilated as effortlessly, as brutally, as relentlessly as her writings?

CHAPTER 45

LATE AFTERNOON-EARLY EVENING, JULY 21, 1403,
SHREWSBURY PLAIN

The banners of Saints Edward and George fluttered above the royalist troops. King Henry stood beside Sir Walter Blount, a veteran of the Black Prince's campaigns, who was dressed in the king's livery and holding the royal standard. Or more precisely, Blount was one of three such decoys designed to confuse the enemy as to the King of England's real identity. Otherwise, more than five thousand rebels would be focused on one target alone.

Most of July 21 had been wasted with fruitless back and forth negotiations. Thus, the opposing forces had less than two hours before the sun's setting. Had they been fighting in winter—well, they wouldn't be fighting in winter for by this time yeomen and peasants and their farm animals would have already settled in for the night. Leaving forests and fields to the owls, mice, foxes, and hedgehogs who claimed the darkness for their own.

Yet here, in mid-summer, the bells from Shrewsbury would have long since rung compline before darkness made it impossible for men to kill each other.

The weather remained far too hot and humid. Hours ago, Matthew's arming squire had buckled him into his armor, which exacerbated his discomfort. For no good reason Matthew's heart would increase its speed; his breathing become oddly labored. While his armor was like a second skin, expertly fitted for maximum comfort, flexibility and protection, Matthew's cuirass felt as if it had been fashioned too tightly, causing him to be overly aware of his breathing. As he also noted that, despite his lack of physical exertion these past several hours, he was sweating more than he should. Was it because he knew the terror that would be unleashed with the first sounding of royal trumpets? Or the consequences for everyone he loved if Henry lost?

But Henry Bolingbroke will not lose.

The royalist forces consisted of three wings arranged in a checkerboard pattern of men-at-arms alternating with archers. Prince Hal was positioned to the left of his father the king; Henry in the center; to Henry's right the forces of the twenty-six-year-old Earl of Stafford.

Matthew was part of the king's formation, close to the royal standard bearer and Henry himself. Lancelot and Serill would fight near him; Lancelot's oldest brother, Arthur, stood three rows to the front, easily recognizable by his painted helm. The other three Ravenne brothers who'd answered Henry's call —Perceval, Tristan and Bors—were fighting under the banner of Edmund Stafford, 5th Earl of Stafford.

The Earl of Stafford was young, courageous and eager to prove himself in battle. What Edmund Stafford was not was a seasoned commander. After having appointed Stafford Constable of England, Henry had ordered him to lead the advance. The earl, thus honored, would soon give the command for the vanguard to march forward.

A selfless act of bravery, Matthew knew. For unless God were merciful, Edmund Stafford had presented himself as a sacrificial offering, willingly bleeding out in order to protect his sovereign.

As would Stafford's men. Since they were largely militia, their physical protection was slipshod. No ordinary soldier could afford plate armor, so they would be particularly vulnerable to the archers' sting. In other words, once Hotspur's war bows were unleashed, Stafford's vanguard would be cut down like grain before a monstrous scythe.

But full armor should protect Perceval, Tristan and Bors. The rest was up to them. And God.

Matthew could sense the increased tension, felt the familiar combination of excitement, fear and determination that caused his stomach to roil before each engagement.

Knowing that the time was upon them, King Henry mounted his destrier and rode the length of his formation before returning to its center. Pitching his voice at a lower register to better carry, Henry addressed his men.

"You are doing God's work by defending your rightful king," he began. He spoke of courage, honor and duty. Sincerely, if not eloquently.

For as much as Mathew loved Henry Bolingbroke, his liege was no orator.

Matthew remembered another day, nearly fifty years past, before the Battle of Poitiers. When Edward the Black Prince had walked among his men, exhorting them to vanquish the far superior forces of the French. Even now Matthew fancied he could hear Edward of Woodstock's voice, see the fall light upon his golden hair, the way his armor seemed to be outlined in a holy nimbus. The euphoria that had come over Matthew when facing his first battle knowing, down to his very marrow, that the English would prevail. How could they fail with the Black Prince at their helm?

Henry Bolingbroke was no Edward, who, along with his father, had possessed that rare charisma which caused men to follow them out of sheer love and loyalty. Whether to death or victory it made no difference.

Henry's personality was…smaller, though every bit as intense. It would be enough.

It has to be.

While Henry was finishing his speech, Matthew noticed a murmuration of starlings dipping and swirling, coming together and breaking apart in the sky over Harry Hotspur's army. Darkening this tiny part of Shropshire, as would the arrows of Hotspur's archers all too soon.

The mournful blast of a trumpet pierced the hot, humid air. Then a clarion's call, followed by the beating of sticks upon kettle drums. The clanking of shields, weapons and armor as the Earl of Stafford's vanguard readied to move out.

Scattered war cries. Shouts of "En avant banner!" The Earl of Stafford's vanguard began its march toward the hillock upon which the rebel army awaited. Harry Hotspur had chosen his terrain well, particularly in regards to his dreaded Cheshire archers, many of whom still wore the white hart in honor of their dead King Richard. In addition to Hotspur's superior position, the royalists would be marching with the sun's rays directly in their eyes. They would also have to cross a treacherous pea field, as well as detour around two marshy ponds. All of which would further slow their advance.

"When will Hotspur loose his arrows?" Serill asked. He was standing between his father and Lancelot. Unconsciously, he touched his breastplate beneath which his talisman, the book *Mon Coeur*, was safely nestled in his aketon.

Matthew turned to study his son, hoping Serill's query did not confirm Matthew's secret worry, that his son would prove as lackluster a warrior as had his brother. Mercifully, Matthew saw no fear in Serill's eyes. Simply a younger version of himself—though at Serill's age Matthew had already been a veteran of the Poitiers and Rheims campaigns. Matthew's eyes had long been leached of the eager innocence still visible in his son's.

"Stafford is well within range," Matthew replied. "Any time."

Lancelot cradled his polished black helm against the right tasset protecting his upper thigh. "I pray my brothers are as ready as I am," he said, a small frown between his eyes. He raised a hand to his forehead to shield his eyes against the lowering sun, as if that might somehow help him see his brothers among the colorful jupons, plainer brigandines and gambesons.

"Hart blood flows through their veins as well as Ravenne," Matthew said, instantly regretting his flippant—and misguided—response. Lancelot of Glastonbury possessed more warrior blood than his seven brothers combined. If one knight walked away from this battle, Matthew knew it would be his sister's sixth son. But Arthur, Tristan, Perceval and Bors? Rather than martial skills, their fates would depend on God's beneficence— and blind luck.

Hoping to distract from his thoughtless comment, Matthew reached out to touch Lancelot's gauntlet. Upon its surface a motto had been painted in scarlet.

"It is as it is," Matthew read, pleased. With those words his nephew was paying homage to their great king, for that had been one of the third Edward's mottos.

A half-smile. "Acceptance. Wise words to live by," Lancelot said.

They once more turned their attention to Stafford's advancement, easily monitored by his blue, yellow and red banner. Farther in the distance, upon the hillock, the great Percy lion trembled in a breeze from the east. Flashes of armor danced like the light from a thousand tiny suns.

Three hundred yards.

Well within archers' range.

Kettle drums boomed as if in time to the beating of the army's heart. Dust hung like a dirty fog around the knees of Stafford's advancing men. The murmuration of starlings, which had been swooping and swirling and blackening the sky, had abruptly disappeared.

Matthew sensed that the fury's unleashing was imminent. As if Lancelot and Serill were complete martial virgins, as if they'd not trained for combat nearly every day of their lives, he could not help but offer a final piece of advice. "A simple way to remember in the heat of battle—if they face you, they are enemy. If they face the same direction, they are ours."

He pulled the retaining chain anchoring his great helm to shift it so he could grasp it between his gloved hands and raise it above his head.

"The rain of arrows will be short, particularly since they will be saving some firepower for our advancement. Bodkins will not pierce armor from that range. Only danger is the eye slits so when our turn comes do not look up. And after the arrows…"

Matthew did not finish. For, even as he positioned his helm upon his head, atop his bascinet, he knew. Before he heard or saw, before the trumpets even blasted their warning.

How many times had he heard that thwump of thousands of simultaneously released bow strings? Witnessed the manner in which thousands of shafts would darken the heavens? Like the murmuration of starlings? Or, as he had so often thought when viewing their flight, like that of wild geese in winter. With one goose always in the lead.

As there would always be the lead arrow.

The first thunk.

Followed by the deluge.

First screams.

First fallen bodies.

The Earl of Stafford's vanguard reached the pea field, thick with stakes as high as a man upon which pea plants had been twined. In the night Hotspur's men had untangled the vines and tied them together in order to impede enemy progress. Now, Stafford's foot soldiers had to hack through tendrils that clung relentlessly to boots and greaves and sabatons, that pulled men down as if they were fingers grasping upward from the grave.

Thus, the first slaughter began. The Earl of Stafford's men, according to chroniclers, "fell as fast as leaves fall in autumn after the hoar frost."

Chaos. Screaming, bucking horses; screaming men mad with pain or battle frenzy. More volleys. Gaps in the formation. Air thick with terror; the first coppery smell of released blood.

Stafford's archers tried unsuccessfully to return fire. Unprotected as they were while readying their bows, they toppled over by the dozens.

Hotspur's troops, led by a mounted Earl of Douglas, swarmed down the incline, waving their weapons and yelling the Percy motto, "Esperance, Percy!"

The Earl of Stafford's banner struggled forward. Stafford himself urging troops who could not hear him above the din. Douglas hacking his way toward Stafford and his banner.

Hundreds already fallen. Again, the chroniclers: "like apples fallen in the autumn when stirred by the south west wind."

Troops began deserting, running back toward the baggage train. Yet, even if Stafford's men fled the field, King Henry and his eldest son, Prince Hal, would press forward. Matthew knew that the battle would not be lost with the annihilation of Stafford's vanguard.

Still...

Beside Matthew, Lancelot made the sign of the cross. Doubtless praying for the safety of Perceval, Tristan and Bors, who were in the thick of it. Matthew was sending his own prayers heavenward. How could he face his sister if her boys were killed?

As suddenly as if it were a giant flower plucked from the earth, Stafford's banner disappeared.

Triumphant shouts. Meaning, Matthew knew, that Stafford himself had been killed.

Easy enough to predict what would happen next.

Like insects swarming upon a carcass, deserters skittered back toward the royal baggage train, pursued by rebels. Once at the rear, rebel and royalist alike began grabbing booty and horses from the train before fleeing the battlefield all together.

A rout.

Hotspur's archers had already begun racing down the slope to retrieve spent arrows, ripping shafts from the wounded and dying and dead. So that when King Henry moved out, he would be treated to a similar deadly welcome.

In the space of minutes, nearly four thousand royalist troops had been killed or had fled.

Leaving Harry Hotspur's men believing that the battle had already been won.

While many of Henry's believed the king's cause was already lost.

King Henry had already sent a message to his eldest son, ordering Prince Hal to attack Hotspur's right flank, thus disrupting archers even now planting their arrows point down in the earth. Anticipating the second command to fire, this time against the Usurper himself.

Knowing that he must not show panic, Henry addressed those around him.

"Courage! Do not falter! God is on our side!"

He raised a gauntleted fist. Trumpeters signaled the advance. Drums beat their rhythmic tattoo. Pause. Repeat.

"St. George!" cried Henry's men. "St. George!"

Matthew did not waste his oddly labored breath on shouts that would not be heard beyond his great helm. His throat was already raw from the cloying dust. Mercifully, the air was beginning to cool. More importantly, once both sides engaged, all physical discomforts would be forgotten in the struggle for survival.

Approaching the pea field where the last of Stafford's vanguard grappled with the rebels.

Steady.

Gripping his pollaxe, Matthew called a silent warning to his son, Lancelot and Arthur and all those around him. Dread, a tangible thing. Inhaling it along with air. It was ever the same, though when on horseback it was the destriers who trembled—albeit more with excitement than fear. For such horses, like their masters, had been trained for precisely these engagements.

Anticipating the moment when Hotspur would unleash his archers. After which Hotspur's men would race down the hill, and the final battle would be joined.

Nearing twilight. A full moon would soon peek above the horizon, as if it were a shy bystander uncertain whether to oversee the remaining slaughter. Hours left with enough light to see, imperfectly. But well enough to kill.

The din was too great for Matthew to actually hear when the archers released their fusillade. Instinct caused him to raise his shield just in time to deflect the first missiles.

As did Serill and Lancelot.

Around them, soldiers began crumpling. One minute, marching forward, the next, falling clumsily or gracefully, as if yanked off their feet by invisible strings. Bodkins easily pierced the hodgepodge of old brigandines and gambesons, linen jacks; hauberks of outmoded mail; the iron helmets, bascinets and caps discarded by wealthier knights.

They reached the now badly trampled pea field. Stepping around obstructions that had once been men and horses.

Soon the two sides would be close enough to engage in hand-to-hand combat. And soon after that, Harry Hotspur would throw everything he had, on foot and horseback, into a final charge.

On command, King Henry's archers returned fire. A dense crosshatch of arrows darkened the heavens.

As Matthew predicted, the second fusillade of enemy arrows proved even shorter than the first. Already it was easing. Imperceptibly. Then like stray drops following a summer squall, slackening. Ceasing all together.

Hotspur's men engaged Henry's first line.

Matthew shifted his pollaxe.

And made ready for his final battle.

Prince Hal, who at sixteen was already a seasoned commander, had done precisely what his father commanded. He and his men slammed Hotspur's right flank, slashing, snapping, tearing like hungry wolves at an enemy thrown off balance by the surprise attack.

It was at this moment that fate intervened for the first time that day in the shape of an arrow. When Prince Hal raised his visor in order to better survey maneuvers, he was hit in the face by a shaft. Burrowing deep below his eye nearly to his nose. Life threatening. And yet, the prince, aided by seasoned commanders, continued his onslaught. Or so said the chroniclers. Though, if the prince could indeed effectively fight after such a grievous wound, he already deserved the warrior reputation he would carry through the ages as Henry V. Whether it was Prince Hal, or Prince Hal aided by his commanders, his forces relentlessly hammered the rebel column, pushing even the Cheshire archers into the center.

Closer to Harry Hotspur himself.

CHAPTER 46

EVENING, SHREWSBURY PLAIN

*P*erched atop his destrier, Harry Hotspur surveyed the battlefield. Watching the chaotic dance below—the dipping, bobbing banners, as well as the royal standard, tall and straight and motionless near the center— mocking him.

Or extending an invitation?

"Come, if you would claim me," it seemed to say, as if it were a mistress beckoning her beloved.

Aye, that I will.

But not for some lover's tryst.

While Hotspur watched, he calculated the weaknesses and strengths of both armies, sifting through the confusion to the strategy beneath. For there was always a strategy. As there was a path to victory, no matter the odds.

It was true that the Usurper had surprised him by moving his troops so quickly that Hotspur had been unable to rendezvous with his father and Owen Glendower. Still, their great King Edward had won against overwhelming odds. As had the Black Prince. Hotspur enjoyed the superior terrain, and his men were far more experienced than the Usurper's troops, many of whom had no martial experience beyond the required forty days per year.

What Harry Hotspur did not have was time.

King Henry's main body alone contained more men than all of Hotspur's. He might have swept thousands off the field, but the numerical odds remained against him. Nor did Hotspur underestimate the Usurper's courage or tactical skills. Or the skills of young Prince Hal. If the Usurper's formation did not buckle in the manner of Edmund Stafford's, it could easily overrun Hotspur's lines.

Victory would belong to the false king.

A full moon edged upward though a sky only marginally darkened by streaks of pink and lavender. Hours of adequate light left.

I must even the odds.

Harry Hotspur swiveled in his saddle to survey his household knights. One hundred mounted warriors, all wearing the blue and yellow Percy livery, each identifiable by the pennon positioned right below the individual spear tip of his resting lance. There should have been more, but some like his worthless cousin, Reginald Luci, had somehow disappeared along the way to Shrewsbury. Which might be all for the better.

Berwick was no place for amateurs.

Hotspur's one hundred knights had all fought against the Welsh and the Scots; all were acquainted with both the risk and glory associated with this battle. Hotspur picked out the faces of those yet unhelmeted. He caught the gaze of Gerald Halle, short and squat and with the strength of ten. The Earl of Douglas, former enemy and experienced commander, who'd so ably dispatched the Earl of Stafford. Others from old families. Risking their lives and their family's futures to wipe out the Usurper.

Counting on me to lead them to victory.

Harry Hotspur made a decision. While known for his impetuosity, Hotspur had survived thirty-nine years by obeying his instincts. And his instincts urged him to act. Battles were not won from defensive positions. Battles were not won by the faint of heart.

One hundred mounted knights scattering thousands of foot soldiers?

It could be done. It has been done. I will do it.

Hotspur's gaze once more swept the Usurper's forces. Calculating how easily they might be pushed to panic when faced by his cavalry.

There was nothing more terrifying to a foot soldier—especially a poorly trained foot soldier. The baron and his men could quickly smash through their ranks, causing them to break and run so that claiming his prize would be a simple thing. First, the Usurper's standard. Then the Usurper himself.

Of course, should Hotspur's charge be blunted, should royalist soldiers have time to surround him, they would crawl all over him and his men-at-arms like flies upon a corpse.

And corpses we will be. He thought suddenly of his crescent shaped sword, left behind by a careless squire. As he remembered the shiver that had passed through him when he'd learned of the name of the hamlet where they'd camped. Berwick. This, so the wizard had prophesied, was where he, Henry Percy the Younger, would die. At a place called Berwick. And without his favorite sword.

But great men command their own destinies, Harry Hotspur reminded himself. *At least until God decrees otherwise.*

The Usurper's kettle drums rumbled like thunder before a gathering storm.

Hotspur gave the command to a runner, who passed it down the line. Knights lowered visors or settled great helms upon heads; removed swords from scabbards; couched lances.

Hotspur unsheathed his own sword, the sword that was not his talisman, and raised it over his head.

The knights charged, blue Percy lion streaming overhead.

"Esperance! Esperance, Percy!" they cried.

The caparisoned chargers were a blur of color, arranged in such close formation that their riders galloped knee to knee, couched lances pointing into the heart of the Usurper's formation. Down the hill toward the royalists, horse's hooves causing the ground to shake like an earthquake. Trailed by running foot soldiers, as well as the green and white liveried archers who had replaced their longbows with war hammers, swords and mallets.

Hotspur's cavalry slammed into King Henry's first line. Following the initial charge with lances, they cut, slashed, and beat with swords and maces and morning stars and war hammers that could easily pierce kettle hats and bascinets to the skulls beneath.

The first line pushed into the second. Destriers reared and kicked, downing or trampling fallen soldiers with as much eagerness as their riders.

Harry Hotspur's soldiers attacked with a desperate fury. The field was a jumbled mass of thrusting, cutting weapons, straining men, maimed and falling bodies.

The final battle had been joined.

MARY ELLEN JOHNSON

~

With the engagement of Hotspur and his cavalry, the din had increased tenfold. In the background, the ubiquitous kettle drums urged royalist troops to maintain order despite the unfolding carnage. Dying men, gutted men. Severed limbs. Headless torsos. Thrashing, shrieking horses. Blood soaking into the trampled field like contaminated rain.

The royal momentum had stalled.

The second line crashed into the first.

The third into the second.

Matthew wielded his pollaxe with disciplined fury. On foot a pollaxe was an all-purpose death-dealer, more effective than swords, which were virtually useless against full plate armor. A mindless task to block blows, trip those careless enough to enter Matthew's range before burying the weapon's spike into poorly protected chests. To use its axe to bash heads or, in one downward stroke, separate limbs from torsos.

It helped that, compared to others in Matthew's past, Hotspur's rebels were mediocre fighters and woefully inexperienced.

How many years had it been since he'd engaged in such brutal hand-to-hand combat? Decades? Though the muscle memory remained, Matthew's breathing was impossibly labored. Yet understanding he must, as always, push past the pain, past the intermittent numbness in his right arm, ignore the sometimes blinding sweat bathing his face.

To dispatch one more rebel. Then another.

Finally, mercifully, the fighting lessened, at least among those not directly engaged with Hotspur's cavalry. A mutual withdrawal in order to catch one's breath, staunch minor wounds, grab water, allow arming squires to replace weapons and equipment.

Nearby, King Henry and George Dunbar, a fiercely loyal Scotsman and enemy of Hotspur's Earl of Douglas, had piled up an impressive number of bodies. Still, if Harry Hotspur made it to the eye of the storm, King Henry should not be so weary he could scarce raise his sword. Time for a strategic withdrawal and re-evaluation.

Matthew removed his great helm, allowed it to fall free down his back until stopped by a retaining chain. Leaving him still protected by a bascinet and aventail but allowing easier communication with those around him.

He called out to Dunbar, pointing with his pollaxe to the rear of the lines.

Dunbar nodded.

The retreat of Dunbar and the king left Sir Walter Blount charged with carrying the royal standard on the field. At the mercy of an enemy who believed Blount to be England's actual sovereign.

Once free of the fighting, Matthew handed his pollaxe to his arming squire before bending over, gauntlets on cuisses, gasping for breath, gratefully gulping in the cooling air.

Dispassionately assessing his physical condition—chest that felt as if it were constricted by an iron band; head pounding as though assaulted by a legion of galloping horses.

Finally, Matthew straightened, gulped water from his flask before handing it to another squire, who hurried to a nearby water barrel to refill. Matthew willed the frantic beating of his heart to slow, the iron band to loosen, the dancing spots before his eyes to recede.

Nearby, the king was being attended by a bevy of squires while Dunbar surveyed the field. As did Matthew. Easy to spot Harry Hotspur on his blue and yellow caparisoned destrier, looming above the milling mass of foot soldiers. No doubt that the baron and his knights had moved closer to the royal standard. But Matthew could chart their path and determine what the rebel leader could not—that he and his men were completely surrounded. With a fierce rush of joy, Matthew knew, aye, he knew that Henry Percy the Younger had gambled and lost. That the baron's life had been reduced from the possibility of decades to the certainty of minutes.

In silent thanks to God and St George and all the saints, Matthew raised his eyes to the heavens. Imagining that his great king Edward, his king's sons, Matthew's parents and his brother gazed down upon him with pride. Acknowledging that once more Matthew Hart had discharged his duty.

It was then Matthew noticed that the normal twilight sky was no longer normal. The earlier pink and scarlet streaks had blurred together, deepening to purple. The full moon, which had begun its ascent as a golden ball, had gradually leached to white. The usual course of things but... Matthew blinked, mistrusting his eyes.

What is happening to a full moon that is no longer full? How can that be?

There were no clouds hiding part of its face, yet there it was. Now a gibbous moon, as if the phases had sped up and were unfolding in real time. Impossible. Matthew wiped his forehead with the padding of his jupon and looked again. He'd not been mistaken.

Meaning?

Matthew felt the hairs stand upon his neck. It must be a trick of the eye. A full moon that was not a full moon; that even as he looked appeared to further shrink, as if being nibbled by some monstrous maw.

A cry emerged from the heart of the battle. Matthew jerked his gaze back to his north star—the royal standard.

Vanished.

"King Henry dead!" came the cry. More forcefully, "The king is dead."

A shiver ran through Matthew. He turned to Henry Bolingbroke, who remained very much alive.

Obviously, Walter Blount, arrayed in royal livery, had been mistaken for England's king. Killed and the royal standard trampled underfoot.

"Henry Percy king!"

Wrong, thank Christ. Still, it was an eerie feeling, as if someone was shouting out the future. And the peculiar sky? Surely another troubling omen.

But for whom?

"Our men will rout," Henry said flatly, jerking his head toward the field.

"Aye." Matthew yanked the chain on his great helm.

Dunbar and the king followed suit.

All knew that if King Henry's men mistakenly believed him to be dead and that all was lost, the falsehood could have the same impact as truth.

Matthew had seen it before—a disciplined force suddenly, unaccountably disintegrating into chaos. Bloody Christ, they'd just witnessed it with the Earl of Stafford's men.

King Henry retrieved his sword from a waiting squire. "Time to finish what the traitors have begun."

"It is as it is," Matthew whispered, before accepting the pollaxe extended by his arming squire and again following his king into the fray.

If the battle did not halt completely, it seemed later to those remembering that it had. Destriers frozen mid-stride; men whose contorted expressions would remain forever thus; raised weapons that would never fall. Had the cacophonous noises abruptly ceased, replaced by an eerie silence, as if all earth's creatures had taken to hiding? Or did memory simply make it so?

The moon had completely vanished, plunging Shrewsbury's plain into total darkness. If every eye was not fastened upon the wonder unfolding above them, witnesses later claimed otherwise. A wind sprang up, gradually blowing away the curtain obliterating the moon's surface. First, behaving like a coy mistress, it revealed itself as the barest sliver of light. Then more, until half its face was uncovered. Then three-quarters. But its color was unlike anything before seen. Neither white nor golden, nor even orange. Blood red. As men gaped, the darkness was gradually banished by a disk so huge and round it was like some monstrous demon's mouth threatening to swallow the entire sky.

Soldiers dropped to their knees or crossed themselves and beseeched God's mercy. Later, in the retelling, some swore that the moon dripped blood. Others that Satan's face appeared. Yet others that armies battled across its surface.

The one thing everyone agreed upon: this particular eclipse was an especially evil omen. But for whom? Harry Hotspur? King Henry? England? The entire world?

As it turned out, there was no need for soothsayers to cast the Christian equivalent of pagan runes in order to interpret the object of its wrath.

Why did Harry Hotspur choose that particular moment to lift his visor? Did he gamble that in the gloaming he would not be targeted by some alert archer? An expertly thrown axe or spear? Or did he expose his face simply because he was in thrall to a wizard's prophecy?

At that moment, a longbowman released the shaft that sealed Harry Hotspur's fate. Silently, it raced toward its destination. To land squarely between the baron's eyes.

What might have been Henry Percy the Younger's last thoughts? Of the errant moon? The prophecies surrounding his demise? Had fear flashed like heat lightning inside his brain, warning him that all was lost? That they'd killed an imposter rather than the Usurper himself?

Or did the baron die believing he had triumphed?

Harry Hotspur tumbled from his horse.

Dead before he hit the ground.

Initially, few saw. Or knew. Or understood.

Then:

"Percy dead!"

The cry was taken up by others.

With increased certainty. Followed by despair.

Morphing into a crescendo of wails.

Knowing that his belief in the rightness of his cause had been vindicated, Matthew Hart experienced a fierce euphoria.

We have saved Henry's throne. Now 'tis simply a matter of mopping up.

Prince Hal's men were already herding Hotspur's right flank like sheep toward a pen; mercilessly slaughtering all those who tried to bolt for Watling Street and, so they hoped, the friendlier faces they would meet in Cheshire.

Matthew spotted Serill and Lancelot, still in the vicinity of the fallen royal standard. Serill, the white of his surcoat flashing in the waning light with his every stroke. Fighting with a frenzy Matthew would have been hardpressed to match in his own youth. Lancelot, feet planted, body angled to the side, shield raised with his left hand, pollaxe in his right, delivering the coup-de-grace to an already toppling solder. Even as Matthew continued his mindless maneuvers and counter maneuvers, he felt something loosen inside before completely falling away. An ancient burden, even now barely articulated. That if he should ever relinquish his sense of responsibility, remove the mantle of duty and obligation from his shoulders, his family, the entire Hart line would fall into ruin. Who besides himself was strong enough to protect those he loved, to continue its warrior legacy?

Aye, well, now he could rid himself of that particular notion, couldn't he?

Already Hotspur's cavalry was breaking rank. A few determined to fight to the death alongside their leader. Others being pulled from their horses or frantically trying to cut their way to the edge of the field and then hie themselves far away, beyond King Henry's vengeance.

Matthew's attention was caught by a particular horse and rider headed in their general direction. The silver rimming the destrier's dark caparison shimmered with each frantic movement of the agitated stallion. His rider, whose helm was topped by an eagle's crest, cut an especially menacing figure. The destrier, who had either been wounded or maddened by the surrounding chaos, reared and kicked. Soldiers tried unsuccessfully to hamstring the horse or grab its bridle, pull the eagle knight from his perch—or more often simply elected to stay out of the way.

Despite the horse's erratic trajectory, Matthew guessed it posed the greatest threat to Serill, who was directly in his path and whose back was to the unfolding danger. The animal could easily trample Serill underfoot before he was even aware.

Matthew spotted the lather coating the horse's muzzle, the rolling eyes, then the arrows sticking out of his hindquarters where he should have been protected by a croupier. A wounded animal driven mad by pain.

Matthew saw a clear path forward—a way he could distract horse and rider or take them out. He could trip the animal with his pollaxe, hamstring it, or, when it reared, bury his spike into the part of its underbelly unprotected by barding. Or focus on the rider, who was flailing about as if he had no real idea how to use a war hammer.

Intending to position himself between the danger and his son, Matthew hacked and thrust and butted his way forward. His lungs screamed in protest; his heart felt as if a giant's hand had reached in to squeeze it to pulp. His vision darkened, mimicking the darkness of the eclipse.

But the distance had closed.

Then, as it sometimes did in battle, everything seemed to slow, to take on the fragmented quality of a dream. After dispatching his latest threat by burying the spear point of his pollaxe in the man's chest, Serill stepped back. In time to see Lancelot, also free of danger, raise his pollaxe and point behind Serill in warning.

Serill spun around. To face the destrier, nearly on top of him.

Matthew could not reach his son in time.

The animal reared. When he crashed back to earth, he would trample Serill. Matthew saw his son plant his feet, bracing himself as expertly as if he'd faced such a threat every day of his life, angle his pollaxe so that its spear would hit the unprotected part of the animal's breast.

The destrier's front legs pawed the night. Descended with a sickening crash upon the spear's wicked point, driving deep into the horse's belly. Immediately halting its momentum. Screams. Like those of similarly wounded men, who had long ago taken up residence in Matthew's nightmares.

Serill had stepped aside, had already withdrawn his sword from its scabbard. Either to finish off the horse or face its rider.

As the eagle knight's mount seemed to shiver and then halt, Matthew watched the knight flailing about, striking empty air with his weapon. Matthew, having stumbled and leapt and forced a pathway to the trio, now stood close enough to engage. Unsheathed the bollock dagger at his right hip while he waited. As soon as the knight hit the ground, Matthew would step in to bury the dagger's blade between gaps in the armor to the flesh beneath.

While Serill, crouched to the side of the mortally wounded animal, would finish it off.

Horse and rider crashed. The knight had not the presence of mind to kick free of his saddle. His right thigh and leg were pinned beneath the dying animal.

Completely focused on dispatching the fallen rider, Matthew lifted his bollock dagger...

Oblivious to the rebel behind him, who had raised his morning star to bury it in Matthew's helm. Not hearing Lancelot scream, "Uncle! Behind!" Not seeing Lancelot trying to reach him before the weapon descended.

Serill, straightening, now aware of the danger. Simultaneously screaming a warning while bolting toward the rebel.

Matthew turning, even as the morning star descended, even as Serill and Lancelot reached the soldier. Lancelot driving a pollaxe into his back; Serill slicing through the tendons behind his knees. Causing the soldier to crumple to the ground.

On top of Matthew.

Who did not move.

CHAPTER 47

CUMBRIA, SWAFFHAM MANOR, EDMUNDSBURY CASTLE

t least bring him home, Margery thought, her hands caressing the profile on the effigy of her husband. In her heart, she already knew there had been a battle, and that Matthew was dead. The dream had warned her.

Had prepared her.

As if anything could prepare her for a life without Matthew Hart.

Around Viviane, she heard women whispering and crossing themselves.

Am I dying? she wondered. *'Twould be just my luck.*

Going through all this pain—well, not so very much pain, and her baby boy was perfection itself—but to be dying.

How can I be dying when I feel fine?

But Viviane had never been dying before. Mayhap some at death's door felt fit as could be.

"Will you weep for me?" she silently queried Lancelot. *Will you see me in the face of our baby boy and wish you'd loved me better?*

Loved me at all?

Dozing. More whispers, voices raised in alarm. Something about a peculiar moon. The word "eclipse" was repeated.

What exactly did that mean?

More precisely, was it a good or bad omen to be born under such an occurrence?

How long would an eclipse last? Moments? A season? Forever? Was it confined to Cumbria Castle, the northern lands, or had it spread throughout the kingdom?

Has the darkness reached you, my Lancelot? Are you safe? I will pray so very hard that you return to me—to us," Viviane promised, before drifting back to sleep.

Rumors had reached Swaffham Manor of the two opposing armies that were camped near Shrewsbury, several days' ride to the west. Even now, this very minute, soldiers could be dying. Even now, England's rightful king might have been killed. Which meant that every man Jane le Babbe loved, if not already dispatched in battle, would be executed immediately afterward.

My babes and I might already be poor as cottars. But what will material losses matter if...if...

Janey rested in her bed, curtains drawn up to catch the summer air from uncovered windows. Beside her, Neddy was sunk into a nest of pillows while her two Bear Dogs stretched beside a cold hearth.

Despite protests from the restless babe inside, Janey managed to maneuver her bulk to face the windows. Strange, how the sky appeared to be changing, though it was easier to mark those changes from the shifting shadows upon the floor than the narrow openings.

Janey's sense of dread increased. Anything out of the ordinary might mean...what? A pending storm? A trick of the light? A slow-moving bank of clouds?

Or something far more ominous?

Fearless and Happiness rose from their sleep. Ears alert, tails stiff, they padded to the windows.

"What is it?" Janey whispered.

The dogs raised their noses, sniffing the night.

Janey's throat constricted; invisible fingers pressed against her windpipe.

Unable to exit her bed without help from her maid, terrified of what she might see once she *did* reach the windows, Janey began to cry.

For all those she loved. For the lives that had been lost, regardless of who won the conflict that even now must be raging.

Thus, warned the heavens.

Nothing will ever be the same.

Janey brought a fist to her mouth and bit down on her knuckles lest her sobs awaken Neddy.

She thought of Elizabeth Ravenne, wished that she could be with her mentor and friend in order to comfort her.

Janey whispered the names to the darkness. "Lancelot. Serill. Matthew. Arthur. Perceval. Tristan. Bors. King Henry. Prince Hal."

A roll call of the dead?

Janey prayed, how she prayed, that God would stay the hand of the Angel of Death.

Even though the night sky seemed to be warning otherwise.

Elizabeth Ravenne removed the reading spectacles that allowed her to decipher the words on the page before her. She had been reading Geoffrey Chaucer's tale about the traveling knight and had become stuck on one sentence:

"This world is but a thoroughfare of woe,/ And we are pilgrims passing to and fro."

Chaucer certainly could express himself more artfully than she ever had.

Best that my words have been turned to ash.

Elizabeth rubbed the bridge of her nose where her spectacles had rested, blew out her bedside candle and slumped into her pillows. Old age brought such a change to sleeping patterns—dozing in the middle of the day or crawling into bed early, only to start awake and chase sleep until the dawn.

Tonight, Elizabeth Ravenne felt particularly restless.

Her gaze turned toward the solar window. A long lance of moonlight spilled upon the rushes. Even as Elizabeth watched, the night, which had appeared unnaturally bright, began to darken. Struggling from her bed, she crossed to the traceried window frame.

The sky was indeed changing. Even as Elizabeth watched, the moon shrank to the size of a fingernail. Before being completely obliterated.

"Mother Mary!" she murmured.

A hushed stillness had descended upon Edmundsbury's keep, its bailey, and, Elizabeth suspected, all the kingdom. It was as if a million insect and animal voices had been stoppered, as if the wind itself was holding its breath. Elizabeth's hand crept to the crucifix she always kept round her neck. Unnatural. A shiver passed through her, though there was yet no stirring of a breeze. No sound from her maids upon their pallets, not even a groan or a loud exhalation of breath.

"What has happened?" she whispered.

Elizabeth thought immediately of her brother and her sons. Her forehead was clammy; her heart hammered so loudly it displaced the unnatural stillness that had gripped the chamber. Elizabeth felt such a terror for her boys, for all those she loved who might be engaged in some great battle or riding to their deaths.

How many of her sons had answered King Henry's initial call? Word traveled so slowly. Lancelot, for certes, and those whose holdings were concentrated in the midlands.

Five of my eight.

Elizabeth blinked, as though the darkness might be due to a malignancy of her eyes rather than of nature. Already, the sky was lightening. Gradually, finally settling on a color that resembled twilight. The moon expanded until it was full and round and red and unspeakably ominous.

"*Alea iacta est*," Elizabeth Ravenne whispered, as if her thoughts were usually in Latin. "The die has been cast."

It was then that the rhyme popped into her thoughts, this in English.

A rhyme that caused Elizabeth to fall to her knees.

"Five sons…ride off to war… Four sons who are no more…"

CHAPTER 48

AFTER THE BATTLE, SHREWSBURY PLAIN

*T*he author of the *Brut* chronicle wrote that the Battle of Shrewsbury was *"the heaviest, and unkindest, and sorest battle that had ever taken place in England. For there was the son against the father, and the brother against the brother, and kin against kin."*

Under the cover of darkness, Harry Hotspur's men fled without fear of pursuit. Looters went among the bodies, consisting primarily of royalists, lifting weapons or anything of value. Long into the night and past dawn, fellow soldiers carried the wounded to a dedicated area where they would be attended by surgeons, barbers or priests.

Serill Hart remained with his father. It was an odd thing. Matthew's helm had been dented so badly it could not be removed until a blacksmith approached Serill, offering help. Vaguely, Serill took note of the man's mane of hair, as thick and long as Lancelot's, though snow white, and he felt a flicker of something… recognition… familiarity? But Serill was too distraught to ponder anything beyond his father's death, and that he must do everything to honor him, to make him proud. Together, he and the smithy worked the helm from Matthew's head, to find that his father's face remained largely untouched.

You look peaceful, Serill thought. And if that were not so, Serill would convince himself otherwise. As he would assure others.

"I have prepared bodies before," said Fulco the Smithy. "That we will do, so he can be properly returned to his lady wife."

Serill was too distraught to wonder at the sudden appearance of this stranger, or what a blacksmith would know about the Earl of Cumbria. Rather, Serill stayed while Fulco the Smithy rode to Shrewsbury to find the herbs, spices, wine, quicksilver, cotton and the balsam that would be used to rub his father's limbs.

To preserve Matthew Hart's body for his final journey.

Lancelot need not worry about descending to hell. He'd already entered it. His beloved uncle gone, and here he was searching among nearly two thousand bodies, scattered over a distance of three miles, dreading to find his brothers. He'd sent several of his retainers to make their way among the rows of wounded, praying desperately that his siblings had survived.

Mayhap they are all alive. Mayhap they have already retreated from the battlefield, back to their demesnes.

Lancelot hoped but did not believe.

He had an idea where Perceval, Tristan and Bors had been positioned within the Earl of Stafford's vanguard. Still, Lancelot did not find the last of his brothers until nearly dawn. Before, he and his squire had passed their torches over horror after horror, seeking the familiar coats of arms or less likely, an unhelmeted face.

All his brothers were in such a state that Lancelot would spend the rest of his life trying to erase those particular images.

As he would make up a pretty tale to spare his mother.

It was not even so very odd that, when he returned to the spot where he'd last seen his oldest brother, Arthur, he of the prettily painted helm who had been in King Henry's column, Lancelot screamed his anger and rage and pain to the heavens.

Or that his was simply another voice added to the cacophony that had descended following the Battle of Shrewsbury's end.

King Henry ordered a mass grave to be dug. When he was taken to the body of Harry Hotspur, His Majesty wept. At one time, he and Hotspur had been kinsmen. They'd grown up together, crusaded together and fought together.

To have it come to this...

Henry first ordered that his nemesis be buried at the market town of Whitchurch. As was so common, rumors immediately circulated that Harry Hotspur was still alive. In no mood to fight yet another revenant, His Majesty ordered the rebel leader's remains returned to Shrewsbury. There, Harry Hotspur was propped up in a sitting position in front of an axe and strung between two millstones. First, he was publicly displayed outside Shrewsbury's gates. After enough people had seen the corpse to determine that the traitor was indeed dead, Harry Hotspur was beheaded and quartered, his parts scattered across the kingdom.

King Henry ordered one quarter sent to York. So that every time Henry Percy the Elder passed through its city gates, he would view the fruits of the Percy rebellion. To further cement the futility of dissent, Henry immediately ordered most of Shrewsbury's rebel leaders executed. More heads were impaled above city gates around the kingdom. The Earl of Douglas, who had fallen and shattered his kneecap while attempting to flee, was spared execution in exchange for an exorbitant ransom. Knowing that the Welshman, Owen Glendower, yet remained free, King Henry also spared most of the common soldiers, showing special favor to the Cheshire archers.

Their loyalty was necessary if Henry was going to crush the final threat to his kingship.

And he would.

CHAPTER 49

AUGUST, 1403, CUMBRIA CASTLE

*E*very day Margery kept watch upon Cumbria Castle's battlements, awaiting Matthew's return. For more than two decades she'd climbed Cumbria's vice to assume her position as a watcher.

Is this what I'd always anticipated? You coming home to me in a coffin?

Once, Margery had fantasized a quiet life, just they two. Perhaps in a village where he might be a miller or a fletcher or a carpenter; where she would be an alewife or a spinner, in addition to being a mother. Where they resided in a tidy cottage, worked a bountiful plot of land, and raised a baker's dozen of healthy children.

But God had denied them those choices.

Matthew Hart had trod a much larger stage—one occupying kings and princes and lords and all those who shape a kingdom's destiny. Participating in wars and rebellions, coronations and funerals, helping orchestrate the deposition of one king and cementing the throne for another. Events already immortalized by chroniclers; events that future generations would ponder and dissect and lecture upon in Oxford and Cambridge and public squares.

You never really belonged to me.

Despite Matthew's passion, his protectiveness, his companionship and certainly his fidelity, Margery had sometimes felt as if she were a tagger-along in the larger story that was Matthew Hart's life. Duty and obligation had been his lodestones.

Now you will have an eternity to mingle among those with whom you shared that stage. And someday soon, if God so deems it, I will join you.

Finally, far in the distance, Margery spotted Matthew's funeral cortege.

Surprisingly, distressingly large.

Aye, certain protocols had to be followed, especially for a lord as powerful as the Earl of Cumbria.

Already, Margery felt tears burn her eyes. As if she had not already shed enough. *At least Serill... and Lancelot...*

Though once in their presence Margery feared she would completely fall apart.

Margery spread her arms wide upon the battlements, as if she were a bird, as if she were embracing the sky itself.

Imagined stepping forward into empty air.

So that she would not have to do what was expected of the Dowager Countess—bend her knee to the new Earl of Cumbria.

Father James waited beside Margery. St. Bosa's Chapel had been draped in black; daily masses were already being said locally and in various Hart demesnes; King Henry had ordered a month's mind at Westminster.

Margery silently addressed her husband. *You would like that, your king publicly acknowledging your loyalty.*

Margery was also quite certain that from Matthew's heavenly perch—all those battlefield indulgences had surely resulted in a speedy entrance to heaven—he was feeling quite pleased with his manner of death.

Odd the things that lodge in one's memory...

1360. The Rheims Campaign. Matthew returns from France wracked by a coughing sickness. So ill he has not the strength to send Margery word of his arrival.

The plague had also returned to London, leaving Matthew and his brother Harry holed up inside Hart's Place. After Harry sent word to Margery, who is employed by the goldsmith she is later forced to marry, she arrives to find her once larger-than-life lover reduced to a skeleton.

"Do not look at me like that," Matthew says, his smile reminiscent of a death mask. Margery hears the rattle in his chest, sees the blood upon the cloth Matthew had put to his mouth following a bout of coughing. His eyes are bright with fever; save for two scarlet spots on his cheeks, Matthew's face is the color of wax.

"'Tis just a slight cough I picked up during the campaign," Matthew says. "It returned during the crossing from France. I've had a bit of trouble shaking it."

"In case you need reminding," counters Harry, "that slight cough killed hundreds. It very nearly killed you."

Matthew raises a bony arm in a gesture of dismissal. "No one dies at twenty-four."

"'Tis a pity someone forgot to tell all those twenty-four-year-olds who will remain forever behind in France."

"At least I know I will not die puking and sweating from some bothersome wasting sickness. 'Twould be no fit end for a knight."

Harry says, "Not even you, brother, can choose the way to die."

"I can choose the way I'll NOT die."

Trumpets announced the imminent arrival of Matthew's funeral procession. Beside her, Father James quietly prayed the rosary while Matthew's retainers, dressed in armor and wearing surcoats bearing the leaping white hart, assumed their positions. Beyond Cumbria's drawbridge, villagers lined the road.

You did *choose your way to die,* Margery thought, again addressing her husband. *Not sick and wasting away or having slipped into senility but dying on the battlefield in service to your king.*

Margery did not torment herself with wonderings about whether Matthew had thought of her during his last moments.

Such sentiments were better left to the young and naively romantic.

I was ever a pale mistress to your first love.

Not so much war, really, as duty and obligation.

How can I begrudge you that? To die the way you lived?

Lancelot and Serill, in full armor save for their helms, were the first to pass through Cumbria's gateway. Faces pale and drawn, as though they themselves were little more than ghosts.

Somewhere behind them, among the other mourners, would be the cart holding Matthew's body. Margery had already decided she would not view it.

My last memory will not be of you wrapped in cerecloth. I will remember that God granted us a long lifetime together. I will harvest those memories instead. As I will comfort myself knowing you have been reunited with all those who have gone before you.

Once Serill dismounted, Margery knew her duty. To curtsy before the new Earl of Cumbria.

It is as it is, she thought, stepping forward to greet her son. *One life passing, another approaching its fullness.*

But before Margery could bend her knees, Serill wrapped her in his arms. So very tightly as to make breathing painful for them both.

Nothing was said.

There were no words…

Lancelot stood behind his cousin, watching the unfolding reunion without really seeing it. He was back on Shrewsbury's battlefield; he was back in Edmundsbury Castle with his grieving mother; he was here in Cumbria Castle with his uncle's coffin only a few cart lengths behind; he was here in Cumbria Castle knowing he should rejoice that he was a new father; he was here in Cumbria Castle knowing he should long to see his wife, still lying-in following her birthing.

Lancelot was here knowing all manner of things. While feeling nothing.

He wasn't sure when he became aware that Viviane Halle numbered among the bystanders. There she was, standing a distance apart from the rest of Cumbria's household. Peculiar, that. His wife was never shy about making her presence known, of elbowing her way to the forefront, demanding to be acknowledged.

Their eyes locked. *I canna do this*, Lancelot thought. He continued gazing at his wife. As if she were a casual acquaintance, mayhap, because he didn't feel *anything*.

'Tis not quite so, he thought, dispassionately assessing his reaction. He felt… distaste. If only a twinge. He could chart their forthcoming reunion as accurately as astrologers read the stars.

Viviane Halle would make everything about Viviane. Viviane's wants. Viviane's needs. Viviane's insecurities. Viviane's pain.

"My brother was killed," he imagined her wailing, while dismissing Lancelot's losses. "You were not here for my delivery… You do not care that I suffered through the most painful labor since the beginning of time… You are not even grateful I've given you an heir…"

I canna do this. The phrase an endless litany. *I canna placate and soothe and remind myself that Viviane Halle is my wife. That she deserves, at the very least, respect and courtesie.*

Following her criticisms, Viviane would fill Lancelot's head with inanities that would immediately leave him wanting to clamp a palm across her mouth and order her to *shut up!* Not even the birth of his son could claim the importance it deserved. Lancelot was groping his way through a fog so dense as to leave him totally disoriented.

After the example of the original Lancelot du Lac, he increasingly considered retreating to a hermitage where he would end his days as a monk.

If Mother did not need me…

Mayhap after Elizabeth Ravenne retired to a nunnery, as she was currently contemplating. Or joined her four sons. Then, Lancelot might squirrel himself away.

Lost as he was in contemplation, Lancelot did not immediately realize when his lady wife had moved to stand in front of him.

Lancelot's lips parted, but he could not speak. Thoughts, impressions penetrated his fog: *Noticeably slimmer… Too soon to have left her lying-in chamber… Eyes black as ripened currants… Plucking currants from bushes near the River Eden… hands stained black with their juices… Hands stained black with blood…*

Lancelot blinked. His lady wife still stood before him, her eyes locked to his.

Leave… disappear…

A second peculiarity. Viviane's emotions had always been tiresomely predictable—ranging from jealousy to frustration to disappointment to disapproval to hurt. And back again.

Today Lancelot discerned something new in her gaze. Could it be….

Opening her arms to her husband, Viviane Halle whispered, "I am so very sorry."

Even as Lancelot instinctively stepped into her embrace, he identified this new emotion.

A marvel.

Viviane Halle appeared to be feeling compassion. Genuine compassion on behalf of another human being.

When Viviane's arms pressed against him, Lancelot did not flinch. Nor was he repelled by her tears. These tears, he knew, were being shed because of *his* losses, *his* pain.

Given the rubble that had once been Lancelot's heart, that was miracle indeed.

CHAPTER 50

AUGUST'S END, 1403, CUMBRIA CASTLE

*M*argery departed Cumbria Castle for her daily walk to the Enchanted Cottage. Thatched roof; exterior walls the color of sunflowers; topaz blue shutters; window boxes currently overflowing with late summer flowers.

Matthew had built the tiny dwelling as a wedding present. It had been their haven from seemingly endless obligations. So many happy hours had been spent in a room a quarter the size of Cumbria's solar.

It *had* been enchanted.

Margery had never cared about the material possessions that accompanied Matthew's position. Being the widow of a prosperous goldsmith had provided comforts enough. All she'd ever wanted from Matthew Hart was his love.

What will happen to me when Serill claims his legacy?

As soon as Janey, who'd been delivered of a third son, recovered enough to travel, the Harts would take up residence at Cumbria Castle.

Should I remain here? Return to London and the Shop of the Unicorn? Retire to a nunnery? Imitate Matthew's former lover and wall myself inside an anchorhold?

Ceding mistress of Cumbria Castle to Janey would be a relief. And

Margery's grandbabes would provide distraction enough to at least partially fill her days.

Still... what do I really want?

What was important to Margery was her connection to Matthew. To that end, she knew she would feel his presence no matter where she resided. Even now, she sensed him near. Which made it easy to pretend he was off hawking or hunting—or on another campaign.

Whether a trick of the mind or Matthew's actual presence, it brought Margery comfort. Absently, she touched the wooden robin around her neck, the robin she'd given Matthew as his talisman before the Battle of Shrewsbury. The morning of Serill's departure, he had slipped it into her hand.

Increasingly, Margery thought of her grandmother, Maria Rendell, and of the men Maria had loved. She thought of the Cherry Fair, of the arc of one's life, which lasted little longer than the cherry blossoms. All so achingly beautiful. All so transitory.

Yet the blossoms ever returned. Renewal, as well as dying, was part of God's plan.

And now, here it is, nearing August's end. With fall around the corner. My first fall without you.

Margery pushed open the wooden door to the Enchanted Cottage. Beside the jugs of water and wine and the simple repast Dru the Caretaker always left, a large bouquet of cut wildflowers had been lain upon the table.

"Lovely," Margery whispered. Dru must have gathered the flowers before leaving for the orchard where Cumbria's apple crop was being harvested.

Crossing to the cupboard, Margery retrieved a pitcher in which to place the bouquet. After pouring in the proper amount of water, she carefully inserted various flowers. Yellows, blues, purples and reds, particularly vibrant in contrast to the dull grey of the pitcher.

Suddenly, inexplicably Margery thought of Fulco the Smithy.

Were you at Shrewsbury? I pray not. That you remain safe and well.

She would not think beyond that, that Fulco the Smithy might number among the dead.

Margery felt that familiar prickling behind her eyes, warning her of more tears. So many gone. All the length of England, churches and chapels and cathedrals swathed in black; grieving families. Reminiscent of plague times. Only this plague had been caused by men.

Why am I thinking of Fulco? Strange how a man with whom she'd spent so little time could remain such a presence. Perhaps it was simply because after she and Matthew parted, Fulco had resurrected feelings she'd assumed long-dead. More than resurrected. Fulco had introduced her to darker passions than she'd experienced before or since.

Whenever her thoughts drifted to that long-ago May, Margery rationalized them away.

'Tis simply that when lovers realize their time is fleeting, every emotion is heightened.

Which also explained the fantasy she'd later constructed. Deluding herself that Fulco's every subsequent action and thought had somehow included Margery Watson.

Nonsense, of course. With aging, one learns to put aside childish things.

Bending forward, Margery closed her eyes to better inhale the delicate fragrances wafting from the pitcher.

"Margery Watson."

That familiar voice. Low and deep. A voice she'd seldom heard when their mouths had been used for actions other than speaking.

Margery exhaled. Took note of the escalating rhythm of her heart. Turned to see Fulco the Smithy standing in the open doorway.

Surprised, yet not. She'd hadn't seen him in how long? Five years, preceding the joust-that-never-was in which King Richard had banished Henry Bolingbroke and Thomas Mowbray from England.

"The flowers are lovely," Margery said, knowing Fulco had gathered them.

A flash of white teeth against swarthy skin. Margery studied her one-time lover. While Fulco's hair was completely white, he had maintained his impressive physique. His sleeveless linen tunic revealed the muscular arms that were a trademark of his craft. Beneath the loose ties threading the front of his tunic, Margery spotted the pendant he'd fashioned of her naked body.

Which he'd promised to always wear.

Their gazes held. How very odd that Fulco looked at her as he had during those nights by the River Stour. As if nearly a quarter century had not passed. As if she were still young and desirable.

Fulco stepped through the doorway. "I told you I would wait."

He halted a few steps away from the table where Margery stood. Close enough she might stretch out her arm to touch him. She suppressed the urge to back away in order to maintain a proper distance.

"I am an old woman." Her voice sounded steadier than she felt. "Who has lost the man she loves."

"One of the men you love," Fulco the Smithy corrected.

Margery gazed into those dark eyes, so little changed. The way he was looking at her... "Were you there, at Shrewsbury?"

Fulco nodded. He did not elaborate. Apparently, they were back to communicating with a minimum of words.

Fulco's hand crept up to the pendant; his huge fingers closed around Margery's image. "Remember?" he whispered.

Margery felt the power of him, of his hold upon her.

"Aye."

From his position atop his forge wagon, Fulco extends a scarred and calloused palm. Beckons. "Come with me."

Margery reaches up to place her hand in his. She knows her lover is leaving Canterbury, that he will ply his trade in other parts of England.

"I so wish..." If only they could disappear into an enchanted underworld where decades would pass like days, where they would never grow old, where they would ever remain together.

However, Fulco is no faerie lord. And Margery is too old to indulge in fantasies. Even though her relationship with Matthew has ended, she cannot follow a near-stranger who is probably incapable of providing the barest comforts.

How long will passion last when our nights are spent sleeping under your wagon? Before life's hardships drive us apart?

Yet, the part of Margery whose blood is as base as Fulco's yearns to cast aside her well-ordered life...

"My home be a half-day's walk from here," said Fulco. "Less by wagon." His gaze swept the room's interior before returning to her. "Comfortable enough. Larger than this. My business prospers. I can provide any comforts you need. If ye'll but come with me. Where you belong."

Margery grimaced. "I've no idea where that might be." How does one continue when your *raison d'etre* no longer exists?

As a young woman, Margery had felt trapped between two worlds—that of her peasant mother and her noble father. Between her love for Matthew and her loyalty to her stepbrother Thurold and the radical priest John Ball. She'd wrongly assumed she'd reconciled those feelings.

As a Dowager Countess, I could live in luxury. As the widow of a prosperous goldsmith, I could return to London and the Shop of the Unicorn. Which do I want? Or do I desire something altogether different?

Fulco had moved so close Margery fancied she could feel his body heat.

"If you will but come with me, I'll na leave thee. Just we two."

"I've Serill and my grandbabes—"

"You can visit whenever you please. I'll not deny thee any happiness. So long as you return to me."

Another few inches. Face to face. Fulco settled his hands upon Margery's waist. His expression held that oh, so familiar mixture of yearning and desire.

She did not twist away. "What a scandal we would be!" She laughed. The first time in how long?

"A blacksmith and his helpmeet? Who's to notice? And when you return to Cumbria, it can be astride a fine palfrey and wearing your prettiest gowns. "

"Play at a lady when I choose and a blacksmith's leman otherwise? What a fanciful notion."

Against her ear, Fulco whispered, "I canna promise I'll make thee happy. But I promise to spend the rest of my days trying."

Margery allowed herself to rest her cheek against Fulco's broad chest. It was not Matthew's, could never be Matthew's, could never be as dear. But it was familiar and dear in its own way.

"Life is short," Fulco said. "I'll wager we've already passed our allotted time."

Margery smiled against his tunic. "I have, for certes."

"You be the lone woman I've desired, Margery Watson. Grant me this. Grant me you."

Fulco's arms tightened against her. Her pendant pressed into her cheek. He was not Matthew. No man could be Matthew. No man could take Matthew's place.

But Fulco?

Leaning back in his arms, Margery tilted her chin up to better view him. "A pretty cottage?"

"Beautiful."

"With soft feather mattresses?"

"And hot and cold running water for your bathing, as they say 'tis at Windsor Castle." Fulco brushed her lips with his own. "Should you wish."

"And you would not leave?" Margery's voice broke. Knowing no one could make such a promise, let alone keep it.

"Never," Fulco said with such passion she could almost believe 'twas so.

Not Matthew. Not Matthew.

"I will go with you, Fulco the Smithy," Margery said.

And for the first time in so very long, she found herself at peace.

ABOUT THE AUTHOR

Mary Ellen Johnson's writing career was sparked by her passion for Medieval England. Her first medieval historical, *The Lion and the Leopard*, was followed by *The Landlord's Black-Eyed Daughter*, a historical novel based on the Alfred Noyes poem, "The Highwayman." (Published under the pseudonym, Mary Ellen Dennis.) *Landlord* was chosen as one of the top 100 historical romances of 2013.

After taking a twenty year detour in a quixotic quest to change the world--rather like Arthurian knights' quests to find the holy grail, which ended in similar failure — Mary Ellen has happily returned to historical fiction writing and her favorite time period, the tumultuous fourteenth century. Her six book series, *Knights of England*, follows the fortunes of the characters (and their progeny) introduced in *The Lion and the Leopard* through the Black Death, the reign of that most gloriously medieval of monarchs, Edward III, the 1381 Peasants' Revolt, the deposition and murder of Richard II in 1399 and the beginning reign of the king whose reign inadvertently laid the groundwork for the Wars of the Roses.

There is nothing Mary Ellen loves more than bringing Medieval England alive for the reader. She particularly enjoys researching battles, campaigns, the daily lives of both lord and peasant, and trying to figure out our ancestors' thought processes, particularly how they viewed their world. Oh, and did she mention the castles and cathedrals? Mary Ellen likes to say her favorite place in all the world is standing before the tomb of the Black Prince in Canterbury

Cathedral. (Hyperbole, of course, since Mary Ellen is not that well-traveled and her favorite places are probably wherever her kids and grandkids reside.)

However—and the very recounting gives her chills—a distant cousin recently shared the results of her years-long genealogical research on the family tree. When flipping back and back through the centuries, Mary Ellen began finding names that were hauntingly familiar—John of Gaunt, Edward the Black Prince, Edward II, Edward III, even Richard the Lionheart! All the historical characters she's spent a lifetime reading and writing about! How can that be? Genetic memory? Reincarnation? She has no idea but you can bet she'll be exploring the possibilities in future novels!

In the meantime, Mary Ellen hopes you'll enjoy reading *The Lion and the Leopard, A Knight There Was, Within a Forest Dark* and *Lords Among the Ruins* as much as she's enjoyed writing them.

www.MaryEllenJohnsonAuthor.com

 facebook.com/mejauthor

www.ingramcontent.com/pod-product-compliance
Lightning Source LLC
Chambersburg PA
CBHW020645030726
47498CB00002B/375